My War With Hemingway

James Charles

Published by Rogue Phoenix Press
Copyright © 2015

ISBN: 978-1-62420-115-8

Credits
Cover Artist: Designs by Ms G
Editor: Sherry Derr-Wille

Dedication

To the American Veteran

Chapter One
I'm All Broken. They've Broken Me. E.H.

"Zach!" Micah yells from behind me. "Get back!"

I glance back at him and hold up a clenched fist. He stops, yet I edge closer to the young Afghan boy, no more than ten, eleven years old. He is screaming, crying and flailing his arms. A vest of explosives covers his Perahan Tunban, Afghan robe. "It's okay," I say shouldering my rifle and putting my hands up to show him I mean no harm. "It's okay."

"Powell!" Sergeant Evans yells at me from near where Micah and the rest of my squad now huddle for cover behind a pushcart full of Afghan vegetables. "What the hell's wrong with you? Get your ass back here."

The boy, hysterical, falls to his knees with his hands raised to the sky as if he's appealing to Allah. Out of the corner of my eye I notice ten Taliban fighters scurrying up the dirty village street heading right for me, yet they don't seem to be real. They are like ghosts to me, or perhaps I'm a ghost to them and they can't see me. It doesn't matter. Nothing really matters, except this child in front of me who's caught between heaven and hell.

I am calm, yet determined, as I kneel next to the boy, and struggle to dislodge the vest, strapped and buckled tightly on his backside. He sobs while I try to set him free. "It's going to be okay," I say again, grappling with great difficulty to get the vest off.

In an instant, I hear a rifle report and the boy's head explodes like a pumpkin being dropped from a second floor balcony. His body droops into my arms and I look down at his lifeless body hanging on mine. I stand, sigh, and wipe something bloody from my hands onto my Army Combat Uniform, ACU's.

The Taliban fighters, screaming like banshees, are almost upon me. They pop off a few rounds, the bullets whizzing past me. I turn and head toward my patrol.

A blast knocks me to the ground.

Small arms fire rattles off from every direction as I high-crawl over to a ditch, a pain stabbing me in my shoulder. I glance over to where the boy had been. He is gone, having blown up anyway. One of the Taliban fighters must have controlled the detonating device, probably a cell phone. What animals, using children like that. No, I can't denigrate animals. Animals are higher species than they are.

I lie there, trapped in the crossfire, my squad engaged in the firefight. With bullets zipping over my head, I'm unable to get over to my squad, so I lay my head on the Afghan dirt and think how these past six months have been nothing more than a vacation in hell. These Taliban just keep coming and coming and coming. This will go on forever until everyone is dead.

I roll over onto my side and notice the boy's brain matter splattered all over my ACU's. The smell makes me nauseous and my hands shake. My clothes are soaked from summer sweat, the pain in my shoulder is intense. I reach up and massage my shoulder only to discover it is leaking blood like a sieve. *I can't* bleed to death here, in a ditch in Afghanistan. I just turned twenty-two.

I glimpse my buddies, Micah, Julio and Aaron engaging the enemy. They are my best friends. We have been together now four and a half years and have been through so much together in combat and back on base.

Then I recall how this day began like any other, routinely trudging along on foot patrol, but realize it will now end in a different way, for me at least. I hope my buddies all make it, even if I don't. Sweat drips from my brow. I lay my head down, close my eyes, and drift off into darkness.

~ * ~

I awake, lift my head and realize I'm sitting at a small table in the corner of a cheap, disheveled and darkened motel room on Bourbon Street early one Sunday morning. I notice dirty clothes and empty beer bottles strewn around.

I can't seem to erase that scene from my mind, or anything about the wars. I can't turn my head off. I think about that event, like it happened yesterday, yet it has now been six months. I'll never forget the terror in that young boy's innocent brown eyes just before he died. I'll forever see that event, as well as the other horrors, play out over and over again. *I've got to make it stop.*

I look down at a handgun on the table in front of me, sigh deeply, then grip a bottle of whiskey, raise it to my lips and guzzle. I slam the bottle onto the table, wipe the dribble from my chin with the back of my hand and pick up the gun, cradling it in my palm. Staring at it for the longest time, I engage its cold steel slide, chambering a round. It reminds me that death is cold, like when, as a child, I kissed my mother in her casket.

"That is how it came to be for me, too," a voice behind me says.

I whip around and face a young man standing behind me dressed in a military uniform. It looks old-fashioned, with a large belt worn over the coat at the waist, and a leather, buckled strap that hangs over the right shoulder and under the left armpit. He steps forward, snatches the gun from me and limps over to the window where he swipes the curtain open with the back of his hand, pulling it apart and peering out. Sunshine streaks into the room. I squint and shield my eyes.

"A cheap motel," he says. "On Bourbon Street. How fitting."

In disbelief, my vision a little blurry, I watch as he ambles back over to me, pries the bottle of whiskey from my hand and helps himself to a nip.

"Potent," he says banging the bottle down. "Does the trick." He has a youthful face and a full head of black hair combed over the top.

"What the hell?" I look back at the door. "How did you get in here?"

He studies me a moment and says, "Look kid, the world breaks everyone and afterward many are strong in the broken places."

"What?" I say, my voice agitated.

He drops the magazine from the gun and ejects the round from the chamber. It bounces on the table. He gestures to my shoulder, the one I injured in Afghanistan and says, "The body can heal itself. The mind?" He shakes his head. "Not so easy."

I close my eyes and rub them with my palms. When I open them, he still stands there gazing at me. I look past him, scanning the room.

He finishes another swallow, looks the room over and says, "What the hell you looking for?"

I crinkle my brow. "Did Julio put you up to this?"

"Who's Julio?"

"You an actor? How much did they pay you?" I wrestle my bottle of whiskey out of his grip and swig more.

"Actor?" He snorts. "They're pretentious dandies."

I catch my breath from the whiskey, narrow my eyes and say, "Dandies? What kinda talk is that?"

He smiles. "You're funny, kid."

"Who the hell are you anyway?" I snap. "What's with the old uniform? You in costume for a show?"

He peers down at his uniform, frowns, then takes hold of the whiskey again. "Most call me Hem. You can call me Stein." He takes another pull from the bottle.

I lean forward resting my elbows on the table, close my eyes, and massage the back of my neck with my hands.

"Look, kid," he says, sitting next to me and glancing around the messy room. "You'll never know 'til you have lived through the worst what the best can be."

4

I look over at him and scowl as he twirls the base of the bottle around on the table by its neck. I look away again, down at the floor, and whisper to myself, "Am I that drunk?"

"Drinking lets you see things you normally can't when you're sober."

I turn back to him, examining his dark brown eyes and mahogany-colored complexion. He spins the gun around on the table like a roulette wheel and says, "You were like all the others. No catalogue of horrors ever kept men from war."

"Yeah. *Now* I get it. I can't go back, yet again."

"*Now* there are things greater than yourself to consider."

I hear someone fumbling to open the door behind me. I turn to look and see my buddies burst into the room. "Let's go, gringo," Julio says.

Micah says, "Yeah, we need to get goin'."

I turn to face the mystery man, but he has disappeared. I look the room over but he is nowhere. Julio slumps onto one of the double beds near the window and Aaron crashes on the other. Micah pulls the drapes open allowing the sun to illuminate the room and stands over me looking at the gun, a nine-millimeter Beretta. "That yours?" he says.

"What? Yeah. Thought about cleaning it just now."

His eyes bore through me. "You shouldn't be carryin' around a concealed weapon. You outta your mind?"

I shrug. "I figure this is the South. Everybody's packing down here."

"Don't mess with the South, mister," he says in his Alabama accent.

"We've all had breakfast," Aaron says. "You hungry?"

I pull myself up from the table, using it to steady me. "No. I just had mine." I motion to the bottle of whiskey.

"Damn," Aaron says peering at me. "You didn't get enough last night?"

"I'm taking a shower." I stagger into the bathroom, drop my boxers and jump in the shower before the water warms up. I rub my face and blow mist onto the shower wall. *What just happened? What was I thinking?* I stand there for the longest time leaning against the shower wall trying to get a grip on reality. *I have to pull myself together.* I have to play it cool. For the guys.

A few minutes later, I drag myself out of the shower and towel off. In the room, Aaron is stuffing clothes in his pack while Julio lies on a bed with his eyes closed. Micah inspects the whiskey bottle and grimaces at me.

"Don't start on me with your bible-thumping," I say drying my buzz-cut head with a hand towel.

"You know I've given up on tryin' to save your soul from eternal damnation," he says.

I drop the towel from around my waist and pull on a pair of boxers. "Stop staring at my ass," I say, throwing the towel at him.

It lands on his head. He pulls it off and throws it back at me. "Your skinny butt?" he says. "I won't ask if you don't tell."

"Funny," I say.

"Girls, stop your quarreling," Julio says. "My head's pounding." Aaron throws a dirty sock at him. It lands on his face. "Hey," Julio says. "That ain't mine." He throws it on the floor.

"Quarreling?" I say. "Where'd an East LA Cholo like you learn to talk like that?" I pull on a pair of shorts.

"Mexican-American is the correct way to address me, Private. Besides, I'm more of a patriotic American than you are. You know my great-grandfather was a decorated World War II soldier in Patton's army."

"Yeah, yeah, yeah. I've heard it all before. Hey, did I ever tell you, you remind me of a young Ricardo Montalban?"

"What? Ricardo Montalban? How old are you?"

"I used to watch old shows on TV Land. *Fantasy Island*? You're the spitting image of him."

"Freak," he says closing his eyes.

I pick up a pair of dirty boxers and drop them on his head. "Dammit, homie," he says, tossing them on the floor. "That's your nasty ass shit."

"What're you guys up so early for anyway?" I pull my socks and shoes on.

"Early?" Aaron says. "While Sleeping Beauty slept the morning away, we've already had breakfast and roamed the streets, fool."

"Stop calling me fool, bro."

"Listen white boy. Just get your drunk ass moving or I'll have to kick it again."

"We're closin' in on checkout time," Micah says. "We need you to pack up so we can get back to Bragg on time."

"Hey," I say, "we should stop at your place in Tuscaloosa. Perhaps Elise or some of Penny's friends would like to see me." I pick up my clothes and stuff them in my pack. I sniff a dirty shirt, shrug, and pull it on over my head.

"I wouldn't let any of them near you," he says.

"If you don't, I'm gonna put a skirt on you, pretty boy. What with those baby blues, blond hair and your rock-solid abs." I try to pinch his cheek, but he slaps my hand away. "You're so sexy."

"Knock it off. You're not my type, scrawny northerner and all. I like a little muscle, you know." He drops the whiskey bottle in the trashcan and shoulders his pack.

I glare at him and stuff the Beretta and the clip in my pack. With the palm of my hand, I slap the sole of Julio's shoe. "Let's go, Amigo."

Julio rises from the bed, moaning. He grabs his pack and heads out behind Micah and Aaron. I lift the bottle from the trashcan and guzzle the rest. *I think I fooled them. I think I got away with it.* I toss the bottle back into the trashcan and follow.

~ * ~

The car pulling over to gas up wakes me. "Get up sleepy head," Aaron says slapping me upside my head.

Swatting at his hand, I say, "Where are we?"

"Just south of Montgomery," Micah says pulling into the gas station. Micah drives, not only because the car is his, but also because he is the only one without a hangover. He doesn't drink. Aaron and I ride in the backseat of his new Dodge Charger, a gift from his father for service to our country. Of course, it helps that his father is a Baptist minister in one of those mega-churches where everyone buys tickets to heaven during the Sunday broadcast.

I'm in luck. There's a liquor store across the street. I bolt from the Charger, run across the street and purchase a bottle of Jim, Kentucky Bourbon. Back in the car, I pop Jim's top and take a hearty swig. Micah, pumping the gas, looks in and frowns.

Aaron plays a hand-held video game next to me in the back seat. Julio returns from the restroom, hopping into the front seat. Micah returns the nozzle to the pump, gets in and turns over the engine. He puts a CD of Lynyrd Skynyrd's *Second Helping* into the car's player and cranks up the volume for *Sweet Home Alabama*. Julio frowns and says, "My head, homie. Really? Redneck music?"

Micah lowers the volume a bit and grins at him. While I stare out the window admiring the beauty of southern, then central Alabama, I think about what happened back there in that Bourbon Street dive. *What was I doing?* I look over at Aaron and up front at Micah and Julio. They are like my brothers, if I had any. We have been through so much together and I can't let them down like that, especially with our third deployment coming, this time back to Iraq.

We're on a four-day pass between deployments. I joined the army right after high school and met these fools in basic training. We all had our reasons. Julio Salas's was to get out of the barrio. Aaron Glover for the same reasons with Southside Chicago, and Micah Reid, well, I haven't really figured him out yet after five years together. He also convinced the rest of us to reenlist. A band of brothers he says, and we all have to stick together. Micah enlisted, putting his football scholarship with the University of Alabama on hold. Go figure. Well, we've survived one tour in

Iraq and one in Afghanistan helping one another through the slow and the boring, and the sometimes intense times in combat, as well as drunken escapades off base. Me, Julio, Aaron and some of the others have gotten drunk and laid, but not Micah. He's a good god-fearing boy who won't be with a girl before he's married.

I wrack my numb brain thinking of that strange man back in New Orleans. It's like dreaming about people with whom you've never met. It wasn't a dream. Was it? What was he saying, and what was with the old uniform? It's as if he put on Julio's grandfather's World War II uniform from a trunk in the attic or something, but it didn't look like any WWII uniform I've seen. *I must be out of my damn mind.* In any event, I pull my journal from my pack, tap my pencil against my lips and to the best of my recollection, transcribe what he said to me. From memory, I draw his face. Aaron looks over at the finished sketch. "Your boyfriend?" he says.

"Knock it off." I reach over and pinch his big black nose. We start wrestling but I hold my own and push him off. I open up Jim and take a good gulp. Micah looks back at me in the rearview mirror. "What?" I say, inflecting my voice.

"You're gonna have withdrawals in Iraq, Zach."

I top Jim off, wipe my lips and say, "I've got you, bitch, to hold me through the night."

He shakes his head. I doodle and write some notations in my journal. The journals I use have durable leather covers from an Indian company I found on the Internet, probably someone's incarnated relative. "So just what *do* you write in that diary all the time?" Julio teases looking back at me.

"What idiots you guys are. It's not a diary. It's a journal."

"Ooooh. A journal." He reaches over and grabs it.

"Dammit," I say struggling with him to get it back. He does after I put him in a headlock.

"You fools're gonna get us in an accident," Micah says.

"Look," I say opening to a page. "It has narrative and illustrations of our battles. Okay?"

"Narrative?" Julio says. "Illustrations? Awright, awright, psycho. You need to see a shrink."

"I need to see a shrink? You freaks keep it all bottled up inside. At least I let out."

"We're worried about you," Aaron says. "Let momma take care of you, my sweet boy." He teases me as he strokes my head.

I swipe at his hand, but miss. "Take care of me? You can't take care of yourself."

I stow my journal in my pack and stare out the window as we loop around Atlanta on Interstate 20. We transition to 95 north toward Fayetteville and head for Fort Bragg. I snuggle up with Jim, and while hugging the door, I hope like hell I can hold it together for this deployment, let alone survive it.

Chapter Two
Groundhog Day

Six months later I am on foot patrol with our platoon. I've made it this far, with only six months to go, yet I am physically and mentally exhausted. If I can just not get shot, or better yet killed, I'm finished. I've had enough killing for ten thousands wars.

Day in and day out for the past six months we've patrolled the shitty, hostile streets of Baghdad as part of the president's surge. It's what we call Groundhog Day. Routinely we patrol, wax, or kill an insurgent or two, then do it all over again the next day. Occasionally one of our own poor bastards gets waxed. You never think it's going to be you; it's going to be the guy next to you.

A hotter than hell day in November, Jimmy Howard and I bring up the rear of the patrol. A pudgy-faced African-American, all of eighteen years old, this is his first deployment. He's a replacement for Private Davis who was killed in Afghanistan. Jimmy is also as green as they come. At formation one morning before our first foot patrol, I saw how jittery he was so I threw my arm around his shoulder and told him I had his back.

The platoon halts and Jimmy and I take a lunch break on the corner of a bombed-out building. Breakfast, lunch and dinner, when out on patrol, consist of MRE's, Meals Ready to Eat, or better yet, Meals Refusing to Exit.

I guess that is what they are designed to do, constipate you so you're not having to crap all over the place in the field. You have more important things to do. Not hungry, I draw Jimmy in my journal concentrating on his field of fire and say, "Why did you sign up?"

"To help my grandmamma pay her bills. The checks go straight into our joint account. She's a diabetic and my grandpapa died coming home from the plant one night. He didn't leave much for her and she can't work."

"Really? How'd he die?"

"He was shot by accident in a drive-by. He was in the wrong place at the wrong time."

I think how we have our own version of combat on the streets of America.

"He was a real good man," Jimmy goes on. "He worked for Chrysler. They gave grandmamma a small bit of money for the funeral, and he had a little pension from his job, but that money don't go far because he didn't reach his full retirement age."

"I'm sorry."

"Thanks."

"What about your parents?"

"I never knew them. My momma died of a drug overdose when I was two, and I never knew who my father was."

I nod, leave it at that. "Here." I pass him the journal with the page open to the sketch I made.

"Wow," he says. "That's good. Looks just like me." He passes it back and I stuff it in my ACU pocket.

Silence. I scan the smelly street, but can't see much activity except a grungy mutt scavenging for food. I worry insurgents might be planning something as a woman rushes by covered from head to toe. At least I hope it's a woman and not an insurgent in disguise. "What're you gonna do when you get out?" I ask.

"Get out? I'll probably re-up. There's nothing to go back to in Detroit. I could then support grandmamma for a long time. Her medical bills are a lot."

"Suppose you're right. Not much for me to go back to either. My old man hasn't been called back to General Motors yet, if he will ever. Delivers pizzas. I have to get out or I'll go crazy." *If I'm not already.*

Sergeant Miller, a lifer with a death wish, moves the platoon out down the street a few minutes later. The only hostile activity we encounter is the indignant stares of the Shiite majority living here. Jimmy says, "You're all tangled up, Zach." He straightens the strap on my pack.

"Thanks, Dad." I trudge along gripping my M-4 combat assault rifle. She hugs me wherever I go, whether in the latrine or on my cot, the dining facility, what we call the DFAC, or when we do PT or play ball. I named my rifle Alice, after Alice Kramden from *The Honeymooners.* I used to watch the show as a kid on TV Land. Their antics made me laugh. It's good to remember that out here. "One of these days," her husband Ralph would say, "POW. Right in the kisser. Straight to the moon, Alice." I always hoped she would one day want to go to the moon to get away from him, and take me with her.

Merchants glare at us, yet continue with their business. Most people in this world are like anyone else. They want to make a living to support their families and could care less of engaging in petty politics. Although, it seems, politics engages in them.

A couple miles down the road, Miller directs us into defensive positions. There's an insurgent nest we need to address and this time my squad will sit in support in the rear, covering. I take a deep breath as we huddle near broken down storefronts. Civilians in the area scatter.

Micah nods from his team's position near the corner of a building on the other side of the street. Small arms fire crackles from the assault team in Fourth Squad up near the nest. It's progressing according to the playbook and we should be able to mop up and head out in short order.

A second later, AK-47 fire rattles out from atop surrounding buildings. An RPG explodes near the frontal assault element sending debris into the air. I get down prone trying to shield myself. Ambushed and surrounded like ducks in a pond, this operation is now going south, fast. Realizing I hadn't been paying attention to Jimmy, I see him lying a few feet behind me in front of a hookah lounge. "Zach," he shouts. "I'm hit."

Julio is hunkered down in front of me behind a burnt out Volvo wagon. He too sees Jimmy. I signal to Julio to cover me. As he opens fire on the insurgents pinning us down, I sling Alice over my shoulder and sprint over to Jimmy, grabbing him under his armpits and dragging him into an alley next to a pile of garbage. "I don't feel too good, Zach," he says, his breathing labored.

I cradle his head in my lap, facing away from me so I can ensure my field of fire is covered. I pull his pack off and rip open his ACU shirt breaking off the buttons. "Hold on, Jimmy." I tear his T-shirt back and he spits up blood. "Damn," I murmur.

"How bad is it, Zach? It hurts real bad."

I wipe blood off his chest with his torn shirt and see three entry wounds. As soon as I wipe the blood away, the wounds gush once again, covering his chest. I rip open and apply his first aid compress covering two of the wounds but I have to use his torn shirt to cover the other.

Bullets whiz all around us as if dozens of bees are buzzing in my ear. An insurgent jumps up in a nest and shouts something about Allah while holding his AK above his head. Johnny Reddens, whom I dubbed Johnny Redneck, from Georgia, is our sharpshooter. He adjusts his Leupold LR/T riflescope, squeezes off one shot killing the insurgent.

Our squad Sergeant Evans rushes over. With Jimmy's blood all over my hands, I say, "It's bad, Sergeant."

He barks into his radio headset, "Waters, get over here, goddammit." Jimmy is ashen and drifting in and out of consciousness. "Hold on, Howard," Evans says.

"Zach?" Jimmy whispers.

"I'm right here, Jimmy." I grab and squeeze his hand while applying pressure on his wounds with the other. "We're getting the doc and he's gonna patch you up. You'll be reenlisting real soon."

"Okay." He coughs, a little bit of blood spurts out from between his lips. "Zach?"

"Yes, Jimmy?"

His eyes catch mine. "You've been a good friend to me."

"Yeah, well," I say. "You're not going anywhere, you hear me, Jimmy?" I press down onto his wounds trying, in vain, to stop the bleeding.

"Tell my grandmamma I loved her, Zach."

"Sure, Jimmy. Sure, I will."

His eyes flicker as he squints from the sun. Looking at Evans he says, "Is that you, Jesus? Take care of my grandmamma." I push down hard on the compresses trying to stem the flow, but my hands slip and slide in his blood. "I'm'a comin', Jesus," Jimmy says. "I'm'a comin'."

Waters crawls over and assesses Jimmy, checking his pulse. "Jimmy? Jimmy?" Waters says. Nothing. Waters looks at me and shakes his head.

"You gotta to do something," I say wiping some blood away from Jimmy's chest, discovering the wounds have stopped gushing.

"I'm sorry, Zach. He's gone."

With my bloody hands, I grab Waters by his ACU shirt and say, "You gotta save him."

Waters pushes my hands down. "Zach, get hold of yourself." He hustles off.

"Get focused, Powell," Evans says crawling off.

All alone, looking down at Jimmy's pale black face, I place his head on his pack and close his eyelids. I try to wipe his blood off my hands onto my ACU shirt and pants, but I can't seem to get it all off.

I lie back down prone, and glimpse Micah and his team hunkered down on the other side of the street. Platoon leader, Lieutenant Petersen, who's younger than me, crawls toward Sergeant Miller. An enemy sniper shoots Petersen in the neck. He grabs his neck and falls over onto the street.

This is not good. This is really not going well. I put my head down and rub the sand out of my eyes, getting Jimmy's blood on my face. It makes me nauseous and I can't seem to catch my breath. My heart races, my hands shake and I feel woozy.

"They wrote in the old days that it is sweet and fitting to die for one's country," Stein says suddenly appearing in his old uniform and lying next to me. "However, in modern war, there is nothing sweet nor fitting in your dying. You will die like a dog for no good reason."

In disbelief, because I haven't seen this character since back in New Orleans in my drunken stupor, and still no clue who this fool is, I say, almost trancelike, "It's always the young ones."

"It always will be." He pats me on my war shoulder, crouches low, and darts off carrying a vintage military ambulance stretcher.

I squint and shake my unsteady head and see Miller rushing forward, grabbing Petersen under the armpits and pulling him toward the side of the street. A plume of red mist spews forth from in-between Miller's shoulders and he slumps over Petersen, short of cover.

Damn. Could this get any worse? Our guys stop firing and the insurgents do too. The scene is quiet, save for an occasional sniper round. There is no movement coming from either Petersen or Miller. Evans yells into his headset, "Everyone stay put." He crawls over to Micah and I watch them argue. Aaron pulls up next to me and says, "This is bad? Ain't it?"

"Yeah. We'll get out of it," I say, not believing it. I always wondered why people in situations such as this say things they know are futile. However, it now makes sense. It is either nerves, or a psychological tool to calm those in distress. At present, both reasons seem to apply.

Johnny Redneck shouts, "Fuck you, Johnny Jihad." He opens fire on a sniper nest and Aaron and David Zimmer engage as well. I want to laugh, because Johnny Redneck is yelling at Johnny Jihad? *He is one crazy son-of-bitch.* David Zimmer, from Minnesota, is just as crazy as the rest of us.

I notice Micah looking over at Miller lying in the street bleeding to death, yet flailing his arms about as insurgents take pot shots at him. Micah sprints toward Miller and Petersen as insurgents pop off several rounds at him too. Like the quarterback he was in high school evading sackers, he dodges the bullets and makes it, grabs Miller and drags him back for cover. Petersen, it seems, is already gone. He does not move and has stopped grasping his bleeding neck. I didn't know Petersen well because, as an officer, he kept his distance.

Micah says something to Miller, who is conscious. He tears open Miller's ACU and applies his first aid compress. He then slings his weapon over his back, grabs Miller's weapon and signals for us to cover him. He runs up the street and dives like a quarterback for a first down on a quarterback sneak into a position occupied by two guys from Third Squad. We cease-fire and Aaron says, "He's got angel's wings."

"He's got something," I say shaking my head. "A damn death wish."

All quiet and everyone waits, including the insurgents. A minute goes by, then two, three and four. It feels like days, weeks. Johnny Redneck scans the building above me. "You want to know the irony?" I say.

"Irony? What're you talkin' about?"

"It's just that here we are, in the heat of battle, we're scared to death, wanting nothing more than to get out of it, to go back to base, or home…"

"Yeah? So?"

"So, this is just what we signed up for. It's our job." He shakes his head and Johnny Redneck discharges a round. A second later an insurgent falls from the nest above us landing three feet away. Johnny gives me a thumbs up. "Good shot, Johnny," I whisper to myself, trying to calm my nerves.

With insurgents firing on them, Micah and Danny Cox, a fast-on-his feet kid, hurry into a storefront and head up the stairs. A moment later a grenade explodes on the rooftop, then M4 rifles sputter. Thirty seconds later Micah and Cox run from the storefront and down the street where Micah grabs one of our injured guys and pulls him to cover while Cox grabs another. They administer first aid.

Whew. Although, I realize we are still in a world of hurt out here. For an eternity, all is still and quiet until someone shouts in Arabic and the insurgents open fire again.

I flinch and grab my cheek, feeling a stinging wound. Either a bullet fragment or some other debris has nicked me. Blood trickles down my cheek so I press my hand on the wound to stop the bleeding.

Danny Cox opens fire, covering Micah, who sprints across the battleground dodging debris and bullets and grabs another one of our injured guys, dragging him for cover. I can't believe what I am seeing. It seems as if I am watching one of those fantastical movies where Rambo or Chuck Norris runs around the battlefield. He jumps up again, unscathed, and runs across the battlefield another way, dodging more rounds and takes up another position against a wall of a storefront. He drops Miller's rifle and pulls his own off his back. "What the hell's he doing now?" I say to Aaron.

"I dunno," he says. "You're right. He's got a death wish."

Micah disappears behind the back of the store and hurries up to the rooftop where the insurgent nest waits for him. Evans screams into his headset again, "Hold your positions, goddammit."

Someone shouts and gunfire pops out from the rooftop where Micah went. He jumps up and struggles with an insurgent. "Dammit. I can't take this. Cover me," I say to Aaron before rushing over to Evans.

"I told you to stay put," he says.

"Stay put? Micah needs support."

We look up, see him unsheathe his combat knife and stab the insurgent in the chest. "Yeah, well, he's disobeying orders," Evans says. "I told him to take up a defensive position and wait for reinforcements."

"Yeah, me too," I say. "Disobeying orders." I sprint for the storefront where Micah went with bullets kicking up dirt at my feet. I trip and crash onto the street, my brain bucket bouncing off the pavement.

Someone pulls me for cover, rolls me over and sits me up against a VW van. He kneels, opens my first aid pouch, tears the packet open and applies the dressing to my cheek, tying the ends together on the other side of my head. "A little flesh wound. Not serious," Stein says.

I gape at him and say, my voice quivering, "I don't think I'm gonna make it."

He analyzes me. "A man is at his loneliest when he fears death. He came into this world alone, and will go out alone."

I stare blankly at him. Micah slides onto the dirt next to me on the opposite side. "Zach? You okay?" He jostles my shoulder.

"What?" I say shaking my wobbly head and looking over at this Stein character, but he's disappeared again. *Damn.*

"You're hit."

"It's nothing. A ricochet." I feel the compress against my cheek. *Huh.*

"Well, I gotta take out that other nest," he points.

"You're trying to get yourself waxed."

"Don't be ridiculous." He stands behind the van and scans the scene like General Patton. "Cover me." He is off in a flash.

"Crazy bastard," I grumble, getting into a prone position. I aim Alice at another one of the nests and squeeze off a three-round burst. Micah makes it for cover in an alley, however, just as he does, and I cease-fire, one of the insurgents stands up shouting and clenching his fist. *Are they all idiots?* I aim at him, but Alice clicks. She's out of ammo. I drop the magazine and slam in another.

Too late. The insurgent fires a few rounds at Micah as he runs out of the alley and dashes up the street. A small red cloud puffs up around his right knee. He dives onto the hard, unpaved street and rolls over behind an abandoned pushcart.

I stand up, with bullets harassing me, and race over to him as he struggles to get up, his knee buckling under him. I drag him to the side of the street behind a truck.

"Darn it," he says. "They're slaughtering them up there."

"Yeah, darn it," I say tearing his pant leg open. He pulls his ACU shirt off over his head and rips off a couple of strands. "Here. Tie it off."

"Wait a minute." I hose his knee down with water from my CamelBak and blot the wound with a piece of his shirt. His kneecap is shattered and hanging outside in the wrong position. I apply a piece of his shirt to the wound and tie it off around his knee. "Just stay put. I'll see what's going on."

"I've got to take out that other nest," he says.

"Take out the…What? You're in no condition."

He looks back at Aaron and shoots him hand signals. "When I move," he says, "concentrate fire in that direction." He points.

"Your knee is mush. You can't…" With that, he is off, limping on his injured leg, his rifle used as a crutch. Aaron and I open fire and Johnny Redneck squeezes off a few rounds. Silence.

More silence. Evans signals for us to stay put, again. Micah stands up from inside the nest and waves all clear. I wait, for what, I don't know.

A few minutes pass and Julio appears just as Micah hobbles over, wincing in pain. "We've got more hajjis up near the front of the platoon," Julio says. "I'm not sure how many."

"We need to get to the radio," I say.

Evans hustles over. "Goddammit, Reid," he says. "You're disobeying orders."

I say, "Sarge, we don't know if Wells got off a call or not."

"We need to get to that radio, Sarge," Julio says.

Evans scans our anxious faces and purses his lips. "Okay. Okay, you and Powell go."

"Good plan," Micah says. "I'm going to take out that other nest."

"You're in no shape for that." Evans looks at his mangled knee, blood seeping through the impromptu bandage.

"Gotta go, Sarge," Micah says, dragging his injured leg like a Zombie.

"Shit," Evans says. "Go!" he yells to Julio and me. "Go!"

We sprint up the street, hugging the storefronts where we come upon two buddies from Fourth Squad, dead where they lie. Julio signals to stop. I

20

look over at Evans who catches up with Micah and Cox. A shot cries out striking Evans. *Damn.* We're dropping like flies. We *are* going to die like dogs here on this Baghdad street. They try to revive Evans, but he is dead. A moment later Micah and Cox rush around the corner of the building. Julio and I wait.

An occasional sniper round breaks the still, city heat. "Look," I say pointing to a body lying in the street. "It's Wells."

"Yeah," Julio says. "We've got to get that radio."

"I'll get it," I say, not believing I say it. "Cover me."

Julio discharges a few rounds. I sprint into the street, grab Wells and try to drag his body backwards, but it will not budge. While unhooking the Manpack tactical radio from the body, Julio's gun jams. A shot pops out and strikes me. I fall face first onto the street. That's it. *I'm dead!*

Chapter Three
A Farewell to Combat

The moon lights my path as I stroll down a street I don't recognize. Fog swirls at my feet and I smell salt water lingering in the heavy, tropical air. Voices can be heard coming from a nearby house.

A strange honking sound startles me and I turn to see a brand new 1934 Plymouth DeLuxe, four-door sedan speeding up the street. Jumping out of its way and hugging the street sign, I look up and read the sign, "*Whitehead Street*?" The Plymouth pulls into the driveway of a two-story house I'm standing in front of, palm trees swaying in the gentle evening air. A young couple, the woman in a dress with butterfly sleeves and nylon stockings and the man in a suit with exaggerated shoulder pads, roll out of the Plymouth and hurry into the house. I follow them.

A porch encircles the upper level of the limestone walls. Approaching the open front door, a white, six-toed cat greets me, encircling my feet. "That's Snowball," Stein says. "Come on, kid. We've been expecting you." With a drink in one hand, he grabs my war shoulder with the other and leads me into the foyer and to the living room where a chandelier hangs above me. A large, gorgeous Circassian walnut chest-on-chest sits against a wall. "This is my wife, Pauline," he says heading over to a wet bar nearby.

Pauline has a narrow face with short hair, parted to one side. She wears a purple floral chiffon dress that hangs loosely on her slim figure.

"Zachary, Ma'am. Pleasure to meet you." I shake her hand.

"Pleasure's all mine," she says, smiling. I glance around the room and see a couple dozen partiers drinking, dancing and flirting. There is finger food on a table next to the wet bar stocked with booze. A small band plays a slow jazz tune in the corner of the room. I notice two books, *The Sun Also Rises* and *A Farewell to Arms* prominently displayed on the coffee table. I pick one up, scanning the cover.

"What do you think?" Stein says handing me a tumbler of whiskey. This time he's dressed in wool slacks, a white dress shirt with an open collar and a sports coat, yet his clothes seem dated, similar to clothes worn in old black and white movies. He has a thick, dark brown mustache and appears to be in his thirties now.

"About what?" I say setting the book down and sipping.

"My books, kid."

I glance back down at the books and over at him. "I've never read them."

"Well, what're you waiting for?"

"There's a war on you know."

He chuckles. "There's always a war." He smiles at a gorgeous blonde woman passing by.

I sip again, squinting at him, wondering how the hell I got here and what the hell is going on. "Thanks for the drink. You have no idea how much I needed this."

"Forget it. Look, an intelligent man is sometimes forced to be drunk to spend time with his fools." He clinks glasses with me and downs his drink.

"Are you saying I'm an intelligent man, or one of your fools?" I follow suit and tip my tumbler again.

He laughs. "Drinking, kid," he says putting his arm around my shoulder, "is the way to end the day."

"An intelligent man, fools, ending the day. You're a real philosopher."

23

"I like ya, kid," he says, squeezing my shoulder. "You have potential." He pours us another round. The band strikes up a swing jazz tune and Pauline snatches me up and spins me round. We hit the dance floor and the moves from a 1930's version of the Charleston come out of me from nowhere, although Pauline performs much better. I have no idea where that came from.

After the dance, I land on the couch, out of breath, Pauline next to me. "Hem," she commands. "Another round." He fills two tumblers at the bar, saunters over and sits next to me handing Pauline and me our tumblers.

"He's cute," she says to him, but winking at me. She runs her fingers through my hair. "His lovely brown hair, these mysterious brown eyes and look at these luscious eyelashes." She runs her finger over one. "Why do some men have such perfect ones while we women struggle so with ours?" Stein is not paying attention, but flirting with that lovely young blonde woman next to him.

"My, Zachary, you're in great, solid shape," Pauline says caressing my bicep.

"Hard army regimen over the past five years, Ma'am."

"Well," she says, leaning over and whispering in my ear. "You come back and visit anytime you like."

"I'd like that ma'am, but..." I look down at my army ACU's, my combat boots, and up at her again. "But..."

~ * ~

I must be dead because I cannot move, yet I open my eyes and see the chaotic ambush still playing out before me. I think of that strange dream, if that's what it was, and wonder where it took place as one of those pesky Baghdad sand flies lands on my nose. I am unable to swat it.

"The first and final thing you have to do in this world is to last in it, and not be smashed by it," Stein says kneeling next to me. "Man is not made for defeat." He scans the carnage. "A man can be destroyed but not defeated."

He drags me by my armpits behind a car where he rips my ACU shirt open and tears my T-Shirt back. As my vision becomes clearer, I see that it's Julio, not Stein. "The bullet went clean through your shoulder, Zach," Julio says. "Came out your front. You're gonna be all right."

He cuts his compress in half with his knife and presses one piece against the entry wound on the back of my shoulder. *Damn, this is the same shoulder I injured in Afghanistan.* The other piece he applies to the exit wound a few inches above and to the left of my left nipple. I look down at it, dazed, and thank God I still have it. I can't imagine going through the rest of my life without my nipple. Then I wonder why men have nipples. It's not as if men are going to nurse a baby. *Funny.*

He tears my T-shirt and ties it around my upper body to hold the compresses in place. "It must have just missed your lung," he says.

I stare at him, saying nothing. Using the radio Wells had, he calls for assistance. "Stay put, Zach." He sprints over to Aaron.

I sit, feeling useless. I can at least try to take up a defensive position. Reaching down and grabbing Alice, I wince in pain. It feels as if I have a spear through my shoulder. I have to help. Lying down on my good side, I try to sight the nest, but can't. A shot or two breaks the ghostly silence every couple of minutes. It is just a cat and mouse game at this point. Another crackle from a rifle, someone wails something concerning Allah, and expires. Aaron hustles over. "You okay?" he says.

"No. You?"

He sighs and lies next to me, his face tight. "Dunno. We're pinned down by that nest."

"Micah and Cox are trying to get at it." Someone shouts from the nest above and we hear a shot from an M4. "Can you see anything?"

"No. I'll check." He hustles off.

All alone, I try to sight Alice again, but can't. Faint, soaked in sweat, yet feeling cold, blood leaks from my wound. My eyes flutter shut.

~ * ~

Then I'm standing on a dock staring at a beautiful wooden fishing boat in a harbor, the name on its stern, *Pilar*. A warm, salty breeze blows across my face. "Hurry up, kid," Stein says. "Get in."

I jump onto the back of the boat. "Grab that line," he says pointing. I release the mooring line off the port quarter. A Hispanic man dressed in a white boating uniform and captain's cap cranks over the boat's engine. He guns it and we edge away from the dock. "Captain's Gregorio Fuentes," Stein says.

"Nice to meet you, sir."

Fuentes has a long and weathered face, whereas Stein has a rounder, fuller one. Stein is older now, perhaps in his forties. He has a thick mustache, a stubbly beard, and wears a loose-fitting Guayabera shirt, khaki cargo shorts and a Greek fisherman's cap. "A beauty, huh, kid?"

"Yeah," I say examining the boat.

"She's thirty-eight feet, sturdy built by Wheeler Shipyards in New York City of all places. Fine operation, though. Bought her in thirty-four." Fuentes navigates through the harbor and we head out into the beautiful turquoise sea.

"Pilar?" I say.

"You need to read my book, kid. She's the heroine in *For Whom the Bell Tolls*."

I nod. "We going fishing?"

He looks up at Fuentes and they laugh. "You could say. Not marlin, but U-boats."

"U-boats? In this?"

"Hell, yes. U-boats regularly stop fishing boats to confiscate provisions, water, and fish. When they pull aside, we spray the deck crew with these." He grabs a Tommy gun from the storage bin under the bench seat and slaps it against his palm. He swings it around in front of me. I crouch down and away from the muzzle and he chuckles. "Relax, kid. I only shoot Nazis."

"Nazis?"

"That's right. Then we throw grenades and satchel charges down the hatch."

I glance at Fuentes piloting the boat. He smiles back at me. *Are they out of their minds?* "Where are we?" I say.

"I'm not out of my mind and what do you mean where are we? We just left Havana Harbor. U-boats have been spotted all throughout the Caribbean." He sets the Tommy gun down and pulls out a small, flat liquor bottle from his pants pocket. "Here." He tosses it to me.

I catch it in the nick of time. "Thanks." I pull the cork out with my teeth and take a filling swallow. I pucker, replace the cork and toss it back to him.

He does the same and pockets it. "Good shit, huh? Nothing like Caribbean rum."

"You don't know how much I needed that," I say to him gripping the pole that holds up the wooden canopy as Pilar rocks along. I gaze out at the open sea.

He comes up beside me and pats me on my injured shoulder. "Nothing like a man and the sea," he says.

"I've never been out on the sea."

"I didn't until I went to Europe for the Great War. Grew up on the lakes in Michigan. Since then, I haven't looked back. This is the place to be. If Darwin's right, that we evolved from the sea, then that's why I have an affinity for it." He digs around in the storage bin under the seat, this time pulling out a pair of binoculars and searches the horizon. "Chasing Nazi bastards is a lot of fun," he says.

"Have you killed many?"

"None," he says lowering the binoculars and squinting. "There's always a first time, however."

It could be the last time. I look at his disappointed frown.

"Last time, hell." he says, perking up again. "Then we have an excuse to fish and get zozzled." He sits in the angler's chair. Pilar slices through the water as if to say she is in charge. Although, the sea will get its way in the end because it is forever, everything else is not. "What do you know, kid?"

"Nothing."

"Good answer. Too many people have it in their heads they know much, and when it dribbles out, it confirms they know very little." He shifts in the angler's chair and puts the binoculars back up to his eyes. "Remember, when people talk, listen completely. I have learned a great deal from listening. Most people never listen."

I hold onto the canopy pole thinking: *What the hell kind of a dream is this?*

"Who says it's a dream?" he says. "You never heard of time travel, H.G. Wells?"

"Sure. But…"

"But nothing. You'll be back in your time soon enough. We are all hostages to our time." He lurches forward and points at the horizon. "Gregorio. What the hell's that? Abeam to starboard."

Gregorio steers Pilar toward whatever this crazy SOB sees. It just occurs to me that I didn't verbalize anything about this being a dream to him, or them being out of their minds, or it being the last time. I shake it off as Pilar races toward the Nazis.

Stein staggers against the rocking of the boat over to the storage bin under the seat. He grabs a Tommy gun and tosses it to me. He clutches onto two World War II era pineapple grenades and flings me one. I juggle it. He swigs more rum and hands it back to me. I do the same and pocket it so we don't get too drunk with loaded Tommy guns flailing about. He steadies himself holding onto the pole, focusing on the craft we race for, like a dog with its head out the car window.

I shake my head. *Am I to die at the hands of Nazis?* I can't die chasing Nazis around the Caribbean. I should die in Iraq. I hold on as Pilar speeds forward. With the naked eye, I can't see anything but the sun glistening off the crystal clear blue water. As we close in for the kill, we discover our Nazis are two Cubans in a small fishing boat. We pull up beside them. "Hola," Stein says. "Buenas tardes."

I glance over at Gregorio who shrugs his shoulders. Stein rattles something off in Spanish at the two men. They look terrorized, their faces wide with fear at the sight of the Tommy guns we hold on them. One of the men says, "No Nazis, Señor."

Stein waves at them and says, "Gracias. Adios." He turns and says to Gregorio, "Let's go. They haven't seen any Nazis." We stow the Tommy guns and grenades. "Give me a pinch," he says. He takes yet another swallow and passes it back. I take another hit as well, if for nothing but to calm my nerves. "Hell," he says. "Let's drop a line and see what we can get."

Gregorio trolls and Stein prepares a fishing pole. "Been fishing, kid?"

"No," I say watching him drop the line and place the pole in the rod holder.

"No? It's pure happiness. Happiness in intelligent people is the rarest thing I know. That is why I commune with nature." He shifts in the angler's chair. "Fishing, living with nature, camping. Man fishes. Animals hunt. Man hunts. Man is an animal."

"What about war?" I say, the humid Caribbean air soaking my ACU shirt.

"What about war?"

"Is man hunting one another in war?"

"There is no hunting like the hunting of man, and those who have hunted armed men long enough and liked it, never care for anything else thereafter."

I consider this while gripping the canopy pole, Pilar rocking as she trolls. I gaze out over the calm Caribbean Sea. It seems so peaceful. I feel so serene and complete. Perhaps he is right about all of this. Perhaps he is right.

~ * ~

"Wake up, Zach," Aaron says shaking my shoulders.

"What?" I feel groggy and disoriented. It's as though I am zozzled. *Zozzled? What the hell?*

"Are you back with us, Zach?" Micah says.

"Huh? Yeah." I squint at him kneeling over me.

A man with a vest of explosives holding a detonating device in his hand runs toward Danny Cox who is covering the position with the guys from Third Squad. The man screams, "Allah Akbar." Aaron and Micah try to get a fix on the man, but it's too late. The man blows himself up, his body reduced to pieces the size of a basketball.

After the body parts settle, we see Cox lying near the blast. The two guys from Third are dead. I jump up with Aaron, flinching in pain from the shot I took. Together with Micah, who staggers like Frankenstein because he can't bend his knee, we hurry to render aid. We're horrified by what we see. Cox's legs are lying near him, blown off above the knees. He's also missing one arm above the elbow. "We've got to move fast," Micah says. "Tear off your shirts for tourniquets." Aaron and I do. Cox is conscious, but in shock. He doesn't cry, scream or say anything. He looks at us like a kid awakening from a long nap. We tear his clothes for tourniquets and tighten them with our combat knives.

A bullet kicks up dirt near us. We hit the ground, rolling over. A sniper in a storefront doorway sights for another shot. "Enough," Micah says. He uses his rifle as a crutch, stands on his good leg, and limps forward, charging. He swings his crutch, or rather rifle, up to his waist and pumps off one quick round after another, like the Duke walking down a western street. The sniper returns fire, but misses. Micah shoots the insurgent who falls over dead. Micah slides down against the wall, his injured leg buckling sideways.

30

An Apache attack helicopter swoops in out of nowhere and destroys the last insurgent nest. It hovers for a couple minutes until Humvees from a platoon-size military police unit storm the scene. The Apache swings around and disappears over the rooftops.

The landscape looks like one out of hell, Armageddon in fact. Bodies lie all over the place. A medic jumps from a Humvee and assesses the wounded. He first attends to Cox. "You guys saved his life," the medic says. "You injured?" he says to me.

"No. No, I'll be okay. Take care of him." Ambulances arrive and medics put Cox in one. It speeds off. Aaron sits on the ground next to Cox's legs and arm looking at the blood all over his hands. "You okay?" I ask him. His pale black face looks up, staring. "Aaron?" I say shaking him by the shoulder. "Medic!" I shout. One runs over. "Can you look after him? Shock."

"Over there," I say to another medic running by. "Follow me." My face twists in pain from my wound. I shuffle over to Micah, followed by the medic. When we get to him, he too is pale, and in and out of consciousness.

"Stay with us, soldier," the medic says to Micah.

"Whaddaya think, doc?" I say.

"It's bad. He's lost a lot of blood. I don't know if we can save the leg."

"You gotta save the leg. He's a star quarterback on his way to the NFL."

The medic sighs and looks at me with wide eyes. I grab his arm. "Don't let them take the leg. I'm begging you."

"Awright. Awright," he says pushing my arm down. "I'll try my best."

They load Micah onto a stretcher, hustle him over to the ambulance and zip away. I slide down against the wall of the storefront, the searing pain stabbing me in the shoulder. My bandages seep. I sit there alone, all alone, feeling sick. My hands shake and my head spins.

"The only thing that could spoil a day was people," a young Stein says standing over me holding that vintage military stretcher. "People were always the limiters of happiness except for the very few that were as good as spring itself."

I squint from the sun streaming around him. He slides down and sits next to me. I study him and say, my voice cracking, "I shouldn't be alive, Hem."

"Look, kid. Every man's life ends the same way. It is only the details of how he lived and how he died that distinguish one man from another."

I stare at him in disbelief, my mouth wide open.

"Forget your personal tragedy. We are all cursed from the start and you especially have to hurt like hell before you can write seriously. When you get the damned hurt, use it…don't cheat it."

"Write?" I say squinting at him. "What the hell're you talking about?"

He smiles, pats my knee and stands. I watch him stroll off down the street. I feel so cold. So alone. I close my eyes and darkness envelopes me, yet again.

Chapter Four
There Are No Heroes… E.H.

"There's nothing here for me!" I shout at my father. "I don't want to work in a dead-end job like you."

My father sits on the couch, four empty beer cans on the coffee table in front of him. His beer belly hangs out over his belt. He belches. "What the hell're you gonna do then?" he says.

"I'm gonna enlist in the army after graduation." I grab his last unopened beer can and pop it open, taking a swig.

"If your mother were here she wouldn't let you do that."

"Enlist or drink?"

"Both." He wipes foam off his stubbly beard.

"My mother?" I say pacing in front of him, a Bills game flickering on the television behind me.

"Get outta the way. I can't see the game." He struggles to look around me.

"You can't see the game? You can't see shit in front of your nose."

"Goddammit, Zachary. If I was only a few years younger I would spank your ass like I used to."

"Oh, yeah? Thanks. I'll always bear the psychological scars of that."

"What? Psycho-scars. I hardly spanked you."

I chug the beer and throw the can on the table.

"If only your mother were here."

"You already said that. Besides, you saw to that, didn't you?" I head for the door.

"You don't know what you're talkin' about." He gulps his beer.

I turn to face him. "You know, you're right. I don't know what I'm talking about *because* you've never told me about it."

He waves his arm at me and says, "Ahhhh."

"What does that mean? Ahhhh?" I wave my arm imitating him. He looks past me, staring at the game. "Well, what was it then?"

He continues ignoring me.

"I deserve to know the truth. She was my mother."

"It does no good to dig this up." He looks past me at the game.

"Dig it up? That's the Powell way. Bury the truth. Drink it away."

"Dammit, Zachary. Your mother was a sick woman." He points to the side of his head. "It's best you don't know these things."

I mimic his gesture, pointing at my head. "Sick woman? In her head? Really. Because of you."

"No," he snaps, polishing off the beer and throwing the can on the table. "You drank my last beer."

I stand and wait, staring at him. He continues to look past me at the game. At last, sensing my stare, he looks up. "Look, she had what you'd call depression."

"Depression? You're kidding? Who wouldn't in this place?"

"I don't like your tone." He looks back at the TV.

I stare him down some more. Silence. He knows I'm waiting for an answer. He says, "There was nothing anyone could do."

"Nothing anyone could do? You mean you did nothing."

"I tried to help her, but she didn't want help. She shut me out."

I shake my head. "I don't believe that. When someone's sick, why wouldn't they get help? Let someone help them?"

"I don't know. I don't know."

I storm out of our small one story house. We live in the old-town section of the city, Lockport, New York, north of West Avenue, which is part of State Highway 31. This town had been a boomtown first during the Erie Canal days of the nineteenth century, then again during the birth and growth of General Motors in the twentieth century. I run over to Outwater Memorial Park, take out my journal and sit on a bench to write and doodle, as I have done over the years.

~ * ~

Groggy, I awake in the Landstuhl Regional Medical Center in Germany, notice an IV in my arm, a bandage on my cheek, and a bandage over my wound on my shoulder, both front and back. Several minutes pass before a nurse enters. A cute Latina, she checks my IV. "How're you feeling, Private?"

"Are you an angel?" I clear my dry throat.

She smiles and checks my vitals beeping on a monitor.

"I bet you get that all the time?" I say.

"You're gonna recover just fine," she says entering data into a computer. "I'm Captain Herrera and you let me know if you need anything."

"Thanks, Captain. My unit?"

"I'll find someone to come and speak with you. Can I get you anything?"

"I had a journal in my ACU pocket."

"It's right here." She pulls from under my bed a plastic bag containing my personals and hands it to me.

"Oh, and whiskey?"

She smirks, shakes her head and checks on the guy next to me.

I hate the stench of hospitals. The smell of medicine, plastic tubes, and other putrid smells all make me sick. A couple hours pass until an orderly makes her rounds, giving me juice and Jell-O. I don't have much of an appetite so I drink the juice and leave the Jell-O for later.

After she departs, and there is no one pretty to look at, I lie there for the longest time staring at the ceiling. Damn, I need a drink, if nothing but to mask the unpleasant smell of this hospital. I wonder who is injured, dead or not. I think of Micah and wonder if he is nearby. Not only do I hope he's alive, I hope they didn't take his leg. I detail and sketch the ambush.

~ * ~

Captain Herrera makes her rounds later that day. "You'll make a complete recovery, Private Powell." She checks my IV. "You'll be out of here soon."

"I'm looking forward to it. After you discharge me, I'm taking you out for a schnitzel and beer."

"You're cute, but I'm too old for you." She checks my bandages.

"Too old? Get out. What're you twenty-two, twenty four tops?" She smiles and removes the bandage on my cheek. I breathe in through my nose, catching a whiff of her perfume. "How bad is it?"

"The scar?"

I nod.

"Just a scratch."

"My good looks are ruined."

"You're just as cute as ever."

"You see. You gotta sister?"

"You don't give up, do you?" She wipes my wound with an antiseptic swab. "I have three sisters, but they're all back in San Antonio."

"Really? That's exactly where I'm going to live when I get out."

"Oh?" She applies a fresh bandage. "Then I'll introduce you to my papa when you get there."

"Your papa?"

36

She tapes the bandage to my face. "Yes, my papa. After he approves, he'll chaperone and then the wedding and, then you know how it goes."

"Can't we just elope?"

"Not a chance." She checks my other bandages. "You're lucky. The bullet missed everything vital."

"I know. See how lucky I am? You stick with me and we could be lucky together."

"I'll see you in the morning." She smiles again and checks the guy next to me. I watch her work until she disappears through the door.

I look at the other guy who's still under sedation and unconscious. I don't recognize him. He has a bandage over his face with only his nose showing, a tube stuck up one nostril for breathing or feeding and he has an IV and wires stuck in all over his body. He's also missing an arm. It's a stub below his elbow. I don't want to end up like that. I would rather be killed in action than have to go through the next fifty or sixty years of my life with missing limbs. I think of Danny Cox. *Damn.*

I close my eyes and worry about Micah and his football career. Most likely, he has none. I see him over and over again in my mind running around that street. He really killed a lot of insurgents and saved many of us from certain death. I think of what I did and try to put the pieces together, reconstructing the ambush. I think of the guys killed. At least I'm here in the hospital and won't have to see the fallen soldier memorials for them. I don't think I could handle the ceremonies looking at their boots, brain buckets and rifles.

"There are no heroes in war," Stein says, dressed in his uniform and sitting in the chair next to me. "We all offer our bodies and only a few are chosen, but it shouldn't reflect any special credit on those that are chosen."

"You always jump in at the most relevant times."

"Yes, well, when we ponder life's mysteries, we ponder our fate." He hands me a black and white photograph.

I examine it. It shows him, at the same age he is now, lying in a hospital bed, his legs wrapped in bandages.

"I was injured from mortar and machine gun fire fired by the Austrian army on the Italian Front. I was just an ambulance driver and should not have been injured like that."

"Really?" I hand the photograph back to him.

"There is no illusion as to glory," he says. "It is ephemeral." He puts the photo in his breast pocket and stands.

"At least you give me more to think about."

He pats me on my leg and walks to the foot of my bed.

"So what do I do now?"

"Do? Take note."

"Take note?"

"Keep living, kid. Remember, the past is bygone."

"No kidding?" I raise an eyebrow.

"Look, wise guy, live life to the fullest. It all ends at some point." He turns and limps on his injured leg out the door.

It all ends at some point? This guy is nuttier than I am.

I lie there for the longest time staring at my journal, the ceiling, and the door. I take in a deep breath, but it feels as if an elephant sits on my chest.

~ * ~

The sun glints off the spectacular snow-capped mountains this early misty morning. I have not seen them before. Shouldering my M91 Carcano carbine, I trudge through the thick muck, the puttees around my boots dirty from the hike.

Loud rumbling in the distance sounds like thunder, but I realize it's artillery. "Someone's shelling someone," I mumble to myself, itching from my grey-green Italian uniform.

A minute later, a new Ford Model-T ambulance speeds down the muddy path. A nineteen-year old Stein pulls up. "Get in," he barks in Italian.

I climb into the passenger seat. "Where are we?" I say in Italian, holding on as the ambulance picks up speed again, bumping around in the ruts we hit.

"What do you mean where are we?" he says concentrating on the road ahead. "We're along the Italian-Austrian front."

"What's that town back there?" Why am I speaking Italian? How am I speaking Italian? I don't know Italian.

"Schio. Damn, kid, where you from?"

"I don't remember."

"Oh, shell shock," he says under his breath. He extracts a whiskey bottle from his pocket and hands it to me.

I pop the cork and take a hit. "It's beautiful, this country, Italy."

He glances over at me, nodding, as if I'm a delicate flower. "You're kidding? Of course it's beautiful."

I sense distress in his voice. "But what?"

"It's beautiful all right. But man has a way of fucking it all up. Just wait and see."

A few minutes later, we pull up behind some vehicles parked near military tents. He jumps out and hurries over to the Italians there attending to wounded soldiers. I hop out of the ambulance and wait. Stein nods to the others and says, "Si." He runs back to the ambulance and grabs a stretcher. "Give me a hand, kid."

I sling the Italian rifle over my back and help load an injured soldier onto the stretcher. His legs are mangled and he has taken shrapnel to his face. They have already bandaged his head and I can't see his eyes or half of his face as a result.

An Austrian artillery shell explodes several yards from us. Dirt and debris shoot upwards. It knocks me on my ass. Shrapnel from the shell passes over me. *Damn! Shrapnel again?* Although, I'm not hit.

More artillery shells impact nearby. I stand and grab one end of the stretcher while Stein grabs the other. We rush over to the ambulance and load the soldier. He grabs another stretcher and we repeat the action for yet another injured soldier. "Thanks, kid," he says climbing into the ambulance. "I'll be right back." He tears off the way we came.

An Italian officer shouts at me. I scamper and jump into a nearby trench where four soldiers guard a sector squeezing off shots at the enemy line. I join in and pop off a few rounds.

An explosion knocks me to the ground. I black out.

~ * ~

"You're gonna be all right, kid," Stein says as he and another ambulance driver load me onto a stretcher.

I have a bandage around my shoulder and I can't move. "I just got here," I say.

"Well, you're going home now." They slide me into the ambulance. He gets in and speeds off, the ambulance bumping along.

I look over at another injured soldier lying next to me. I know this guy. His breathing is shallow, yet he looks over at me, blood bubbling out from between his lips. It's Jimmy Howard. "Is that you, Zach?"

"It's me, Jimmy."

"Tell my grandmamma I loved her, Zach."

"Sure, Jimmy. Sure, I will."

He takes his last breath and expires. I look up at the roof of the ambulance as it rocks along the rutty road. A tear rolls down the side of my face and into my ear.

Chapter Five
Start Over

"Some of the guys are gettin' a game together," Micah says standing at the foot of my cot tossing a football up and down. "You in?"

"Naw."

"You're in, or I'm gonna drag you out there."

"I don't feel like it," I snap.

"Zachary, you need to." He waits. "Come on."

I ignore him.

"Let's go," he says pulling my leg, dislodging me from my cot. "Don't make me kick your butt."

"Awright, awright, pretty boy." I sigh, close my journal and follow him out to the dusty field behind my shitty connex, the oven it is. Although the sun is setting over Baghdad, it's still hot as hell.

We form up in teams, six guys to a team and set up sidelines and end zones using empty shipping crates. Micah heads the opposing team as, what else, the quarterback. We are no match for him because he can scramble and hit his receivers every time. I cover Aaron on a long pass but he catches the ball as it sails over my head. He runs it in for the touchdown, Micah high-fiving him. "We'll give you guys a handicap," he says, slapping me on my war shoulder. "We'll spot you two touchdowns."

41

"You're a real sport," I say panting from the run. "No thanks. We don't take handouts."

"I am, aren't I?" he says. "A good sport and all?"

I smirk at him as his team lines up. Danny Cox kicks off and David Zimmer catches the ball. I block for him, but Julio knocks me on my ass. "That's for always cheating in cards," he says running after Zimmer who runs for an additional ten yards. I get up and dust myself off.

I carry the ball on second down and run for a touchdown because 'semi-tractor trailer' Johnny Redneck blocks the guys in my path. Aaron did manage to tackle me in the end zone. Johnny Redneck, David Zimmer, and the rest of my team celebrate by jumping on me. "Hey," I say. "I can't breathe down here!" They roll off laughing.

~ * ~

The train slowing outside the suburbs of Detroit wakes me. I recall that dream and guess it's better than a nightmare.

Six months to the day since that ambush, I discharged and am on my way to keep a promise I made.

While I watch the neighborhoods of Detroit pass by, I wonder how I got in to Columbia University. Many schools have programs for veterans, and I think because of this they granted me admission, or felt pity on a poor fool.

I daydream of the others, Aaron and Julio who finished out the tour in Iraq without me, and Micah, who went back to Bragg with me to convalesce and finish our enlistments. I'm glad they didn't take his leg. They gave him a new titanium knee. I can't believe Aaron is now enrolled in the police academy in Chicago. I am sure his mother and sister are overjoyed with his return. Julio, who was promoted to sergeant and took over for Sergeant Evans, decided to get out and return to East LA to work at his parents' restaurant. I read an email from David Zimmer who discharged and enrolled at the Labovitz School of Business and Economics at The University of Duluth.

The porter shoots me a dirty look passing by as I sip Jim from my flask. "Wurp," Stein says sitting across from me.

"What the hell do you want?" I snap at him while twisting the top back on.

"Give me some of that panther sweat." He motions to my flask.

I hand it to him. "Wurp? Panther sweat? This is the twenty-first century, dude."

He gulps. "This all you drink?" He hands it back. "Dude? It was always the kids who coined vernacular."

"Look, Hem. The war's over. I've made it. What're you doing here?"

"What am I doing here? What kind of gratitude is this?"

"Thanks for everything, but I've gotta get on with it."

"You will."

The train jerks and slows. I look out the window at Detroit's skyscrapers and back at Stein, but he is gone. *Damn.* I wish he'd stop doing that.

I disembark at the Amtrak station on West Vernor Highway and hail a taxicab. "I need to go to this address in Brightmoor." I hand the black cab driver a slip of paper with Jimmy's grandmother's address. He takes the paper and frowns at me in the rearview mirror.

I say, "I'm looking for the grandmother of a friend I served with in the army."

"Okay. It's your funeral," he says putting the cab into gear.

It doesn't seem fair, somehow, I reflect. Jimmy was a deeply religious soul who loved his grandmamma and his country, although his country hadn't always loved his kind back. If there's a heaven, I hope he is there, or he can have my ticket. I sigh and think how I only knew him for a year, since after we returned from our tour in Afghanistan. I sort of took him under my apprenticeship, if that is the word, although I guess I really didn't take care of him after all.

I watch the city that is Detroit pass me by. The downtown buildings glisten in the sun, seeming to say that we are still here, despite the decline and blight that has hit Detroit over the past three decades. We pass through some rough neighborhoods, areas that, if I get out of the cab, I'll be shot for just being a white boy.

In the Brightmoor area of Detroit a light rain sprinkles from the darkening gray sky. The cabbie drives down a street with dilapidated houses, the grass in the front yards overgrown. Old appliances litter the front yards and driveways and there is no street traffic at all. We stop at a boarded up and abandoned house, the cabbie looking back at me in the rearview mirror. "This is it?" I say glancing at him.

"Sure is," he says.

"Please wait here, sir."

"I'm keeping the meter running," he snaps.

"That's okay." I climb out, look around and see an elderly man sitting on a front porch of a house across the street. I look back at Jimmy's rundown house, then back at the man and approach. "Excuse me, sir?"

"What're you doin' round here, boy?"

"I'm a newly discharged veteran and I served with Jimmy Howard." I stop in front of his porch.

"That right?"

"Yes, sir."

"A veteran?"

I nod. "We served together in Iraq."

"You don' say?" He looks me over. "I'm a veteran too."

"Really?"

"Korean war."

I nod and look back at Jimmy's house again. "Can you tell me where Jimmy's grandmother is?"

"She loose her house. She inna nursin' home."

"Oh. Can you tell me where?"

He studies me some more. "You seem like a good boy."

"Thank you, sir."

"Wait here." He stands and goes into his house and emerges a minute later with the name of the nursing home and its address scribbled on a slip of paper. He hands it to me. "You bes be gittin' outta here befoe' sundown."

"Right. Thank you, sir." I walk back to the cab and hand the driver the paper. "We have to go to this place."

We drive a few blocks and pull up to an old dirty brick building. "Sunshine Villas," the cabbie says pulling over to the curb. I examine the building. Hardly any sunshine, and not quite villas, it looks more like a rundown concentration camp block. I climb out of the cab and sling my backpack over my shoulder. The cabbie drives off leaving me standing there looking down the rain-soaked street, the clouds blotting out the sun. People walk past me shooting daggers from their eyes. I ring the buzzer to the front door. "Yeah? Who is it?" a voice squawks at me from the speaker box.

"I'm here to see Beatrice Jordan." A moment later the buzzer sounds and I open the door. Walking into the foyer, no one is there so I amble down a short hallway and come upon a nurses' station. A woman dressed as a nurse looks up at me from the Jet magazine she reads, her eyes narrowing. "Who're you?"

"I was a friend of Jimmy Howard. I believe his grandmother lives here. Mrs. Jordan?"

She squints.

"I promised Jimmy I would see his grandmother."

She looks me up and down. "Room fifteen, on the right." She lowers her eyes to continue reading her magazine.

"Thank you." I wander down the hall, passing two elderly people sitting in wheelchairs against the wall. One is asleep, or so I hope, his head hanging down and the other looks at me as if I'm an alien. I find room fifteen, stop at the door and see a woman inside in a wheelchair, her head drooping over with a TV blaring down from the wall. I knock.

Nothing. I knock again and say, "Hello? Mrs. Jordan?"

Nothing. I creep into the room and approach the woman from behind. I see a picture of Jimmy in his army uniform sitting on the shelf, a big and proud smile on his face. "Hi. Mrs. Jordan?" I walk around in front of her and she looks up at me. "Mrs. Jordan?"

"Yes?" she says. She appears drained of life and looks to be in her seventies. Jimmy never told me how old she is. In any event, she doesn't look well. Jimmy said she has diabetes, and I can see it is taking a toll on her. She is overweight and her skin is graying.

"I was a friend of your grandson, Jimmy." I compete with the squawking television.

"Jimmy?" Her eyesight, and perhaps her hearing must be failing because she looks past me at the wrong spot. "Is Jimmy here?" she says, her voice rising.

"Aw, no," I say, drawing out the two words and kneeling down to take her right hand in my two hands. "I served with him in the war, Ma'am."

"Jimmy is a soldier," she says, her face lighting up.

"Yes," I say drawing it out as well. "We were friends in the army."

"He's gonna take care of me now." She smiles at me.

I know the Pentagon must have sent a representative to inform her, much like that scene from the movie *Private Ryan*. I play along. "Yes. Yes he is ma'am."

"When you see my boy, you tell him I'll have the house ready for him."

"I will ma'am. I will tell him." I rub her hand and set it back down onto the arm of the wheelchair. She continues to smile at me. "Well, I came here to tell you that Jimmy loved you, er, loves you, very much. He talks about you all the time." She just smiles at me. I smile back at her. "Well, you take care now, Mrs. Jordan."

She looks up at the screeching television. I back away and stop at the nurses' station. "Thank you." The nurse looks up, frowns. "May I ask you how old Mrs. Jordan is?"

"She's sixty-five." She lowers her head to read her magazine. I nod, edge away, walk back to the foyer and whip out my phone to call a taxi. Out on the street the sun is setting and dark clouds spit on me. People passing by gawk as I swig Jim from my flask. I feel some sense of closure with Jimmy, but I will never, ever, forget him dying in my lap on that Baghdad street.

~ * ~

The train rolls into the Buffalo station where my sister's boyfriend, Brad, picks me up. Brad is shorter than me and has long, greasy hair and a silly grin half the time. "How's she doing?" I ask climbing into their crappy nineteen ninety-eight Chevy Chevalier.

"She's having contractions," he says pulling out of the station.

"Shouldn't she be at the hospital?"

"They say not yet." A warm summer day, we head to Lockport, his driving scaring me more than combat as he speeds and swerves around cars in our path. "So, you're some sort of a war hero?" he says slapping me on my war shoulder. "We saw you in the paper."

"Yeah, something like that." The goof, only three years older than me, is brain dead from smoking weed. "How's business?"

"Business is good, man," he says. "People love subs. But you wouldn't believe how hard this job is, the stress and all."

I nod, raise my eyebrow. He passes a car on Transit Road, just making it back into our lane before a truck swishes by. "So you're going to college?"

"Yeah."

"What're you gonna be? A lawyer or something?"

"Or something."

"Well, I heard your father say he is proud of you no matter what."

"No matter what? What does that mean?"

"I mean, he's happy you're back alive and all…"

"But what?"

"I dunno. He just wishes you'd come home."

"Come home? For what?"

"What more could you want than this? We got everything."

"The world."

"You were always funny, man."

"Were?"

"You see?" He snorts. I look out the window and watch the activity along Transit Road realizing I just arrived, but wanting nothing more than to turn around and get the hell out of here.

~ * ~

In Kristen's apartment Brad shakes me awake at two o'clock in the morning. "The baby's coming," he says grabbing a small duffle bag next to the couch I'm sleeping on. "Let's go." I jump up, run into Kristen's bedroom and help Brad get her into the car.

A nurse rushes a moaning Kristen into the delivery room in a wheelchair. I halt in the waiting room while they allow Brad inside. I surf the net on my phone for at least an hour until a nurse escorts a woozy and pale Brad back out and helps him sit in a chair. "What happened?" I ask the nurse who places a cold compress on his forehead.

"She delivered," the nurse says. "The blood and mess did him in. You have a healthy baby girl. We'll bring them into the observation room in a few minutes." She heads back into the delivery room.

I notice my old man outside the lobby arriving. He drops an empty beer bottle into the trashcan there and ambles inside. "I got here as soon as I could," he says clearing his throat.

I know he delivers pizzas until two in the morning when the pizzeria closes, but drinking and driving?

"How is she?"

"She's fine," I say. "Baby girl."

He glances at Brad and sits next to me. "What's wrong with him?"

"Too much trauma."

He shakes his head. Silence for a time, then, "I saw you in the paper."

"Yeah?"

"Good job over there."

"Thanks."

There is a long pause. "Kristen tells me you're going to college?"

"Yeah. Columbia."

"That a good school?"

My poor father, he has no clue. "It's an Ivy league school."

"Really? How you gonna afford that?"

"G.I. Bill, a job for expenses. I'll cover it."

"Good. That's good."

Good? That's all he knows to say. "Well, you guys want some coffee, or something?" I ask.

"No," Dad says.

Brad shakes his head.

I stroll over to the vending machine, slip some coins in and purchase a candy bar and a cup of coffee. I glance over my shoulder at the two of them sitting there in the reception area and turn back to splash some Jim in my coffee.

A few minutes later the nurse comes out. "You can come over to the window," she says.

"Come on, Bradley," Dad says getting up and following me to the window. "Get your ass up and see your new daughter and future wife."

I stand with Dad looking in through the window, Brad hovering behind us. Kristen lies there smiling on the rollaway hospital bed holding her new daughter. I am so joyful to see life come into this world after I have seen so much life go out of it these past few years.

~ * ~

I ride the train to Union Station in D.C., hail a cab and make my way to the Holiday Inn on Rhode Island Avenue. It is late, so I nurse Jim, cuddle up with him and continue reading Stein's book, *A Farewell to Arms* that I bought back at the station in Buffalo and started reading on the train.

At nearly two in the morning, just as I finish the book, I hear a knock on the door. I get up and let Stein in holding a bottle of Teacher's Blended Scotch whisky. "Not bad, huh?" he says.

I look up and down the outdoor corridor outside my room, then close the door and follow him back inside. He sits in the chair at a table next to the bed. "What the hell, man?" I say to him.

"The book, kid. What did you think?"

"The book?" I sigh and tilt my head to the side, shake it off and sit on the edge of my bed. "Well, your prose wouldn't make it in today's market."

"Why not?"

"The average American wants easy-to-read action. Basic reading level is about eighth grade."

"What the hell happened?"

"Television, I suppose."

"Crying shame."

"She dies in the end," I say setting the book down on the table. "What the hell's up with that?"

He takes a nip and says, "Love is only temporary in this world."

"Oh? That's comforting."

"What about you?"

"What about me?" I reach for his bottle, take a swig.

"Ever been in love, kid?"

"No. Not really. Thought I was with a girl in school, but she blew me off."

He takes back his bottle, pounds some back. "Well, there's still time. When you do…"

"If I do."

He pats my leg, stands and hands me his bottle. "If, is the recurrent question, isn't it?"

"You have a way with words, don't you?"

"You're kidding, right?" He saunters across the room, opens the door, and heads out into the night. I rub my eyes, get up and close the door after the nut.

~ * ~

I awake the next morning lying on the edge of the bed, my feet on the floor, holding an empty bottle of Teacher's Blended Scotch Whisky as the sun streams in through the cheap, thin curtains. I look at the bottle and think, I've never bought this brand in my whole life. *Huh.*

I squint, sit up, toss the bottle into the trashcan, and dress in my army dress blues. I think back to the time when, while on leave with Micah, Julio and Aaron after our first tour in Iraq, that we went to Micah's sister's wedding in Tuscaloosa. Seems like a million years ago.

Rummaging around in my pack, I pull out a bottle of Jim, twist his top off and take a swallow. I toss him onto the bed thinking the Secret Service probably won't let me take him inside. I rinse with some mouthwash and spit it out in the bathroom sink.

I call a cab and head out to the White House where I meet up with Aaron, Julio, Micah and his girlfriend, Penelope, and Micah's pastor father and his wife. Pastor Reid towers over me at six feet four inches by three tics. He grips my hand squeezing the blood out of it. "I'm so proud of you boys," he says in a deep, melodic voice that has a hypnotizing effect.

"Nice to see you again, Pastor," I say taking my hand back and massaging it. "Nice to see you again, Ma'am," I say to Micah's mother, a traditional wife who doesn't have much to say. "And you, Penny," I say to Micah's girlfriend, a gorgeous and well-proportioned young woman with long auburn hair. Again, similar to when I met her at the wedding, Micah hangs back, not fully engaged in her presence, let alone her beauty. In fact, he never kept a picture of her with him in combat because he once told us he didn't want to look at it and become depressed while humping it through one godforsaken Afghan or Iraqi village after another. I could never figure him out. I'd be staring at her picture all the time. Like I told Stein, I've never had a girlfriend, or a girl as hot as this! I would never have enlisted if I had his life.

An escort arrives and takes us to the Oval Office where the President greets us, thanks us, and talks of what we did and how proud he is of all of us. The White House photographer snaps pictures, one of the President and Micah, then one with Aaron, Micah, Julio and me. He takes one with Micah and his family, then one with the whole group.

A page leads us to the East Room, one of those rooms that holds so much history, from dead presidents to weddings and other receptions. Here I sit, in the front row, adjacent to the Secretary of Defense, the Vice-President and other dignitaries. I shoot Julio a look of awe, and he shoots me one of 'where the hell are we'?

The President comes in and the ceremony begins. We watch him place the Medal of Honor around Micah's neck. The President then reads the citation:

"For conspicuous gallantry and intrepidity at the risk of his life above and beyond the call of duty while engaged in an action against an enemy of the United States."

I listen as the President tells the story of the ambush, how Micah put his personal safety aside time and again, and ran around like a madman killing all of the enemy, yet saving many of our lives. In the hospital in

Germany and back at Bragg while convalescing, investigators conducted an inquiry of the ambush. Micah was recommended for the Medal of Honor while some of the others, including myself, received other awards at an on-base ceremony before discharging. I recently read where most recipients of the Medal of Honor received it posthumously. Rarely do recipients receive the nation's highest honor while they're living. I guess God kept this boy alive for some reason. Makes no sense.

As the president rambles on, I daydream and see Jimmy again, and Sergeant Evans, from Scranton, Pennsylvania. I smile and remember how Evans always said, "Scraaannnton." I recall how his snoring on base drove me crazy. I think of some of the others, all dead. Yet, I'm alive? It doesn't seem fair, somehow. I sigh.

After the ceremony, everyone mingles for a few minutes. Standing there with Aaron, Julio and Micah, this man approaches and says, "I'm so proud of you soldiers." He shakes our hands.

"Thank you, sir," we say.

"I thank you," the Chairman of the Joint Chiefs of Staff says, a four-star admiral.

I feel a hand on my war shoulder. "How are you boys getting along?"

I turn and say to the Vice-President, "Fine, sir. Thank you."

"Nice to meet you, sir," Julio says.

The Vice-President shakes our hands. "Let's get a picture," he says to the White House photographer. "Scott, you've got to get in this picture," he says to the Secretary of Defense. "Mr. President?"

I can't believe this. Standing together with Aaron, Micah and Julio, the President and the Secretary of Defense join the Vice-President and the Chairman of the Joint Chiefs of Staff while the White House photographer snaps a few pictures.

After handshaking and backslapping all around, we bid farewell and depart for the Willard Intercontinental Hotel, one block from the White House. Micah and his family are staying here. While sitting at The Round Robin and Scotch Bar, just off the lobby, where Mark Twain and Walt

Whitman drank, I Google the hotel and discover it was first opened in 1818 and has been at the center of the political world in D.C. since. Dignitaries and political leaders stay here. Swanky is an understatement. The main lobby has extravagant draperies, furniture, and carpets, and all look like they belong in a European palace.

We have dinner at the Occidental Grill and Seafood Restaurant decorated with historic pictures on the walls of the rich and famous, including presidents. The pastor pays for the whole affair.

"When Micah finishes at the university," Penny says, "we'll get married."

I nod at her, smile and sip an expensive scotch. I glance over at Micah who is stone-faced, staring at his steak and twirling his peas around on his plate.

After dinner Micah and I see Julio and Aaron off at the curb. We watch as the taxi whisks them away to the airport. "You were real quiet," I say to Micah.

He looks over at me. "Yeah." He kicks at a stone near his foot and pulls on the medal on its blue-starred ribbon around his neck. "Just tired I guess."

I nod. "Well, here's my cab," I say as the taxi pulls up. "Let's keep in touch. I guess I'll see you at your wedding?"

"What? Yeah, sure, Zach."

I play punch him on his shoulder, hop into my cab and ride back to the motel where I spend the night drinking Jim, documenting the event in my journal, and watching *Sergeant York* with Stein on a classic channel.

~ * ~

The next day I drag my drunk ass out of bed and take the train to New York City and check into a youth hostel in Chelsea for a few days. A few days are all that I can take, as the kids there are stoned-out travelers from Europe.

I meet with an admissions advisor and enroll in the general studies program because I haven't decided what I want to do. Next, with the help of Facilities Housing, I sign a lease for an apartment share off Riverside Drive and am assigned to a three-bedroom apartment for nine hundred dollars a month. The apartments are in the Morningside Heights area near the university on the upper west side of Manhattan. The apartment is small, yet fully furnished and the utilities are included. It is not quite like the barracks at Bragg, but similar because I will share the common areas with my apartment mates, whomever they may be. At least I will have my own room and not have to listen to others snoring, although I flash back to Sergeant Evans and his snoring, the poor bastard. He was a hard ass, like many sergeants, but he'll never get to snore again.

I check out the jobs listed with the university, food service, event security, and campus beautification, but these don't interest me. Strolling down Amsterdam Avenue, I look in several shops and a few restaurants. Hungry, I stop in front of a bar and grill called Duffy's. It's a brick front building, with one door and a large picture window revealing patrons eating at the bar and at small tables along the wall. I open the door and stroll in.

The bar stretches from the front near the door to the rear. It reminds me of an old western saloon. The bar edge is padded and a long brass footrest goes from one end to the other. Small tables and chairs line the wall opposite the bar. I pull up to the bar and sit.

A moment later a middle-aged bartender comes over. "What'll ya have?"

"Whiskey," I say. "On the rocks, please." I feel like Henry Fonda in some dusty western. The bartender fetches my drink. He is balding, slim, and has bad teeth. I notice an older man, perhaps in his sixties, sitting at the end of the bar talking with another man of the same age. The bartender returns with my glass of whiskey. "Thanks," I say.

"Anything to eat?" he says.

"Yeah. What do you have?"

He reaches under the bar and pulls out a menu. "Not from around here, huh?"

"No." He drops the menu in front of me. "Thanks. I'm from upstate." I pick the menu up.

"At university?"

"Yeah. Start in the fall."

He wipes the bar in front of me. "Why so early?"

"I was just discharged from the army and wanted to get settled and look for a job." I scan the menu.

"Really? You in the wars?" He considers the scar on my cheek.

"Yeah."

"Which one?"

"Both."

"No kiddin'?"

"No. I'll have the burger and fries, please."

"Sure." He places the order with the cook in the kitchen at the end of the bar and walks over to the old man and says something to him. The old man looks down the bar at me. I look away and sip my whiskey.

The old man saunters over. He is short with red cheeks, like Santa Claus with a thin white beard. "I'm told you were in the wars," he says, his voice deep and raspy.

"Yes, sir." I don't know what to make of this, not wanting to get into an argument.

"Name's Duffy," he says offering his hand. "This is my joint. It's been in my family for three generations. My father was Duffy, my grandfather was Duffy."

"Zachary Powell, sir, Mr. Duffy."

"Just call me Duffy." He sits on a stool. "Now what the hell're you doing in New York, son?"

"Well, I'm enrolled at the university."

"Yeah, but a veteran in a liberal college like that? You're not the norm there."

"Yes, well I figured that. For some reason they granted me admission. I wanted to live in and get the feel for the big city."

"Oh, you'll get that all right." The bartender delivers my meal.

"Thanks," I say.

"It's on the house," Duffy says.

"No, no. I'd like to pay."

"You ain't paying, son."

"Oh, okay. Thanks.

"I'm a Vietnam veteran."

I nod and take a bite of my burger.

"So, I hear you're job hunting?"

"Yeah. University jobs seemed boring."

He smiles. "It's your lucky day. I'm looking for help."

"Oh?"

"I need someone to do a little of everything and fill in where needed. You would do some bartending, a little short order, clean up."

I finish chewing another bite. "Well…"

"We'd work around your classes, of course."

"Wow. I mean, I just walk in off the street and you offer me a job?"

"I can spot a good kid when I see him." He pauses. "Look, Zachary. I believe in helping veterans like you get on with life. Whaddaya thinking of doing? For a profession?"

"I have no idea." I sip my bourbon.

"Whaddaya say? About the job?"

"Okay. Okay, I'll do it. When can I start?"

"Take your time. When do you wanna start?"

"Tomorrow?"

"Tomorrow? You don't wanna see the city sites first?"

"Naw. I've got four years for that."

"Suit yourself." He sticks out his hand and I shake it.

~ * ~

I start working the next day at Duffy's and within a few days have figured out the menu and learned how to slap a burger on the grill, not that it's difficult. I take some orders, pour some beers and a few shots, and clean up when the joint closes at four in the morning. All summer long, I work four days a week. Duffy is too generous, or so I believe. He pays me fifteen dollars an hour to start. That, and free booze, what more could I ask for? At the bar, checking emails on my laptop one day, I say to Bud, "You've worked for Duffy for a while?"

"Ten years now. Knew his daughters in school."

"He's a real good guy," I say closing my laptop.

"You have no idea. He saved my life."

"Really?"

"I'm a recovering alcoholic."

"No kidding? You can work here?"

"Duffy took me in, got me sober and off the street." He wipes the bar down. "He had a friend who got me into AA. I work here because doing this keeps me sober. I see drunks come and go and know I don't want to be like them. Know when to stop them from drinking when they've had too much."

"Huh," I say, sipping my whiskey.

~ * ~

The rest of the summer passes and I sack away some funds for expenses. Stein shows up to mess with me once in a while. *Crazy bastard.*

Two apartment mates move in a couple weeks before classes start. Basir el-Masri is Egyptian, average size, dark complexion, he is a quiet young man. Dale Hatwick comes from a wealthy family from Long Island.

Tall, with an athletic build, girls come easy for him. I wonder whether if it is because of his wealth or his good looks. Probably a bit of both.

The second week after classes begin I have some down time on a Saturday afternoon before heading over to Duffy's. I'm in the living room reading a textbook on American studies when Basir comes in. Dale is making a sandwich in the kitchen. "Hey," I say to Basir.

He nods and sits on the couch adjacent from me. Silence for a long moment. "You were in the army?"

"Huh? Yeah."

"Did you fight in Iraq?"

"And Afghanistan."

He scrutinizes me. "Why did you do that?"

I shrug. "Just had to."

"You did not have to join."

"No, I didn't. But, I did. I signed a contract, and I had to go where my country sent me."

He stares me down.

"Look, Basir, right, wrong, it doesn't matter. I did it, it's over and I'm here now to get on with my life. If I hadn't joined up, I wouldn't be here at this university now and couldn't have afforded it."

He doesn't respond.

"You?"

"What about me?"

"How can you afford this university?"

He shrugs.

"What does your father do?"

"He owns a company in Cairo."

"Really?"

"It is a tourist company."

"Hey, look. I don't judge you or anyone for being rich, and I hope no one judges me for doing what I've done." Dale stands behind me chewing on his sandwich. I say to Basir, "Let's just be friends?" I reach over and force a handshake.

"Yeah," Dale says. "Let's go find a party to crash."

"Ah, later, dude. Some of us work for a living."

"Yeah, well, someday I will. I mean, everyone works too hard. We all need to relax more."

"Right. Well, nice chatting with you chaps." I drop my textbook on my bed and head out to Duffy's.

~ * ~

Julio discharges a few rounds. I sprint into the street, grab Wells and try to drag his body backwards, but it will not budge. While unhooking the Manpack tactical radio from the body, Julio's gun jams. A shot rings out and strikes me. I fall face first onto the street, my brain bucket bouncing on the hard surface. That's it. *I'm dead.*

I can't move. I open my eyes and look up at Micah, Julio, Aaron and Jimmy standing over me. "He was such a good soldier," Julio says.

"Yeah," Aaron says. "And a good friend."

"Let's say a prayer," Micah says. They take their brain buckets off and hold them in their hands. "Lord, we pray for our comrade, Zach."

"I'm not dead. Help me up." However, I can't move and they can't hear me. Immobile, it's as if *I am* dead.

Micah continues, "Lord, I am a sailor out on the ocean, far from land as I can be, but I am not afraid no, I will never worry 'cause the light of your lighthouse shines on me."

"What the hell?" I murmur, but no one hears me.

They start singing and swaying like a southern gospel choir, dressed in choir robes, yet they are wearing ACU's. They sing, "Shine on me. Shine on me. Let the light of your lighthouse, Shine on me."

"I'm not dead!" I scream and jolt upright in my bed.

Dale and Basir rush into my room. "Dude," Dale says. "You're dreaming. You okay?"

"What?" I look around the room, sweat dripping from my brow. "Yeah. Yeah, I'm okay."

They back out and return to their rooms. It is four forty-two in the morning. I grab Jim off my nightstand, take a good swallow, stagger to the bathroom and wipe my face with a towel. I have to change my T-shirt because it is soaked in sweat.

I return to my room and sit on the edge of my bed for a long time staring at the floor. Reaching over and opening the nightstand, I pick up my Beretta and inspect it, New Orleans flashing back. I could get into real trouble having this in New York and not registering it. I stare at it for the longest time, shake it off, return it to its holster, push it to the back of the drawer and swig some more Jim.

"You know, I drink to make other people more interesting," he says.

"No kidding?" I look over at Stein standing there at the foot of my bed with his signature bushy mustache. "You're saying I'm not interesting?"

He chortles. "You're getting there, kid."

"I woke from my nightmare, so this can't be another one," I say with droopy eyes.

"You saying I'm a nightmare?" He sits on the edge of the bed next to me, reaches for the flask and takes a hearty swallow. "Well, Poe said, 'all we see or seem is but a dream within a dream.'" He hands Jim back.

I take another sip. "Yeah. I think I've heard that." Twisting the top back on, I look at him and say, "Am I completely mad?"

He laughs. "All writers are mad, kid."

"Writers?"

"It's an exclusive club."

"I don't wanna be in your club. I just want to turn it all off."

"You almost did."

"Yeah. I never thanked you for that."

"Don't mention it." He pats my war shoulder and stands looking down at me. "Look, people want simple answers. There are no simple answers. The world is simple, but man cannot accept it. He cannot just accept it as it is. He has tried to explain this simple world, but he only complicates it in the end."

I nod a little and draw out the word, "Okay."

"Don't worry. It can be a long, slow dance."

"Whatever you say, Papa. Whatever you say." He walks out of the room and down the hallway. I rub my face and look at my flask cradled in my hand.

~ * ~

My freshman year flies by and my grades are good. I struggle to keep busy with my classes, work at Duffy's, and hit the clubs with Dale, who usually sneaks off with some hot girl. I don't, but instead hang with my friend, Jim from Kentucky, who always tucks me in at night. Stein shows up at times to chat with me and I continue to have nightmares of the wars. Jim doesn't do a very good job of washing it all away. Sometimes I see Jimmy and wake up with his blood all over my hands. I always run into the bathroom to wash them. While walking to Duffy's one day a car backfired. I jumped behind a truck looking to see where the shot came from. Two ladies next to me scurried on, reacting as though I was a lunatic.

I receive regular updates from my army pals, Julio in Los Angeles working at his parent's restaurant, Micah in Alabama at the university, Aaron in Chicago who finished the police academy and is now on patrol, and some of the others including David Zimmer and Johnny Redneck. The guys still in, including Sergeant Miller who made a full recovery, are deploying again, this time for Afghanistan. I feel guilty, and lonely, and long to be there with them. *If that isn't crazy.*

My sophomore year begins like my first. However, my life is going to take a turn.

Chapter Six
What the Best Can Be

During the third week of the fall semester on a Tuesday morning I arrive to class early to get a good seat. I review a section in the textbook to prepare for the lecture, a general studies class on political science.

She sits next to me. There are empty seats all over the room, but she sits next to me? Gorgeous is an understatement. She is slim, yet shapely, and has warm hazel eyes. She smiles at me, curling her lips. "Hi," she says.

"Hi." I smile and look away like a shy high school boy. If she puts those perfect lips together and whistles, I'll melt like an ice cube. She has an oversized book bag full of texts.

She settles in and takes the text out. "I'm Jessica," she says, offering her hand.

"Oh," I say, fumbling with my textbook. "Zach."

We shake. Her hand is delicate, soft and warm.

She opens her book to the chapter I'm reviewing. "Just reading it now?"

"No," I say. "I read it last night, but wanted to review some of the key points."

She glances at the clock on the wall. "I didn't have time to read it. Could you give me a summation?"

"Ah, sure." *Why the hell am I so nervous?* "Well, it's essentially about Thomas Hobbes' moral and political philosophy, where he believed that in order to live in a state of nature without fear and civil conflict we should give our obedience to an unaccountable sovereign."

"That was well said."

"Thanks." Damn, my heart is racing and my palms are sweaty. The instructor rolls in and everyone settles down. He is perhaps in his sixties, prematurely bald, but has one of those ridiculous ponytails that some balding men have. I wonder what the point is. You had lost all of your hair, except on the back of your head, so you grow it long there to compensate? Whatever.

I don't hear much of the lecture, and try to stay calm because I smell sweet perfume or body lotion drifting my way from Jessica. Several times she flicks her long, light-brown and silky hair to her side where she wraps it over her ear, catching me looking at her. She smiles, and I look away like a kid caught with his hand in the cookie jar. *What an idiot.*

The class breaks up and I place my text and notebook in my backpack, watching her out of the corner of my eye as she readies herself for departure. She exits the row and I follow her out into the hallway where she turns and says, "I'll see you again on Thursday?"

Those smoky hazel eyes, slightly tilted upwards, knock me over. "Ah, sure," I say readjusting my pack. "Yes. I'll see you then."

"Perhaps we could study together sometime?"

"Yeah. That would be great."

"Okay. I'll see you Thursday."

"Yes. Nice to meet you, Jessica."

She smiles again, turns and walks down the hallway. Like a dog in heat, I stand there watching her hips sway in her tight-fitting jeans. Someone jabs me in the side. "You perv," Dale says. "She's hot."

"Yeah, well, don't you even think of it."

"Yeah?" he smirks.

"Yeah."

"Or what?"

"Are you kidding? What do you think I did in Iraq and Afghanistan?"

"Awright," he says. "I get it, psycho. It's cool."

"You have a class here?"

"Yeah. Catch you later." He enters the lecture hall and I head off in the opposite direction.

~ * ~

I stroll into Duffy's for my shift at four o'clock. During happy hour, the business is brisk. I take and deliver orders to the tables, pour a few beers. Most of the patrons are businesspersons and university staff heading home. Around eight o'clock Duffy gears up to head out. "How's the semester starting off, Zach?"

"Okay, I guess."

"Hey, you seem to have a zip in your step tonight."

"A what?"

"A little spring in your step. Haven't see that from you before."

"Yeah?"

"Who is she?"

"You can tell?"

"I've been a bartender all my life, son. Bartenders know life and can read people."

"Wow. Well, I only just met her today in class. Damn, I could've croaked from a heart attack."

"You've been with a lot of girls?"

"A few. I'm not a slut, you know."

He grins. "With this one, you sense something different?"

"I don't know." I shrug. "She wants to study together."

"Ah. That's how it begins, my boy."

"Yeah?"

"Yeah." He pats me on my war shoulder and departs. *Why does everyone always pat me on that shoulder?*

The activity in the bar has slowed so I take out my laptop and check emails. While sipping a whiskey, I read one from Micah:

Zach, Thanks for your last email. Plans have changed. I can't say too much, but it's not working out. I have to take some time off. I have to go to Minnesota. You shouldn't email me as I can't answer them anyway. Micah

I think it through for a moment. Situation? Minnesota? An Alabama boy going to Minnesota? What for? I reply anyway:

Micah, Okay. Let me know if you need anything. Hope everything is all right. Zach

He has to take some time off from the University of Alabama? I hope it isn't something combat-related, like depression or something. After all, he had been such a superhero that maybe it has all caught up with him.

I notice a customer has finished his beer. I tap out another for him.

~ * ~

An explosion knocks me to my feet. "What the hell?" David Zimmer says lying on the ground next to me looking like a skittish cat. In shorts and T-shirts, we just returned from PT. We jump to our feet and see a puff of smoke rising above the DFAC. "First, set up a perimeter," Sergeant Miller shouts. "Third, follow me." I shoulder Alice and run after the others.

A small fire from the blast smolders as we approach the DFAC. We run inside and find our platoon medic, Chris Waters, is already on site administering aid to survivors. "There're kits there," he points to a box of first aid supplies. "Help those guys over there." Ten, eleven soldiers perhaps, lie around, injured, stunned and disoriented. We spread out and assist the injured, some digging through the rubble.

I hurry over to a guy who sits against an upturned table holding his arm. He is Private Luther King, from Headquarters Company, a supply clerk. He has what appears to be a broken arm and shrapnel wounds. His

ACU shirt is torn across his chest. He'll live, but with scars the rest of his life.

"It's gonna be okay," I say to him. "Let's get your shirt off." I rip it off, inspect his arm, and see that it is not a compound fracture, but is broken nevertheless. A putrid smell permeates the area. It smells like burnt flesh, if that is what it smells like. I use King's torn shirt and make a sling for his arm. I tie it around his neck. "That'll do until they get you to the hospital."

He stares at me, his mouth open. I scan the smoky room, now swarming with soldiers aiding the wounded and digging through the debris. "You're a clerk at HQ, aren't you?" I say trying to bring him out of his state of shock.

"Yeah," he says.

I help him up and lead him to the door, weaving our way through the scattered debris. "Where're you from?"

"Dallas," he says.

"Really? You a Cowboys fan?"

"Yeah. You?"

"You kidding? Bills fan." I lead him outside as ambulances pull up, medics and others hustling around. "Over here," I say, motioning to medics who just arrived. "You'll be okay now," I say to King.

The medics take over. I hustle back inside and assess the chaos, wipe soot from my brow and see charred pieces of tables and chairs, food, blood and some body parts mixed together on the floor in an odd scene that gives me a shiver. How can I ever eat in a dining facility again?

"Over here!" Aaron shouts. "This guy's alive." He digs through some debris near the center of the blast. I rush over to him, medic Waters right behind me. The soldier underneath the rubble stirs, yet he is missing an arm, blown off just below his elbow. It is Tom Bilkens, the guy who had hollered at us minutes earlier as we jogged by during PT. The stump leaks blood, but seems cauterized by the fire that smolders nearby. We lift him onto a stretcher and carry him to an ambulance.

I watch the ambulance speed away. I didn't really know Bilkens, but he seemed like a good soldier. He was somewhat of a wise cracker, but I shouldn't complain about that.

Julio is helping another injured soldier into an ambulance. I look over at Aaron who has blood all over his PT shorts and shirt. "We better get back in there," I say to him. He looks over at me, nods and follows me back inside.

Aaron digs under an overturned table. "I got someone," he says, pulling on an arm there. It dislodges and he holds it up. He drops it and looks at me in horror.

~ * ~

I jolt upright in my bed, soaked in sweat, and see Stein sitting there on the side of my bed sipping from my flask. "Hey," I say in an agitated voice. "Do you mind?"

He shrugs, tosses me the flask. I take a swig to catch my breath and wipe the sweat off my face with my T-shirt. I look down and realize it is one of my PT shirts from the army. I rip if off and toss it at the trashcan. "Was it a trigger?" I ask him.

"Could be," he says. "Almost anything could be."

"That's not reassuring." I crawl out of bed and stand there dripping. "What's it gonna take?"

"Time. Support."

"I don't know what's worse. That, or you showing up to screw with me."

"Look, kid. I don't show up to screw with you. You show up to screw with me."

"Ah," I say waving my hand at him, "you're crazy." I make my way to the shower and stand there letting the cold water run over my body, almost like I did in New Orleans the first time the SOB showed up.

I towel off and discover he has departed and left the door to my room open. I wrap the towel around my waist and shuffle down the hall to see if he's there messing with my roommates. He isn't. I find Dale in the kitchen. "What're you doing for Halloween, Zach?" he says chomping on a bagel.

"Nothing. You?" I grab a bagel from his bag.

"I'm having a party at my parent's house. Costumes and all."

"Really?"

"Don't worry. The folks will be out of town," he mumbles, chewing.

"Worry? Me? Never."

"Hey, why don't you invite your girlfriend?"

"She's not my girlfriend. I just met her."

"Well, ask her. I'll have a town car pick you up." He punches me on my shoulder. *Damn.*

"A town car? You're kidding?"

"Why not? The house is over on Long Island in Plandome. You can't take the subway there."

"I'll let you know." I head back to my room, dress, sip some Jim, head out to class and arrive early where I find Jessica already sitting near where we sat on Tuesday. *Interesting.* There is almost no one else in the room. I shuffle down the aisle. She looks up as I sit next to her. "Hi," I say.

"Hi, Zach." Her smile is so cute I may crumble to pieces and they'll have to use a dustpan to sweep me up. "This time I came prepared," she says.

"Great," I say opening my text. "I read it, but maybe you can help me understand it this time," I lie. I just want her to talk to me. Other students filter in.

"Okay. Well, basically, John Locke greatly influenced western political thought, especially Thomas Jefferson who believed that mankind had basic human and individual rights, or natural rights, such as life, liberty, property and that government's role is to ensure or protect these rights, not grant them." She has a slight New England accent, although I have no idea where she is from, or anything else about her.

I nod. "I see," I say. *I see?* What was that? Why am I so nervous?

Professor West meanders in, drops his briefcase on the desk at the front of the room, and blathers on. I listen and take notes trying to look straight ahead, but I can't help but glance over at Jessica. Again, several times our eyes meet. She smiles at me and tucks her hair behind her ear, revealing her slender neck. *On my side no less.* I turn to Professor West and stare at him, if only to calm myself.

The lecture breaks up and I follow Jessica into the hallway. "So, you want to get together and study?" she says.

"Yeah. Sure."

"I have a class in a few minutes, but, why don't you meet me in front of University Hall? Say, in an hour and a half?"

"Okay. I'll be there."

"See you then."

She strolls off. Again I'm transfixed as she disappears down the hallway.

This is the only class I have on Tuesdays and Thursdays. Usually I go back to the apartment for a while before heading to Duffy's, but I trot right over to University Hall where I wait on a bench, trying to read a chapter for another class, but I can't concentrate. My mind wanders from what is up with Micah, to my old unit now in Afghanistan, and back to the most beautiful girl I have ever met or seen in this world. *And she wants to study with me?* I sip some Jim from my flask to calm me.

I wait for a while, get up and pace around in front of the hall. I sit again and take crackers from my backpack, break some up and sprinkle them near my feet. The pigeons swarm me. I've heard stories of New York City pigeons and how aggressive they are, but now I know that it is true. They are fearless. One sits on the armrest next to me giving me the eye, as if he is saying, in a New York twang, "Hey buddy, keep sprinkling. I'm not full here." I break up and sprinkle the last of the crackers just as Jessica approaches.

"Did they steal your lunch?" she says.

"Almost." I stand up.

"You know," she says looking around, "it's such a beautiful day, why don't we go for a walk in Morningside Park?"

A walk in the park? "Okay."

We cross 120th Street and wander into the park where I notice young men tossing a football around. "You know those guys?" Jessica says.

"No. No, it just reminded me of some friends I used to hang with. We'd get a game together once in a while." As we walk along a path I have the strangest feeling those games we played were so long ago, decades, centuries it seems.

"So, Zach?"

"Yes?"

"Where are you from?"

"Let's play a game."

"I'm listening," she says smiling.

"You get one question, and then I get one question."

"Okay."

"And may I carry your books?"

"Wow. That never happens anymore."

"I believe in chivalry." I reach for her book bag. "Your first question, madam."

"Where are you from?"

I tell her. We turn up one path and meander down another. "You, my lady?"

"I'm from near Greenwich, Connecticut, a place called Round Hill."

"Is it a nice place?"

"Is that one of your official questions?"

"If you insist." A squirrel runs across our path carrying a large acorn in its mouth. It stops. We stop. It looks at us, then scurries on. "What was that all about?" I ask.

"I always wonder what they are thinking when they see us giants walking around." She starts walking again.

I start walking too. "He just thought," and I say this next line imitating James Cagney, "don't even think about trying to take this acorn from me, mistar. Ya see, mistar?"

She giggles. "So, you don't know anything about Connecticut?"

"No. Nothing. Why?"

"Well," she says smiling again, "where I'm from is a nice little town."

"Great. I'll have to visit someday."

She smiles yet again.

"Why so smiley?" I say smiling back at her. *I can't believe this.* I'm acting like a high school kid in puppy love.

"Oh, nothing." We approach a park bench. "Shall we sit a few minutes?" We sit. "So, tell me, Zach. You're not right out of high school like many of the others, the rich ones."

Here it comes. I contemplate what I'm going to say as I say it. "No. I worked for a few years to get the money for all of this."

"What kind of work?"

"Ah, wait a minute. I have a question, or two."

"One." She holds her index finger up.

"Are you right out of high school?"

"No. Thanks for the compliment. I'm an old broad, I just turned twenty."

"Yeah, I thought you resembled my grandmother."

She curls her lips. "I'm a sophomore," she says, "but I took a year off to travel with a friend. We saw Europe."

"I'm a sophomore too. I haven't seen you around."

"Guess we just never had a class together. Too bad." She smiles yet again.

Too bad?

"What kind of work did you do?" she says.

"Well, my work involved a lot of travel too, with friends."

"Yes?" she says, pulling it out of me.

"I was in the army."

"Oh? In the wars?"

I nod.

"Really?" she says. "A veteran. Well, I think that is just admirable. All these rich, party boys walking around, their daddies paying their way, and you served your country. Now I hope your country is repaying you and paying for your degree."

"Not entirely, but a good portion."

She glances at me, then averts her eyes.

"What?" I say, smiling.

"Oh, I…I…shouldn't ask."

"No. No, go ahead."

"Did you get that little scar on your cheek from a combat wound?" She crinkles her brow.

I feel flush and nod.

"Oh," she says, "I'm sorry. No…no, Zach, it actually looks attractive and has character."

It actually looks attractive and has character? I put my hand up to my face to hide the scar and feel like crawling into that squirrel hole I saw one shimmy into a few moments ago to beat him up and steal his acorn. I don't know what to say. Here I sit with the smartest and most gorgeous girl I have ever known in all my life, and it is all over before it begins. I knew this was too good to be true. Why is she interested in me? I want to grab Jim to comfort me, but don't. My eyes water and I look away. I can't believe I'm falling apart like this. *What the hell's wrong with me*? I wipe at my eye closest to her pretending I have dust in it or something. I hope she didn't notice my emotional breakdown.

I didn't get all of it. A tear rolls down my cheek. I quickly wipe it away. *What is she going to think of me? What a loser!* "I…I…"

She reaches over and holds my hand, pulling it down to her side. I don't know what to make of this. "I have a confession," she says.

I sit there like a garden gnome.

"I saw you sitting in class last Thursday," she says, "and rushed to class to sit next to you on Tuesday."

I am speechless.

"And after we spoke," she says, "I wanted to meet up with you after class, but I figured it was too soon and you might think I was stalking you."

She was worried of stalking me?

"Now I know it was the right move. I like you, Zach."

She likes me? She doesn't know that I'm a psycho, lunatic, crazy veteran, killer.

"Of course you're very smart and funny," she goes on, "well-travelled and all, but it's your handsome face I find very appealing."

I force a chuckle. "Oh? And not my hot body?"

"Are you kidding?" She smiles. "Oh course, but I don't give in that easy."

"Oh? Well, I don't either," I lie.

We watch the squirrel stick his head out of his hole, spot us, and dash off to a nearby tree where he scoots up and runs along a limb. "You hungry?" she says still holding my hand.

"Yeah. What're you in the mood for?"

"I don't know." She thinks a moment. "I think a greasy burger and fries."

"A girl after my own heart. I know just the place."

We head out of the park and down Amsterdam. I tell her my family history, or just the good parts. "Yeah, someone told me that place has good burgers," she says.

"I can vouch. I actually work there part-time."

"Oh, then we gotta go in."

"After you." I hold the door open for her. Bud works the bar and Duffy sits on his stool talking with his cronies he grew up with. They see me come in with Jessica. I sit her at a table and head over to Bud to get menus. Bud raises his eyebrows at me. I return to Jessica to take her order.

Duffy rolls off his stool and saunters over. "Hey, son."

"Jessica, this is Mr. Duffy. Mr. Duffy, Jessica."

"Just Duffy," Duffy says. "Pleasure's all mine, Jessica." He shakes her hand. "Sit down, you," he says to me.

"I was going to get her order," I say.

"Sit your butt down." I sit across from her. "What'll you kids have?"

"I would love a burger and fries," she says. "And a diet soda. Thank you."

"You got it. Zach?"

"Same. Burger, fries, whiskey."

"Coming right up." He places the order with Bud.

"He seems like a nice guy," she says.

"Yeah. He's been real good to me." I think a moment.

"But what?" she says.

"I don't know. I'm just thinking how fortunate I've been since I came to New York. I've heard horror stories about how awful people are here and what a big bad city this is." I pause. "Enough of me. I want to know all about you."

"Not much really. Like I said, I grew up in an area near Greenwich."

"And your family?"

"An older brother."

"Doing?"

"Law school. He'll work for my father. Corporate law. Embarrassing, huh?"

"Why do you say that?"

"Zach, my father's a multi-millionaire."

"You're embarrassed?"

"I was born with a silver spoon in my mouth."

"I'm meeting my share lately. Which reminds me. Would you like to go with me to a Halloween party at my roommate's house?"

"A silver spoon kid? Only if you protect me."

"Chivalry, my lady, will be my pleasure." Bud brings over our drinks followed a few minutes later with our meals. We eat and talk more of our families. I tell her about my new niece and a little bit about some of my army buddies, Micah, Julio, Aaron and the others. I do not, however, tell her about Jimmy, the others lost, or any of the horrors I saw.

While eating, I look at the shiny, silver, heart-shaped pendant dangling on a necklace resting in the groove at the base of her neck where the two collarbones meet.

After we finish, I get up and I stroll over to pay. Duffy steps in. He puts my money back in my pocket. "Duffy. This was a date."

"Get outta here," he says.

"You're too good to me."

"I said, get outta here."

I hold the door open for Jessica and walk her back to her campus apartment. "Well, I'll see you, what on Tuesday?" I say.

"No. I'll see you tomorrow, right?"

"Tomorrow?" I say drawing out the word.

"You promised we'd do some studying."

"Absolutely." *I can study with you until the cows come home.*

"At four o'clock? Let's meet again in front of University Hall."

"I'll be there." I watch her climb the steps to her apartment. *Wow. What just happened?* On the way to my apartment, I bump into an old lady on the street, almost knocking her down. I apologize and steady her.

At the apartment, I find Dale and Basir watching television. Dale is channel surfing for something interesting and Basir is holding a textbook trying to read, but not really focused on it. "Find something and stop on a channel," Basir says.

"Here." Dale tosses him the remote.

I plop down onto the couch next to Basir. He scowls at me. "I'm coming to your party, Dale," I say.

"She said yes? I knew you had it in you, dawg." He flings a throw pillow at me. "Now, if we can just get Ramses here to come."

"Stop calling me that," Basir says in his Arabic accent.

"It's true, right?" Dale says.

"What is true?" Basir says.

"Ramses, Mubarak. You still have a pharaoh, a ruler after ten thousand years."

"You do not know what you are talking about."

"Aw, leave him alone," I say to Dale.

"Not until he says he's coming."

"Why would I go to an American infidel event like that?"

"Because there'll be white American women who'd love to get some of that mysterious Middle Eastern dark meat." He throws a pillow at Basir striking him in the shoulder.

"American decadence." He shakes his head. "I have heard all about it."

"I'll protect you," I say.

"Oh? Really, soldier boy?"

"Yeah. No matter what you say, I'll be your loyal friend." I pat him on his knee.

"That is nice," he says.

"Then it's settled," Dale says.

"Yeah. It's settled." I toss the throw pillow back at him. I go into my room and fall asleep reading a textbook for a class on research practices while thinking of Jessica.

~ * ~

Sand blows across the street, obscuring my visibility. I have to pull my goggles down from atop of my brain bucket to cover my eyes. I see Aaron and Jimmy running ahead of me. A barrage of bullets zing all around. I take cover behind a vegetable pushcart, reach down and grab a few dates, toss them in my mouth. *Tasty.* "Move on, Powell, goddammit," Sergeant Evans shouts at me. I glare at him. He too pulls his goggles down to guard against the blowing sand that pelts us before hustling up the street.

I follow, but can't see three feet in front of me now. Someone shouts and I stop at the edge of a bullet-pocked building, scan the area, but no one is in sight. *Where did everyone go?* "Zach. Where are you?" That sounded like a woman's voice. Battling the strong blowing sand dinging my goggles, I move on. "Zach?"

I make it to the other side of the building where a ray of light strikes me. Gripping Alice in my right hand, I hold up my left hand to shield my eyes.

Shadows dance around ahead of me in the middle of a barren, dirt patch of the road. Edging forward, the blowing sand ceases to harass me. I stop behind the guys standing there in a circle surrounding a black-shrouded body on the ground. Julio, Aaron, Jimmy, Micah, and Sergeant Evans look back at me. They open the circle letting me enter. "Who is that?" I say scanning their faces, their goggles still covering their eyes.

Julio stands rigid pointing at the body on the ground. The others stand rigid as well pointing at the shroud. I move closer to the body, the circle closing behind me, sling Alice over my back, kneel down and look at the shroud. I lift my goggles up onto my helmet and look up at all of my comrades pointing at *me* now.

Reaching for the shroud, I pull it back to reveal the body of beautiful Jessica. "Jessica?" I grab and embrace her, cradling her in my arms.

"You have to see and start fighting," she whispers in my ear.

"What? I don't understand." I look at her smooth, soft skin and see her heart-shaped silver pendant around her neck shining up at me. Looking closer at it, I see my reflection and realize there are no eyes in my sockets. How can that be?

Dropping her onto the ground, I claw at my empty eye sockets and jump up in my bed struggling to break free of the sheets wrapped around me. My body is soaked in sweat and my hands shake. Grabbing Jim, I fumble with his top, but manage to pry him open and down a good gulp. I toss the flask onto the bed, lie back and try to catch my breath.

This shouldn't be happening anymore. I'm not in combat or going back. I really like this Jessica. She said she likes me. Would she want to be with me when she learns I'm certifiable?

I look the room over. I expect you know who would show up, but he doesn't. Just as well, because he would just talk in circles and drive me crazier. After toweling off, I grab my laptop and check emails. Nothing from Micah. I open a new email from Julio.

Zach, How's school? You going to be a great philosopher now? Guess what? I'm getting married to my high school sweetheart. You're invited to the wedding. The wedding's going to be a week before Christmas. Jackie's pregnant. Yeah, I know. I let it rip. At least the kid won't be born until after we're married. My grandmother scolded me, made me go to confession. I'll send details later. Adios. Julio

I write him back.

Julio, I didn't know you had it in you. I'll try and make it. Hey, I might not need one of your sisters after all. I met this great girl. I hope it goes somewhere. Did you hear that Micah took time off from school? I don't know what's up. Must be crazy. Catch you later. Zach

I close the laptop and place it aside. It is almost six in the morning, so I hit the shower before the others rise.

~ * ~

For the next few weeks I study with Jessica, we walk in the park and just hang out and talk. While dropping her off at her apartment one day, she catches me off-guard, leans in and grabs the back of my head, pulling me in for a kiss. I think I'm on the way to the moon, without Alice. I don't need her anymore.

79

Chapter Seven
Damn You, Jim.

The town car picks me up at seven o'clock on All Hallows' Eve and drives over to Jessica's. Basir has gone on ahead with Dale so we can be alone. I pull up to find Cinderella in a blue dress with white dovetails, a choker, headband and glovelettes. She climbs in and sits next to me in the back of the car. "Wow," I say. "I hope I don't turn into a pumpkin at the stroke of midnight."

She giggles upon seeing me dressed like Prince Charming with a blue jacket, white pants with gold stripes down the legs, red waist sash, black cape and a gold shoulder sash. The driver pulls out and we head across Manhattan for Long Island. "You decided on your major?" I inquire.

"English and Comparative Literature. Then I'll decide what to do with it."

"You're an intellectual then?" I say with a poor imitation New England inflection.

"I wouldn't say that. I think you're more of an intellectual with your life experience, more so than the rest of these boys."

"Me? Life experience? I'm just a babe in the woods."

"Oh come on, Zach. I hope you tell me all about the wars and your time in combat."

I shrug.

"You know, I come from a very conservative family. My father's law firm takes big corporate cases. He hangs out in political circles. He supported the wars and is very pro-military."

"Really?"

"Yeah, but although he supports all of that, my brother would never be allowed to join the military and actually fight."

"Yeah, that's left up to poor fools like me."

"I didn't mean that." She squeezes my hand and I look out the car window thinking this is too good to be true.

We drive across the Robert F. Kennedy Bridge and over the Triborough Bridge to the Grand Central Parkway and pull up to Dale's house In Plandome. I jump out, run around and escort Cinderella up the sidewalk. I can't believe the size of this house. *So this is how the wealthy live?* Dale told me his father is a venture capitalist and his mother a socialite. The sign on the front door says: Come in, get a drink, mingle, and have a scary-good time. I follow her into the foyer. The living room off to the right is huge, a large dining room opens to the left. Two dozen kids pack the place already getting drunk and stoned.

Pulling up to the wet bar, manned by two hot girls dressed like Playboy Bunnies, Jessica smiles at me and I raise an eyebrow. "Whiskey on the rocks," I say to the blond bunny.

"White wine," Jessica says.

The bunny hands us our poison. A person dressed as a condom walks by and I glance at Jessica sipping her wine. "May the farce be with you," Darth Vader says pulling up in front of us. He lifts his mask. "Cinderella," Dale says taking her hand, flipping and kissing it. "You lucky dawg," he whispers to me.

"This is Jessica," I say to him frowning.

"Pleasure to meet you," Jessica says taking her hand back.

"The pleasure should be all mine." He winks at me. "Fill these out," he says handing us slips of paper, "and drop them in the fish bowl by the door. It's a costume contest. Okay, you kids mingle and have fun."

"He's juiced," she says.

"Damn drunks," I say to her sipping my booze. We look around, confer, fill out our papers and drop them in the fishbowl. "You want to dance?" I ask. She nods. I knock back my drink and set it on the coffee table. Lady Gaga is playing. We dance and watch a guy dressed in a white rabbit suit with a waistcoat swing by with a hot, young Lady Godiva in a skin-tight flesh-colored leotard. "Hey, Zach," the rabbit says.

"Yeah?"

"It is me."

"Basir?" I break out in a hearty laugh. "The White rabbit?"

"Yeah. Dale got it for me. He says it is from Alice in Wonderland."

"No kidding?" The White Rabbit and Godiva dance off.

A cloud of marijuana hangs in the air. "Let's go out back," I say. I lead Jessica out back where others hang out in their costumes. A few partiers have taken off their clothes and are jumping in and out of the pool, some making out.

The backyard has a gazebo, a large barbeque area and the sizeable pool. A few minutes later Darth Vader calls the crowd to the backyard for the costume contest. He staggers around trying to organize the event, his Playboy Bunnies assisting him. Jessica and I stand near the back and try to remain anonymous. Dale rambles on awarding scariest costume to a guy dressed as an ax murderer and sexiest to Magenta, from the Rocky Horror Picture Show. "And cutest couple," he shouts. "Cinderella and Prince Charming." Everyone whoops and hollers. I feel embarrassed, as does Jessica. "Now, the winners come over here."

"What's he up to?" I say to Jessica.

She shrugs and we creep over to him as he pours whiskey into shot glasses lined up on a table. He steadies himself and swigs. He grabs a shot glass and hands it to Jessica and one to me, ax murderer and Magenta. "To, Halloween," he says.

"You like whiskey?" I say to Jessica clinking her glass with mine.

"Not really. But one shot." We knock them back, she puckers and sets her shot glass onto the table. Dale pours her another. "No, I can't," she says.

I set mine down too, but Dale pours me another one. "You can't stop now," he begs. He hands me my shot glass then picks up Jessica's and clinks with me.

We dump them down our throats. "Okay, that's enough," I say.

"We're just getting started," he says pouring two more. Jessica grabs me by the hand just in time and we return to the living room where we dance some more. The marijuana cloud makes me dizzy and I have to sit on the couch. I catch my breath and look around the room at several couples making out and Lady Godiva flirting with the White Rabbit. *Wow. Am I hallucinating like Alice in Wonderland?* Jessica and I talk for a while, but the marijuana cloud lingering overhead makes me high. It's a good thing I'm not still in the army and have a piss test in the morning. "I have to find the ladies room," she says.

"Okay. I'll be right here." I watch her proceed up the staircase where several people are hanging around. Dale saunters by with his two bunnies, waves at me and heads upstairs too. I wait for what seems like an eternity.

I wait some more. Five minutes? Ten minutes? What is taking her so long? I grow impatient and meander up the staircase to search for her figuring I can take a leak as well. Pushing my way through the crowd looking for both Jessica and the bathroom, I come upon an open door to a bedroom where three couples, one on the bed, one on the floor and one on a sofa are screwing the hell out of one another. *Jeeze.* Actually, Little Red Riding Hood is blowing The Jolly Green Giant. "Hey, man," Fidel Castro behind me, says. "The line's back there."

"Oh. Right." *Damn.* Hell of a party Dale throws. I find the bathroom at the end of the hallway, the door wide open as well. Betty Boop sits on the toilet blowing Elmer Fudd. *What the hell is this?* I stand and wait.

"What?" Betty snaps.

"I gotta piss," I say.

"Go piss in the pool," Fudd says.

"Okay, okay." I turn around and head up the hallway where I find another bathroom unoccupied, so I take a leak. I then proceed the way I came zigzagging through the crowd of kids loitering in the hallway. Out of the corner of my eye, I catch a glimpse of Henry the VIII embracing Cinderella. I turn away for a split second, but look back. They are now standing close together, Henry with his arm around her and whispering in her ear. Go figure it would be Henry the VIII. He'll have me beheaded.

I shoot down the stairs and hurry out into the backyard, standing there gawking at the partiers. They seem to be staring at me. I snatch a whiskey bottle off the table and guzzle it. Scanning the happy crowd, I take another large gulp, and yet another.

I wander over to the pool, sit in a chair and take another sip of whiskey. Am I being too much of a gentleman? I really like her and I thought she liked me. Should I have made the move on her? Clearly Henry upstairs is. Why haven't I made the moves on her? Am I a fool to believe that a rich girl such as her could be with a poor soldier-boy like me?

I chug more Jim, look down at the water and see myself sitting in my second grade class doodling in my notepad.

As school ends, Ms. Pendleton says to me just before going through the door, "Zachary, may I see you a minute?"

With my oversized backpack weighing me down, I saunter over to her. "Yes, Ms. Pendleton."

She holds up that writing assignment we did, the one where she instructed us to write about what we wished for most of all. "I want to tell you," she says, sniffling and struggling to hold back tears, "I was very impressed with your paper."

I stare at her with long, puppy-dog eyes.

"I'm sorry about your mother," she says. "You did a wonderful job showing how much you loved her."

I continue to stare at her.

She hands me my paper with a happy face. I look at the drawing showing my mother standing next to me, her arm around my shoulder. The words at the bottom of the paper read:

I miss you mommy.

Why did you leave me mommy?

I glance at a semi-nude couple swimming by in the pool and think of my comrades, both dead and alive. Scenes of good times together on base and around Fayetteville flash through my mind. *Why do I wish I was back there just now?* I take another hearty gulp of whiskey and look at the bottle. Not much left. I look around for Stein, but he doesn't show. I tilt the bottle up to my lips and chug the rest of it. I savor the last drop and throw the bottle in the pool.

I get up and grab another bottle off the table and start on it. Revelers around me are having a good time as I stagger back to the pool, look down at the water and see my mother smiling up at me. She leads me to the school bus, strokes my shaggy brown hair and kisses my cheek. I get on the bus and take my seat, watching her wave goodbye as the bus pulls away. My vision blurs and my head spins. I lean forward and fall into the pool.

~ * ~

Daddy screams, "Ruth!"

I am seven years old when Kristen, my older sister by three years, runs into the hall from her room the same time I do. She looks at me with her large, brown eyes, wide with terror.

Daddy comes from the bathroom and sees us. "Get back in your rooms, goddammit." He has a beer belly and beer breath. Kristen runs into her room, but I double-back into the hall after Daddy goes into the kitchen. I hear him talking on the phone, but cannot understand what he says.

I sneak into the bathroom and open the door. Mommy lies in the tub, the water all red and her head rests against the wall. She is not moving and her arm is outstretched, blood dripping from her wrist onto the floor. "Mommy?" I whisper, rubbing my tired eyes. I shake her wrist, getting blood on my hand. "Mommy?"

I make my way into the kitchen and see Daddy sitting at the table crying, his head down. "Daddy? Mommy's in the bathtub and she won't talk to me."

"I told you to get back in your room, Zachary. Now, get back there and stay. You hear?"

I bolt for my room, slam the door and crawl into bed and cry as a siren screams up the street. A minute later, there are voices in the hallway and something banging around. This lasts for a few minutes until all grows quiet again. Later, I hear Daddy crying in his bedroom.

At the funeral, no one tells me the truth why Mommy died. Grandma tells me she has gone to heaven. I gawk at Mommy in that box, but it does not look like her. She looks like a plastic doll with a long, beautiful white dress. I watch the men lower her box into the ground. *Why are you sleeping in a box in the ground, Mommy?*

"It's a damn tragedy, kid," Stein says suddenly appearing next to me.

"Dammit. You scared the crap outta me." We are standing together watching myself as a little boy weeping next to the grave. He hands me a silver flask.

I take a swig, my lips puckering. "What's this?" I hand the flask back.

"Absinthe." He takes a hit too.

"Stuff's wicked. Is it legal?"

"They tried to ban it in fifteen. Who cares?" He shrugs and we turn and walk away, leaving everyone behind sniffling.

We weave our way through the headstones, the cool autumn air rustling yellow and orange maple leaves at our feet. "My father shot and killed himself," he says.

"Really? Sorry." We walk onto a boat dock on Lake Ontario. "Toronto is just over there," I say signaling with my head.

"Yeah. I wrote for a couple of rags there."

"No kidding? So you were a hell of a writer."

He laughs. "Well, some debated that."

I sigh and look out over the lake.

He says, "It's *not* easy."

"Yeah?"

"Yeah. I have a lot of experience in this. But, what the hell? Let's go for a swim." He hands me his flask and jumps off the dock. *Yeah, what the hell?* I set the flask down and jump in after him.

~ * ~

I open my eyes as two guys pull me from the pool. "Is he breathing?" one of them says as they lay me down.

"I think so," says Fred Flintstone.

I spit up water.

"Zach!" Jessica screams running up to me. She kneels down and wipes the water from my face with her dress. "Let's get him upstairs."

Fred and Yosemite Sam help me up because I am too drunk to stand on my own, so they throw my arms over their shoulders and drag me along. Upstairs, they set me on a bed where I fall backwards. Where's Jessica? I can't see Jessica. Fred and Sam are taking my clothes off. *I hope they don't take advantage of me.* Struggling to keep my eyes open, they pull my pants off and someone unrolls one sock, then another. Fred and Sam pull me up in the bed and I struggle with them, fighting and punching. "Zach," Jessica says holding my arms down. "You're okay. It's okay." She says something to Fred and Sam and the door closes. I can't seem to focus or keep my eyes open.

~ * ~

Stein says, "Grab that there, will ya, kid?" He points at a large, menacing rifle on the back of a World War II era Jeep. We're in the middle of some dry, barren plain.

I hand it to him. "What is it?"

"A CZ-550, bolt-action Safari gun, what some might call an elephant gun." He cradles the gun and takes a nip from his flask. He hands me the flask and I do the same.

"We shooting elephants? That legal?"

"Legal? What're you talking about?"

I hand him his flask and look out over the landscape, zebras passing by in the distance. "What is this place?"

"Uganda, kid."

"Uganda? Is it safe here?"

"Safe?" He squints and walks off into scrub nearby. He is in his fifties, has a white beard and a solid full frame. I follow him, dressed as he is in khaki shorts, a safari shirt and bush hat. I look ridiculous. He crouches behind underbrush and sees something scampering across the plain.

I kneel next to him, but can't make out what he sees. He sights his riflescope. "What is it?" I ask.

"Don't know," he says following the beast with the rifle as it moves closer.

"It doesn't look like anything. It looks like nothing."

"No," he says putting his finger on the trigger. "I know exactly what this is."

The large, dark cloud swoops in. "Well?" I say, an edge in my voice.

"It's fear, kid." He pulls the trigger and the rifle pops. Fear disintegrates within inches of us.

"How can that be?" I ask him. "You know what I've faced."

"Fear masquerades in different ways." He stands and I do too. "Let's go," he says patting me on my war shoulder. "Your girl is waiting back at base camp." I follow him over to the jeep.

~ * ~

I open my eyes and catch the sun streaming in through the window. I'm in a bed, somewhere, the covers pulled up to my belly button. Whose bed is this? Whose room is this? Whose house is this? There is someone sleeping next to me. I look down and see a full head of brown, silky hair. It is Cinderella, dressed in a large Yankee T-shirt. She is gently breathing. My head pounds and I feel sick. She stirs, stretches, and looks up at me. "Good morning, handsome," she says.

Oh God, I want to wake up next to her every morning, but not like this! "Good morning." I clear my throat.

"How are you?"

"I…ah, don't really know."

"You drank too much and fell in the pool. I was so worried about you." She places her hand on my chest.

"I'm so embarrassed. No, ashamed." I look away from her.

"Forget it. I got so drunk once my parents had to send our head servant to pick me up. I never heard the end of that."

"Your head servant?"

"He was our butler at the time."

"Oh? Just a butler. Well, I feel like an ass. I talked of chivalry and you end up looking after me."

"My pleasure."

89

Her pleasure? What pleasure, looking after some drunken fool? "Yeah, but what happened? I mean, the last thing I remember was looking for you because you had taken so long in the restroom."

"I'm sorry. I didn't know that. I ran into a high school friend and we shared a laugh. I then came downstairs and heard all the commotion and saw the guys dragging you out of the pool."

"Yikes." I look away. *What an ass.*

She reaches over, grabs my chin and rolls my head to face hers. "Forget it. You were just in a party mood and having fun."

I gaze into those tender hazel eyes, her hair lying across my chest. She smells so sweet as she runs her finger over the exit wound near my nipple. "Another war wound?" she says.

I nod. She moves her index finger over it again several times although her pinky finger encounters my nipple a couple of times. *Oh no. Get down, you. Not now.* "Does it hurt?" she says.

I shake my head.

She lays her arm across my chest and leans in to kiss me. I close my eyes and we hold the kiss. We pull apart a little bit and she says, "I like you, Zachary Powell. You're not like the other boys. The ones I grew up with. They *only* wanted sex. I hope we can develop our relationship."

"I'd like that."

She kisses me again and I am Jell-O. "Shall we see if there are any other living beings around here?" she says.

"Okay."

She climbs off the bed and I do too. Stark naked, and you know who hasn't completely deflated, I quickly turn away and grab the bed sheets, pulling them up around my waist. She giggles. "I've already seen everything."

She's already seen everything? I haven't seen anything. "You didn't take advantage of me?"

"Me? No. I can't speak for Fred Flintstone and Yosemite Sam."

"Who?" I stand there resembling Julius Cesar in his toga.

90

"Your costume is all wet. Let me see what I can find." There's an adjoining bedroom next to this one with a bathroom in the middle. She heads in there and I follow. The door to the other bedroom is wide open so we peek in. "Oh my," she says.

"Wow," I say seeing Dale sleeping there with the two bunnies, one on each side.

"Hey," Dale says beginning to stir. "Everyone have a good time?"

"Yeah," I lie.

"Zach fell in the pool last night," Jessica says. "His clothes are all wet. You have a robe or something?"

"Fell in the pool?" Dale laughs. The bunnies awake and stretch. "There's a robe on the back of that door," he says pointing to the door behind us.

"Thanks." I grab the robe and quickly pull it on.

"You guys hungry?" Dale says. "There's plenty of food in the fridge, bagels, muffins on the counter, coffee. Help yourself."

"Great," I say. Just before we turn to depart, Dale smothers his head into the breasts of one of the bunnies. He then grabs the covers and pulls them over their heads.

We descend the staircase and see empty beer bottles and other trash all over the place; it reminds me of New Orleans. A few partygoers sleep on the couch and the floor. On our way to the kitchen, we see the White Rabbit sleeping with Lady Godiva on the couch. *Alice in Wonderland indeed.*

I find a jug of orange juice in the refrigerator and when Jessica is not looking, I pour a jigger of whiskey from a nearby bottle into my cup, just enough to sooth my hangover. We eat breakfast as the deadbeat drunks wake up and trickle out. I dress in a pair of Dale's jeans and a T-shirt and he has a town car drive Jessica and me back to Manhattan.

~ * ~

Over the course of the next couple of weeks I attend class, work at Duffy's, and hang out with Jessica studying. Each time while dropping her off at her flat we kiss goodbye. We still haven't had sex. I want to, but...

"It'll be okay," she says one day sitting on our bench in Morningside Park.

"Thanksgiving? At your house? With your parents? I think it's way too soon."

"No, it'll be fine. I've had friends over before."

I hesitate. "I don't know, Jessica."

"It's all right, Zach. I promise." She squeezes my hand.

I sigh. "If you really insist."

"I really insist." She nods and smiles.

"Okay, I guess."

~ * ~

The next day we shop for clothes. She helps me choose some outfits for the occasion including a new suit, a top-of-the-line brand. "I will look like a highfalutin prep school New Englander."

"You'll fit right in."

I force a smile. *I hope so.*

Chapter Eight
She Loves Me?

Jessica's father has a town car pick us up the day before Thanksgiving.

Off Round Hill Road near Greenwich, Connecticut, we drive through a security gate and up a circular block-lined driveway. The estate has gardens, rock-outcroppings and mature evergreens. We pull up to a huge six-bedroom stone-and-clapboard colonial estate. The driver pops the trunk and helps Jessica out. I roll out and grab my gym-style overnight bag in one hand and sling my garment bag over my shoulder. We walk up to the house. "Nice," I say.

"Embarrassing, huh?" I follow her in. "Mother?" We stop in the columned portico of the spectacular entrance, a grand staircase before me leading to the second floor. Hardwood floors, a large marble fireplace in the living room and floor-to-ceiling windows complete the house.

Jessica's mother saunters in from the back of the cavernous home. She resembles Jessica, except her hair is short and sassy and she has Jessica's eyes. "Mother, this is my friend from Columbia, Zachary."

Her mother slows a little upon seeing us standing there. "Oh," she says, acting as though she's sort of surprised to see me.

"Pleasure to meet you, Mrs. Patterson." I shake her hand and Jessica kisses her cheek.

"Yes, well, nice to meet you, Zachary," she says. "You might want to put your bags in your room and freshen up? This way." She glances at Jessica, who ignores her.

"Yes. Thank you ma'am." I follow her and Jessica upstairs, feeling awkward, as if I have just arrived at the Hilton and her mother is the concierge. They lead me into one of the bedrooms, large enough for my father's house to fit into. Mrs. Patterson moves Jessica along and out the door, closing it behind them. In awe of this room and house, it seems as if I have entered an enchanted castle. Hearing them talking outside the room, I tiptoe over and listen. "You said you were bringing a friend," her mother says in a hushed voice.

"And I brought a friend," Jessica says sharply, not in a hushed voice.

"You didn't say a boyfriend."

"What difference does that make?"

"What do you know about this boy?"

"Enough to know I like him, mother." With that, their voices trail off down the hallway.

Oh no. I knew this was a bad idea. Now I feel like the uninvited houseguest. I have two nights to sweat through this. I dig in my bag and find my flask, take a good hit and replace the cap. I then take a gulp of mouthwash, meander into the bathroom and spit it out. I splash some water on my face and towel off after taking a pee. I exit the room and head downstairs to the living room where Jessica waits on a large plush couch. I slink into the room feeling like an interloper. "Everything okay?"

"Well, no, I guess. I have to be honest with you. I didn't tell my parents I was bringing my boyfriend. They assumed a girlfriend. I'm sorry." She tilts those smoky hazel eyes up at me while curling those lips.

Sorry? How can I ever be mad at her with those eyes, those lips? "Oh," I say pulling up near her on the sofa. "Well, as long as your father doesn't shoot me."

"He might."

94

Won't be the first time I've been shot. Again with that smile. *I can't take this.* She leans in to kiss me. I hesitate. "I don't want to get too close and have your mother come in and scream at me."

"Mother, scmother." She grabs the back of my head, pulls me in, and plants a wet one.

Just then, an older Latina enters the room. "Oh, I am so sorry," she says.

I almost jump out of my slacks. "It's okay, Clara," Jessica says. "This is my friend, Zach."

"Hi," I say.

"May I get you anything, Miss Jess?"

"No, thank you," she says. "Zach?"

"No, thank you." Clara departs. "Miss Jess? I like the sound of that."

"She's called me that since I was a small child."

"Well, I'm stealing it from her." I look out the window at the large yard and long driveway. "Your father isn't going to take this well?"

"I don't care." She squeezes my hand. "Don't worry about him. He's just a little over-protective. I'm his only daughter after all."

"Oh, great. That doesn't help."

"Come on, Zach. You were a soldier in two wars, which by the way, you have yet to tell me about."

I say nothing.

"You don't want to tell me."

I shake my head. "It's really ugly stuff. You don't want to hear about that."

"Okay. But if you want to talk about it, I'm a good listener."

"Let's just concentrate on the future," I say. "I've started a new chapter in my life and I really can't believe how good it is." Is this what Stein meant? *Crazy SOB.*

"Well, don't worry about my parents. I really love them, but they're so controlling. I'm twenty and I just can't breathe sometimes. Enough of them. Let's go for a walk."

We put on light jackets and stroll around the expansive estate. She wraps her arm around mine and it feels as if I have eyes upon me from within the house. She leads me down a path to a horse stable. "What is this?"

"Horses, silly."

"I know. I see horses, but you have horses?" We stand at the fence of the corral where four horses mingle. A shiny black mare trots up to me. "She's absolutely beautiful."

"That's Lilly," she says standing back watching. Lilly extends her head over the fence and nudges me by the arm, her nostril breath blowing on me. I stroke her nose. "Wow," Jess says. "I don't believe it. She's taken by you. That almost never happens." Lilly continues to nudge me, so I continue to stroke her nose and her neck. The other horses come over to investigate. Jess doesn't take her eyes off me as I look at her and smile. I turn back to give Lilly my full attention as if I'm a little boy meeting his new puppy.

We stroll back to the house and Jess leads me into the recreation room where a nine-foot billiards table calls out to me. I used to play pool with the guys back at Bragg, so many centuries ago. Jimmy always beat me. Jess and I play a game and a few minutes later a car pulls up to the front of the house. "Father's home," she says.

"Yikes. Judgment day has arrived."

"Don't be nervous." *Damn, I've stared down terrorists and been pinned down under fire, but I am scared as hell right now.* Sensing this, she says, "Relax."

"Protect me," I say squeezing her hand.

I follow her to her father's study where he and his wife finish a conversation. "Father, this is Zachary Powell. My friend from Columbia." Her mother leaves the room.

"Pleased to meet your, sir," I say extending my hand.

He shakes it. He stands an inch shorter than me, is perhaps fifty, and appears to be in good shape. "Zachary," he says, glancing at our entwined hands. "Would you like a drink?"

Would I like a drink? "Yes, sir."

"Scotch?"

"Rocks, please. Thank you, sir." He tweezes a couple of ice cubes from an ice cube tray and splashes some scotch from a decanter into a cocktail glass. He hands it to me and hoists his glass signaling a toasting gesture. We sip. "Very smooth," I say.

"Glen Burns," he says. "Single malt. You know your scotch whisky?"

"Not in a connoisseur sort of way, but some." I notice Jess, who hasn't let up on her grip, acting a little uncomfortable. *She's uncomfortable?*

"Why don't you see what your mother wants to do for dinner?" he says to her.

"I would like to take you, sir, your lovely wife and daughter out for dinner. A place of your choice, of course."

"Zach, you don't have to do that," Jess says.

"No. No, I'd like to."

"That would be fine," her father says.

That would be fine? I'm sure he's figured me out by now, that I am some poor hick boy trampling on his domain, stealing or defiling his daughter, and how will I pay? He sees right through the fancy new clothes I wear. Jess goes to inform her mother. Mr. Patterson says, "So, Zach…" Here it comes, *Get the hell outta here and don't ever come back…* "Tell me about yourself. Sit. Please. Where are you from?" He waves to a leather couch nearby.

We sit. "Well, I'm from a moderately sized town east of Niagara Falls. Lockport. General Motors town."

"Really? I know it." He sips his scotch.

He knows it. Then he knows I'm just a poor blue-collar working-class white-trash nobody. He probably wonders how I ever got into Columbia and how can I afford it. I might as well get the hell outta here. "So tell me, Zach. Shouldn't you have finished college by now?"

"I served in the army, sir."

"Oh. I see. The wars?"

"Yes, sir." I can see him contemplating what to say as he takes another sip: *You're a psycho, nutcase, lunatic, war veteran who will go berserk, kill my daughter, and perhaps shoot up the campus.*

"Combat?"

I finish a sip. "Yes. Army Ranger."

"Really?" He nods. "You saw some action then?"

"A little."

"Well, I do thank you for your service to this country." *Why do I feel that that was condescending?* He downs the rest of his scotch, so I do the same. "Let's get the ladies," he says. I follow him into the hallway where Jess and her mother meet us. Mr. Patterson helps his wife into her evening coat, and I do the same for Jess. I catch Mrs. Patterson watching me like a mother hen ready to pouch on this weasel for stealing her chick. We exit the house and climb into a new, black, four-door Lexus LS.

I sit in the backseat with Jess who holds my hand, squeezing it the whole ride while glancing at me and smiling several times. We pull up to a five-star restaurant in Greenwich. The valet parks the car and at the door the Maître d' greets Mr. Patterson by name, seating us promptly.

Everyone orders a cocktail, whiskey for me, and wine for Patterson and the women. Mr. Patterson orders an appetizer, La Ballade Gourmande, a pâté with veal, pork and bacon smothered in Dijon mustard and balsamic reduction. Very tasty. "Zach was in the service, Mary," Mr. Patterson says.

"Oh?" she says after sipping her wine. "Did you see much action?"

"Some, ma'am. It was mostly slow, boring." Jess watches me.

"You don't have any war tales to tell?" her mother says playing with the stem on her wine glass.

War Tales? Yeah, tales indeed. "No. It's really not that exciting."

"What are your plans after school?" Mr. Patterson says.

"I'm really not sure. I'm just trying to figure it out right now."

"I see," he says. *Why does that sound wrong? Who are these people?*

During our main course, Patterson says, "Did Jessica tell you of her ancestry?"

"Father, I don't think Zach wants to hear about that."

"No. It's okay. I love history, where we came from. Please, Mr. Patterson. Go on."

"Well, she's a decedent of Roger Patterson." Jess fidgets. "Roger Patterson was a founding father," her father says, continuing.

"Really?" I pretend to be impressed.

"He was one of only a few men to sign both the Declaration and the Constitution." I nod, shovel in the rest of my vegetables. "How about you, Zach?"

"My Ancestry?" I say. "I don't know all of the details, but I know my ancestors came here before the revolution." It is true, but I want to one-up the SOB. "My name originates in Wales," I continue, "although my more immediate relatives came from Worcestershire County."

"Like the sauce?" Jess chimes in.

"Yes, like the sauce."

During most of the dinner Mrs. Patterson mostly keeps quiet, sipping her glasses of wine. I think she has three while we eat dinner. The only thing that bothers me is her glare, as if she's trying to incinerate me. I want to bring it to her attention, but in another life perhaps.

After dessert, the bill comes. Mr. Patterson reaches for it, perhaps because of instinct, but I grab it first. "No," I say. "I want to treat." He raises an eyebrow. The arrogant bastard didn't believe me, or wanted to embarrass me. I toss my credit card onto the tray without peeking at the bill.

We finish our drinks just as the waiter returns the check holder with my credit card, the bill, and the credit card slip. I slide my credit card back into my wallet and read the total to figure the tip. The total is three hundred and twelve dollars. *Damn, someone drank a lot.* I figure twenty percent and apply it.

We drive back to the estate, Mr. Patterson rambling on concerning the economy and the decline of the American empire, or something.

"Well, it's late," Mr. Patterson says upon entering his grand domain. "Everyone should turn in now." He looks squarely at Jess. Her mother is already climbing the staircase.

"If you need anything," Jess says to me, "you can just call Clara on the intercom."

"Okay. Thanks."

Inside my room, I sit on the edge of my bed and take my shoes and socks off, stand and undress, tossing my clothes on a chair. I jump into the shower and blow the mist onto the shower wall. I think back to New Orleans. Did Stein really save my life that day?

After a hot, steamy shower, I exit the bathroom with the towel wrapped around my waist. I rummage through my bag and find a pair of underwear, toss them on the bed, and grab my toothbrush and paste. I return to the bathroom and brush my teeth. I rinse, spit, and go back over to the bed. I drop my towel to the floor, grab my underwear and while pulling them up, Jess opens the door and slips in as if she's evading a freight train speeding down the hallway. Just as quickly, she closes the door. "What're you doing?" I say. "Are you crazy?"

She only wears a large T-shirt that hangs just below her waist. She hurries over to me. "Yes. I think I'm crazy for you." She pushes me backwards and I fall over onto the bed, coming to rest on my back. Because of her parents, is she enjoying this defiance, this danger? She jumps on top of me and kisses me.

In between passionate kisses, I try to speak. "I don't," kiss, "think," kiss, "this," kiss, "is," kiss, "a," kiss, "good," kiss, "idea."

"Oh, I do," she says. Her hair cascades onto my face and chest as she works my lips with hers.

I get an erection. "You father will kill me. He probably has the means to make me disappear or something."

"My father is a scheming troll," she says while kissing me.

"Wow. Tell me how you really feel."

She stops and looks me right in the eyes. "I really feel like doing this."

"Your parents are right down the hall," I plead.

She kisses my neck. "This tells me you do too," she says squeezing my boy.

"I do. I do. It's just not the right time." She rolls off me, lays her head on my chest and runs her fingers through my hair that has grown in since leaving the army. It is not too long, but I'm now able to comb it over on top with a little glob of gel. "I really do like you, Jess. But we can't do this now. Here."

"I more than like you, Zach," she says kissing my chest. "I think I'm falling in love with you. I don't know how I'm going to concentrate on my studies now."

"Funny. We'll get you through your studies." We lie there for a few minutes. "Why did you go to Columbia and not Yale like your brother?"

"Are you kidding? I didn't want my brother spying on me and reporting to daddy."

"So, you don't think I won them over?"

"I don't care. I enjoy being with you, Zach. You're different. I've had a couple of boyfriends, but they were typical. They just wanted sex. You're really sweet and such a gentleman."

I run my fingers through her hair and we continue lying together for a few minutes. "We better say goodnight," I say.

"Goodnight," she says.

"You have to go back to your own room."

"Oh, all right." She gives me a long wet kiss. I escort her to the door where she looks me up and down. "I could eat you from head to toe."

"I bet you say that to all the guys."

We embrace and kiss again. "Like I just said, you've been a real gentleman, Zachary Powell. When I get you back to New York, look out."

"Promises, promises." She opens the door and sneaks back to her room.

Lying on the bed staring at the ceiling, I flash back to Iraq and Afghanistan where I used to stare at my connex roof, or at the stars out on patrol. I hope the guys in my unit are holding it together. I can't believe how my life has turned around. I would never have dreamed this. Somehow I've survived and now have this? I hope I can win over her parents. I could be with this girl the rest of my life. I roll over and see my bag on the nightstand. I stare at it awhile, reminding me of the difficult times in combat when I couldn't fall asleep and longed for Jim. After several minutes, I grab Jim and he jumps down my throat.

~ * ~

The next day we hang out around the house. Jess's mother supervises the help as they prepare the feast to come. Her brother, Andrew and his girlfriend, Denise arrive at noon. Andrew is an inch or two shorter than me and resembles his father. No doubt, he will join his father's law firm just as Jess's father has planned for him. I wonder what he has planned for her? After what I experienced last night, I guess she wants to go her own way and escape his grip.

We youngsters nibble on sandwich squares in the recreation room at noon while Jess's father works the phones concerning cases in his study. "How many guys did you kill in the wars?" Andrew says chewing on a square.

"Andrew," Jess says furrowing her brow.

"Oh come on, Jess. It's kinda cool."

"I don't know," I say.

"You don't know?" he says.

"I didn't keep a body count."

"A body count? That means more than one."

I shrug.

"Well," he says, "you did what you had to do to get those towel-heads under control."

"Andrew," Denise says. She is very cute, yet prim. "That's not appropriate."

"You think they were appropriate with our guys?"

"I just think…"

"So Andrew," I say steering the conversation, "what area of the law are you interested in practicing?"

He is on to me, but nods. "The firm mainly practices corporate, but has a small criminal division. It's sexier." He rubs up against Denise.

"Andrew," she says, blushing.

"Let's go see the horses," Jess huffs. "Why not go for a ride?"

"You two lovebirds go on," Andrew says. "You don't need us hanging around pestering you."

Jess dresses in jodhpurs and women's medium-height field boots, a white blouse and a black riding jacket. I follow her out dressed in jeans, a new dress shirt and a light jacket. "I've ridden horses a couple of times back home on an uncle's farm, but it's been a while."

"It's like riding a bicycle," she says. "Don't worry."

Don't worry? I hope I don't fall off. I help her, but she really doesn't need my help. She knows what she is doing. She readies the horses and prepares the saddles. Then, to my amazement, she hoists the saddles onto the horses as she climbs this ladder setup. I stand there useless. She helps me onto Dutch, a brown stallion with a patch of white down his nose and climbs atop Lilly.

Dutch is gentle and cooperative and follows Lilly as Jess guides her along. We trot down a path, through the main gate and follow a trail for a couple of miles around the edges of town. It feels so serene and I feel so alive. The bright November sun shines down upon me and a flash goes through my mind. I think of Sergeant Miller and the others in Afghanistan and feel guilty. I think of Jimmy and wonder what happened to Micah.

I watch Jess atop Lilly, her hair gently blowing in the breeze. She wears one of those jockey caps professional riders wear. Not only does she look so sexy in that, but I catch myself staring at her tight little well-rounded ass snuggled there in her saddle. *Am I in the enchanted forest?*

We circle around and make it back to the corral. I climb down from Dutch and lead him by his bridle over to the water trough. Jess, still atop Lilly, leans over, strokes and whispers in Lilly's ear about how beautiful she is. I think Lilly understands because she neighs and swishes her tail around. I help Jess jump down and she whirls around, hugs and kisses me. I hold the pose for a few moments, but pull away a little. "Your parents could be watching."

"I hope so," she says kissing me again. Lilly neighs. "Jealous," she says leading Lilly to the water. I help her take the saddles off, brush and rub the horses down.

We return to the house and I take a shower. This time Jess sneaks in and waits by my bed as I step out of the shower. I don't see her as I towel off walking right out into the bedroom. I quickly wrap the towel around me. "Jess."

"I fondled you last night," she says standing up to hug and kiss me, "so there's nothing to be embarrassed about."

"I know. But your father."

"What's he need to see it for? Inspection?"

"Funny."

She presses her body up against mine, her average-sized, but firm breasts, tight against my chest. My heart races. "Jess?" her mother calls out from the hallway. I pull back.

"I'm in here, Mother," she calls out.

"Are you outta your mind?" I whisper to her.

"What are you doing in there?" her mother says approaching the door.

I zip into the bathroom as her mother opens the door to the bedroom. I listen through the door. "Talking to Zach," Jess says.

"I don't know if I like what's going on," her mother whispers.

"Nothing's going on, Mother."

"You had better not be, well, you know."

"Be what?"

"Jess, I'm warning you."

"I'm twenty years old, you know."

"Lower your voice. We'll talk about this later."

I think I hear her mother leaving, but I hear her say, "Come on, Jess. Out."

I hear the bedroom door close. I open the bathroom door and peek out. The coast is clear, so I drape the towel over the shower door and dress in a suit, minus a tie we bought on our outing the week before. Knowing what is going on behind the scenes makes me want to get the hell out of here tomorrow morning as fast as I can. I knock back a sizable portion of Jim and creep down the stairs, slinking my way into the grandiose dining room. The table is set and could seat twenty people if needed.

The others arrive from different areas of the house. Mrs. Patterson enters carrying a bottle of white and a bottle of red wine. Upon seeing me, she says, "My, I must say, you *do* look dashing in that suit, Zachary." She places the wine bottles on the table.

"Thank you, Mrs. Patterson." I almost fall over, as she hasn't paid me any compliment up until now. Jess happens upon the scene the very moment her mother says that. "Trying to steal my boyfriend, mother?" If I wasn't nervous enough, I am now.

Mr. Patterson is the last to arrive. Clara and another woman serve the meal. I wonder why they aren't home with their families. I hope Patterson pays them well. Of course, just as this goes through my mind, Patterson pops the question. "Why aren't you home with your family this year, Zachary?"

Jess, frowns, not pleased with the inquisition. "Well, my mother passed away when I was young. My father is spending Thanksgiving with my grandmother in a care facility and my sister is with her boyfriend's family."

"Uh huh," he says pouring some wine for himself. *Uh Huh? Uh huh what? That I don't have a neat little perfect family like yours?* Clara and this other woman bring out the dishes to pass. Jess sits across from me, her mother at one end of the table, and of course, her father at the head. Andrew sits next to Jess and Denise next to me.

The meal goes well, although I only have one modest serving. I do, however, drink a few glasses of wine. The conversation centers on a case her father is litigating. I only listen. The discussion, which Andrew is in on, centers on constitutional rights of corporations. At times Jess rolls her eyes when no one but me is watching her. Out of nowhere her father says, "What do you think, Zach?"

"Father," Jess says, "this is not a law class."

"No, Jess," I say. "It's okay." I put my fork down and take a sip of wine. "Well, sir, I think that only persons have standing as parties under due process of law. That's the fundamental question, as to whether corporations are persons. However, the central issue is if a corporation is considered natural, like a person, then to what degree. Me, as a person, I have very little power to influence the actions of government. However, a corporation, as an entity, wields more power, by virtue of its wealth, and therefore the question comes down to equal access." I glance at Jess and she is holding her fork level above her plate in suspended animation. Mr. Patterson has stopped eating and holds his utensils steady as well.

"In effect," I continue, "the same holds true of wealthy individuals. A wealthy person can write a check for a million dollars to a candidate's Super-Pac who in turn, will, most undoubtedly give that donor access. If I, in being a less than wealthy person, contributed twenty dollars to a senator's campaign, would the senator call me back if I left him a message, or would he call back the individual who donated a million dollars? If we are truly all considered equal politically, as Jefferson espoused, one man, or woman," I smile at Jess, "and one vote, and not my one dollar to a wealthy person's or corporation's million dollars, then I think government must safeguard my truly unequal access and balance it."

No one says anything. In fact, Andrew has his mouth wide open. Mrs. Patterson, who had tipped her wine glass up to her lips, has held it there during my entire oration. "It's about fairness and equal access," I say. "Don't you think, sir?" I cut a piece of turkey in half on my plate, fork it, and place it delicately into my mouth.

After dinner and a movie, *The Dark Knight*, we head to our respective rooms where Jess kisses me goodnight. "As much as I would love it," I whisper to her in the hallway, "you gotta stay outta here. I'm locking the door."

"Then I'll break it down," she says kissing me again before heading to her room where she waves at her door, blows a kiss, and goes in. I close the door and flop onto the bed with my clothes still on. *Damn, am I in some sort of dream world?*

"I don't think so," he says.

"Jesus, Hem. Stop doing that." I sit up as he sits and hands me his flask. I swig. "Absinthe again?"

"Your girl's airtight." He takes the flask back.

"Airtight? More nineteen twenties lingo?"

"Hey, that was a hell of a time, ya know."

"Yeah. I've heard. Then it all went to pot."

He shrugs. "It always does."

"It's been awhile. Where've you been?"

"You've been busy."

"But why now?"

"You're conflicted."

"Conflicted? What're you my shrink?"

"She's inviting you in, kid."

"Yeah," I sigh, "I know."

"You have to let it go."

"But…"

"But nothing. We shot fear in the eye."

I nod.

He gets up and goes to the door. "You want me to go a few rounds with the bastard?" He play punches the air.

"No. I can fight my own battles."

"Have it your way." He opens the door and tiptoes down the hall. I have to get up and close the door after the loon.

~ * ~

The next morning Patterson and his wife see us off. He probably thinks this is the last time he will ever see me. *Well, I have news for him.*

The driver drops Jess at her apartment. Outside her stoop she whispers in my ear, "I'll see you later." She gives me a quick kiss and goes in. After the driver drops me off at my apartment, I grab my computer and head over to Duffy's. I promised I would fill in today so Bud could have the day with his family.

Duffy is not in today either. The noontime crowd shuffles in, but it is not too busy. Liam is the main cook who opens up today. I work the bar and pour myself a helping now and again. Liam is a cousin of Duffy's, and at fifty-two years old, has never worked anywhere else. He treats me well, although he likes to grab my head and rub his knuckles across it. He is married with two small grandkids from his only daughter. Not the best Irish Catholic, I figure.

Business picks up, but by three in the afternoon, it dies down again. Standing at the bar, I open my laptop and check emails. Nothing from Micah. I sip some whiskey and read an email from Aaron:

Zach, Drew my weapon for the first time the other night. Some punk drug dealer. He surrendered. Never fired a shot. Oh well. Watch out for those NYC girls. Aaron

I write back:

Aaron, Hey, I'm going to Julio's wedding over Christmas break. I have a girlfriend. Can you believe it? Never thought that would happen. I won't need your sister now. I'll take the train and blow on through your hood after that. Zach

No other emails. I tap out a couple of beers for two guys who stroll in and another for a guy at a table reading a book. I then read a story on my computer concerning the war in Afghanistan. It centers on two Afghan soldiers who turned on their American trainers, killing three. Wonderful. Jess walks in and hurries right over, planting a kiss on my lips. Liam gives me a smile and a nod. "Did you work on your paper?" I ask.

"Uh huh," she says. "Worked on it. But, I couldn't stop thinking of you."

"Really? Not one second passes without me thinking of you."

"Oh, you just said that to best me."

"Maybe," I say smiling and closing my laptop.

"There's always tomorrow for paper writing."

"You hungry?" I ask.

"Not for food." She curls those lips and tilts those eyes at me. "Let's get outta here."

Liam pats me on my war shoulder. "Go on, get outta here."

"You sure?"

"I got this," he says rubbing my head with his knuckles.

I hold her hand as we cross the street and head back to my apartment. I don't even get the door closed before she pushes me up against the wall. I drop my computer on the chair next to the door and she is all over me. Trying to get the words out between kisses, I say, "I don't know if anyone's here."

"Hello?" she calls out. "Dale? Basir?" She hurries around and surveys their rooms. "Nope. No one here." She jumps into my arms, wrapping her legs around my waist and kisses me. In this position, I carry her to my room, close the door, and fall over with her onto the bed. We tear one another's clothes off. "Wow," I say struggling again between kisses. "You're an animal."

She kisses me on my abs and works her way up to my nipples. She gently kisses my bullet scar and ravishes my neck. She works her way across my chest, then my abdomen, and goes down on me.

At last, I reciprocate, kissing her breasts. I kiss her belly and explore her with my tongue, her moaning so loud I worry someone will hear and I'll get evicted.

I come up for air, locate a condom from my nightstand, tear open the packet with my teeth, and roll it on. She climbs on top and writhes, moving up and down. We enjoy intercourse for several minutes. I try as long as I can to hold it, wanting it to last forever.

But I can't.

She stays on top and holds on. We are so out of breath neither of us speaks. Several minutes pass. I can tell her heartbeat is returning to normal. "Are you okay?" I say.

She kisses me and rolls off. "I *am* in love with you." She toys with my nipple, the one I almost lost. I take a deep breath and exhale. "What was that for?" she says.

I shrug.

"Zachary," she says, an upturn in her voice.

"It's just that, well, I've never done it like this before."

"What?" she says pulling her head up to look in my eyes.

"Well, I've never, you now, made love before. It was always only sex."

"Oh? How was it?"

"Extraordinary," I whisper in her ear while running my fingers through her hair. "I have this deep feeling in my gut. I've never felt this intensity before." A tear runs down my cheek. I turn away trying to hide it from her, but she sees it and wipes at it with her finger.

She snuggles up and lays her head on my shoulder, saying, "I know what you mean."

I kiss her on the top of her head. Her hair smells so sweet. We lie there in silence for the longest time holding one another and kissing some more. I fondle her breasts, kissing them. She plays with my penis and this time she lies back. Yet again we enjoy sweet intercourse.

I pivot to her side, still inside, and while holding her, I drift off to sleep not aware of what happens next until she tells me some time later.

She lies there listening to me breathe. She then gets up and shuffles into the bathroom. When she comes back to bed, she glances at my opened nightstand drawer. She reaches in and pulls out one of my many journals. She opens the leather bound cover and looks at the entry there on the first page. It reads: Afghanistan June 2005. The illustration next to the heading depicts several dead Taliban on the ground and American soldiers standing over them. She lies down and reads the entry.

Somewhere in Uruzgan Province. Humped it over a mountain today. What a god-forsaken place. A tiny village, don't remember its name, they're all the same, little kids came out. Reid kicked a soccer ball around with several of them, no more than twelve years old. Interpreter told Miller all the males over twelve have been forcefully conscripted by the Taliban. Elders report most of their boys are dead. Those who refused to join, were shot on the spot. Several girls in a makeshift school were raped and tortured. We gathered intel and moved out after lunch, those delicious MRE's.

June 20th. Located the bastards in a valley, took up surveillance. Waited another day to strike. We counted twenty-six Taliban. LT and Miller mapped it out. Attack at dawn. Took shifts on sentry. Mine, two to three.

Attack began on schedule. Squad line formation. We hit them hard, waxed many on initial assault. Never knew what hit them. Had them surrounded. Turkey shoot, Johnny Redneck said. Mopped up. Some bastard pretended to be dead. Zimmer saw him twitch, struggling to detonate a grenade. Grenade, Zimmer screamed. Everyone dove for cover, except Reid, another crazy SOB with a death wish, who blasted Johnny Jihad to hell. Some other Taliban idiot moaned nearby. I planted one shot in his head waxing him. Humped it back to base without incident. No causalities. Mission accomplished!

July 4th. America is on vacation and here I am walking through a poppy field. I picked one. Evans says I could get rich off that one. I trimmed it with my knife. Stuck it in my brain bucket.

July 5th. Almost lost Johnny Redneck today. Bastard's crazy. Sniper shot and missed, but bullet tore through his pack. He threw it to the ground, cussed like hell. Bullet actually shredded his romance novel. Go figure. We read anything we can get our hands on over here. Surrounded the sniper. Cox got him, but not dead. Redneck rushed the bastard and slit his throat with his combat knife. He then cut the Tali's ear off. Miller had to intervene and stop him from keeping it. Pissed him off.

She flips through the pages and reads another passage halfway through:

August 9th. I laughed at the grim reaper today. Told him to fuck off. Son of a bitch waved his bony finger at me and said, ah, ah, ah. I'll get you one day. I told him not today. He scowled and flew off like one of those dementors from Harry Potter. On patrol I tried to get a suicide vest off a young kid, but a Taliban waxed him, The bullet meant for me. Then, the Tali blew him up anyway. Shrapnel tore into my shoulder. Stung like hell, but they patched me up. A day later they got me to the aid station. Doc took them out, returned me to duty.

August 14th. No action the last few days. Bored out of our damn minds. Not today, however. Salas got dinged by a sniper on patrol. The round hit his itty bitty toe. Took the tip off. Reid, Glover, Zimmer, Redneck and me tracked the sniper down. Redneck, a hell of a shot, plugged him in the gut from two hundred yards. We rushed him and Glover lit him up. Emptied his mag into him. We sat there, the dead Taliban beside us, and had lunch until the others cleared a nearby house.

She closes the journal and returns it to the nightstand. Next, she picks up a small black case with the words inscribed on its cover: Bronze Star Medal. She opens the case, examines the star and the red ribbon with a V for valor on it. She closes the case, puts it back into the drawer and finds another case that holds one of my two purple hearts. She runs her finger over George Washington, closes the case and puts it back. She closes the drawer, turns out the nightstand light and snuggles up next to me, and while listening to me breathe, falls asleep.

Chapter Nine
You Can Stay Away Now

The next few weeks are hectic. I study with Jess, we take exams in most of our classes, I work at Duffy's, and we make love. Yeah, make love. I can't believe this is happening to me. I have this feeling in my gut, while holding onto her tightly after lovemaking. I don't want to let go of her. I remember Stein saying that 'Love is only temporary in this world.'

For Christmas, I book my train ride across the country. Jess is heading home, as is Dale. Basir, however, doesn't celebrate Christmas, so he will have the run of the apartment. "I'm really going to miss you," Jess says to me while strolling to an exam one day.

I squeeze her hand, sigh and look away.

"What?" she says stopping me at the door to her exam room.

I try to hide the tear I'm fighting from rolling down my cheek. "Zach?" She swings me around to look in my eyes. "What's wrong?"

I shake my head.

"What is it, Zachary Powell?" She holds both of my hands.

I continue to struggle with the tear as students walk past and glance at us. "It's just that, I don't know. Along comes an angel." The tear breaks loose and runs down my cheek. She wipes at it before I can, hugs me and buries her head in my chest.

"Awright you two," Dale says walking past. "Get a room." He moves on.

I wipe my wet eyes with my fingers and she enters her exam room. I head over to Duffy's, make myself a burger, pour a whiskey and check emails. Nothing from Micah. He has disappeared from the face of the earth. I write an email to Julio detailing my arrival time in Los Angeles and later head back to my apartment where Basir is reading in the living room. "Hey," I say.

"Zach," he says.

I sit down on the sofa, pull out a textbook, one for another general studies class, Fundamentals of Western Philosophy, and skim a passage. "Why don't you come with me?"

He shrugs.

"What're you going to do around here the whole time?"

He shrugs again.

"You'd get to see the whole USA and experience our different cultures."

"I have had quite a bit of your decadent American culture."

"You seem to have had a good time experiencing it. You should round it out with a little more. Come on, we'll have fun. You'll like Julio and Aaron."

"Well…" He looks down at his book.

"That's it, you're going."

"I did not say that," he snaps, glancing back up at me.

"No, but you're thinking about it."

"Well…"

"I'll get you a ticket. I'm buying."

"That does not matter. I could buy my own ticket."

"You could, but it's my Christmas present to you."

"Do not get me started on that."

114

"You can get me a Ramadan gift some time."

"It does not work that way."

"Well, whatever Muslims do."

"Contrary to your American misperceptions, we are really generous people."

"I know that. I never fought and killed nice people."

"Ha, ha."

"So, it's settled. You're going with me, and it's my treat." I push his shoulder.

He bites his lip. "Okay. I guess. Just keep me away from these American women. All they want to do is use me for my body."

I laugh. Basir isn't unattractive, only average. He is shorter than me and hairier than a grizzly bear. I'm sure some women find that attractive.

~ * ~

I buy a ticket for Basir the next day and together we ride the subway to Pennsylvania Station. We board our train and Basir sits across from me as we traverse the country.

I call Jess when we clear the station. She answers after the second ring saying, "I love you."

"I love me too," I say.

"Zachary."

"Of course I love you, silly, as you say." Someone is talking in the background and she says something to this person. "Jess?"

"Just a second, Zach." Her voice is muffled as if she has smothered the phone against her body. "Zach?"

"Yes?"

"Hang on a second." I wait for a minute until she says, "Okay. Where are you now?"

"We're in West Virginia. Is everything okay?"

"What? Oh, yes."

"What was all that?"

"Oh, nothing. Just my father ordering me around." Her breathing rate picks up, as if she is jogging or walking fast.

"Are you sure?"

"Don't worry."

"Where are you?" I say, glancing at Basir who frowns at me.

"I'm heading out to the stables to take Lilly out for a ride."

"Oh. I wish I was there."

"I wish you were here," she says.

Silence for a long moment. I hear her open the stall door. "My good baby," she whispers.

"Good baby?"

"Lilly," she says. "You're my good boy."

"That makes you my good girl," I say. Basir frowns again.

"Well, I'll call you later," she says.

"Okay." Silence, but she doesn't hang up. "You still there?" I say.

"Yes. You have to hang up," she says.

"No," I say. "You have to hang up first."

"No," she says. "I'm not hanging up until you hang up."

"I'm not hanging up until you hang up."

Basir says, "Give me the phone."

I hesitate. "Hang on," I say to Jess. "Basir wants to say something. I miss you so much." I hand the phone to him.

"Hello, Miss Jessica?" A moment, then he says, "I will hang up on you so that way he does not have to. Okay?" Another moment, then, "Goodbye," he says. He hands the phone back to me after pushing the end button. "I could not take that any longer."

"Thanks. You're a real sweetheart."

"What is a sweetheart?"

"A good friend," I say. He nods.

116

~ * ~

We pull into Union Station in Los Angeles almost three days after leaving New York.

We disembark and make our way into the main terminal. Los Angeles' Union Station, a national landmark, I Googled on my phone, has a Southwest mission theme with terra cotta tiles and travertine marble that highlights spectacular floor designs. The station is full of travelers coming and going or waiting around for loved ones or trains.

Outside, Julio texts me saying he is five minutes away. I text him back saying he should not be texting while driving.

He pulls up in a brand new, red Chevy Camaro and jumps out. "Are you kidding?" I say.

"Nice huh?" He punches my shoulder.

"Ouch," I say. "That's my war wound."

We embrace. "That's why I hit you there."

"This is Basir." They exchange handshakes. Julio opens the door for Basir to crawl in the back and tosses our backpacks in the trunk while I sit in the passenger seat. He pulls out and drives onto one of those famous LA freeways, accelerating to eighty miles an hour in a split second. "You don't have to show off," I say.

"I drive like this all the time. Relax, this is my hood and I know it like the curvature of my fiancé's body."

"Funny," I say holding onto the door handle for my life. I look back at Basir.

"Now *I* know all of you Americans are crazy," he says.

We exit the freeway at an off-ramp called Eastern Avenue and a right onto City Terrace. "Now don't go wandering around out on your own," Julio says. "Basir could pass, but a white boy like you. Well, you'd probably be kidnapped and sold into slavery in one of those Mexican drug gangs and be somebody's bitch."

"Wonderful," I say. "Is this the America I fought for?"

"It's Mexica-America, amigo," he says with a thick Mexican accent and making some gang-sign with his hands on top of the steering wheel. We pull up to a large house just off Cesar Chavez Avenue. It is larger than most we passed in this area.

"Is this the Beverley Hills of East LA?" I say.

"You got that right, homie." We enter the house. "Mama made us dinner." We drop our backpacks on a chair in the foyer. The house is large inside as well, with an old wooden dining table like something out of a Clint Eastwood movie to the left in the dining room, and leather brown furniture in the living room. In fact, the whole house looks right out of one of those Mexican or spaghetti westerns.

We sit at the kitchen table. Julio pulls from the oven some enchiladas, refried beans and rice. He grabs three beers from the refrigerator, pops the tops and we dig in. "Cheers," he says.

We finish eating and I have another beer to squelch the hot salsa. "May I go to your bathroom?" Basir says.

"You may." Julio leads him to the bathroom. He comes back after a minute. "He's going to take a shower and go to bed," he says. "Another beer?"

I nod, put my empty plate by the sink. "That was delicious."

"That's my mama. The best of East LA, man." He retrieves two more beers from the fridge and sits at the table. I sit opposite him and take a swig of beer.

Silence.

"You miss it?" he says.

"I did at first, the guys and all, but now that I've found this amazing girl, I don't."

He nods. "I think of the guys still fighting."

Silence, another sip of beer. "You have dreams?" I say.

"Like nightmares?" He nods. "Sometimes. But with Jackie right there, she helps me get back to sleep."

"Huh," I utter swigging more beer. "It's normal, I guess."

"Yeah." He takes a long swig of beer. "Well, wait to you meet her. I've known her since the third grade."

"Wow. Childhood sweetheart. True romance."

"Fuck yeah. She's so hot."

"Yeah? Where're your sisters?"

"I told you I'd never let them near you."

"Relax. Jess is the only girl I'll ever have from now on. My days of philandering are over."

"They better be. What's with your pal there? Basir?"

"Wealthy Egyptian family. Studying to be a doctor. Pretends to be a hard ass on America and us Americans, but I think he really likes it here. We went to a Halloween party where this hot chick got him drunk and popped his cherry."

"Really?" He laughs. "Well, we should turn in. We've got a lot to do tomorrow." I follow him into his room. Basir lies there on the bed reading a textbook after finishing his shower.

"Somebody smells fresh," I say. "Where am I crashing?" I look the room over.

"There." Julio points to his bed.

"Oh no," I say.

"Guys sleep together all the time in my culture," Basir says. "It does not mean we are gay."

"Yeah, well, just keep your ass on your side of the bed."

"Shower's in there," Julio says. "I'll see you in the morning. I'm off to snuggle with mi muchacha." He slaps me on my back.

"Gee, thanks," I say grabbing my pack and heading for the shower.

~ * ~

The next day we have some time until the rehearsal and dinner so Julio drives us to Venice Beach. We zip down one freeway, and come upon a freeway jam downtown. We transition to another freeway and can see the Hollywood sign up on the hill. The hill is larger and the sign looks smaller from all of the pictures I have seen.

We start at Muscle Beach where all these Schwarzenegger-types press weights. "Damn," I say. "His arms are bigger than my thighs."

Along the boardwalk, we happen upon musicians, magicians, palm readers, artists selling their wares, and tourists buying cheap trinkets from street venders. The weather is warm this December day and people actually lie around on the sand and frolic in the water. A game of pick-up-ball plays out on the basketball court. Some guy is eating fire on a stick, dropping it down his throat and pulling it back out. Tourists toss coins into his hat on the ground.

We come upon an old man in a wheelchair. He is missing a leg and wears a worn vintage olive drab army jacket. He is balding on top, but his hair is long on its sides. He looks like David Crosby. He has a dirty beard and a placard that says: 'Vietnam Vet. I won't lie. Need money for booze.' I stop as Julio and Basir walk on ahead of me. "What's your poison?" I say to the man.

"Whiskey," he says squinting from the bright sun, "but I'll settle for beer."

"A man after my own heart. Hang on." I enter a liquor store and buy two bottles of Jim. Julio and Basir intercept me as I exit the store.

"Whaddaya doing?" Julio says.

"We have time, right?" They follow me over to the vet. I hand him one bottle and keep one for myself.

"No one's ever bought me booze like this before," he says, his face lighting up. In heaven, he twists the top off, as do I with mine.

120

"Cheers," I say tilting my bottle and taking a gulp. He takes one as well and I sit down on the grass next to him. Julio and Basir stand there glaring at me as if I've lost my mind. "He's a vet," I say to Julio passing him the bottle. He takes a nip and passes it to Basir, who shakes his head. "We're vets too," I say to the man.

"Really? Iraq?" He has a gruff, deep voice, probably from all of the booze for the past forty or so years.

"And Afghanistan."

"No kiddin'. Pretty fucked up, huh?"

"Aren't they all?"

He grunts, takes another swig.

"I'm Zach, this is Julio and Basir."

He squints at them. "Ya bring him home with you?"

"No," I laugh. "He's from Egypt."

"Egypt? We fightin' a war there now too?"

"No. We're actually students together at Columbia, in New York City." He squints at Basir again and takes another swig. "Where were you in 'Nam?" I say.

"Hundred First. Central Highlands, A Shau Valley and some action at Ap Bia Mountain, they called it Hamburger Hill."

"No shit?" I think of the movie we used to watch on base.

"I'll be right over there," Julio says pointing to a crowd gathered around an acrobat, Basir following him.

I sit quietly with the man for a couple minutes. "Where you from?"

"Wisconsin. Madison."

"How'd you end up here?"

"Discharged here and never left. Can't beat the weather."

"Yeah, I guess so." I look over at Julio and Basir standing with the crowd watching the acrobat jump around on one hand while tied up like a pretzel. I take another nip. "Never wanted to go back?"

"To Vietnam?"

I chuckle. He frowns. "No, Wisconsin. Any family there?"

"No. Cold as hell and everyone's dead. Sister somewhere."

"How'd it happen?" I motion with the bottle to his leg.

"Landmine, out on patrol in one of those fuckin' rice paddies."

I take another swig, think a moment. "They have a VA nearby?"

"What, you need it?"

"No. Just wondering."

"Just wondering? Yeah, they got a VA."

"You go to it?"

"I've been there. Waste of time and I got no need for it. They don't do shit anyway."

Julio and Basir come back over after the show. "We gotta go, Zach, if we're gonna beat rush hour."

I knock back more Jim and pass it to Julio who does too. He lifts the bottle at Basir, who shakes his head again. I stand to go and Julio hands me the bottle, three quarters full. "Here." I give it to the man.

He takes it. "Thanks. Must be Christmas. Name's Chuck."

"Merry Christmas, Chuck. Take care of yourself." I reach into my wallet and hand him a twenty-dollar bill. "Buy yourself some lunch."

We walk back down the boardwalk. "Are you nuts?" Julio says.

"What?"

"You're just contributing to his alcoholism and misery. He'll probably drink himself to death tonight with all that whiskey."

"Yeah, he might. He's already given up. This country, in those days unlike us, forced him to go to Vietnam, and when he came back, shit on him. If he wants to just drink away his pain, who're we to say?" Julio doesn't respond. I watch Basir turn his head to look at a passing bikini-clad blond roller-skater. "I saw that," I say.

"What?" Basir says.

"I think you need to confess to Muhammad, or Allah, or whatever you do."

"That is why we cover them up in our countries."

"What because you don't trust yourself?"

"It is not like that," he says.

"What's it like then?"

"We respect our women."

"Oh really? What, by not letting them vote, run for office, drive cars?"

"That is in Arabia."

"Oh, okay."

"America did not either."

"True, but we do now."

"Children," Julio says. "Let's not start another war." We make it back to Julio's car and out onto the freeway a few minutes later and head back to East LA.

~ * ~

At the rehearsal, I meet Jacqueline, a cute, short girl. Her pregnancy is just beginning to show, so it won't be too noticeable at the wedding. Julio's parents host the rehearsal dinner at their restaurant, one that occupies half of the block. They have a spacious banquet-style room that holds a hundred people.

After the rehearsal, while waiting for the dinner to start, I call Jess. "Hang on, Zach," she says.

I hear someone talking in the background, then hear her close a door and talk softly. "What was that?" I say.

"Nothing. Privacy. How's the wedding going?"

"Fine, but I wish it was ours."

"Are you proposing?" she says.

"I could be."

"Hum," she says. "Let me think. I will," she blurts out. "But let's wait until we graduate."

"I agree." Silence. I hear her sigh. "I heard that."

"Parents are driving me crazy. I don't want to talk about it. I want to talk about you, me, us."

"You, me, us. I could write a song." Everyone starts to take his or her seat behind me at the tables in the banquet room. "Hey, they're getting ready for dinner. I have to tell you, Jess, I'm the only white guy in the room, perhaps within ten miles."

"That's funny," she says.

"Yeah, real funny. Well, I gotta go. I really love you, Jess."

"You're kidding? I just want you for your hot body, Zach."

"I figured that."

"I can't wait 'til you get back," she says. "You're all mine."

"Now let's hang up on the count of three."

"Okay, promise?"

"Yes, dear."

"One, two," we count at the same time, "three."

Nothing. "You didn't hang up," I say.

"You didn't either," she says.

"All right. This time," I say. "I'm not kidding. One, two, three." I click the phone off. I hope she did too.

~ * ~

The wedding the next day goes off without a hitch and is a beautiful one. At one point Julio looks over at me with the largest smile. I think of our time together. We have gotten drunk together, gotten laid together, fought together, and laughed together. I remember the time during our tour in Afghanistan when a Taliban threw a grenade and it landed between us while we lie there on the ground. Without hesitation, he picked it up and threw it back at the Taliban killing them with their own hand bomb. We never said anything to one another. I shot him a look of, 'I can't believe you just did that,' while he shot me a look of, 'I can't believe I just did that.' Or, the other time when he fell into a rut, twisting his ankle with a hail of bullets whizzing all around. I crawled through a patch of mud, a foot thick, holding Alice above the fray. Johnny Redneck jumped up from behind a large rock where he took cover and laid down suppressing fire blasting the Taliban as I grabbed Julio and dragged him back behind the line. We lived through other minor incidents as well. It all seems like a million years ago.

"You may now kiss the bride," the priest says.

This is the second wedding I have attended with Julio. I think back to Micah's sister's wedding. I hope he will soon be at mine. I wonder where the hell he is. I hope he's not in an asylum, if they still do that.

At the reception the best man, one of Julio's school friends, makes a toast. Julio's father and a couple of his friends do as well. I then propose one. "Julio was the best buddy a soldier could have," I say holding my champagne flute. "I couldn't have made it without him. Although, he thinks he was my daddy. He knows who his daddy was." Someone whistles. "No, seriously," I say, "I know he's gonna make the best daddy and husband in the world from how he looked after us." I raise my flute. "To the newlyweds." Everybody cheers and takes a drink.

~ * ~

The next morning Julio's mother cooks Basir and me a hot breakfast of hash browns and eggs rancheros with tortillas. After breakfast, Julio's father drives us to Union Station. I check my phone and read an email from Aaron confirming our arrival in Chicago. There is an email from Johnny Redneck to everyone. It reads:

Hey, Got a job here in Georgia at the Smart Mart. I work the late shift. Going to get married to my girl, Betty. We're expecting. It's been hard getting back into this civilian world. Wanted to shoot some fucker for cutting me off in my truck the other day. Asshole shot me the bird. Good thing he high-tailed it outta there before I grabbed my rifle off the rack. See y'all. Johnny

125

I reply:

Hey, Congratulations, you redneck son-of-a-bitch. I don't know about you populating the world, however. No, have fun. Here in LA at Julio's wedding. He's having a baby too. WTF? Anyway, stopping in Chicago to see Aaron. He's Chicago's finest now. How about that? Me? A college intellectual. Actually found a girl too. See ya, Johnny. Zach

Basir and I board our train. Pulling out of LA, sitting next to one another I say, "What did you think?

"LA reminds me of Cairo."

"Yeah?"

"How big it is, the weather is the same."

Silence for a minute. "What is it?" I say watching him stare out the window at the passing city.

"I was thinking of Egypt."

"How so?"

"It is my country, but you Americans, it is somehow different here. Everyone seems happier, even though there is this recession. In Egypt, most of us are happy about our families, but there is a feeling under the surface, I guess I mean politically."

"I don't really understand Egyptian politics."

"Well, Mubarak, the so-called president, is not elected by the people, or any of the government. There is a sense of nothing. People are not connected to the government. We really have no liberties."

"People don't feel too connected here either."

"At least you Americans have the option of voting out your president and government. We do not. Most of the Arab world is like this."

"What's it gonna take?" I say.

"Probably bloody revolution, I think." He pauses. "Revolution." He nods and turns, staring out the window again.

We have a few hours in San Francisco between trains so we head down to the Embarcadero. We have dinner and watch the hustle and bustle of this famous waterfront. I analyze Basir and convince myself he is having a good time. We head back to the station and board our train.

~ * ~

The train pulls into Salt Lake City. I rent a car telling Basir I have to visit an old friend. He sits back and enjoys the view of the Rocky Mountains as I drive along Interstate 84. I turn the radio on and we listen to some country music.

At the junction of route 93, I drive north through Shoshone to route 75. On 75, I drive on into Ketchum, the valley before us spectacular. It is winter and a fresh dusting of snow has fallen on the ground. "I have never been in a car in snow before," Basir says. "Do not get me killed."

"Don't worry. I grew up in snow."

"It is beautiful."

"Yes it is," I say pulling into a café.

In the café, our presence provokes a few stares from some of the patrons. When we sit in a booth, Basir's Arabic accent makes the waitress nervous, her hand trembling a little. I whisper to her when he goes to the restroom, "He's not a terrorist. We're just students."

She frowns, says, "Oh," and turns our order over to the cook.

We have a nice lunch and head over to the Ketchum cemetery on Main Street. Basir says, "Your friend is here?"

"Yeah." I park the car. We get out, Basir following me as we walk to the northeast corner where two large evergreens sway gently overhead. I locate the large granite slab that covers Stein's tomb. I scrape half an inch of snow off with my bare hands to read the inscription on top. It simply reads: *Ernest Miller Hemingway, July 21, 1899-July 2, 1961.*

"This is the American writer?" Basir says standing next to me.

"Yeah." I stick my cold hands in my jacket pockets.

"How is he your friend?"

"Just is."

We stand for a couple of minutes until he says, "I will wait for you in the car."I nod, scan the cemetery and study the marker again, the wind-chill penetrating through to my bones. I take a generous nip from my flask to warm me and put it and my hands back in my pockets. "Cold place you picked here. What happened to the Caribbean?"

"It's where I ended up," Stein says standing beside me.

I pull my hands from my jacket, cup them to my mouth, and breathe into them. I look at the mountains and back at him. "Well, it's been nice knowing you, but you can stay away now. I don't need your weird chitchats, you showing up at strange times to screw with my head anymore."

"I told you, I don't show up to screw with you. You show up to screw with me." He tips his flask and offers me some.

"What have you got for me now?" I say, taking it and swigging.

"Teacher's Blended Scotch Whisky. Like I brought to you in D.C. My favorite, unlike the shit you drink."

I scowl, say, "I'm not rich, ya know." I take a nip and hand it back to him. "Well, ciao. Nice knowing ya." I pat him on his shoulder, leave him standing there and return to the rental. In the car I can still see him staring down at his grave. "Look over there, Basir. By the grave. What do you see?"

He looks. "What?"

"You see a man standing there?"

"No."

I glance back at the grave but he is gone. *Damn.*

We drive over to Stein's memorial on Trail Creek Road near the Sun Valley Lodge. I park the car and we climb out traversing a hundred or so feet where we come upon Stein's bronze bust atop a pile of flat stones with a diverted stream running near its edge. He gazes out at the majestic Rocky Mountains. Basir stands beside me. The inscription on the memorial reads:

> *Best   of   all   he   loved   the   fall*
> *The   leaves   yellow   on   cottonwoods*
> *Leaves   floating   on   trout   streams*
> *And   above   the   hills*
> *The   high   blue   windless   skies*
> *...Now he will be a part of them forever.*

We return to the car and drive over to the Hemingway Exhibit at the Ketchum/Sun Valley Heritage & Ski Museum and look at his pictures and memorabilia.

On our way back to Salt Lake City, Basir says, "So, he was a great American writer?"

"Yeah. It was a different time. A different world. I'd like to say it was a simpler time, but it never was."

We return the car early the next morning after driving through the night. While waiting for our train to Chicago, my phone rings and I fumble and punch the button. "Jess?"

"Zach. I had to find the right time to call."

"Not the parents again?"

She sighs. "I am so angry at them."

"They're just worried about their little girl. We can always run away together."

"That sounds like a plan," her voice lighting up. "Where are you?"

"Salt Lake. We're going to stay a day and a night in Chicago and then back to New York."

"I'll be there when you get back. I have to get out of here."

"Great," I say. "I can't wait to see you."

"Let's spend the whole weekend together in bed," she says.

"Didn't one of the Beatles do that?"

"Yeah, I think so, but they did it for some political statement. Hey, we could do it for a statement to my parents."

"Great. Your father will have me locked up or committed."

"I'll rescue you then."

"Hey, we're getting ready to board."

"Okay. Call me in Chicago."

"I will. I really miss you, Jess."

"I love you, Zach."

After breakfast in the dining car, I start reading *The Sun Also Rises* that I purchased in Ketchum. What strikes me is the tough guys and the main character, Jake, a World War I veteran, his personal predicament, and the heavy drinking. I also find exciting Jake's main squeeze, Lady Brett Ashley, who personifies the sexual freedom of the roaring nineteen twenties. While reading, my mind wanders back to Jess.

We disembark the train at Chicago's Union Station on Canal Street later the next morning. We wait at the curb outside the terminal until a few minutes later I hear the "whoop, whoop" of a police cruiser. It pulls over and Aaron gets out. "Put your hands up where I can see them."

"Funny," I say. He is dressed in his Chicago uniform, all pressed and immaculate. We hug. "Don't you look spiffy? This is Basir." They shake hands.

We climb into the backseat. "And Officer Randall," Aaron says. Basir and I exchange handshakes with Aaron's senior partner behind the wheel. We head for Southside Chicago, their beat. "I'm off at eight," Aaron says. "We'll drop you at the house. Momma has your beds set up. How's Julio?"

"Happy."

"And this girl you found?"

"I'm in love, Aaron. Can you believe it?"

"Love? What do you know about love?"

"Didn't know much, until now. I only know it now that I feel it. Hey, whatever happened to that girl you met in the army?"

"Carla? Didn't work out."

We pull up to a brick bungalow in the Pullman area of Southside Chicago. It has a front porch, one and a half stories and a full basement. Aaron lets us in. His mother, a woman barely fifty, greets us with a hug. Aaron returns to his patrol.

130

"I know you boys must be hungry," Aaron's mother says. "I cooked up a meal." She takes our backpacks, sets them on the couch and leads us to the kitchen. There, Aaron's mother serves us beef ribs, potatoes and green beans. She sits with us while we eat and says, "I want to thank you for all you did to help him in the wars."

"I should be thanking you. He always looked out for me."

"I worried so much about all you boys. I can't help but feel so sorry for the mothers of those boys killed over there." She looks down at the table.

"Yes, Ma'am. Well, we're home now. You must be real proud of him as a police officer."

She forces a smile. Silence and she stares at the table.

"What is it ma'am?"

"I'm worried about him, Zach. You were one of his best friends, so I think I can tell you."

"Tell me what?" I stop eating.

"Well. He's just…he has a lot of nightmares. I hear him talkin' in his sleep. Screaming sometimes."

I hesitate and say, "I've had them too."

"What happened over there?"

"Well, what happens in war. I would not even want to begin to describe it to you."

She sniffles and smiles to cover it up.

We finish our meal and she shows us the house. She made up two pullout sofas in the basement that doubles as the recreation room. Basir sits in bed reading a pre-medical book while I continue reading Stein's book when Aaron pulls in after his shift at eight-thirty. The main characters are drinking and watching the running of the bulls in Pamplona. Not the way I want to go, being gored, no matter how much I drank.

Aaron comes down to talk. "So, what're you going to do with your life, Zach?"

"No idea." I close Stein's book and set it aside. "I could do almost anything."

"You should go into politics, or something."

"Or something. Hey, your mother is real nice. What does she do again?"

"She's a nurse at County."

"Oh, yeah. Right."

Silence.

"Can you believe it's been this long already?" he says. "Since we got out?"

"Yeah. Seems like so long ago."

Silence again. It feels as if we are strangers, despite having spent six years together. "What is it?" I say.

"I don't know. It's just that, if it wasn't for my job, I think I'd go crazy."

"How so?"

"I mean, I wasn't honest about Carla." I wait for him to continue. "She broke up with me."

"Really? What happened?"

"I dunno. It's just that I can't sleep. Get agitated. I got rough with her."

We pause.

"I've had nightmares," I whisper so Basir doesn't hear.

"Yeah?"

"I have to tell you. I'm not having as many since being with this girl, Jessica."

"Huh. I have them less when I'm working all the time and real tired. If I take time off, and have too much time on my hands, I can't sleep. Need to keep busy, I guess."

I peek over at Basir who has drifted off. I lower my voice. "Before Jessica, I missed you guys and the army. Can you believe that?"

"I know."

"Now, not so much."

"Want a drink?"

"Whaddaya got?"

"Scotch. Glen Burns."

"No kidding?"

"Why?"

"Jessica's father. He's a rich blueblood. He thought he was impressing me with his."

"Really?" He takes out a bottle and two tumblers from a cabinet near the TV and pours. "She's rich?"

"Yeah." We toast, clink and take a nip. "He doesn't like me."

"Who couldn't like you?"

"An upper crust asshole."

"Fuck him," he says raising his glass. "You love this girl?"

"I do. I really do, bro."

"She loves you and doesn't care where you come from? Then, fuck him." We finish off the round. He pours one more. "To, true love."

We clink and down the round. He puts the bottle back in the cabinet and takes my glass. "Get some rest. I'll show you guys Capone's city tomorrow." He goes upstairs and I doze off reading Stein's book.

~ * ~

I stand at the altar watching her walk down the aisle. Her face is veiled, and a long wedding train is held by Micah, Julio, Aaron and Jimmy.

A congregation sits in the pews dressed in military ACU's. They have no faces, however. When she arrives at the altar next to me, she turns to her bridesmaid who lifts the veil off her head. She turns to face me.

It's not Jess. It's her father and he holds my Beretta up in front of my face. "Who were you fooling?" he says. He places the Beretta in my palm. "It's the only way."

"I really love her. I've never loved anyone before." Tears drip from my eyes.

"It's over," he says raising his voice. "You are from two different worlds."

"No, please, sir. I promise to always love her. Take care of her. Please."

"You should have done it in New Orleans."

I stare at the Beretta in my hand. "Please, sir. I'm begging you." Tears stream down my face. "I love her. I really do."

"Now, or I'll do it for you."

"Jess?" I look around the room. "Jess? Where are you?"

Patterson grabs my hand and closes it around the gun, forcing it up to the side of my head. He wraps my index finger around the trigger. The soldiers in the pews open fire, shooting up the place.

I jump up in bed in a cold sweat, breathing heavily and look around the room. The morning sun shines in through the basement window.

Sitting up on the edge of the sofa bed, I dig around in my pack, find my flask and take a big swallow. "You should have let me at him," he says punching at the air again.

I hand Stein the flask, my hands shaking. "I don't want his money, or hers she stands to inherit. I only want his daughter."

"You know how that sounds to a father?" He sips.

"I'm a swell guy, right?"

"Yeah, you're a swell fella." He hands Jim back to me. "Look, kid. No one you love is ever truly lost."

"What the hell does that mean?"

"It means, the one you love is always close to your heart."

"Okay. You're spinning my head." I smell something delicious coming from upstairs in the kitchen and glance in that direction. Basir begins to stir and I look back at Stein, but as usual, he has disappeared. I examine Jim in my palm, then twist his top back on and use my T-shirt to wipe the sweat off my stomach and forehead. I pull on a fresh shirt, jeans, socks and shoes and head up to the kitchen where I find a girl, late teens cooking breakfast. "Hi," I say.

"You're Zach?" she says.

"And you are LaShanda. Your brother kept it a secret how beautiful you are."

"Well, I'll scold him then." She scrapes scrambled eggs onto some dishes, drops two sausages onto a plate and grabs toast from the toaster. "Here you go," she says handing me the plate.

"Thanks."

Aaron saunters in rubbing his eyes and yawning. "Hey," he says. "Sis, look at you." He pats her behind.

She makes a face and says, "You didn't tell me how cute he is," she says to Aaron, but winking at me. "For a white boy."

"See," I say. "I told you I was good enough for your sister." I slap him on his torso.

"Yeah, knock it off," Aaron says. Basir joins us for breakfast.

After we eat, Aaron shows us the Chicago sights. We ride up one hundred and eight stories to the Skydeck of the Sears Tower and stand in one of those glass balconies, the building swaying in the wind. We take in a Bulls game. They lose, but it might be the one and only time I see game at the United Center so it was worth it for me.

~ * ~

The next morning Aaron drives us to the station. "Thanks for everything," I say hugging him.

"No problem."

"I'll see you at my wedding then. As soon as we finish school."

"Let me plan your bachelor party."

"You got it, bro."

On the train, I place a call to Jess, but it goes to voice mail. I leave a message, "It's me, Zach. Duh. Who else would it be? I'll send you a text too. Miss you. Love you."

I finish reading Stein's book. Jake and Brett talk of what might have been. Sad.

Chapter Ten
Jesus Loves Me, This I know

For the rest of year two at Columbia Jess and I are inseparable. We study, hang out around campus, and at Duffy's.

She surprises me for my birthday in July. I hustle down the steps to my apartment and jump into a cab where she waits. "You're not going to tell me?"

She shakes her head. "Nope." The cabbie pulls out, zips across Central Park at 97th Street and turns south on Fifth Avenue. We pull up in front of The Plaza at Fifth Avenue and Central Park South. "Let's go," she says.

I jump out and together we head inside. At the reception desk she checks in and gets a room key. In the elevator she says, holding onto my arm, "You're mine for the whole weekend. Happy birthday." She kisses me.

We enter a Deluxe Courtyard Room with a king bed, a sitting area with a writing desk, and a bathroom with inlaid earth stone with a separate bath and shower. The room and furniture transport me back to the late nineteenth or early twentieth century.

For the first twenty-four hours we never leave the room, making love, ordering from room service and watching classic movies. At the end of *Casablanca*, as Rick watches Ilsa board the plane with Victor Laszlo, I look down at Jess snuggled up beside me and flash back to my unit, my buddies, and hope like hell Miller and the others are holding it together. They would never believe what I have and where I am. Stein was right, that crazy bastard. "What're you thinking?" she says, looking up and catching me staring at her.

I stroke her hair and shake my head.

"Zachary," she says drawing it out. "What?"

"Pinch me so I know you're real." She does, right on my nose. "Ouch." I look back at the television as the plane flies away. Bogart strolls off with Claude Rains and says, "'Louie, I think this is the beginning of a beautiful friendship.'"

"This is all real, Zachary Powell." She pulls up tight and turns my head to face hers. "I told you," she says. "Not only are you smoking hot, but you are not like all the others. I want nothing to do with those spoiled rich boys my parents want me to be with. I can guarantee you they'd all be cheating on me and screwing their personal assistants within a year. My parents have said we are young, and this will pass. Blah, Blah, Blah." She puts her lips up to my ear and whispers, "I will tell you. This will not pass. They are my parents and I love them, but we can show them what true love is and how we can make it without them. On our own. Without their money." She looks me over. "Okay?"

I nod and she plants a kiss on me. We snuggle up and I fall asleep with her head resting on my chest.

~ * ~

"Jimmy!" I scream jumping up in bed in the middle of the night. His blood is all over my hands. Jess sits up next to me. I wipe sweat from my brow with my palm and lie back to catch my breath. She snuggles up, holding me tightly until I relax, never saying a word. I fall back to sleep with her head on my shoulder, her arm draped over my chest and holding my hand.

~ * ~

During the beginning of year three, Jess and I join the junior staff at the Columbia Spectator, the university's student newspaper. She convinces me to major in journalism. This is after her confession to me about reading my journals.

Sitting on our bench in Morningside Park waiting for her, I review notes for a class. It is almost a year this winter break since I returned from Chicago. I have sent emails to Micah, even a letter to his parents, but I've heard nothing. Didn't we promise to stay in touch? Jess strolls up and sits next to me, kissing me for the longest time. "How was your class?" I ask her after she lets up.

"Good," she says snuggling. We sit for many minutes like this and watch the squirrels work on getting ready for winter. I notice a man sitting on a bench nearby. It occurs to me that he has turned to look at us several times. "You see that man over there? On that bench?"

She nods.

"You know," I say, "I think I've seen him someplace before."

"Doesn't look familiar to me." The man is in his fifties, perhaps, and wears a gray flat cap and a large overcoat.

"Well, let's go," I say. As we walk back to the university, I look to see if the man is following, but he is not. I kiss Jess goodbye. "See you later."

Sitting in a journalism course, it dawns on me where I have seen that man in the park before. He had come into Duffy's and I had served him a sandwich and a beer. It must be a coincidence.

After seeing a Broadway musical that weekend, we stroll through Times Square, our arms entwined. I stop dead in my tracks and gawk at the side of one of the buildings. What is it?" she says, glancing at me, then back to where I'm staring. "Are you looking up at the guy there?"

"Yeah. It's Micah."

"From your journals? The Medal of Honor hero? The one you went to the White House with?"

"Yeah. That's him." I continue to stare at the advertisement on the side of a building.

"He's cute," she says. "What a body."

"Yeah, that he is."

Micah is posing in one of those sexy underwear ads. His body and abs are still rock solid. He has grown his hair a little longer like mine. "I guess he hit the big time getting a modeling job like that," she says.

"Yeah. I guess so." I look at her. "We've got to find him. He knows where I'm going to school here. I wonder why he hasn't been in touch."

"Maybe he's been real busy."

"I don't know. Something's not right."

"You can try and find out his modeling agency from the underwear company."

"Good idea." Two blocks away, we find one of those famous New York pizzerias that specializes in thin crust. Out of the corner of my eye, I see that man again, the one from the park and from Duffy's. "Look." I point.

"Yeah. That looks like that man from the park," she says.

"It is the man from the park and I saw him glance over at us. What the hell is with this guy? Wait here." I look both ways and dash across the street. The man sees me coming and hightails it, although I catch up, jump in front of him and block his path. "Hey. What the hell, mister?" I say.

"Excuse me," he says, pushing, trying to get past me.

"Don't play with me, sir. We caught you."

"I don't know what you're talking about." His eyes dart around the street. "I'll call for help if you try and mug me."

"Mug you? You're joking?"

He tries to push past me, but again I block his path. Jess jogs over. "Why are you following us?" she says.

"You people are crazy." He reaches into his pocket.

I react and shield Jess in case the man pulls a weapon, but he takes his phone out. "I'll call the police if you don't get out of my way." He waves the phone in my face and pushes past us.

I let him go and he hurries off down the street, my adrenaline surging, as if I were in combat. "What was all of that?" she says.

"I don't know, but if we see him again we need to file a complaint. He's gonna call the police on us?" I shake my head and lead her by her arm back across the street to the pizza parlor.

~ * ~

It takes me a couple days, but I track down someone at the underwear company who told me the advertising agency they use. I play phone tag for a few days with several people who are reluctant to give me any information, but after begging them to give Micah my number, he calls on my way to class a week later. "Hey," I say. "What happened?"

"It's a long story. I'm sorry I didn't contact you." He sounds subdued, unlike the gregarious Micah I knew.

"Naw. Forget it. You know I'm here at Columbia."

"I know, but my old email and phone accounts were cut off, well, I don't know when. I thought about trying to contact you many times, but couldn't get up the courage, I guess."

"Courage? You? Are you nuts?"

"Some would say."

"Well, it's been far too long."

"Yeah," he says. "I've actually been in New York for a few months now."

"Making quite a living, I can see."

"I'll have to tell you all about it over dinner."

"I've actually got a girlfriend, can you believe it? Me? We should all get together."

"Sure. I'd like to meet her."

Silence for a moment. Then, I say, "I just can't believe you're doing what you're doing."

"Well, someone at the agency came across the video of the medal ceremony at the White House and tracked me down."

"No kidding?"

"She said she just had to find me after seeing me in that starring role."

"I understand, what with those big baby blues, that blond hair, and those abs and all. You're such a stud."

"That I am, huh?"

"Awright, don't get stuck on yourself."

"I gotta go, Zach. I've got a shoot."

"A shoot? Listen to you."

"Hey, why don't you and, what's your girl's name?"

"Jessica."

"Jessica. Come on over Friday night to my place. I live with this fantastic cook."

"Really? Is it serious?"

He chuckles. "Yeah. You could say."

He gives me the address, in Midtown Manhattan. I disconnect the call. Wow. I can't wait to hear what caused him to drop out of the University of Alabama and everything else he has been up to.

~ * ~

Jess and I hop on the subway and zip down to Midtown Friday night. The building is one of those swanky new towers near the Midtown Tunnel. I look at Jess and she looks back at me. "What do you think?" I say.

"I think someone's making some good money." A door attendant lets us in. We pass through a security checkpoint and ride the elevator up to the twenty-third floor where we buzz the door to Micah's apartment. The door opens and Micah lets us in. "Hey," he says.

"Hey." We hug. "This is Jessica."

"Nice to meet you," Micah says, hugging her too.

"Nice to meet you, Micah. I've heard so much about you."

"Oh really?"

"All complimentary I can report."

"Can't be anything else." He smiles at me.

"Hello," a voice calls out. An attractive man, perhaps a few years older than the rest of us, approaches from the kitchen wearing a cook's apron. He could be a model too.

"This is Peter," Micah says. "Peter, Zach and Jessica."

Peter hugs Jess. "Nice to meet you," he says. "And you," he says, giving me a big hug, taking me aback. "I've heard so much about you."

"All lies, I can assure you," I say peering at Micah. He closes the door behind us. As we move into the living room my mind begins to whirl. It all starts to click, however I have to be careful my mouth doesn't drop open like it did on the street when I saw the advertisement.

Micah says, "What would you like to drink?"

"Wine, if you have some," Jess says.

"Of course," Peter says. "White or red?"

"White. Thank you."

"And Zach?"

"Whiskey?"

"Coming right up." Peter moseys off.

Following Micah into the living room, I glance at Jess. She smiles, indicating it is clear as the day is long to her. "Can I get the tour?" she says.

"Sure," Micah says. He leads us on the guided tour. The apartment is larger than the house I grew up in. It has three large bedrooms, three bathrooms, a large living room and a kitchen you could shoot a television cooking show in. In the hallway we stop and look at Micah's Medal of Honor display case hanging on the wall. Jess reads the citation accompanying it and examines the medal hanging on the blue-starred ribbon. The picture of Aaron, Julio, Micah and me with the President in the Oval Office hangs next to it.

"The building is only five years old," Micah says as he leads us into the kitchen where Peter hands us our drinks. In shock at this whole revelation, I want to down the entire contents, but decide to sip it lest it become obvious. "Peter owns the Le Parisien Grande," Micah says. "Have you been?"

"Never heard of it," I say sipping my booze. Jess nods. "What?" I say. "You know of it?"

"Yeah," she says. "It's the best French restaurant in New York. It's been on all the cooking shows. Five star."

"Why thank you," Peter says.

"It's also one of the most expensive," Micah says frowning.

"Well there you go," I say. "That's why I haven't been."

"You come in any time and it's my treat," Peter says touching my arm. "Any friend of Micah's is a friend of mine."

"I'll do that," I say. "Thanks."

"I've been in a couple of times," Jess says. "With my parents of course."

"Well, that's no fun," Peter says leading us back into the living room.

"It is when daddy's paying," she says. I raise an eyebrow at Jess when she looks over at me smiling.

"Please. Sit," Peter says. The living room has a large three-sided sofa and some sort of an oversized modern-art coffee table in a sunken portion of the room. This apartment has to have cost at least a million dollars, perhaps more. *Damn, everyone's rich but me.* Peter returns to the kitchen where he continues to prepare whatever he is cooking. It smells great.

Silence.

I sip my drink, glance at Micah, and quickly away. "I've struggled all my life, Zach."

"No. No, it's okay." I look back at him. "I have no problem with…with…"

"With what I am?"

"Come on, Micah."

"You can say it. Gay."

"It's just I thought it was your strict religious convictions and Penny as to why you didn't pick up girls with the rest of us."

"Yeah, my religious beliefs." He frowns and takes a sip of soda, because he still doesn't drink.

"How did Penny take it?"

"Hurt. When I got back, I enrolled at UA and still tried to hide it. Yeah, I always used my religion as an excuse not to have sex with her. Oh, we made out, but it didn't work for me. Nothing happened. I knew I couldn't go through with it. So, I finally came out to her."

I take a sip. Jess sips her wine.

"She cried and asked what was wrong with her. I told her nothin'. I told her how for years I had to not look at the guys in the locker room because I would get excited, not always a rise, but in my gut, a feeling. I told her I thought girls were very pretty, but I just didn't get excited, sexually, you know."

I think he reads my mind.

"No, I wasn't attracted to you, Zach and never stared at your butt and all. You don't have the vibe."

"Hey. Now I'm hurt."

"You're a good-lookin' guy, but not my type," he says smiling.

"No, but he is my type," Jess says rubbing my leg.

"Aw, thanks," I say teasing her.

"Did you ever have anyone, before Peter?" Jess says.

He nods. "One guy in high school. He moved away in the eleventh grade. We were on the football team. We'd hang out after practice, and then, well, you just knew."

Football players. Huh. Makes sense, all those hard-bodies. I try to hide my surprise by sipping my drink.

"Gay guys just know it and gravitate to one another," he says. "There's a certain vibe. Some call it gaydar."

"Gaydar?" I say. "What like radar? Who knew?"

He nods. "No one does, except gays, because you have to sneak around and hide in the closet. And in the south? Believe me, there are guys screwin' each other all the time, but they have to hide unless they get their Bibles thrown at them."

"And speaking of Bibles. Your father?"

"Yeah. For all my life, I heard nothin' but this was a sin and fags would burn in hell. I struggled so much with why did I feel this way? Why wasn't I attracted to girls? Why did God do this to me? I tried so hard, prayed, to not be gay. These religious folks just don't get it. Why would we choose to be this? Why would we put ourselves through so much pain, and scorn?"

He sips his soda and continues, "It just makes me so mad that these people can't accept we are born this way, God made us this way. I mean, my father is the one who sent me to that clinic in Minnesota to cure homosexuals. It's all a lie, no matter what they tell you. You can't cure homosexuality because it's not a disease. I fought it. I hid it. I used to hate myself. I wanted to die."

I look at Jess. "He purposely played the hero, putting himself in the line of fire. I knew it. You *were* trying to kill yourself."

"You're right. I would have died if they had let me go back into combat."

"Well, I'm glad they didn't," I say.

"That's two of us," Peter says entering the living room. "Dinner is served."

We move into the dining room. As we situate ourselves, Peter announces, "We're having Artichoke Tartlets as an appetizer. Our main course is roasted beef tenderloin and an easy wine shallot sauce. Our side dish will be herbed beans Provencale, which is creamy white beans mixed with garlic and herbs from Provence. Our dessert is Apple Clafouti, a vanilla custard with fresh apples, lemon zest and cinnamon."

"Wow," I say. "This is fantastic."

"I wanted it to be romantic," Peter says smiling at Micah.

"Okay, okay," Micah says. "Get on with it."

"Yes, captain." Peter serves the appetizer.

"Don't insult us enlisted men," Micah teases him. I try to hide my smile. "What?" Micah says.

"Oh, you two are just too cute."

"Now who's funny? You always said funny. Funny. It drove me nuts."

"Funny. So what about your parents and family?" I say.

"I think my mother suspected when she met Eddy, the guy from the team I hung out with all the time. I think she chose to ignore it, or pretend it wasn't true. I used to keep sports magazines all around showin' all of these buff guys, with their hot abs in my room. I'd leave underwear ads on my bed. Mother walked in and caught me with some of those ads doing, well, you know."

I raise an eyebrow. Jess catches me and shakes her head. "You didn't masturbate?" she says.

"Jess," I say embarrassed.

"This is delicious," Jess says to Peter, tasting the appetizer.

"Thanks," he says.

"Yes," I say nibbling on mine too. "Your father?" I say wincing.

"Well, it's exactly what you can imagine. He disowned me. Said I needed to pray harder after I told him I tried and prayed for years to not be gay. He said it was a choice and the devil had hold of me. I said no, God made me this way and perhaps it was a test to see if Father would still love me. I reminded him Jesus is the lovin' son of our Father and his first and foremost message was to love one another. I asked did Jesus not love all his children? The rich, the poor, the young, the old, the sick, the wicked, even the whore? I said Jesus loves straight people, and he loves gays."

He takes a breath. I can see this still troubles him. Although, I feel sorrier for his father than I do for him. He says, "I told Father I hoped I would die in combat and that was why I joined, but God didn't do it. Why? Why did God not kill me if I am this horrific creature? I said perhaps it was because he loves me and he made me this way."

146

Again he pauses and sips his soda. "So I went to this clinic in Minnesota," he says, "basically as a prisoner, to be cured. I lasted three weeks. It was a lot of prayin', down on our knees. This Mormon guy and I drooled over one another. Again, the gaydar. It took all of our power not to give in to temptation." He chuckles. "Temptation, can you believe that term?"

Peter squeezes Micah's titanium knee.

"We went at it in his room by the second week. It was like letting off steam that had built for years, ever since Eddy in high school."

"Wow," I say. "I'm so sorry."

"Don't be. Well, I got outta there by the end of the third week and went to my sister's, and they both support me, where I was contacted by this modeling agent. I met Peter on a business dinner with my agent here in New York, can you believe it? At his restaurant, and the rest is true love."

"I'm so happy for you, Micah," Jess says.

"I am too," I say. "Really. I can't imagine how hard this has been for you. I have no problem with this, Micah. We were great buddies, are great buddies, looking out for each other in the service and I will always be your buddy. I only wish I could have helped you through this."

"Thanks. I'm sorry for not contactin' you. I didn't know how you would take it and I wanted to leave my military past behind."

"Well," I say, "what matters is we're your friends, your new family and to hell with them." I raise my cocktail glass. Everyone clinks. "To friends."

Micah says, "Thanks."

I finish my whiskey and Peter pours me another. We finished eating and lounge around for a few more hours talking in the living room, me telling stories of Mr. Hero, Medal of Honor winner, while Micah tells silly stories of my antics. We say our goodbyes at nearly one o'clock in the morning and depart. Peter orders a taxicab and prepays it. He doesn't want us traipsing around Manhattan at this hour.

At Jess's apartment I wait until she is inside. I turn to head back to my flat when I notice someone watching from across the street. It looks like the man I confronted outside the pizzeria. I jog over to him. He sees me coming and hustles up the street in the opposite direction. "Hey," I call out. "You again?" I sprint after him but he quickly climbs into a sedan parked there, turns the engine over and I pound on the trunk as it speeds away. I catch my breath. That's it. I have to make a police report. What the hell is going on here?

Chapter Eleven
You Can't Go Home Again

I made the police report and never heard from them.

Our junior year flies by and I am the happiest man on the face of the earth. Jess and I spend every day together and we work at the paper. In August we rent a car and drive all throughout New England, staying in old romantic bed and breakfasts. Jess spends less and less time at her parents' house, only going on holidays, although she informs me they don't approve of our relationship. We both decide, however, we don't need their approval. Also, I guess Stein got the message, because I haven't seen him in so long. My nightmares happen less frequently and with Jess not far away, they are just about nonexistent now.

I head back to the apartment one night in December during my senior year after a slow shift at Duffy's. Basir is watching the news with reports on the events unfolding in Tunisia. I sit on the couch and watch the protesting on television. "What do you think will happen?" I say.

"What always happens. A brutal crackdown. Much bloodshed."

I wait for him to say more, but he stares transfixed at the protesting and listens to the commentary. "I have to admit," I say, "I don't know much about the political situation there."

"It is similar to our situation in Egypt."

We watch as police clash with demonstrators outside a government ministry, hosing them down and beating them with batons. Basir continues to stare at the television. "Well," I say. "I hope it works out."

~ * ~

The next day I'm standing with Jess on the street, the town car her father sent waits. She won't let go of me. I have to see my father, Kristen and my niece, Holly, and Jess has to attend a Christmas celebration. We kiss goodbye, I open the door and she climbs in. I watch as it disappears down the street on its way to Connecticut.

I take the subway down to Penn Station where I catch a train to Buffalo.

On the train, I read another of Stein's books, *For Whom the Bell Tolls*. Speaking of dictators with Basir, Francisco Franco fits right into my earlier conversation with him. Here we are in the twenty-first century and the world still deals with dictators, just like Franco. I come across the character Pilar, for whom Stein named his boat in Cuba. I flash back to that episode with him. *Nutcase.* Pilar, a strong woman and the de facto leader of the anti-fascist guerilla band of misfits, was the wife of Pablo, the true leader of the group.

I stand in the freezing sleet outside the train station in Buffalo waiting for Brad. "Damn," I whisper clapping my hands together. He should have been here twenty minutes ago.

At last, Kristen's rusting Chevy Chevalier pulls up to the curb. I open the door and see Kristen behind the wheel. Holly is crying in the child seat in the back. In fact, I see tears rolling down Kristen's cheeks. "What is it?" I say. "Do you want me to drive?"

She nods and we exchange seats. "Brad left me," she says.

"I knew it." I pound my fist on the steering wheel as we pull out of the parking lot. "I'm gonna kill that son-of-a-bitch, pot-head."

"No. No. It's my fault."

150

"How the hell is it your fault?"

"I was too demanding, ordering him around."

"What does that mean?"

"I don't know. I just wanted him all to myself, that's all."

"What're you talking about?"

She turns to comfort Holly. "I should've let him go out with his friends when he wanted to. I nagged him that he was spending too much time with them and not enough time with me."

"Well, hell yeah. He has an obligation to be with you since you are the mother of his child and his future wife."

"There's not gonna be any marriage."

I pound the wheel again. "I'm really gonna kill him, Kristen. I swear I'm gonna kill him." I look over at her, her eyes soaked with tears and swollen red from crying. "What about Dad?"

"He can't do too much. He's not well, Zach."

"I know he drinks too much."

"No, he has something wrong with his kidneys."

"What's wrong with them?"

"The doctors say they're not working like they're supposed to."

I turn on the windshield wipers, but they are frozen to the windshield. "Damn." I stop the car and shake them loose. I climb back in the car and drive off again, the wipers heavy with sleet and doing a poor job at wiping the slush off. "What do the doctors say they can do?"

"He has to do dialysis. They say he is not a good candidate for a transplant because of his drinking and he has diabetes."

"Are you gonna be okay? I mean, do you have enough money?"

"I'll be okay."

Kristen works full-time at Lock City Bar and Grill, a dive owned by a friend of my dad's. "Is Brad helping with the baby? Money and all?" She doesn't answer. "Dammit," I say. "I knew it. You need to file some papers, with the court. I can help with that."

"You have too much to worry about."

"I have nothing to worry about except you and Holly. I'll send you some money."

"No, no. You have that expensive college to pay for."

"I've got extra." She sniffles and tries to hush Holly.

This is going to be a great Christmas. I miss Jess so much and it has only been a few hours. I wonder if she is out on a ride with Lilly, that big, black beautiful horse. How the hell am I gonna take a week in this depressing environment?

~ * ~

The next day I head over to see Dad. Upon entering the house, I can see that it is a wreck. There are dirty dishes in the sink, pizza boxes stacked near the door, and empty beer cans all over the coffee table.

"Dad? Dad?" I sneak into his bedroom and find him lying there in filth, unshaven. "Dad?" Shaking him, he grunts and looks up at me, groggy and incoherent.

"Zach? Is that you?" He squints at me as I open the drawn drapes.

"Jesus, Dad. Are you okay?" I help him into the bathroom. He stares up at me while sitting on the toilet. I do what I have to do and bathe him, but it's not pretty. After the tub, I help him into the living room and set him on the sofa. The house smells like a barnyard. I head into the kitchen and find a stack of unopened and unpaid bills there on the table. I see final notices, overdue house payments, and all kinds of delinquent stuff.

I clean up the place, peeking into the living room where Dad sits staring at the wall. *Damn.* He is only sixty-three years old. I wash the dishes, bag up the trash, and vacuum. "You want something to eat?" I say to him.

"Can you give me the remote?" I do and he turns the TV on. "And get me a beer?"

"I don't think..." He looks up at me with long and drawn eyes. What the hell, I figure. It's like Chuck on Venice Beach. What's the point? Either I get him a beer or he'll get one himself.

After I clean the place up and throw his dirty clothes that are lying around all over the floor into a hamper, I find the phone book and go through it. I call the hospital and track down his doctor who calls me back a couple hours later. "Come into my office tomorrow at two o'clock," the doctor, says, "and I'll get the paperwork together for you to declare him indigent. He'll become a ward of the state and be put into a facility where at least he'll get the care he needs."

"Thanks, Doctor." I hang up the phone, read the bills, statements, and overdue notices on the kitchen table. I discover my father has no insurance and no money. I sit there at the kitchen table, the television blaring in the living room, my father drinking his third beer, and I want to cry. I find a half-full bottle of Jim in the cupboard, down a large quantity and catch my breath.

"The slings and arrows of despair can help produce your best work," an older Stein says walking into the kitchen. I stare at the goof as he saunters over and sits next to me. He fingers through the stack of bills. "Jesus, kid. What a mess." He takes Jim from me and pounds him back.

"Slings and arrows? Who're you, Shakespeare?"

He slams the bottle onto the table. "Don't wise crack me, kid."

"Look, Hem, this is my damn nightmare." I knockback some more Jim.

"Then leave me out of it." He wrestles Jim from me and sucks on his neck.

"You're driving me outta my freakin' mind, Papa." I reach over and snatch Jim back. "Stop drinking all my booze."

"A bottle of booze can be your best friend, but it can be your worst enemy."

"Dammit, Hem." I jump up, clutch Jim, and leave the pest sitting at the table staring after me.

I call Jess on the way to Lynch's Pool Hall. No answer, so I leave a message. I toss Jim's empty ass in the trash dumpster outside Lynch's, enter and find Brad sitting in the corner stoned out of his mind. He is all smiles, like a happy stoner, and has no clue. I know it is futile to beat his ass, so I just leave and head back to Kristen's.

~ * ~

The next day the four of us, Kristen, Holly, Dad and me, have a Christmas dinner comprised of ready-made takeout food from the supermarket. I bought the whole full-course ham dinner with side dishes and lugged it over to Kristen's.

That night I call Jess, no answer, so I leave another message. I also send her a text. Unlike her not to call me back and tell me how much she loves me and tease me about missing my handsome face and all the rest. I'm getting worried.

A day later I drive Dad to the nursing home where he will spend his final days. I remember Jimmy's mother in that Detroit home. *Damn.* I hope I die before I get old. I think I've heard that in a song before. Dad says nothing and never protests.

Just before leaving town I find a jewelry store and purchase an engagement ring, complete with a good-sized diamond. They wrap it up in a little blue gift box.

On the overnight train to New York, I leave another message for Jess and send another text. What could she be doing that she wouldn't answer? Now I'm really worried. I sip some Jim to calm me and fall asleep while reading Stein's book.

~ * ~

The train stopping in Poughkeepsie jolts me awake. I finish Stein's book as the train speeds down the Hudson River Valley. A happy ending? Depends on your disposition. I finger back to a page I earmarked in chapter eighteen. I read it again: "Here it is the shift from deadliness to normal family life that is the strangest," Robert Jordan says.

I check for messages. None. I have texted Jess every day, left voice messages, but she hasn't answered. Something is wrong, so I head right over to her apartment and check with her roommates. They have not seen or heard from her although she is due back tomorrow.

Back in my room, I search for her parents' phone numbers, but find none listed. I call and leave a message with Patterson's receptionist at the firm. No one calls me back. This is not right. Something *is* definitely wrong.

Chapter Twelve
Johnny Be Good

Jess is due back tomorrow. I'll find out then what happened.

I run over to Duffy's because I promised to fill in today for Bud. While dropping an order off with Liam, several patrons move in to watch blaring, breaking news on the television. "What's going on?" I ask.

A patron says, "Some nut shot up a convenience store and is holed up there with hostages."

"Huh," I say. "Where?"

"Someplace in Georgia."

I wipe the bar down with my back to the television. I pick up two beer glasses, top them off, and walk them over to customers. "We can now confirm the identity of the shooter," the bleach-blonde anchor from one of those national cable news channels says. "His name...Can we get that picture up on the screen? His name is John William Reddens."

I jerk to a halt, spilling the beer all over me, the two patrons, and everywhere. "Hey." One man yells at me jumping up from his table. I turn to look at the television, still holding the beer glasses, a quarter empty now. The TV shows a picture of Johnny Redneck in his Army dress uniform. "He's a former clerk at the store," the anchor says.

Duffy jumps off his stool and rushes over. Still turned and gawking at the television, I place the beer glasses on the table in front of the stunned customers who are wiping the beer from their clothes. "What is it?" Duffy says.

"I'm so sorry," I say to the customers. "He was in my unit," I say to Duffy.

Duffy looks up at the television and says to Liam, indicating the beer-soaked patrons, "Can you get this cleaned up?" Liam rushes over with a wet rag. "Everything's on the house," Duffy says to the two men. I move over and stand behind the patrons at the bar, Duffy following and halting next to me.

"We can now confirm that there are three dead, and at least five hostages inside with the gunman," the reporter says, her big fake eyelashes dancing up and down. "We're not sure the motive, but have confirmed Reddens lost his job at the store." She puts her finger up to her earpiece. "We're being told the police are trying to negotiate with Reddens to release two children inside the store."

"I have to get down there," I say to Duffy.

"Georgia?" he says. "By the time you get there, it'll be over."

"I've gotta to do something." My eyes sear through him.

He sighs, looks around, his fleshy Irish cheeks crimson red. "Okay. My car's out back."

We jump into Duffy's Cadillac CTS-V Sedan and zip across Manhattan toward LaGuardia. I call an airline on the way and find a flight leaving for Atlanta in one hour. I give the operator, Carl, who's probably in India, my credit card number. "I know it could be over or that I wouldn't be able to do much," I say to Duffy, "but I know this guy. He was a good soldier."

He glances at me. "I get it, son. You gotta do what you gotta do." He drops me at the terminal, I rush in and print up my ticket at the kiosk, go through security and make it to the gate with three minutes to spare before boarding.

In my seat I find the number for the Columbus police and work the receptionist who connects me to a desk sergeant. "There is nothing you can do here."

"No, no. You don't understand. I know him. I served with him in the wars. I can talk to him."

The flight attendant comes by. "We're getting ready for takeoff. You have to turn off your phone."

"Okay," I say to the attendant. "Sergeant, listen," I say into my phone, "I'm coming down there. I'm gonna rent a car and drive like hell to get there before you blast your way in."

"What's your name again?"

"Zachary Powell. Talk to your superiors. Don't kill him. I have to hang up now for take-off. For god's sake, don't go blasting in there and kill him." I turn the phone off as we taxi to the end of the runway.

For the next hour and a half, I'm a wreck. This ordeal could be long over before I get there. However, would the police really risk the lives of the hostages, especially the children? I buy a few of those small bottles of Jim and slam them back while in flight.

We land, I disembark and hurry down the jet way. When I emerge into the terminal, two attentive Georgia state troopers are waiting. One compares me to a photograph he holds. "Zachary Powell?" says the older man.

"Yes?"

"Come with us." They lead me outside the terminal where I climb into the back of a cruiser. We pull out onto an interstate and zip along at break-neck speed, at least a hundred miles an hour, sometimes more, with the sirens shattering the still, nighttime air. All of the cars on the interstate move aside to let us pass by. Neither man says anything, so I don't either.

We speed into Columbus just after sundown. We pull up to a large black van and the troopers rush me inside where people work phones and computers. "Zachary Powell?"

"Yes."

158

"I'm special agent Boyd of the FBI and this is Chief Hollenbeck of the Columbus Police Department." Boyd, in his thirties and clean cut, is dressed in black, swat-like fatigues. He wears a sidearm. "When we got the call from police HQ we ran a check on you at the Pentagon. Bronze Star, huh?"

"Yes, sir."

"I'm not sure what you can do," Boyd says, sighing. "We're really out of options."

"I can talk to him." The two men glance at one another, then back at me. "What is it?" I ask.

"He's completely deranged," Boyd says. "He's talking nonsense, something about jihadists and hajjis."

"You gotta let me talk to him."

"He's not answering his phone. Infrared can confirm the five hostages are alive. He's pacing back and forth near them, but we can't get a shot off."

"Please. Don't shoot him. I'm begging you. Please. Get me close. Let me talk to him."

Boyd studies me. "We're gonna have to storm the place soon and end this."

"He'll listen to me. Please. Just get me close enough." I scan their faces. Hollenbeck reminds me of my father. He must be around the same age, with balding gray hair, and a similar build, minus the beer belly.

Boyd nods at Hollenbeck and hands me a bulletproof vest and gives me a bullhorn. They escort me down the street where we stop behind a police car and take cover. Hollenbeck switches the bullhorn on. I edge out from behind the car and walk slowly toward the store. "Johnny?" I say. "Johnny? It's Zach. Zach Powell. I'm here to talk with you."

Nothing.

"Johnny? It's Zach. I'm just outside." A shadow moves around inside. I wait. The front door opens up a crack. "Johnny?"

"That you, Zach?"

159

"Yeah. It's me, Johnny." I move closer, holding the bullhorn at my side now. "I need to talk to you."

"You out there with no cover?"

Damn. He's Cracked. "Yeah, Johnny. I need cover."

"I, ah…I don't know, Zach. They wanna wax me."

"No one's gonna kill anyone. I'm not gonna let that happen." I set the bullhorn down beside me. "I need to come inside, Johnny."

Silence. I wait.

"Can I come inside?"

"I dunno, Zach. You see, they're all cryin'."

"Who's crying, Johnny?"

"These people in here."

In fact, he is crying too. "Johnny, please. I need to come in. It'll be all right. I promise." I glance at the men behind me, the store surrounded with snipers, police cars, and Boyd and Hollenbeck watching me through night vision goggles. "Look, Johnny," I say facing the store front again. "I completely trust you. See?" I take my bulletproof vest off and toss it onto the ground beside me. I pull out my wallet, my cell phone, keys, everything, and set them on the ground. "I'm unarmed and have nothing on me." I hold my hands up.

"I guess it'll be okay," he says.

"Okay. I'm coming in, Johnny." I approach cautiously, slowly, nervously. Johnny opens the door, grabs my arm and pulls me into the store. He slams the door behind me, locking it. He runs up to me, points the handgun at my chest, and says, "It's not gonna work, Zach."

"What's not gonna work, Johnny?" I say holding my hands up above my head. "It's okay, Johnny. It's okay. What's not gonna work?" Two men, one woman and two young children, both girls, huddle close together on the floor near cereal boxes. The girls have to be no more than seven years old. The children sob and the adults sniffle.

"Betty left me, Zach. She took my baby." He weeps and lowers his gun. Only problem now is that he waves it around the room. There are three bodies on the floor in the next aisle with blood pools near their heads. "I lost my job, Zach."

"We can get through this, Johnny. You have to trust me." I lower my hands, but not all the way.

He looks at me, his eyes swollen from crying. "You think so, Zach?"

"Yes, but you have to trust me, Johnny. Please." I lower my hands to my side.

"How do we do that, Zach?"

I look at the hostages. "You have to let these people go, Johnny. They haven't done anything wrong."

"Let them go?" He wipes tears from his eyes with the back of his hand, the one with the gun, and paces. "Oh, I dunno. That guy over there," he points to one of the bodies, "he laughed at me. Called me names. Made fun of me. He's the manager. Fired me, Zach. Said I couldn't get along with people and was scarin' the customers. Called me a crazy soldier boy. I'm a veteran, Zach. You're a veteran. We shouldn't be treated like that." He sniffles.

"You're right, Johnny." I raise my hands to help calm him. "You're absolutely right. But these people here, did they do anything wrong?"

He looks at the two girls who are crying and the terrified adults. He raises his hand, the one with the gun, up to his forehead, and using the back of his hand, rubs it. "I dunno, Zach. I just dunno."

"Johnny. Why don't we let the children go? Children are innocent."

"I dunno. They could have IED's, Zach." He examines the children's faces.

"Not these girls, Johnny. Look at them." They are cute little blonde girls, with bows in their hair. "Please, Johnny. It will be really good of you and show you are a true hero if you do."

"Well, I guess. You really think so, Zach?"

"I do. Will you allow me to let them go? Right out that front door?"

He wipes some more tears from his eyes. He thinks a minute. "Don't know. Guess it'll be okay."

"Okay. I'm gonna get them, Johnny, and walk them to the front door now. Okay?"

"Are you sure, Zach?"

"I'm sure, Johnny. Please?"

He nods. "Okay, Zach. You're a good friend, for a northerner."

I smile. "Thanks, Johnny. I love the south. I love you as a real true friend." I take a deep breath and walk over to the hostages not knowing if he will snap again. "It's gonna be okay," I say to the hostages.

"Please," the woman begs, tears streaming down her face. "They're my babies."

"You give them to me and I'm gonna have them walk right out the front door, ma'am." I hold up my arms to them.

The woman nods in between sniffles. "Go with this nice man," the woman says to the girls.

The girls are hesitant at first, but the mother releases them. The girls, bawling, step forward while Johnny paces back and forth waving the gun around. I embrace them in my arms, one on each side, pick them up, and walk them to the front door. I unlock and open it shouting, "We're coming out. Hold your fire." I carry them out and set them down. "Run to those nice policemen over there." They run right into the arms of a black-clad swat man holding an automatic rifle. He leads them away and I go back in the store. "It's me, Johnny."

He closes the door behind me, jittery, like a jackrabbit. "I've done a really bad thing, huh, Zach?"

"I can't lie to you, Johnny. But you did a really good thing just now. They will look favorably on that."

"You think so?"

"Yes. We can get through this. We're in this together, Johnny, just like back in the unit. We'll embrace the suck, Johnny."

He paces again. "I dunno. They're gonna wax me now, Zach. This is Georgia, you know. Hey. I didn't know you was in Georgia?"

162

"I just happened to be passing by when I thought I could stop and help."

"I knew it. I knew you was one of the best buddies in the unit. I mean, where is everyone else? You was always such a joker, but you always stepped up. You're a real pal, Zach." He slaps me on my war shoulder.

"Everyone else is also very worried and they would like to help too, but they couldn't get here just now." He continues pacing. I have to get these other people out of here. Scanning the store, I say, "What do we do now, Johnny?"

"I dunno. I mean, I can't go back. They won't let it be all the same."

"You're right, Johnny. Nothing's ever the same, but we can work through this. What do you think?"

"I dunno." He rubs the gun across his forehead again. "I dunno."

I look over at the three hostages huddled there on the floor, their faces sheet-white. I am not sure what color mine is, but it feels hot. "I don't want to see any more people get hurt. Why don't we let them go too?"

"Oh, but they're adults, Zach. They're responsible. They started this war. They must be held accountable. They put us through hell."

"What're they responsible for, Johnny?"

"The war, Zach. They started this. We can't let them go."

"We don't want to hurt them, Johnny."

"No. But someone has to be held accountable."

"Well, why don't you hold me accountable?"

He weeps and waves the gun around. "You're innocent, Zach. Just like me. We're innocents, don't you know?" He points the gun at the hostages. "They're not like us. They're not innocents like us, Zach."

I step in front of the muzzle and put my palms up. "Well, we're all sinners, Johnny." *Where did that come from?*

"It's not a sin in a war, Zach. The Bible says so."

"Yeah, so I'm told." I wonder, because he might think he's still in combat, at least in his mind, if he'll be forgiven.

He slides down onto the floor facing me. I stand with my back to the hostages facing him. "Can I sit next to you, Johnny?" He nods and wipes tears away. I move over and slide down next to him. We sit there for a moment. How the hell am I going to get that gun from him? I know I can't make any hasty moves because Johnny is bigger and stronger than I am.

Silence, except for some sniffling from the hostages. I turn my head and nod at them. "Whadda we gonna do now, Zach?"

"We're going to relax, and take our time to think. Okay, Johnny?"

"Okay."

We wait. My heart is racing. A minute passes. Then five. Maybe ten. "Everyone okay?" I say.

The hostages nod and sniffle. "Johnny?"

He nods too.

"What should we do, Johnny?"

"I dunno, Zach. They're gonna wax me."

He's back to that line. "No one's gonna kill you, Johnny. They promised me."

"This is Georgia, Zach. They give ya the needle down here."

"No. Not you, Johnny. You're a veteran. A war hero. They have programs to help you."

"I don't know anything but soldierin'. I was good at it. They don't care about that. I tried and tried and tried to get work. No one would give me a decent job. I took this minimum wage job, but I can't support Betty and the baby on that. I have no skill 'cept shootin'."

"We'll figure something out."

"I dunno, Zach. Look over there." He waves his gun at the three bodies on the floor nearby.

He is right about Georgia. He could get the needle, but clearly, he isn't in control of his faculties. *For God's sakes.* "You know, if you let these people go, they will take that into consideration."

"But they won't let me go." He sobs.

Again, he is right, but I can't say it. "If you let them go, you still have me. For a hostage."

"You're not a hostage, Zach. You can walk out that door anytime you like." He waves the gun at the front door.

Damn, that didn't work. "Look Johnny, Betty wants to see you walk out that door too. We all do. Why don't we do that? Walk out the door, together? We'll leave these people here. You and me. Out the door together. Just like on a patrol. Together again. Whaddaya say?"

He sobs some more. "Betty left me. I lost my job. I've lost everythin'." He blubbers now. "I get edgy, Zach. I have nightmares. I snap at people. I can't concentrate."

"We can get you help for that, Johnny."

"I dunno, Zach. I was only good in the army. I was good at killin' the enemy. That's all I know how to do."

Damn. This is not working. I'm not a professional.

"I can't go out there now. There's nothing left for me. Don't ya see?"

I do, but I can't say that. "No Johnny. We'll find something for you. You have people who love you."

"I dunno, Zach. It's all over. Don't ya know?"

"No, Johnny. I can't accept that. It's never that bad. There's always hope."

"I dunno. What am I gonna do?"

"Please, Johnny. Let these people go? For me?" He looks at me, his eyes flooded with tears. "Please." I stare into his eyes and wait. "Please. Give me the gun." I hold out my hand.

He nods, but waves his gun at the hostages. "Okay," I say nodding to them. "It's okay." I get up, slowly, and help them to their feet. I walk them to the door, open it, and they sprint off.

I turn to Johnny who still sits and blubbers like a baby. "I'm so sorry, Zach," he says, tears streaming down his cheeks.

It's like a movie, played out in slow motion. Yeah, one of those slow-motion scenes. He lifts the gun and puts the muzzle in his mouth. I lunge for him, jumping, screaming, "No!!!!!!!!"

He pulls the trigger before I fall onto him. We crash together into the cereal boxes. The whole episode seems surreal, or unreal. I roll over, look up and see that he has blown his brains out all over the cereal boxes. I wail, "No, Johnny. No Johnny. No, Johnny." and cradle his head in my lap just as I had with Jimmy.

It seems like an eternity before the swat team bursts through the door and swarms me. They drag me off Johnny's body. I try to resist, holding on tightly. Agent Boyd grabs and wraps me in his arms. He leads me away from the scene and puts his hands up to shield me from the television cameras. Their lights are so bright they almost blind me. Reporters shout questions as Boyd hustles me past them.

~ * ~

I sit in the back of one of those black suburban FBI SUV's staring out the window. The interstate sign reads Atlanta, five miles. We drive into the garage of the Federal Building there. Boyd takes me up to an FBI office where he hands me my wallet, cell phone, keys and backpack. He gives me an FBI T-shirt to wear, seeing as my shirt has Johnny's blood all over it.

I clean up in the bathroom at nearly five in the morning. I'm exhausted, to say the least. It reminds me of long military days. Another agent takes my statement.

Boyd drives me to the airport later that morning, walks me to the gate and says, "You should talk to someone. Professionally."

"Okay," I lie.

During the whole flight back to New York, I stare out the window of the plane at the eastern seaboard of the United States. It looks so beautiful, so peaceful, so simple, so innocent.

166

~ * ~

He stands beside me. We read the inscription:

> *Best   of   all   he   loved   the   fall*
> *The   leaves   yellow   on   cottonwoods*
> *Leaves   floating   on   trout   streams*
> *And   above   the   hills*
> *The   high   blue   windless   skies*
> *...Now he will be a part of them forever.*

"Poignant, huh?"

"Yeah," I say, glancing over at Stein. I turn and follow him along Trail Creek Path. The leaves on the trees have turned spectacular colors of reds and yellows and the bright blue sky above reflects on the stream beside me. The wind cries out. "Where're we going?"

"For a walk."

I draw a deep breath, the fresh and clean Idaho air filling my lungs. I feel so peaceful and at ease. It is like heaven here. "What do you think?" I say.

"You've got a lot of balls, kid."

"Yeah, I guess so. Crazy balls maybe."

He smiles. "Winter's coming." He wears his black angler's hat that covers his graying hair and his full white beard has grown scraggly. He cradles a shotgun in his arm.

"Who're we gonna shoot?"

"Hopefully no one." He stops, reaches into his long coat, and extracts a flask. He twists the top, takes a nip and passes it to me.

I look at it, cradled in my hand like a gun. I contemplate it. It calls out to me. I take a swallow. "Damn, that's good. You always come along at the right time." I pass his flask back to him. He stuffs it in his pocket and we continue walking.

Silence.

I hear the wind speaking in tongues through the trees. A bird chirps nearby as we turn the corner near the bend in the creek. I see a nineteen-fifties vintage car driving down a road, then hear a gunshot and jump to the ground searching for cover. "Jesus, kid. Relax." He jogs up the path ahead of me. I rise to my feet and hustle after him.

Around another bend in the creek, I happen upon him standing over the body of a man who wears army ACU's. He has no face, although it appears it hasn't been blown off by a blast. It is just faceless. "Another one," Stein says.

I kneel next to the body and inspect the nametag on the uniform. It reads: Veteran. I look up at him standing over me and say, "What do I do now?"

"Bleed," he says.

"Bleed? What're you talking about?"

"Sit down at your typewriter and bleed."

Chapter Thirteen
She Loves Me Not?

My head bounces off the window as the plane touches down. My heart races and I'm sweaty. The man next to me glances at me as if I'm diseased.

The first order of business in the terminal is to stop at the bar and get a drink to calm me. In the cab on the way back to Manhattan, I work my phone. No messages. I call Jess, but this time I get a not in service message. *What the hell is this?* I text her too but it bounces back undeliverable. Okay, there is something really wrong now. I call Patterson's office and leave another message with the receptionist.

The cabbie drops me off and I run up the steps to my apartment where I catch Basir in the living room getting ready to leave for a class. His mouth drops open. "What?" I snap.

"You are all over the news."

I head to my room but Dale intercepts me coming from the bathroom, Basir following. "They say you are some kind of a hero," Basir says.

"It's bullshit."

"What the fuck, dude?" Dale says. They stand at my door. "You okay?" he says.

"Look," I say narrowing my eyes at them, "I don't wanna talk about it. Did Jess come looking for me?"

Dale shakes his head and looks at Basir who shakes his as well.

I slam the door on them, sit on my bed and see the wrapped jewelry box on top of my nightstand. I tip my flask, suck it dry, grab my pack and head out for the university; she must be there. Detouring to buy a bottle of Jim, two old ladies walking past give me a dirty look when I stop to fill my flask on the street corner. I jam the flask into my jacket pocket and put the rest of Jim in my pack. A text comes through from Micah:

Zach, You okay? I'm in Paris on a shoot. Wasn't paying attention to the news. Johnny was a good soldier. Call me. Micah

I text back:

I'm fine. It's nothing. Yeah. He was a hell of a soldier, wasn't he? He served his country. End of story.

I make my way over to the campus newspaper's office. Everyone stops what he or she is doing and stares when I walk in. I enter Terri's office, my student mentor and advisor. She's a senior, but is actually two years younger than I am. I like her, she is smart, and even though she is one of those fiercely anti-war, military or whatever people, she has great compassion for me and the other war veterans on campus. "You don't have to do anything you don't want to do," she says, "but I want you to think about this."

I look at her and say nothing.

"Consider writing something. About it, not about it. I don't care. Whatever you want to do. I promise you I will have it published on the front page. I will honor your voice."

I nod, brushing my hair from my eyes.

"Good. That's all I ask."

"Have you heard from Jessica?"

"You don't know?"

"Don't know what?"

"She suddenly dropped out. Withdrew. No one's heard from her."

"I didn't know that."

"That's all I know, Zach. I'm sorry."

Dumbfounded, I leave the newspaper office and hurry back to my apartment. Approaching my stoop lost in deep thought regarding why Jess has dropped out, why she isn't returning my calls, texts and emails, a man runs up to me and thrusts a microphone into my face almost bumping it into my nose. "Zachary Powell?" he says. "Can you talk to me about what happened in Georgia?" He's from one of the major cable news channels, is well dressed in a suit and tie, and looks like he should be dating Barbie.

"I really can't tal…" Out of nowhere, several reporters swarm me shouting questions.

"Zachary, can we get your take?"

"Can you tell us what happened?"

"Did he really shoot himself?"

"Reports indicate a police sniper killed him."

"Was he crazy?"

"Did he threaten to kill those children?"

"Did Reddens really kill all those children in Iraq?"

I run up the steps of my apartment with the reporters in tow, hurry in and close the door behind me. They continue shouting through the door.

I run into my room and tap out the piece on Johnny. It bleeds from my fingers. I don't elaborate on the incident in Georgia. Rather, I write a story of a good soldier, a buddy, who volunteered to serve his country, followed orders, and was always there to back you up in combat. I write that he was an individual who cared deeply about his family and his country. I end with a short dissertation on a veteran who came home to find a home that didn't know what to do with him and had nothing to give him. I email it to Terri.

I call Patterson's law firm and speak to the receptionist again. "Well, can you *please, please* have him call me? Thank you." I give her my number, again.

I mope around the apartment waiting for a callback. Nothing. Two hours later, I call again and leave yet another message.

I turn on the television and watch the protesting in Egypt against President Mubarak that has grown larger and stronger in recent days. Basir strolls in. "There is a reporter at the door looking for you."

"Tell him to go away."

He sits and drops his books on the coffee table. I notice him studying the images from Tahrir Square. "I am going," he says.

"Going where?"

He nods at the television screen.

"Egypt?" I say glimpsing the protesting on the screen.

"Yes. My brother is there. I have to go and support him."

I pat him on his shoulder and go into my room. I call Duffy, tell him I can't make it in to work, and sprint out the front door.

On the stoop, I notice the coast is clear so I bolt down the steps and across the street. I jog over to Amsterdam and hail a cab. I instruct the cabbie to take me to a car rental office where I rent a sedan and head out for Connecticut.

~ * ~

All the way to Greenwich, my mind whirls. I haven't seen or spoken to Jess since before we went on break, over a week ago. This is not like her. This is not the Jess I know. We have been together now for just over two years. What have they done to her?

While driving, I ponder my most recent visit with Stein and chuckle. I should have studied psychology.

I drive up to her parent's house and take a swig of Jim, just to calm my nerves. I climb out of my rental and push the intercom box at the gate. As the phone rings, the security camera swings around and zooms in on me. "Hello?" I say.

I wait. Nothing.

I push the button again. It dials a second time. Once more, the intercom clicks. "Hello?" I say again.

"It's over, Zachary," she says through the intercom.

"Mrs. Patterson? Is that you?" Just then, it starts raining. I have no raincoat or umbrella.

"You're not to see Jessica anymore."

"What're you talking about?"

"You have to forget about her and get on with your life."

"I don't understand." The rain showers grow heavy soaking me.

"You need to go now." The intercom clicks off. The red light goes out on the security camera. I redial.

Nothing. What did she mean? Why are they so cruel? The intercom rings and rings. It finally stops ringing after a couple of minutes. I redial it yet again.

Mrs. Paterson answers: "You have to leave now or I'll call the police."

"The police? That's not necessary. Mrs. Patterson, I just need to talk with her."

"That's not possible." The intercom clicks off again. I look around, soaked to the bone. For the longest time, I stand there thinking of what to do. A black sedan pulls up and stops behind me. The driver's window lowers halfway. "You need to leave or we'll call the police."

I look over at the man I chased in New York, the man who had been following and spying on us. "You?" I say approaching him. He rolls the window up and drives off. "Come back here." I stand there in the middle of the roadway, the rain coming down in sheets. I look back at the wrought iron gate surrounding the estate, keeping me out as if it were the White House, which, by the way, *I have been in you assholes.*

I slosh through a water puddle, soaking my shoes, and crawl back into my rental. I stare at the gate, then glance up the road for any sign of that asshole I am going to *beat the shit out of next time I have the chance.* After a few minutes sitting there dripping, I work my phone and Google Mr. Patterson's law firm.

I drive into Greenwich. Unseasonably warm this time of year, although the temperature is now dropping as it's late in the afternoon.

The Patterson building is an older one, built sometime in the 1920's. The name on the building, *The Patterson Building*, is etched in limestone above the door. First Connecticut Bank welcomes customers on the first floor and professional offices fill out floors two and three. The law firm occupies the top two floors of the five-story building.

I park the car at a meter on the street and take a good hit of Jim. I take a deep breath, exhale and wipe my lips with the back of my hand. I make my way into the large marble-floored lobby where a security guard at a kiosk examines me, water dripping from my pants. "Zachary Powell. I'm here to see Mr. Patterson."

He checks his log, looks back up at me and says, "I don't see you listed."

"I don't have an appointment."

"You need to call the firm and make one."

"No, I don't." I walk past him and head to the elevator where I push the button.

He rises from his chair and chases me. He is a man in his fifties or sixties, gray hair and balding, and not much of a threat. "You can't go up there," he says in an authoritative voice.

"Actually, I can. You mean I may not go up there. Look, pops, you try and stop me and I'll have to neutralize you. Got it?" He narrows his eyes and reaches for my arm. I pull away as the elevator door opens. "You don't want to do that," I say. He grabs his radio and calls for assistance as I enter the elevator and the door closes on him.

I ride up to the fifth floor. The elevator door opens on a lobby with plush carpets and a secretary sitting there in front of large glass doors behind her like Saint Peter guarding the gates of heaven. She is on the phone and her face tightens when she sees me. She is in her thirties, well dressed and proper. I slosh over to her and wait.

She starts to put the phone down in its cradle, but other lines light up on the pad so she holds it steady, glaring at me. "May I help you?" she manages to squeak out.

"I'm here to see Mr. Patterson."

"Do you have an appointment?"

"No. But he'll see me."

"Could you please have a seat and I'll inquire?"

I spot a cloth sofa and chairs against the wall. "I'll stand so I don't get your furniture wet."

She half-smiles, half-smirks and pushes a lighted button on her phone console. "Yes?" she says. She peers up at me and says into the phone, trying to obscure what she saying, "Yes. Right here."

This means trouble. I peek through the glass doors and see a conference room with several people sitting around a large table. I can just make out Mr. Patterson sitting there at the head of it.

The elevator doors behind me open and the security guard exits with two other security guards following him. "There he is." the old man from the lobby says. The other two are not in much better shape than the lobby one. They are rent-a-cop types who can't do much of anything except call the police or log visitors in and out of the building.

I push the door to the offices open and hurry across the floor to the conference room. The security guards chase after me. Lawyers, paralegals and clerks stand up to see the uproar as I make it to the conference room and burst in. I startle everyone in the room, not only with my intrusion, but also with my appearance. Everyone is well dressed in expensive suits, in contrast to my dripping T-shirt and jeans. "I need to speak with you, Mr. Patterson."

He stands and tries to maintain his composure, but I sense outrage in his voice as he says, "I cannot talk to you here. Now."

The security guards rush over and grab my arms and wrestle with me. "I'm sorry, Mr. Patterson," the guard from the lobby says while struggling with me.

"We'll talk about that later," Mr. Patterson says. "You have to go," he says to me.

Using close-quarter combat techniques Uncle Sam taught me, I elbow one of the guards in the pit of his stomach. It takes the wind out of him. Toppling over onto his knees, he gasps for air. I spin around, break free from the second guard and slam the palm of my hand into his chin. He back-pedals into the wall. The third guard, the one from the lobby, I knee in the groin. He collapses, holding his balls and moaning. I back off. "Don't touch me again," I say, my adrenaline exploding.

The lawyers in the room freeze in their seats. No one dares make a move with this clearly deranged person standing before them. Mr. Patterson puts his hands up. "This is not good, Zach."

"Yeah, you're right, Mr. Patterson. You're absolutely right. It's not good." I catch my breath. "It's not any way to treat a veteran from the wars. A recipient of the Bronze Star for Valor in combat. A veteran who put his life on the line so you can have all of this." I wave my arm around the room. "Perhaps I should hire one of your attorneys to litigate on my behalf for the undue stress you have caused me."

With his hands still in the air, he says, "Okay, okay. You're right. Let's go to my office."

He moves for the door, keeping his eye on me. The guards begin to stabilize. I follow Patterson out of the conference room to his office while everyone on the floor stands and watches from their cubicles.

In his office I close and lock the door behind me. He sits behind his desk locked in eye combat with me. I wait for him to say something, but he doesn't. "You're joking, right?" I say.

"You're not to see her again."

"You have no right."

"You and Jessica are from two different worlds. Her path is set for her." He pauses, examines me and says, "I do appreciate what you have done for this country."

"Patronization, sir?" His eyes bore into me. I don't take mine off his. He does then look away, however. "Look me in the eye, sir, and tell me she doesn't love me."

176

He doesn't.

"I deserve respect and to know the truth."

"Look, Zachary, she's young, impressionable," he says glaring at me and leaning back in his high-back leather chair. "We all make mistakes."

"So, you're saying I'm a mistake?"

"I'm not saying that."

"Enlighten me then, sir."

"She's just going to take a different path. The path she's supposed to take."

"I don't believe you." The dripping has subsided, but I'm soaked.

"I don't care what you believe." He shifts. "Go live your life. Be successful at whatever you choose to do. However, *my daughter* is not going to be a part of it."

"She's an adult, you must know. What does she have to say about all of this?"

"That is none of your concern."

"None of my concern? You call yourself an attorney?"

He glares. "I know all about you."

"Then you know how much I care for her and how much she cares for me."

"I know about your drinking."

"Drinking? What? No, you've got it all wrong, sir." I glance through the glass walls and see the office staff standing, watching, pointing and talking. Two uniformed Greenwich police officers are on their way across the floor.

"You've been drinking now, haven't you?"

I'm going to explode. I could just snap his neck like I was taught in Ranger school. "You never answered my question, sir. Look me in the eye and tell me she does not love me."

The police start banging on the door. Mr. Patterson leans forward in his chair and says, "Love is a complicated thing. She was confused. She's getting on with her life and I *suggest* you do the same." He gets up, walks around to the front of his desk, and opens the door letting the police in.

They start shouting orders at me, "Freeze! Put your hands up. "

I ignore them and stare at Patterson. He says to the officers, "It's okay. Everything's fine. He's just leaving."

"Are you pressing charges, Mr. Patterson?" one of the officers says.

"No. No, just let him go. Let him walk out of here."

With my heart pounding, I raise my finger and point it at him, inches from his nose. "I love her, Mr. Patterson." My voices cracks. "I know she loves me."

His face turns red. I turn and walk out of his office that is dead silent. Everyone stares as I pass. The police follow me from a distance until the elevator door closes behind me.

On the drive back to Manhattan, my mind spins as I sip and finish Jim. I look around for Stein, but he doesn't show. I could really use his company now. I don't believe Patterson. He's lying. She loves me. She'll find me soon enough. She knows where I am. She has my phone number. She has my email. She knows my friends and where Micah lives. This is the Smartphone and internet age. They can't keep her from me. Perhaps I can hire a detective and do counterintelligence. No, I don't have money for that. I could stake out the house. Of course, he'll have me arrested, or shot. *I'm not afraid of that.*

I return the car and stop at a Bodega on 114th Street on my way to the apartment. I stand there staring at Jim and Glen on their shelf. I just need a drink, maybe two, just to clear my head. Then I can figure out where she might be. Just a couple jiggers to loosen me up. I splurge and buy a bottle of Glen.

I stroll into Morningside Park and sit on our bench. It's a dark night, it's cold and my clothes haven't dried yet. I check my phone. Nothing. I sit there for the longest time, thinking. What am I expecting? She's not going to show up here in the middle of the night.

I wait. I look around for Stein. Now I need the bastard and he doesn't show?

After several swigs, I drag my drunk ass back to my apartment. She's not here either. No one is. *Where the hell is everyone?*

I curl up on the bed, nursing Glen. God, I hope she's okay. She'll get away soon enough from wherever they sent her, just like Micah did. She'll show up right on cue, jump into my arms, tilt those smoky hazel eyes up at me, and give me a big wet kiss from those gorgeous and sensuous lips. I drink most of Glen and finally pass out staring at the blue gift box on my nightstand.

Chapter Fourteen
Pull Yourself Together, Kid

"Let's go, kid," he says.

I sit up on the edge of a daybed and rub the sleep from my eyes.

"If you don't get your ass up you'll sleep the day away and we'll miss the boat."

"Miss the boat? Where am I?" I say.

"At the Finca Vigia in San Francisco de Paula."

"San Francisco what?"

"Cuba, kid. Cuba." Stein is in his forties with a thick bushy mustache and the beginnings of a gray beard. "Grab that tackle box over there and follow me."

I do as I'm told. We hurry down to the harbor and board Pilar where Fuentes is already waiting. He tips his captain's hat then lights a fire under Pilar. We cruise out of the harbor as fast as she can go.

I have the best time. Stein jabbers on about fishing. He tips a bottle of gin, but has whiskey to give me. Sometimes he drinks other spirits besides whiskey. He says whatever works, works.

I sit on the bench watching him fish. The day is a Caribbean picture perfect one. The blue sky has only small white puffy clouds and the sun glistening on the water sparkles in my eyes. He looks back at me while trolling and says, "I told you I'd box him out for you. I can go a few rounds with the best man." He makes fists and punches at the air.

"Well, I guess I should have taken you up on that then." I chug from a bottle of whiskey.

He snorts. "Every day above earth is a good day, kid."

I analyze him. "Really? Where did that come from?"

"Look, the world is a fine place and worth fighting for and I would hate very much to leave it."

Should I tell him how it ends?

"What's that?"

"Nothing."

He shifts his weight in the angler's chair. "Just know when to get off the dance floor."

"Get off the dance floor?" I say, nodding. "Sure, papa. Whatever you say."

His pole begins to splash around in the water and I watch as he battles a beast for several minutes. He reels in a large marlin and I help him get it onto the boat using a large hook the size of a tackle box. He then gives me a turn at the rod. I actually catch a small marlin a few minutes later. We laugh, drink, and he tells me stories from World War I and his time in Paris. I have one of the greatest days of my life with him there on Pilar, above earth. I wish this time would never end.

~ * ~

But it does. Someone clinks dishes in the kitchen waking me, Glen lying beside me. I tip him to my lips, take a dance, and throw his empty ass in the trashcan. I crawl out of bed and stagger into the kitchen where Dale nibbles on cereal. "You look like shit, dude," he says.

"Thanks. Long night. She's gone."

"What? Where?"

"I don't know. I don't know. Her father was a real prick. I don't know where she is."

"I'm sorry, man. I liked her, and dawg she was hot."

"I need you to remind me?" I grab a box of flakes and dump some in my mouth. Chewing, I say, "Where's Basir?"

"He took a flight out this morning. I had a car take him to the airport."

"Huh," I say dropping flakes on the floor.

"You okay?"

"What? Yeah. Yeah, I'm fine."

"No you're not," he says. What happened?"

"I don't know. They sent her away, poisoned her against me, I don't know. I mean, if she really loves me, and this was not just some school romance, then she'll find me, I guess. Right?"

"Yeah. I hope so." He goes into the living room and turns on the television. I follow him and stand behind the sofa watching the events unfold in Tahrir Square. Protesters are shouting and the military is watching from their tanks. "Do you think they'll attack?" he says.

"Probably. It could be a bloodbath if they do."

"Well," he says. "I hope that crazy Arab doesn't get himself killed. I kinda like him."

"Yeah. Me too," I say.

"Well, I've got a class." Dale departs. I stand there chewing on flakes watching the protesting while listening to analysis from so-called experts.

~ * ~

I can't bring myself to leave the apartment. I mope around for two days, miss a couple of classes, and call in sick to Duffy's. I send Andrew a message through Facebook.

The newshounds must have moved on because I haven't seen any near the apartment. Almost everyone has emailed me about the incident in Georgia. Julio said he went to his room, closed the door and cried for

Johnny. He never acted emotional like that before or at least in front of me. I check phone messages. Kristen left one: "Zach, what were you thinking? I'm worried. Please call me." I don't call her back because I don't need anyone lecturing me about anything and don't want to talk to anyone. I only want to talk with Jess.

On my third day in the apartment, and still no word from Jess, I have to get out of here, otherwise, I'll go crazy. Besides, I'm almost out of booze. It seems I always have to check to make sure I have some on standby.

I attend one of my classes. Sitting there, unable to concentrate, I leave early and head over to the paper where I meet Terri who shows me the edited version of my story on Johnny. "It's very genuine," she says. "And it captures the heart and soul of him. You did a fine job."

"Thanks," I say, brushing my hair from my eyes. I have also let my beard grow out since I last saw Jess.

"Any word on Jess?"

I appreciate her sensibility, not only for her concern for Jess, but her understanding of Johnny. I chuckle. "No. Her parents must have sent her off to live in a convent or something. She's gone. Without a trace."

"I'm sorry, Zach. I know how much you two liked one another."

I nod and look around the office. A flash goes through my mind. "Yes, well, I'm going on a trip for a couple of weeks."

"Oh? Where're you going?" she calls after me as I head across the room.

"I'll send an email. I might have a story or two."

Chapter Fifteen
In a Pickle

I hustle back to the apartment and stuff my backpack with three sets of clothes and another one of Stein's books, *To Have and Have Not*. I hail a cab and pay a huge fare to JFK.

I make my way over to the Egyptair terminal and find an attendant. No one waits there to book a flight, so I hurry right up to her. She shuffles papers, looks up and says, "May I help you?"

"Yes. Please. I need to get to Cairo."

She creases her forehead. "May I see your passport?" I hand it to her. "It's not safe, especially for Americans right now."

"My university roommate is from Cairo and is there now. I have to get there to help him."

She looks me over, returns my passport to me and taps onto the keyboard. "Well," she says glancing up at me, "I have a flight leaving in a couple hours. That is, if it is not cancelled because of, well you know."

"I understand. Is there an available seat?"

"There are many available seats," she snaps.

"I'll book it." I hand her my credit card. "Keep the return flight open, please."

I sign off on a slip. "Thank you very much." I take the ticket from her, sit in a chair and call Basir. He doesn't answer, so I leave a message. I send him a text too.

While waiting for my flight, I start in on Stein's book. More than once, I have to re-read a passage, because my mind drifts to thoughts of Jess. Do her parents think I am trying to weasel in on their money or her money she stands to inherit? Is it because of the wars and they think I am some crazy vet who will go berserk like Johnny? Or, is it just all that blueblood highfalutin class crap?

I hit the bar and down some Jim while watching a correspondent on the television reporting from Cairo that the army has Tahrir Square surrounded with tanks and troops. Good, I might be back in combat before too long. It's all very exciting.

I notice myself in the mirror behind the bar. With my thickening beard and long hair I am beginning to look like a revolutionary, Che Guevara perhaps. Perfect, I'll fit right in.

I board the Egyptair flight which is half-full with mostly Egyptian travelers.

In flight, I continue reading Stein's book. I find Harry Morgan fascinating, and yes, distressing, but I feel for him. It seems like a lot of fun, running contraband between Cuba and Florida. I can picture Stein and me doing that. In any event, Morgan is killed in the end, by revolutionaries no less. The setting reminds me of my dreams of Key West and Cuba, as if I were back there, despite having never been there. Or was I?

As the flight banks over Cairo, I look out my window and see the city alive below, although I can't make out any areas of protest or turmoil or Tahrir Square.

We disembark and funnel through a jet way. The Egyptians corral into one line while I hurry up to a desk all by myself. The attendant, in a sloppy government uniform, glances up at me, then down at a security monitor, and back up at me, as if he is doing a double-take. I present my passport.

He scowls and takes possession of the passport. "What is the nature of your business?" he says in a gruff and tired voice, heavily accented.

"Tourism."

He wrinkles his nose.

"Well, I actually have a friend who is from here. Cairo." I look around. "He should be waiting for me."

As he eyeballs me, he picks up a phone and punches in a number. I wait, rock back and forth on my heels and scan the not so busy terminal. The other passengers from my flight have already made it through the checkpoint and have gone on to collect their luggage. I am virtually all alone. Will they arrest and throw me into some Egyptian prison? Will they torture me suspecting me of being a spy? After the combat I have been in, what the hell did I care? This is an opportunity to be a part of an uprising, one that might bring freedom to the long, repressed Middle East.

He places the phone back into its cradle and scribbles something into his ledger in front of him. I wait.

I wait some more. "Is everything okay?"

He looks back up at me. "It will only be a moment."

Great. A moment? Until what? I wait some more while the official in front of me shuffles papers and looks at his monitor.

A few minutes later, two men in police uniforms approach from the far side of the terminal. *Damn.* This is it. I'm going to be locked up. They are both much older than me, perhaps in their forties. One guy twirls his nightstick and says something to the attendant at the desk. The one with the nightstick says to me in English, accented in Arabic, "Come with us."

I walk with them, one on each side. They lead me to a room with no windows, a small table and two chairs, one on each side. "Stay here," says the man. He closes the door behind me, locking it.

I set my backpack on the table. The room has nothing on the walls, is painted all white, and is twelve by twelve feet square. It reminds me of a police interrogation room, like the ones you see on television cop shows. I sit down and wait, my knee jumping up and down.

I wait some more. Ten minutes pass.

Twenty more minutes pass.

At last, I hear someone talking outside the door in Arabic. I'll be dragged off now to an Egyptian prison and tortured for sure. I must be a spy. Why else would this American come to Egypt at a time like this? They must think my thickening beard and long hair is a ruse.

I hear keys rattling in the door, the knob turns and the door swings opens to reveal the officer. He enters followed by, Basir! "Are you crazy?" he says.

"Probably," I say standing.

"Follow me." He hands me my passport. I grab my pack, shoulder it, and follow him out. We exit the terminal and find an awaiting Mercedes sedan. I climb into the backseat and Basir into the front. "This is my brother, Amir," Basir says. "His English is not so good."

"Hello," Amir says to me driving away.

"Hello," I say. Amir is older than Basir, has long hair, a closely cropped beard, darker skin than Basir, and a larger nose.

"We will go to the house," Basir says to me. "What is it that you think you can do here?"

"Nothing," I say. "I just want to be here to support you."

"This no place for an American."

"Don't worry. I've been in combat you might remember."

He doesn't respond. We weave through the Cairo streets and make our way to El Sarayat in the neighborhood of Maadi, an affluent suburb of Cairo. It has large villas, low-rise buildings, much greenery and a quiet, less congested feel than what I had pictured Cairo to be. We pull into a gated compound. "Wow. This is your house?"

"My father's, yes," Basir says.

"You a young pharaoh or something?"

He doesn't answer, clearly annoyed with my comment, as well as my presence. I have now mixed with more wealthy people in the last two years than I have in my whole life. Probably more than I will ever again.

We stop in front of the palatial Mediterranean-style house. I climb out and follow them inside. I've seen one of Saddam Hussein's palaces in Baghdad and this could almost pass for one.

I follow them upstairs to a bedroom down the hall on the second floor. The large room has posters of soccer players, a couple sports trophies and clothes strewn around. "Drop your backpack there," Basir says pointing to a chair by the door. Amir closes the door behind me, takes out a couple of backpacks from a closet and sets them on the bed while Basir opens a box on the dresser. He pulls out two homemade Molotov cocktails. He and Amir pack the backpacks with the cocktails. "You have one for me?" I say.

"No," Basir barks. He packs bandages, ointments and rubbing alcohol. Amir grabs three water bottles off the desk and tosses one each to Basir and me.

Basir hands me a hooded sweatshirt and says, "You need to wear this and keep your head down. You will stick out as a foreigner. Do not say anything. I cannot get you out of prison easily if you get arrested."

"Right," I say pulling the sweatshirt on over my head. Amir and Basir shoulder their backpacks and I follow them. We scurry out through the front gate and onto the street where Amir hails a cab. "Put the hood up," Basir says to me.

I comply and climb into the backseat with them. Amir talks to the cabbie in Arabic and we speed away.

As we rush through Cairo, the city becomes more dense with high-rises and dirty streets, quite a difference from the lush green neighborhood Basir grew up in. The activity along the route seems to be normal, shops are open, people move around and routine vehicle traffic flows. As we progress, crowds of people walk along in the same direction we head.

The cab pulls over and we jump out. Amir hands the cabbie some Egyptian Pounds and we join the throng of people heading into Tahrir Square.

I follow the brothers who hurry as if they will miss the opening curtain of a show. An army tank parked in the street serves as a checkpoint. We wait with the crowd. Basir whispers to me, "Don't say anything and keep your head down."

"Yeah. You already told me that."

We edge closer to the American-made tank, scrawled with graffiti. As we pass one, the soldiers standing there are talking with activists who have their faces painted with the Egyptian colors. The soldiers are in their late teens and twenties and so too the activists. They could be brothers. We walk past the soldiers and through the barbed-wire checkpoint.

A short distance later, we pass the American University of Cairo, Tahrir Campus. I wonder if I could seek refuge or sanctuary in there if I need to. Probably not. Anyway, I feel high from the energy I absorb from the crowd.

We push our way through the crowd, deeper into the Square, and approach a group of young people singing near a lamppost. A man strums a guitar. It feels like Woodstock, if this is what Woodstock felt like. Amir and Basir hug people, then Basir grabs me by my arm and leads me into the center of the group where he speaks to them. Everyone cheers and moves to hug me. One guy, who gives me a hard stare, does not, however. I smile and play along. "I told them who you are and that you came here to support us," Basir says. "Although, Mohammad is not happy with the American support of the regime or the military."

"Tell him I understand and hope that we can still be friends and work together for a free Egypt." Wow, that sounded like a politician.

Basir rattles that off to Mohammad in Arabic who at least nods at me. The crowd swells as night descends and the orange glow of fires around the square illuminate the protestors' enthusiastic faces. The guitar player strums and sings in Arabic *Blowin' in the Wind*.

Basir talks with a friend and Amir has left our little group and gone somewhere else. "You are not an American spy for our military?"

I turn to face a young woman standing beside me. She speaks English well. "Ah, no, I am not," I say.

Her intense brown eyes focus on me and her complexion is dark olive. Her long, black shiny hair flutters in the mild breeze. "How would we trust you?" she says.

"I don't know, except that Basir knows me. We live together at the university."

She continues to stare. "What is it that you do, Miss, I don't know your name."

"My name is Fajr."

"Nice to meet you, Fajr. What does your name mean, may I ask?"

"Morning prayer."

"That is very nice." She doesn't respond to that. "What do you do?" I ask her.

"What do I do?"

"School? Work?"

"Yes," she says. "I am at university to learn international business."

"Oh."

"What do you do at university?"

"Well, I am studying writing, journalism."

"But you could be a spy."

I smile and shake my head. "No. I can assure you I am not."

"We will see," she says, never once breaking from her hard stare.

Commotion behind us interrupts our conversation. Amir approaches talking loudly to the group that has moved in to hear him. I wait as he speaks to them. "What is he saying?" I say to Fajr.

"He is saying that there are rumors the regime is sending in agitators to attack us."

A man standing on a tank nearby shouts through a megaphone. Fajr listens and I wait for a translation. While I do, I use my phone and take pictures of myself standing amongst the crowd. I paste it to my Facebook page with a caption.

After a few minutes, the man with the megaphone jumps down from the tank. His compatriots hustle him off to another section of the crowd where he gives the same lecture. "Who was that and what did he say?" I ask Fajr.

"That is Mohamed El Baradei, the opposition leader. He predicts the regime will fall soon and that we are the owners of this revolution."

I nod and say, "I am truly very excited and happy for you."

She nods in return and cracks a smile, almost like the Mona Lisa. She is quite beautiful, her shiny black hair blowing across her face. She brushes it aside a couple of times. I think of Jess. Am I fool to be here? What if she is waiting for me back in New York and I am killed on this fool's adventure?

Helicopters fly by and a couple of F-16 fighter jets streak across the sky. I ensure that my hood is up as the crowd shouts at the aircraft, their fists raised into the air. I heard an expert on the television explaining how many of the protesters are sore at America for supporting the government of Hosni Mubarak all these years and that the teargas used by the military to try and quell the revolution earlier is made in the USA, not to mention the tanks, plane and copters.

Fajr joins in the chanting. I listen and pick up some of the phrases. Then, several men on horses and camels storm into the square wielding clubs. Their clubs make direct contact with several protestors, striking them in their heads, on their shoulders, or on their backs.

I rush forward and am surrounded by a dozen attackers who clearly have the upper hand because they are elevated and more mobile. Basir and Amir grab some of their compatriots and pull them to safety. The men on camels are quick and indiscriminate. I jump into the melee and pull a middle-aged woman away from one of the men. He sees what I have done and doubles back, zeroing in on me. He raises his large heavy club and takes a swing at me. I duck and he misses, but he jerks his camel by the reins and it stops short with a loud grunt. He swings at me again. I raise my hands to block the oncoming blow. The club strikes the palms of my hands with a decisive blow. Although it stings, I latch onto the club and pull the man off his camel and onto the ground.

He hits the ground with a thud. I gain control of the club as he tries to get up, but can't because he must have broken or sprained his ankle. His camel stands there chewing its cud. Several male protesters circle around. Mohammad, who hadn't warmed up to me earlier, glances at the injured goon on the ground, then over at me. I toss him the club and he catches it. I turn and do not watch as he beats the man to death.

Many of the men on the camels and horses move on through the crowd hitting others in their path. I walk back amongst the wounded, dazed and angry. I look at my throbbing hands, then make my way back over to the lamppost. Several of the young people I met there are injured. There is blood on the ground and a couple of bodies lie motionless. People scream and cry as I move in closer to see if I can help.

I recognize her clothes. She wears jeans and a sapphire-colored button down shirt, like a typical American teenager. That's all I can recognize. Her face and head, covered in blood, she's been struck by one of the clubs. "Fajr!" I yell, pushing dazed and confused kids out of my path. I sit down and cradle her head in my lap, just as I had done with Jimmy. She is breathing, but unconscious.

Basir runs over and kneels down next to me. He hollers something to the others. A woman wraps Fajr's head in a scarf. Two men lift her up and rush her off. I sit there on my heels, Fajr's blood on my hands.

The turmoil passes, yet fear and rumor permeate the square. "Who were they?" I ask Basir wiping Fajr's blood on my jeans.

"Supporters of the regime," he says. "Security forces."

"Not military?"

He shakes his head while I scan the square. The people, who have all been protesting in a non-violent way, are in shock. The wounded wander around looking for family or friends. Someone shouts from the other side of the square and more scuffles between club-wielding men and protesters break out. A surge of revolutionaries head in that direction. Someone throws a Molotov cocktail and it explodes not far away. People scatter. I

192

hear the tat tat tat of small arms fire. *I am back in combat.* Just then I miss the guys from my unit and hope like hell they are getting along without me.

Basir and I help the wounded. A young man lies dead at my feet. I say, "I'm so sorry, Basir." He nods.

Within an hour, the square is calm, yet rambunc-tious, singing and chanting death to the regime and other things, I'm told. Rumors spread through the crowd from time to time about more attacks coming. I pitch in and help clean our little area of the square. "Death to the regime," everyone chants in Arabic. "Down, down, down, Mubarak." These chants are easy to pick up so I join right in.

I check my phone. Nothing. It's almost midnight. I sit on a crate of water bottles and listen to someone shouting nearby, the crackle of automatic gunfire in the distance. More clashes break out between pro-Mubarak supporters and protesters on the other side of the square. Someone throws Molotov cocktails from nearby buildings. The military pleads with us to disperse, but no one budges. It is all very exciting. I wish I had Alice with me. "We will go back to the house," Basir says to me. "We can rest and get some supplies. Amir will stay here."

"Okay." I follow him out of the square. Pushing our way back through the crowd, several regime goons battle with protesters. Basir steers clear and I stay close on his heels. We make it past the tanks and the university. We walk and we walk. Throngs of people are going both ways. Many head to their homes for the night. Others, the ones who are heading into the square seem like relief pitchers. They will keep up the fight throughout the night.

Basir flags a desperate cabbie a couple miles from the square. We climb in and zip off through the Cairo streets leaving the madness behind us.

~ * ~

I sit with her on our bench in Morningside Park on a warm sunny day. She has intense black eyes, a dark olive complexion and long, black shiny hair that flutters in the mild breeze. She smiles at me and I smile back at her.

A curious squirrel scurries by carrying an acorn in its mouth. He stops, looks at us, then scampers on his way.

She says something to me, but I cannot understand her words. I look up at the blue cloudless sky and hear someone shouting, then the crackle of gunfire. Standing up, I see nothing but the empty park spread out in front of me. What seems odd is that not only has the squirrel disappeared down his hole near the base of the tree, but all of the animals have disappeared. There are no birds, nothing. The park is void of any living creature, human or otherwise.

I turn to look at her, but she is gone. I scan the park, but she has vanished. The air grows bone chilling cold and the sky darkens. I am all alone.

A gun is fired not far from me. I swing around and see Stein jogging down the path holding a large hunting rifle. "Did I get it?" he says stopping in front of me, searching the area.

"Get what?"

"The beast." It's a younger Stein perhaps in his thirties.

"Beast?" I look around. "Not again," I whisper to myself. "Are you out of your mind?" I say to him. "Here? Now?"

"If not here, then where? If not now, then when?" He pulls from his pocket his little friend and takes a sip. "Out of my mind? I told you, all writers are out of their minds." He passes me his flask.

"What's the point of all of this?" I take a swig and hand it back to him.

"The point?" He looks the park over. "Sometimes, there's no point, kid."

"I don't get it."

"Yeah, well, no one gets it. If they say they get it, they're bullshitting you. Look, if you understood everything you'd be god." He notices something on the ground and tracks it.

I follow. "What is it?"

"Don't know." He mumbles something else inaudible.

I peer at the ground and see blood droplets leading along a path. He starts to jog. I hurry after him.

Around the corner, he stops and kneels next to something lying there. I approach and stand over him. "What can I do?" I say looking at the body.

He glances up and nods his head.

"Bleed?"

"I think you're getting the hang of it, kid."

I look back down at Fajr's dead body, her head all bloody.

~ * ~

I jump up on the day bed, my body covered in sweat and my hands shaking. I look the room over, the moon brightly shining on the floor. I make my way over to the window, look out and see the Egyptian moon hanging there in the night sky. It reminds me of the Baghdad moon. I take a swig of Arak that Basir gave me. Arak is a highly alcoholic Arabic drink made from Aniseed. It is clear and colorless.

I make my way to the bathroom and towel off. Basir told me earlier I could use the computer he had on the desk near the bed. I sit down and fire it up. I first check for emails. There is one from Kristen:

Zach, What are you doing? Are you crazy?

She has no idea.

Father is declining and I only hope you survive this stupid journey to see him one last time. Kristen

There are emails from Julio, Aaron, and Micah, but I don't open them. Instead, I feel possessed, hammering out an accounting of the events from yesterday beginning with my crack decision to take a chance to see if I could get into Egypt. I detail how mostly young and hopeful people, who actually comprise a large demographic in Egypt, are struggling for freedom, both economic and political. I end with the beating and death of Fajr. I describe how beautiful she was and how full of energy she had become

195

regarding this revolution, how she embodied the spirit of a new Egypt, and hopefully a new beginning for other oppressed countries in the Middle East. I email the story to Terri and finish the last drop of Arak, hoping Basir has some more nearby.

I hear a knock at the door and Basir enters. "What's the plan?"

"We have to hurry," he says. "I have loaded up some more supplies and a friend is meeting us with a car and some other things. Fajr is dead."

I shake my head. "I am so sorry."

"We must fight on in her name," he says.

Damn. I knew before he told me that she had died. I don't tell him of my dream. How can I? "Yes. We must fight on," I say putting my hand on his shoulder and following him to his room. We load boxes into a VW van parked in front of the house. A young man, Alim, is the owner of the van and a friend of Basir.

We tear off in the van. I sit in the backseat as Alim drives. Alim and Basir speak to one another in Arabic as I watch the streets of Cairo go by teeming with people heading into the city center. "Mubarak has agreed to step down," Basir says to me. "But not until after new presidential elections."

"So it's good news, but not good, good news?" I say.

"Yes. The leaders of the opposition are rejecting this and demanding that he immediately step down."

"You think he will?"

"If the military is truly on our side, but then the military would be in charge." Alim stops the van several blocks from Tahrir Square. He can't get any closer because the streets are clogged with people and cars. He pulls over onto the sidewalk and parks. Basir and Alim exchange a few words. Alim then runs off into the crowd.

Basir and I wait for half an hour for Alim who returns with Amir. Alim waits at the van while Basir, Amir and me each grab a box of supplies and head toward the square. At the checkpoint, the soldiers inspect our boxes. One digs around in Amir's box and one inspects Basir's. Yet another checks mine.

All of a sudden, shouting between Amir and the soldier inspecting his box breaks out, then a struggle.

Basir drops his box and tries to help Amir. Several soldiers jump into the melee and pandemonium breaks out. I drop the one I'm holding. A few water bottles fall out and a couple small tightly wrapped packages. From the bottom of the box, I see what appears to be two grenades. What's in the white packages I can only imagine.

Three soldiers subdue Amir with a knee to his back and another wraps flexi-cuffs on him. Two soldiers knock Basir unconscious. What can I do because I speak no Arabic? Two soldiers start yelling at me while two more grab and cuff me. They throw us into the back of an open-air military truck.

The truck pulls out onto the street and weaves through the city. Basir stirs, sits up and says something to Amir. I assess the situation. Although we are cuffed by our hands, our feet are free. There is only the driver and one passenger.

We slow and stop at an intersection. The truck then edges through it forcing the other cars in the intersection to make way. It seems in Cairo there is no traffic etiquette. "We have to get out of this," I say.

"How can we?" Basir says, his voice cracking.

"We need to jump out before it gets to wherever it's going."

Basir looks at me and says, "I do not know."

"It's our only chance. You want to end up is some prison getting the crap beat out of you?"

"You are right." He communicates this to Amir who then nods at me.

"At the next intersection," I say, "when we slow or stop, doesn't matter, we jump off the back of this truck and make a run for it. We can worry about getting the cuffs off later."

"Okay," Basir says. He relays this plan to Amir.

I survey the approaching intersection and say, "An intersection is coming up." The truck slows as it enters the intersection, but it is not going to stop. We have to make a break for it. "Now!" I yell. I jump off the back and fall onto the street, cushioning the fall by rolling, as if I'm an action star in a Hollywood movie. Amir follows, then Basir jumps. I get up and Amir does too, but Basir must have landed on his ankle and twisted it because he is in pain and cannot stand on it.

The truck stops on the other side of the intersection. "We have to go," I say glancing at the tuck and the two men getting out of it.

"I cannot walk on it," Basir says wincing in pain after trying to put pressure on his foot.

"Tell Amir to push his back up against yours, then his shoulder up against yours hard and it will help as you hop along. I'll hold these guys off."

Basir explains this to Amir. A small crowd has gathered watching the spectacle. I turn and charge the approaching soldiers. They don't know what to make of this lunatic screaming and running at them. They have side arms, but pull out their clubs. I put my head down and charge the driver plowing my shoulder into him like a football player. I knock him off his stride, but the other soldier clubs me on my back. I lose my balance and crash onto the street.

The driver regains his balance and clubs me in the arm. The two of them quickly subdue me and tie my ankles together with flexi-cuffs. They then beat me with their clubs. I shield the blows to my head as best as I can with my arms.

They drag me over to the truck and hoist me into the back of it. As they do, I see the two brothers absorbed by the crowd, disappearing.

The driver clubs me in the face after I drop into the truck bed. I spit up blood. My head hurts and my vision blurs. As I fade to black, I see Jess. I'm so sorry. I'm so sorry, Jess.

~ * ~

My line is taut. My pole bent over, the tip touches the water. I struggle to hold it steady. "Get over to the chair," he yells at me. "Put the pole in the rod holder."

I sit in the angler's chair and wrestle with my pole, managing to get it into the holder. Stein straps me into the angler's chair, and hooks me to the pole. I seem to recall this scene in the original JAWS movie. I only hope that a large fish is on the other end of my line and not JAWS. Whatever it is, it has to be a big fish, because it thrashes my pole this way and that. My pole curves completely over and into the water. The tip of the pole splashes around as I try to steady it.

"Pull back on the pole," Stein says, "and then jerk it forward to reel it in quickly with the slack." He looks similar to the last time I saw him. He wears that Greek fisherman's cap and a fishing vest with lures stuck in it. It reminds me of that colonel character on M*A*S*H.

I pull back on the pole, then with the slack, I spin the reel. My arm tires.

"Be careful not to slack off too much or he'll get away," he says. "Hold it steady."

"Hold it steady? You're kidding?"

"Just concentrate on the art of fishing, kid," he snaps.

Art of fishing? I fight the fish. Stein takes a swig from his flask. I throw him a look of hey, what about me, but he only focuses on the fishing line jumping around in the water.

Ten minutes of pulling back on the line and reeling, my arm feels like rubber. "Don't stop now," he says pulling out the large fishhook from under the bench seat. He leans over the transom. "I see him," he says. "Steady." He raises the hook and just as the fish breaks through the surface of the water, he sinks the hook into its side.

I try to scream from the searing pain, but nothing comes out. The pain bores into my side. I drop the pole and gasp for air. The intense pain of being stabbed shutters throughout my torso. I struggle to sit upright in the angler's chair. The only thing keeping me from sliding out of the chair are the straps holding me in it.

He pulls the catch up onto the boat. It isn't a fish at all, but a man's body. "Hell of a fish," he says looking it over.

Hell of a fish? I look down at the body, my contorted face staring back up at me.

~ * ~

I sit upright abruptly, the pain in my side is great. I have a blindfold over my face and am tied in a chair, a strap holding me so I don't slide onto the floor. The room I'm in smells dank.

"You are American?" he says.

Raising my head, I taste blood in my mouth. "Yes."

I hear him circle around and speak from behind me, "You are a spy, no?"

I have to be careful because even though he speaks English, his questions have their words mixed up. "No. I am a tourist."

"A terrorist?"

"No. A tourist. A student actually."

"A student? Students are mostly agitators."

"Not me. I'm just an observer."

"Interesting time to be observer in Egypt."

It occurs to me I could take another hit at any time, so I prepare myself mentally for one. "My roommate in New York at the university is from Cairo."

"Your roommate have a name?"

200

I hesitate. Basir has done nothing wrong. His family has done nothing wrong. Yet, if I give him the name, would they arrest and torture him? "Mohammad," I squeak out.

"Mohammad," he says, a tone of sarcasm in his voice. "Mohammad have a surname?"

I hesitate again, which leads me to believe he knows I'm lying. "Hussein."

"Hussein?" He says that with a raised voice. Now he is certain I'm lying. "Really?" he says.

"Yes."

"Where does," he hesitates, mimicking me, "Hussein live?"

"Ah, it's- ah, it's the El Sarayat, in the neighborhood of Maadi." That part is true.

Silence, as apparently my torturer contemplates what I have said. "We will go and look for this Mohammad Hussein." He walks around in front of me. "If you are lying, my little friend here will be back." I hear him slap something against his palm a couple of times. I then hear him open a creaky door in front of me.

"Sir? Could I trouble you for some water? And this is really not necessary, this blindfold and keeping me tied to a chair."

"A sense of humor," he says chuckling. "I like that. You Americans are so funny." I hear the door close.

I sit in total darkness. This sensory deprivation is not easy. I am disoriented and nauseous. *Damn, I have to pee.*

~ * ~

I wake to someone screaming in the next cell. I then hear a strange thud, as if someone is punting a football. I think of the times we played. How I long for a game with the guys right now.

More screaming and I hear someone talking in Arabic. Another kick of the football. And, more screaming. Then I realize what I am hearing is someone kicking a body. *Damn.* I guess I'll die in an Egyptian prison after all. Kristen will soon bury father and never know what happened to me. They'll toss my body in the Nile, or put me in a sarcophagus and bury it in a pyramid.

The door of the cell next to mine opens and someone departs from it. The door closes and locks. I hear someone moaning in the cell and listen for some time before passing out again.

~ * ~

The door to my cell creaks open waking me. I hear what appears to be my torturer talking to another man. Someone then leaves the room. "Zachary Powell?" my torturer says.

"Yes, sir."

"You don't look like your photo in your passport."

"No, but it's me. I told you, I'm just a tourist."

"That means nothing. Tourists can be spies."

"But not this tourist."

He chuckles.

"Sir?" He doesn't answer. "I really have to go, you know." I motion with my head to my crotch.

He ignores me and circles the chair. "You work for the CIA? No?"

Okay, who is he? Inspector Clouseau? By the way he poses these questions, he acts like him. "No, sir."

He clubs me in the torso. I jolt upright, grunt loudly, stifling a scream. Bearing the pain, I say, "Sir, I've been polite and cooperative with you and this is how you treat me? Doesn't our government support you? Look, I know the President and the Secretary of Defense, amongst others."

He laughs. "You are a funny boy." He clubs me again.

I grunt, stifling the pain again, then slump over as far as the restraints will allow me. "Okay," I whisper in pain. "You blew it. I'm done with you. I'm finished answering your questions. I demand to speak with my embassy."

"Again with the jokes," he says clubbing me again, this time in the head. It's goodnight, lights out.

~ * ~

I awake on the hard cement floor. They have cut me loose from the chair. My clothes are soaked in sweat and urine. I must have peed. My head hurts. I am hungry and thirsty.

I manage to sit up against a wall, despite my hands tied behind my back and the blindfold still wrapped around my head. I shake. My shoulders are sore and my head is wobbly. I sit for a considerable amount of time trying to regain my equilibrium. I feel sick to my stomach.

Some more time passes. I daydream of Jess. What did they do to her? Do they have her locked up in a place like this?

I hear someone moving around in the cell next to mine. It has been deathly quiet over there for some time. I can smell fresh air coming from somewhere. I use my nose and follow the breeze, crawling along the floor. There must be a crack in the wall near the floor or I am near the door to the cell. I lie down on my stomach and put my lips up to the crack to where the breeze comes from. "Hello," I whisper. "Anyone there?"

The person moving around in the cell stops. I wait. "Hello," I say again.

I then hear the person crawling over to me. "You are American?" the man says.

"I can be whatever you want me to be."

"You maintain a sense of humor in this time."

"I have to, I guess, otherwise I'll go insane."

"It's important to maintain a sense of humor in all that we do."

"Yeah, I try."

"Why are you here?" he inquires.

I tell him the story. "Why are you here?" I say.

"Well, it is perhaps because the regime believes me to be one of the perpetrators of this revolution."

"You speak English very well."

"Yes. I work for Google and started a Facebook page about Khaled Saeed."

"Yes. Yes, I know all of it. We are all Khaled Saeed. That was you?"

"Yes," he says.

Silence.

"What is it?" I say.

"If they killed him," he says, "then what will they do to me?"

What will they do to you? What will they do to me?! "They can't kill you. Everyone knows you are missing and they would only risk a wider uprising, although I can tell you that it is huge now. You would be impressed, as all of Egypt is in uprising."

"Really?"

"The regime is crumbling."

Silence again for a long moment. Then, he says, "This new technology, the internet, lets the oppressed of the world see what we are missing."

"Yeah, well, the government has shut everything down."

"But, they cannot shut us all down."

"No they can't," I say. "No, they can't."

"What is your name, my friend?" he says.

"Zachary Powell."

"I am Wael Ghonim. Pleased to meet you."

"Pleased to meet you, although I wish our introduction was under better circumstances."

"Yes. We must have a drink and a laugh after this is over."

"Yeah. A drink and a laugh." *He has no idea how much I need a drink right now.* "How long have you been in here?"

"I do not know for sure," he says. "Eleven, twelve days perhaps. I have been blindfolded and interrogated the whole time."

Damn. "How long I have been here? I've been in and out of consciousness."

"Three days now."

"Three days? It seems like a few hours, but then again, it seems like weeks."

"I know the feeling. You lose all sense of time under these conditions. That is part of torture."

Silence.

"Someone's coming," I whisper. I hear him shimmy away from the door so I do the same. The door to his cell opens. There is some verbal exchange in Arabic, then I hear everyone walking away. The door to Wael's cell remains open. I hear the sounds of their footsteps recede into the distance at the end of the hallway.

I sit alone and quiet. At this moment I fear for his safety, his life, probably more than my own.

I think of all of the guys, again, both still fighting in Afghanistan and those who have gotten out. I flash back to Johnny and his family and those he left behind who will forever bear the scars of his anguish. I see Jimmy's wide grin and his arm around my shoulder standing at ease in formation.

I really need a drink. Again, where is Stein when I need him? Probably in Uganda on a hunt. *Bastard.* I fidget to get into a more comfortable position, if that is possible. Well, it is not possible because the floor is hard, as are the walls, and my hands tied behind my back with the cuffs are starting to become numb.

I need water. I need food. I begin to have headaches and disorientation from lack of food and water. My body shivers. I need to maintain my sanity. I doze off.

~ * ~

The door opens, waking me. I hear something clang onto the floor. Then the door closes and I hear the person walking off down the hallway.

I sit there a moment wondering what happened. Then, I smell what appears to be bread. I crawl over to the source of the smell. I lean down and sniff. Smells like bread. With my hands still tied behind my back, I lower my head to discover a pan of water there too. I lap at it like a dog for the longest time until it feels like I have reached the bottom of the pan. I manage to manipulate the bread with my mouth and chew on it. It seems to be Egyptian flat bread. It's not an easy thing to do, eat without using your hands. I manage to eat the one piece of flat bread and slide over and sit with my back against the wall.

My stomach starts working on the bread, tearing it apart. I listen to it gurgle, squirt and make all sorts of strange sounds. After my stomach settles down, I doze off again.

~ * ~

I awake to the sound of another pan crashing onto the floor. Again, the person closes the door and walks off. I have no idea how long it has been since the last pan of bread and water. A day? I work on the bread and slurp the water. I can't help it, but I pee sitting there, again. It's degrading. Must be part of the torture, this degradation.

I sit against the wall again and events play out in my mind, like a documentary movie. I see that day in Baghdad when Jimmy died. Then the ambush and Micah running around like Superman. Even though I have just eaten that bread, and drank that water, I sense a sort of emptiness in my gut, not for food, but for those times.

I again picture Jess. I thought we would be together the rest of our lives. I thought we would go on adventures, maybe even write articles together. I thought we would be married one day. I have to put her out of my mind. I doze off.

~ * ~

"In a pickle, huh, kid?"

"Yeah. Whaddaya know?"

"Know? Nobody ever knows," Stein says. We walk down Duval Street in Key West and enter Joe's. I sit with him at the bar. The bar curves rakishly from one side of the room to the other. It's filled with hard-drinking patrons dressed in causal nineteen-thirty polo and safari shirts and slacks. Gamblers at card and pool tables play in the rear. A sign above me reads: Whiskey 15 cents. A large and hearty black man who must weigh at least three hundred pounds serves shots and beer from behind the bar. He slams a whiskey bottle and two shot glasses onto the bar in front of Stein. A one hundred and nineteen pound sailfish hangs on the wall above the bar. "I caught that," Stein says pouring whiskey into a shot glass. He slides one over to me.

"No kidding?" I dump the shot down my throat. "You have no idea how much I needed that." I nod for him to refill me. "Hell of a joint."

"Joes?" he refills my glass. "Yeah. Although, Key West has memories. Heading off to write about the war in Spain." He tips his shot glass to his lips and knocks it back. A beautiful blond woman saunters up to the bar and sits on the other side of him. "Well?" he says to her.

"Next week."

"Good. This is Gellhorn," he says to me. "Martha Gellhorn."

"Nice to meet you ma'am."

"Not from this time, are you?"

"No," I say.

"Give me a glass will Ya, Skinner?" she says to the bartender. He slides one over to her. Stein pours her a whiskey. "Well," she continues, "don't let this nut fill your head with poppycock." She tosses back the whiskey smoothly, without a pucker.

"You don't think his advice is sound?"

"Sound?" She laughs, her sassy shoulder-length hair dancing around her head. "All this coot is good for is a hard drink and a hoot."

"Well said, Gellhorn," he says clinking her glass. "Now tell him how you really feel."

"Spain, huh?" I say.

"Yeah," she says. "If this doesn't get me killed, I might have some stories to tell."

"I remember this, from the history books."

"Yeah, well," he says, "don't go and spoil the ending for me. Nothing worse than a critic giving away too much of the story, if not the ending outright. Bastards. They're all failed writers." He pours us each another round.

We clink glasses and each take a nip. "So what should I do?" I say.

"Do?" Stein says. "Nothing. Everything. Whatever pops into your head. Live for the moment. Seek out adventure."

"Oh, I have certainly done that."

"Look at it this way, you get out of it, you have a hell of a story."

"Yeah," I say. "If, is always the central conjunction, huh?"

He chuckles. "Hey, you're catching on, kid. Look, it's what defines the future."

"Guess so." I down my shot.

"That's not what's bothering you though, huh, kid?" he says, pouring me yet another.

"No. I can't get her out of my mind."

"Yeah. Women are devils." He glances at Gellhorn.

She frowns and says, "Men are pigs."

"I'll drink to that," he says taking another snort. "Look, pain is the best motivator. Love, hate, life, death. The writing comes from the pain associated with such concepts."

"You sound like a whiskey bar philosopher," she says.

"Like the kid says, sound advice." I finish this round. He pours another one for Gellhorn, himself and me. He raises his glass and says, "You've reached the threshold, kid."

"I have, huh?" I take a hearty swallow. The warm and balmy Gulf air sticks to my safari shirt. Safari shirt? I don't wear safari shirts. I look as ridiculous as that day in Uganda. I watch as Stein and Gellhorn flirt with one another. A fight breaks out over a card game in the next room. I see money floating in the air as the table upturns. The fight spills out into the street but Stein and Gellhorn don't move from the bar, so I sit there and ignore the ruckus too, enjoying my whiskey and their company until…

~ * ~

The door to the cell opens startling me. I'm soaked in sweat from the warm Mediterranean climate. My shirt sticks to me. I've been lying on the cement floor in my own sweat and urine.

Two men grab me. They pick me up under my armpits. I try to stand, but my legs wobble. They half-walk and half-drag me out of the cell and down the hallway.

I'm going to be shot. Oh hell. I had hoped to finish my degree and have a few more good times before I died, and find Jess.

They drag me into a room and finally untie my sore wrists. My arms fall to my side and dangle there. I think they might have already begun to atrophy.

The men let go of me. I slide down onto the floor, my legs can't hold me up. They leave the room. I sit there wondering what to do. I smell water. I manage to lift my hands up to my face. I remove the blindfold and try to open my eyes, but have to shut them again because the bright light blinds me. I crack my eyelids open and squint, slowly adjusting my eyes to the light. It takes a couple of minutes but I finally open my eyes fully to realize I am sitting in a shower stall. Or, is it? Is it a gas chamber?

I raise myself up onto my legs and stand there for a couple of minutes regaining my balance. When I'm confident, I reach out and turn on the shower nozzle. The water is cold, but it feels like heaven splashing down upon my dirty and smelly body. I still have my clothes on. I strip down to my undershorts, toss my T-shirt, pants, shoes, and socks aside, and just stand there letting the water cascade down upon me, as well as drink in a lot of it.

I stand under the shower for at least five minutes. The water never warms, but seeing how I am an uninvited guest at this hotel, I don't have room to complain. The water stops flowing. *Huh.*

I look down at my abdomen and waist. I'm bruised all over. It's such good fortune I didn't bleed to death internally, I figure. The door opens and two men enter. They raise a black hood up and put it on my head. They do not cuff me, but lead me down the hallway holding me by my biceps.

They put me in a room and close the door. I lift the hood off. The room is small, has no windows, and only one dangling, poorly lit light bulb above me. A table and two chairs, facing one another, sit in the center of the room. It looks like another interrogation room.

My legs are still not sure of themselves. Dressed only in my dirty undershorts, I sit down in the chair facing the door.

I sit there for some time. How long? I have no idea. It must have been an hour at least.

The door opens and a white man in a Safari shirt and dress slacks, holding a duffle bag, enters. "Zachary Powell?" he says.

"Yes."

He plops the duffle bag onto the table. "Name's Mowry. There're fresh clothes in the bag. Get dressed." I don't ask any questions, but quickly pull on clean underwear and dress pants. He could be FBI, CIA, who cares? "We're going to the embassy to give you a quick medical checkup and then to the airport where I'm to put you on a plane."

"Yes, sir."

"You're lucky," he says. "You have friends in high places."

I don't answer, but slip on a pair of socks and loafers. "We didn't even know you were here and missing," he says, "and you could have been disposed of and no one would have even known, if it wasn't for Wael Ghonim alerting us."

"Is he okay?"

"Okay? He's been treated like a hero since his release. Mubarak has stepped down."

I tear open a plastic package with a new white safari shirt. Safari *shirt? What the...?* I put the shirt on. "How long was I in here?"

"Nine days."

"Nine days?"

He opens the door and I follow him out. Two guards, probably the ones who dragged me out of the shower, stand outside the door. They escort us outside the prison and onto the street. Mowry and I climb into an awaiting black SUV with diplomatic plates and we speed off.

An embassy doctor examines me. It takes an hour to perform a cursory examination, but the doctor tells me there is no serious damage. He says I'm fortunate to not have injuries beyond a few bruises and bumps. Yeah, for some reason I'm fortunate this way, but not others, I guess.

In the SUV on the way to the airport, Mowry hands me my passport. "I read your case file," he says to me.

"I have a case file?"

"You do now. After what you've been through, your military record, and now this, you might want to consider coming to work for us."

"Who's us?"

He studies me. "CIA's always looking for resilience, son." He also hands me two hundred dollars, all in twenties. I don't say anything or ask any questions. He walks me through security and waits there at the gate until I board my flight to New York.

On the flight, I eat the first real meal in days. Again, I order and drink too many of those small shots of liquor. They help me sleep for most of the overnight flight.

Chapter Sixteen
Women are Devils, Men are Pigs

I hail a taxi and make it back to the apartment by mid-morning. Dale sits at his computer in the living room working on a paper, his jaw dropping when he sees me enter. I have no backpack, nothing. "Hey," I say heading to my room.

"Hey," he says staring after me. I zip into my room and grab my computer. Dale pops in and stands leaning against the door. "That's all you have to say? What the hell's with the bruises on your face?"

"Can I borrow your phone? Mine was confiscated, along with my credit card and everything."

He goes to his room and returns with his phone, tosses it to me.

"Did she come looking for me?"

He shakes his head. "Sorry." He heads back into the living room.

I call Kristen first. "Hey, it's me."

"Zach, what're you doing? What were you thinking?"

"Everything's fine, Kristen. I'll tell you all about it someday."

"Well, that may be real soon. Father's not expected to live six months."

"Sorry you have to go through this all alone."

"Zach, what's wrong with you? Egypt? Where have you been for the past ten days? No word at all."

"It's actually kinda funny."

She sighs. "Funny? I should have you locked up."

Locked up? She has no idea. "Look," I say. "I'll try and get up there as soon as I can."

I hang up and call Terri. "It's Zach. I'm back in New York."

"What happened? You okay?"

"I'm fine. I was arrested and sat it out in a jail cell for a few days. Wael Ghonim was in the cell next to me. I think he was instrumental in getting me released."

"Really?"

"I'll write something up and get it over to you."

"Great. Listen, everyone went nuts with your last article. We've got the entire national media hounding us."

"Yeah, well, tell them nothing. I owe my loyalty to you, the paper and the university." I click the phone off and hammer out my story.

~ * ~

Two hours later, I email it to Terri.

I take a hot shower, letting the water roll off me for almost fifteen minutes. Just standing there, my head hung low, I do nothing but breathe. *Wow.* I feel invigorated. I want to jump on a plane and let it take me to some other hot spot to see what trouble I can get into. First, however, I have to finish this degree. I wander out and find Dale in the kitchen. He says, "My folks bought me a townhouse."

"No kidding? Where?" I slug back some Jim.

"Upper East side. Just off of Park Avenue, near 66th."

"What's with you rich folks?"

"I believe in spreading the wealth, man. It's actually in my parent's name, but you can come live there. There are three bedrooms."

"Three bedrooms? Who gets the third?"

"I dunno. I thought I'd offer it to Basir if he comes back."

"He might not."

"Then we'll make it a love shack."

"A love shack?"

"Sure. Escrow closes in a month. We can move in and our last few months at university can be the best yet."

"I'm in." We high-five and I chug some more Jim.

~ * ~

I make up missing assignments and am back on track. My stories of Egypt are well received.

No word from Jess. If she really loves me then she'll find me, I keep reassuring myself. It's that simple. She knows how to find me. I try to keep busy, but my nightmares have returned and are getting worse. In one dream Sergeant Evans lay in the middle of the Baghdad street snoring. *Madness.*

During spring break, I drive to Greenwich and spy on the house. My hair is down to my shoulders now and my beard is full. They shouldn't recognize me. If they do, they'll have me arrested. Although, I'm on a public street, Mr. fancy lawyer. *Try to arrest me you asshole.*

In my rental sedan I cruise up and down the street. I park just past the stables out of view from the house. With high-powered binoculars I purchased, I watch her parents come and go a few times over the course of the long weekend. I observe them get out of their cars, go in the house, then leave hours later, or the next day. I never see Jess, she never shows and she does not ride Lilly. I sit in my car the whole time and don't sleep, much, and eat very little. I do, however, have Jim to keep my belly full.

Sitting near the fence that corrals the horses, I watch Lilly and Dutch frolicking. At one point Lilly ambles over, looks at me and neighs. "Lilly," I say to her through the open window with bloodshot eyes, "tell me where Jess is." She neighs again.

"The first woman I ever really loved called me kid," Stein says sitting next to me in the rental. "She said I was still a kid to her, and always will be."

"Okay. That's too creepy, because that's what you call me."

He chortles. "Well, get over yourself. I'm not in love with you."

"Thank Jesus." I pass him Jim. "So what happened to her? Your first love."

"She left me." He swigs Jim.

"Sorry."

"Broke my heart." He hands Jim back. "Don't think I ever really got over it."

"Why do we do this to ourselves?" I knock back more Jim too.

"We've been trying to figure that out since we stood upright."

"Is that all we are, Neanderthals?"

"Speak for yourself, kid."

"It just doesn't make sense. That asshole is lying to me. I know she loves me. I had the most beautiful girl in the world in love with me, and now she's gone. What did they do to turn her against me?"

"Don't know." He opens the door to go.

"Where're you going?"

"To the John."

"To the John? Out here?"

"Yeah. I'll use that tree over there." He gets out, closes the door and walks over to a tree.

I shake my head in disbelief, tip some Jim and watch him spraying the tree like a dog out for a walk in Central Park.

~ * ~

Two days later, while moping around the apartment, Andrew finally answers my Facebook inquiry:

It's over, Zach. You have to forget about her. Sorry. She's gone. There's nothing I can tell you.

Short and to the point. *Wow*. That's all I merit?

I stop working at Duffy's, thank him for all he has done for me, but don't tell him my dilemma regarding Jess.

Neither Dale nor I have much of anything to move. All I have is my clothes, my journals and a few other personal items. Dale rents a small moving truck and we move out one morning.

The townhouse is a four-story brownstone. The vestibule has a stone floor and opens onto a grand scale living room with two fireplaces. The home has a dumb waiter and wet bar. I nod at Dale upon seeing that and say, "I'll keep that fully stocked, boss."

The dining room has a fireplace as well, and the kitchen is newly modernized. The master bedroom is on the third floor, with another fireplace of course, and a sitting room. There's an outdoor garden area in the back. The other bedrooms are on the fourth floor with fully laid out bathrooms. The staircase continues up to the roof where we discover a small garden. I can see the East River from there. "We'll make this place our open-air man-cave," Dale says as we take in the view. "Just keep the booze flowing and forget about everything else. It's on me."

"You're not going to go far in the corporate world making deals like this."

"Oh, I'll be making money soon enough."

Basir sent me an email:

Zach, all is good. I will be back in the fall to complete my course of study. Basir

~ * ~

One afternoon on a Saturday I sit with Dale in a bar drinking Bourbon. Two ladies flirt with us. They are older, perhaps in their thirties and hungry. They're not unattractive, and will hop on me at the drop of a hat, but for some reason I'm not interested. "No," I say to Dale. "Let me sneak off to the restroom and then you can take them back on your own."

"Dude? You sure?"

"Go on." I meander into the restroom and take a leak, steadying myself on the urinal so I don't fall. Stein stands next to me emptying his load too. I nod at him and return to the bar to discover Dale is gone. So too, the ladies. I sit at the bar and hang with my friend from Kentucky. I don't know how many I've had, I don't count anymore and it doesn't matter. I hear Pete Townsend sing his part of *The Bargain*:

I sit lookin' 'round
I look at my face in the mirror
I know I'm worth nothing, without you
Damn. I kill off Jim, pay the tab and get the hell out of there.

I walk the streets for a time, stop at a bodega and scratch at my long beard. I buy a bottle of Jim and end up sitting on our bench in Morningside Park, waiting for her to show. She does not. At some point, I curl up and pass out.

~ * ~

I jolt up in bed and see Jimmy's blood all over my hands. I rush into the bathroom and scrub them until only my bones are left.

I jump up in bed, scan the room, grab Jim and chug. *Damn*. I make my way into the bathroom and take a leak.

I rent a car and drive to Yale. Stein rides with me to keep me company, but controls the hooch so I don't get too sloshed behind the wheel. Andrew finished school and is now working for his, well, that man, if you can call him that. I guess for Andrew his life is proceeding according to plans.

I walk the campus for three days. Nothing. I think I look in every building and walk the hall of every dorm I can sneak into. Nothing. I sit on benches watching students come and go. Nothing. It is over. I've got to get on with my life. I've got to pull myself together, as Stein keeps reminding me.

However, before returning to Manhattan, I once again spy on the house for a day. Nothing. She's moved away and must have gotten on with her life. Without me. Who am I fooling? I've got to get her out of my head. Hell, I've got to get the wars out of my head. What did Aaron say? Keep busy. *I've got to keep busy.*

Chapter Seventeen
Lost Weekend

One night a week later after dinner with Micah and Peter and a few whiskeys at a local dive, I stumble in at two in the morning. Dale's still up partying with a couple of friends, both drunk and ready to pass out, and three girls from the university. Everyone is plastered. I'm not in much better condition. "You dawwwwwg!" he says staggering over to greet me. He hands me a bottle of whiskey.

"Damn," I say after taking a snort. "Hell of a bunch you have here." I look the room over and pass the booze back to him.

"Come. Sit here," a gorgeous, longhaired brunette with a pale white face says while patting the sofa next to her. I shoot Dale a glance, but he has already moved on to the other girl on another sofa. I sit between the brunette and a cute Hispanic girl with large breasts who smiles at me. "You're cute," she says running her fingers up my chest and fingering my nipple through my shirt.

"Oh, I bet you say that to all the guys."

"Dale hoped you'd be home soon," the Latina says. "Those two are hammered." She motions with her head referencing Dale's two friends now passed out on the floor. "He says you were at your gay army buddy's house for dinner. I would love to go sometime."

The brunette on the other side of me pushes in tighter, her breasts squashed against me, and breathes into my ear. "Yeah. Me too," she says.

I look at her and say, "Why's that?"

"Doesn't it make you hot?" She licks her lips.

"Make me hot? No, can't say it does."

"It makes me sooooooo, hot," she says.

"Does this make you hot then?" the Latina says reaching across me and kissing the brunette, deep tonguing her. I'm frozen, not moving a muscle. They pull apart and the brunette begins to explore my groin. The Latina sticks her tongue in my ear and teases my nipple.

"You like that?" the brunette says.

"Well…I-I…"

The girls are all over me, but… "I'm sorry." I pull away, leaving them frowning. "I'm sorry." I bolt up to my room, slam the door behind me and fall onto my bed lying there on my back catching my breath.

I extract my flask from my jacket pocket, pop the top and guzzle some. I toss the flask onto the top of the nightstand and lie back on the bed again, the room spinning, and gaze at the gift box. I close my eyes and pass out.

~ * ~

The Paris streets teem with life this warm autumn night. People amble around arm and arm smiling in a beautiful mood. I stand on the sidewalk opposite 6 Place Saint-Germain-de-Pres, looking across the street at the restaurant with its veranda and awning stretched out over the sidewalk. Patrons delight in a late night full-course dinner, drinking French red wine. The sign over the awning of the restaurant reads, Les Deux Magots. A nineteen twenty-six B14 Citroen passes by. I am dressed in fine pants, a dress shirt with an open collar and a sports jacket, similar to how Stein dresses. Clean-shaven, my brown hair slicked back, I cross the street and enter Les Deux Magots.

Sitting at a table near a window, he is in his twenties and looks a few years older than the first time I saw him in that motel in New Orleans. I walk up and announce myself, "Lively joint."

"Looking dapper, I must say," Stein comments. "Sit." He signals to the waiter for another glass. He has his own glass and bottle of whiskey. "I want to show you what I'm writing."

He wants to show me what he's writing? "What is it?" I ask.

"I'm calling it, Men Without Women."

"Men Without Women?"

"Yeah. Here." He passes me a manuscript in a folder.

I read the first few lines out loud: "'Manuel Garcia climbed the stairs to Don Miguel Retana's office. He set down his suitcase and knocked on the door. There was no answer.'"

"Take it with you," he says. The waiter brings my glass. I close the folder with the manuscript pages. Stein pours me a full tumbler. "To...well...women. What the hell?" he says clinking my glass and together we gulp a sizable portion.

"I don't get it," I say.

"What?" he says.

"I thought she loved me."

"Forget it. You'll never figure it out."

"Why?"

"Look, kid. Hadley and I are finished."

"Pauline?" I straighten his manuscript and think of him leaving Pauline for Gellhorn, but don't say anything.

"What's that you say?" he says glancing over at me.

"Nothing." *How does he do that?*

"Do what?"

"Nothing." I look around the busy place and see the roaring twenties crowd happily engaged in the moment. I can only wonder what's in store for most of these poor saps in a little more than a decade. I hope they all have a good time now, because it will soon come to an end.

He sees a woman enter. "Here's the answers to your questions, kid. Simone," he calls out to the lady. She saunters over to our table and we stand. "This is Simone de Beauvoir. Simone, Zachary Powell."

She's a plain woman with her hair tied back in a bun atop her head. Slim, not much definition. "Pleased to meet you, Mademoiselle." I reach out to shake her hand. She shakes it, almost cutting off my circulation.

"Just Simone," she says sitting. "You're from another time?"

"Yes, ma'am."

"Yes, ma'am? My, you're a proper one."

The waiter brings yet another glass. Stein fills all three. "Zach here is trying to figure out women."

"Oh really?" she says laughing. "Just remember this." She leans in close to me and whispers, but not soft enough so Stein cannot hear, "Just when you think you have pleased a woman, you have not." She sits erect and sips her whiskey while staring into my eyes. Stein roars and takes a long swill.

~ * ~

The sun streams in warming my face. I am in my bedroom at Dale's. I open my eyes and shield them from the sun's rays, but my hands shake. Lifting my head, I discover I'm still dressed. I sit up, find my flask, swallow and after replacing the cap, toss the flask onto the bed beside me. I peel my clothes off and make my way into the shower.

I let cool water roll off my body for some time.

A few minutes pass until I get out and towel off, drying my beard and long hair. I meander into the bedroom and stop next to the bed where I notice a paperback book lying on the nightstand. I pick it up and examine it. The title reads: *Men Without Women. Huh.* I sit on the bed and finger through it. *Did I buy it in a drunken stupor?* I can't remember.

I head down to the living room, the drunks from last night lie there snoring. I make and pour some coffee, add some Jim, sit out back at a garden table and finish a paper for a class.

At noon, I open the internet browser and hit a bookmark for a national paper. There's a breaking story out of Afghanistan. Details are sketchy, but it has to do with a soldier shooting up a village. "Oh, no."

I run into the house, grab the television remote and turn the TV on. Some bozo interviews a know-it-all pundit, who doesn't know anything. "What's up?" Dale says coming down the stairs with the girls in tow.

I don't answer as the anchor cuts the pundit off in the middle of a sentence, saying, "At least thirteen villagers, including women and children were killed by a soldier who slipped away from his unit during the night," the bozo says. "Apparently his unit suffered some casualties a day before and he snapped, went berserk on this killing spree in retaliation. The Taliban released a statement saying they will avenge this despicable act."

"The Taliban released a statement?!" I shout. "Since when do they have a press release unit?"

Out of the corner of my eye I see the girls slip away as if I'm a lunatic. "Despicable act? What do you think the Taliban does to its own people day in and day out?" I toss the remote on the couch, run up stairs and grab my wallet. I sprint from the house leaving everyone stunned behind me.

I hustle over to Jerry's Gin Joint on Second Avenue and toss my credit card on the bar. Bruce, the bartender, picks it up and puts it in the till. He is in his sixties, and unlike Duffy, is an old hippie, or yippy, something like that. A Rangers game plays on the television and I guzzle the first glass he gives me. Before he can turn around to do anything else, I tap on the rim of my empty tumbler. He fills another and frowns. I stare at the hockey game as Bruce cleans glasses in the sink in front of me. "What's eaten you, Zach?"

"Huh? Nothing." I again tap my empty glass. I really don't know Bruce, and he doesn't know me, although I've stopped in plenty of times, enough for him to know my name, which is not a good thing when you want to be anonymous and drink yourself blotto, as Stein would say. He splashes some more booze in my glass. How much longer will he fill it before he pulls the plug?

"I get it," he says. "You don't want to talk. I'll have you know my ears are the best in the city." I remember Duffy telling me bartenders are keen life observers. As barroom psychiatrists, they should get paid more.

"Thanks." I look up at him. "Hey, you missed the war, didn't you?"

"Missed? Yeah. Burned my draft card and got my head bashed in by cops on the steps of City Hall."

"No kidding?"

"Why you ask?" He dries a glass and puts it in the rack.

"I served in Iraq and Afghanistan."

"Really? Well, you did what you had to do. For me, it was a different time. I judged no one then and I judge no one now."

I nod and press my glass to my lips, tipping it. "A soldier lost it and killed a bunch of Afghan civilians today."

"Jesus. No shit?"

"Yeah. Tragedy, huh?"

"Yeah. That it is." He dries another glass and puts it in the rack. "This thing has been going on forever. We send boys, well now women, off to kill people, and then expect what? I don't blame your buddy. I blame the beast."

"The beast?" I think of Stein.

"The beast in all of us. Some call it evil. I call it the beast. We all have it. Some act on it, some don't. War is that beast in a larger sense."

I chuckle. "Man, what've you been smoking?"

"It's what we all should be smoking."

"Yeah. I'll drink to that." I raise my glass. He has to serve some others so I sit and stare at my love in his tumbler listening to Freddy Mercury sing:

Each morning I get up, I die a little
Can barely stand on my feet

I tip my tumbler and finish him off, signal to Bruce to close out my tab.

He clears my tab, I hustle out and walk the streets of the Upper East Side and down First Avenue past the United Nations. I stand there staring at the flags blowing in the wind. I think back to Tahrir Square and that Egyptian guitar player.

I purchase a bottle of Jim at a bodega. The clerk puts it in a paper bag. I make my way into Central Park and sit on a bench under Denesmouth Arch. I open my precious and take a sip, obscuring the bottle in the bag from people scorning me as they pass by.

A bum, pushing a shopping cart full of his life's possessions, approaches. Dressed in torn and dirty clothes, with a long dirty beard and hair, he looks to be sixty years old. He wears a cardboard sign around his neck. It reads: *Be happy, you're in much better condition than I am.* I chuckle and he stops in front of me. "What's funny?" he says in a raspy voice.

"Your sign, pops?"

"Pops? You snooty?"

"Snooty? What?"

"Got any change?"

"No. I got something better." I raise the bottle from the bag enough so he can see what I have.

"I wouldn't fancy you a bottle bagger."

"You wouldn't fancy? What kind of talk is this?" He sounds like Stein.

He sits next to me on the bench. "Just give me a drop."

I pass it to him and he takes a good gulp. "Damn, dude. Slow down."

"You know how much hustling it takes to acquire a bottle like this?" He passes the bottle back to me.

"No. How much?"

"People are cheap these days."

"There's a recession, ya know."

226

"A recession?" He laughs, and then coughs. "There's always a recession."

It occurs to me as I take a nip that he could have tuberculosis or something. Well, hopefully, drinking will kill me first. "Name's Zach."

"Uh huh," he says.

"Uh huh? That's it?"

"What else is there?" he snorts. "Pass me the sauce."

I do. "You seem like you have your wits."

He finishes his knock back. "Seem? Why? I look like I have none?" He passes Jim back to me.

"What's your story?" I say.

"What's it to you?"

"I'm just making conversation. Relax."

He looks me up and down. "I was an insurance broker. Gave it all up for the simple life."

"No shit?"

He squints. "I cancelled a policy on a family. Mother had a preexisting condition and had reached her maximum limit. She died at home. Horrible, slow and painful death. Bankrupts the family. With coverage, she could have lived. Father then shoots and kills the kids, and turns the gun on himself. He left a letter detailing the whole affair. Named me as the cold-hearted bastard that pushed him over the edge. Cursed me to hell. It was all over the news. My name too. Leaked somehow."

I'm stunned. "Jesus, I'm sorry."

"For them I hope."

I nod. We sit and share the booze and watch people stroll through the park. Everyone seems happy. People with their dogs, people with their children, couples holding hands.

We drink the whole damn bottle. I can barely see him as he grabs his cart and shuffles off into the park. I never see him again.

~ * ~

At 5 Daunou Street, I walk into Harry's New York Bar in Paris. A short walk from The Louvre in the 2nd arrondissement between the Avenue de l'Opera and the Rue de la Paix, it's a quaint little establishment frequented by American expatriates with swinging saloon doors, dark mahogany tables and wood paneled walls. Leather red seating and framed pennants of American universities and crests of English universities hang on the walls. I pull up to the bar and sit next to Stein who is editing a book. "Feels like home," I say to him.

"It's the joint to be in." He slides a tumbler over to me and tops it off.

"Who's that?" I motion with my head to a tall man, must be seven feet. Surrounded by several patrons, he's jabbering on as his audience listens.

Stein looks in that direction. "Primo Carnera. Italian boxer. New heavyweight champion. Just beat the shit out of Leon Sebilo. Knocked him out in the second round."

"No kidding?"

"Yeah. Almost got into a fight with him."

"What're you working on?" I ask, sipping my drink.

"A book. *A Farewell to Arms*."

"Really. What's it about?" I say, knowing what it's about.

"The grim reality of war. The relationship between love and pain."

"Right up my alley." I watch the bartender clean some glasses and I think of Bruce at Jerry's Gin Joint.

"We're getting the hell out of here," he says closing the folder holding the manuscript.

"Pauline?"

"Going to Key West."

"You'll love it there," I say. *Should I stop him from leaving Hadley?*

"What's that?"

228

"Nothing."

"What about you, kid?"

"I don't know. I'm probably like one of your characters in *The Sun Also Rises*."

He sips. "I get it, kid. You've worn a death mask. She's been stalking you for some time. Just remember, I've seen her too." He scrutinizes me. "Look, death is like an old whore in a bar. I'll buy her a drink but I won't go upstairs with her." He tops me off.

"Jesus, you have a way of hitting the nail on the head."

"So buy her drink."

"Buy her a drink?"

"You buy her a drink. But don't go upstairs with her."

I bite my lower lip and shake my head. I hear a piano playing in the basement where the piano bar is located. Someone sings to a jazz tune. This joint, this whole city of lights, certainly now, the nineteen-twenties, is so alive, so happy, so clueless, so lost.

I bid Stein adieu, as he says, and walk the streets of the Left Bank. I watch people pass by. I study their interactions, I investigate their non-interactions. It starts to rain, but I don't care. I walk in Paris in the rain, my dapper suit, soaked through and through, weighing on me.

~ * ~

I awake lying in a strange bed. The room seems familiar, as if I have seen it before. My hands shake a little bit, I seem edgy and my skin is clammy.

I sit up and scan the bedroom and discover I have no clothes on as I pull the sheets off. Odd, I'm clean, like I had a shower. My hair, longer and thicker by the day, and my full beard, smell fresh. I smell body splash or soap. Where the hell am I and what the hell happened to me?

I climb out of bed and make my way to the door where a clean, white cotton robe is draped over a chair. I put it on, open the door and walk into the hallway that seems familiar. *I have been here.* Then I see the display case there on the wall, the medal hanging from its blue-starred ribbon. The picture of us taken in the Oval Office that day hangs beside it. How did I get here? I creep into the living room and hear someone in the kitchen. "Hey," I say, my voice raspy. I clear my throat.

Micah hurries from the kitchen. "Zach. You okay?"

"How'd I get here?" I feel a little lightheaded, so I sit down on the sofa.

He sits next to me. "Zach, you almost killed yourself."

"What're you talking about?"

"Alcohol poisoning."

"What? I only had maybe half a bottle, with some bum in the park."

"You don't remember more than that?"

"More than what?"

"You want some coffee or something?"

I nod.

"Hang on." He fetches a hot, delicious and large mug of coffee and I drink it black. "I don't know anything about the park," he says, "but you must have gone on a binge. They fished you out of the East River."

East River? Damn, That's the second time I've almost drowned. "What day is it?"

"Tuesday. Tuesday morning."

"Wow. Where did Saturday, Sunday and Monday go?" He shakes his head. "How did you find me?" I ask.

"Peter. You ended up near his restaurant. When he heard the sirens, he walked over to see the commotion. The paramedics pulled you from the river. They treated you on scene, and he convinced them to bring you here. Don't worry, he covered everything."

"Damn. I'm sorry for all of the trouble. I'll repay him."

"Forget it." He sighs. "You've got to get some help, Zach."

"What? I'm fine. Had a little fun, that's all." I savor the coffee as it goes down. *Saturday, Sunday, Monday?* I think I saw that movie once on a classic movie channel. Something about a lost weekend. "I really appreciate what you've done for me, Micah." I finish the coffee straight away, not caring how hot it is. I have to get it in me, quick.

He frowns.

"Look, you know me," I continue. "I'll be fine." I get up and take my coffee mug to the kitchen. He stays put on the sofa and watches me return to pass through the living room on my way to the bedroom. "By the way, I took a shower?"

"You had a little help."

"A little help?"

"Relax. I've seen it all before, you remember?"

"Seeing it is not my concern."

"We were gentle with you," he jokes.

"Great." I return to the bedroom and look around. *Gentle?* Two gay guys strip me down and put me in the shower and wash me up? Where're those two girls who wanted to see that? I walk back to the living room. Micah hasn't moved from the sofa. "My clothes?"

"I had to throw them away. They looked like they belonged to a street person."

"Damn. My wallet?"

"Rescued. In the bedroom." I follow him and he pulls my wallet out of the nightstand. He grabs a pair of shorts, a T-shirt and some sandals from a dresser and hands them to me.

"Thanks," I say. "Do you mind?"

"I just bathed you, fool."

"Don't remind me."

He turns his back to me and says, "It's her, isn't it?"

"What? Who?" I pull the shorts on.

"Who do you think?"

"No. No, I'm over her, Micah. She left me. If she really loved me, why hasn't she found me?" I pull the T-shirt on over my head. "No. It's what happened in Afghanistan. I got pissed off, drank a little too much, that's all. It's not like I'm drunk all the time."

"I don't buy it," he says.

I slip the sandals on. "Really, Micah," I say play punching his shoulder. "Thanks. I'll be fine." I head out the door to the apartment and stroll down the hallway to the elevator.

"You can't fool me, Zachary," he yells after me.

Chapter Eighteen
Daddy Dearest

On my way back to Dale's, I purchase a bottle of Jim and take a nip before entering. "Dude, where've you been all weekend?" he says.

"Lost." I run up to my room and grab my phone. There're several voice messages, texts, and emails. I call in. "You have nine new messages," the phone informs me. "First message received, Sunday. 'Zach, dad's dead. Call me.'"

"Damn."

"Next message. 'Zach. Call me back. Dad's dead.'"

"Dammit."

"Next message. 'Zach. Where are you?'" I hear her sobbing. "'Dad hanged himself. Please call me back.'"

I call her back. "I'm on my way."

"Where've you been?" she says, crying into the phone.

"Paris. I'll be there in a few hours." I hang up and run down to Dale. "I need a favor."

"What's up?"

"Can I borrow your car?"

"What for?"

"My father's dead and it's probably faster than getting to the airport, waiting for a plane and all of that."

"I'll drive," he says. "You think I'd let you drive it?" We hustle and pack a change of clothes. I sip some Jim and stuff him in my pack. I follow Dale out to the street and hop into his new Porsche Boxster convertible parked in a coveted parking spot at the curb. He engages the device that folds down the roof. We tear off across Central Park on the 65th Street Transverse and across Denesmouth Arch. *Yikes.* I wonder where my drinking buddy, insurance man is from my lost weekend.

We make it over to the Henry Hudson Parkway where we zip along the Hudson River then connect to Interstate 95. We head up Interstate 80 and speed along the 380 to the 81. On the 90, a trooper pulls Dale over. "Driver's license, registration," the trooper says.

"Sorry, officer," Dale says handing the documents to the man. "Zach's father just died and we're in a hurry to get to, where is it again?" he asks me.

"Lockport, officer."

"Lockport," Dale affirms.

"Sorry for your loss, son," the officer says to me, "but you know you were going a hundred five?" he says to Dale. "This isn't the Autobahn."

"Sorry, sir," Dale says. "You know, officer, Zach here is a veteran of both Iraq and Afghanistan?"

"Really?" To me he says, "But I'll have to give your friend here a ticket." He returns to his cruiser to write the ticket up. We wait until he brings it back and hands it to Dale.

"Sorry," I say to him.

"Forget it. Peanuts." He crumples the ticket, throws it on the floor at my feet and pulls out onto the Thruway.

I pull Jim from my pack, take a swig and offer Dale some, but he shakes his head. He then speeds the rest of the way to Lockport and we pull up to Kristen's apartment. I rush in, Dale following. "I'm so sorry," I say hugging her. She sniffles, shedding tears on my shoulder. "I didn't have my phone with me. Where's his body?"

"Still at the morgue. I contacted the funeral home for arrangements, but you have any idea what it costs?"

"No."

"Well, he had no insurance or anything to cover the costs."

"I'll take care of it," I say. "This is my college buddy, Dale. Kristen." Holly cries in the other room. "Go," I say to her. "I'll make the arrangements."

Dale and I drive to the funeral home. I am shocked to find out how much it costs to die. I place a deposit on my credit card, of all things, and set up a payment plan for the balance. It seems you can charge anything these days, including death. In any event, I buy the basic package that will cost me eight thousand dollars. They have deluxe packages for several thousands more. However, why would you care when you're dead?

~ * ~

The next morning Dale and I buy suits at a department store. I figure I can use a good suit, especially now that I'm finishing school and will be job-hunting soon.

Ten guests show up to the funeral including a couple of dad's cousins and my grandmother who has no clue where she is, what's going on, or who we are.

We bury Dad next to Mom. Staring at her grave the whole time, I flash back to that day in the tub.

I slip Kristen some money, then Dale and I head out. "I want to make one stop," I say to him as we pull out onto the street. "Turn left here."

We drive into the city center. "There," I say, pointing at Lock City Bar and Grill near the locks. Dale follows me inside the dingy lit dive where Kristen works. "Frank," I call out to a short, fat man, my father's old drinking buddy.

He scrutinizes me. "Zach? Is that you?"

"Hard to believe, huh?"

"Yeah, that long hair and beard. You look like a hippie from my generation. Sorry about your old man. We were real pals once. I wanted to get to the funeral, but you know."

"It's okay, Frank. Brad around?"

"Over there." He points to a table by the window. "Hey. I've heard you all over the news."

"Yeah, don't believe the shit you hear." I approach Brad, Dale in tow. "Brad."

He looks up, stoned out of his mind. "Zachareeeeee. Wasup, man?"

"You know my father died."

"Yeah, I heard. Hanged himself or something, huh?"

Adrenaline oozes from my pours and it takes all of my inner peace and love, if I have any left, to control my anger. "You know Kristen and your daughter need you."

"Yeah. Yeah, I'd like to help out, but there's a recession on, man."

"So I've heard."

He squints. "Hey, I seen you on the news."

"I didn't come here to talk about me. I came here to talk about my sister and my niece, your daughter!"

"Take it easy, man. You gotta chill out a little. All that war stuff stress you out. Turn you into a psycho." He struggles to stand. "Well, I gotta go." He falls back into the chair.

That's it. I've had enough. I grab him by his jacket, lift him off the chair and throw him up against the wall where I start pounding on his face. He whimpers and tries to block my blows, but I pulverize him knocking out a couple of teeth, and closing up one or both of his eyes before Dale and Frank pull me off. He falls to the floor crying like a baby, his face bloodied.

Dale and Frank restrain me, saving Brad from certain death, and drag me outside. "You better get outta here," Frank says.

"Right," I agree. Dale and I hop into the Porsche and peel out. In the car, I guzzle some Jim to calm down.

Dale glances at me, grimacing. "You okay?"

"No. Pull over there." We stop at a convenience store in Millersport. I run in and buy a bag of ice. I return to the car and stick my hands in it to stop them from swelling. All the way back to the city, I stare out my window.

~ * ~

I graduate in May, but don't wait around for the ceremony. They can mail me the damn diploma. I have to get the hell out of New York. Get far away. Start over, yet again. I received a few job offers, including one in Pittsburgh and one in Baltimore, however, I decide to write for a small rag in Miami, the *Miami Post Express*. I want to be in a warmer climate and hang out with the kids on spring break.

Before leaving New York I say goodbye to my pals in their hangouts. Last stop, Jerry's Gin Joint. I sit giving Glen a send-off, swirling him around in his tumbler. Bruce comes over and tries to small talk, but I brush him off. I don't want to talk to anyone.

I chug Glen and Bruce tops me off. I hope this gig in Miami is the right move, or should I have taken a job with one of those other papers with the demand they give me an assignment in Syria? That could be a lot of fun.

I make love to Glen in his glass, at least he and Jim won't ever leave me. I tap on the rim for Bruce to refill him. He does, but I say, "Can you just leave the bottle?"

He shakes his head and says, "Sorry. Your friend warned me." *Micah. Damn him.* I have to get the hell out of here and away to where no one knows me. I slam Glen back like drinking water, set the glass down, toss three twenties on the bar and say, "Nice knowing ya, Bruce. Take care." He shrugs, picks up the bills.

I return to the house and pack my clothes, for that's all I have, plus my journals, my laptop, my army citations and medals. Glimpsing the wrapped gift box holding Jess's ring, I start to toss it into the trashcan, but instead drop it into my army issue duffle bag where it bounces off my Beretta. I grab my bags and head downstairs.

Dale walks me out to my newly purchased, pre-owned, black Hummer H1 hardtop. I toss my duffle and gym bag into the backseat. Yeah, a Hummer. Go figure. I high-five Dale and pull out.

Zipping down Park Avenue, Midtown passes me by. I turn onto 42nd Street, weave my way over to and through the Lincoln Tunnel and make the transition to Interstate 95 south. I glance back over my shoulder at New York's skyline, sigh, and swig my buddy.

Chapter Nineteen
Miami's Heat

Before checking in with the paper, or even a motel, I drive over to Miami Beach. The place crawls with bikini-clad girls and boys. I pull over, park and stroll into the first bar I find, the Fancy Flamingo.

Slipping up to the bar, a hot chick in tight fitting short-shorts, her coconut-sized breasts cradled in a skimpy halter-top, says, "Whaddaya have, good-looking?"

"Bourbon. Rocks, please."

"You got it." Her and her breasts bounce along to the other side of the bar where she retrieves a glass, plops some cubes in and splashes on some Jim. Her and her breasts bounce back over to me. "Anything else?"

"No thanks." I take a sip.

"You a tourist?"

"No. Just moving here. Got a job."

"Great. You'll love it here." She waits on someone else.

"I'm sure I will," I whisper to myself watching her boobs dance around in that halter-top. "I'm sure I will." I chug two drinks, drop a twenty spot, and head on over to the paper.

There, in downtown Miami, I'm ushered into the editor's office. Tom Willows is probably in his middle sixties, and looks like shit. He's bald, thin, has a cigarette dangling from his lips, and wears a Hawaiian shirt and shorts with no shoes. I swear he looks like that writer character, Hunter S. Thompson. I read a couple of his books in high school. Willows sits behind his desk, his bare feet up on the windowsill when I enter, and doesn't get up to shake my hand, or offer me a seat. He does, however, lower his feet and put them on the floor under his desk. I have only talked to him on the phone. A brief conversation, he said he had read my stuff and wanted me to come and work for him. Not much of an interview and lasted all but two or three minutes. "You made it," he says.

"Yeah."

"Great. Got an assignment for you." He jumps out of his torn leather chair and leads me into the newsroom. "Your desk," he says pointing, his smoke hanging on his lower lip.

My desk, back-to-back with another, is bare, except for a phone, yet the other one has a laptop, a couple of family photos, and office paraphernalia. The newsroom is small, perhaps ten desks in all and looks as though it hasn't been painted since the nineteen fifties. Piles of files lie stacked against the walls. The atmosphere in the room is stuffy, as if the air conditioner isn't working. "You have to use your own computer," Willows says. "Gold. Over here," he says to a woman nearby.

Gold zigzags between desks and over to us. "This is Powell," Willows says. "Fill him in on Garcia." Willows starts to head back to his office, but turns and says to me, "You'll fit right in, Powell. Oh, and there's no smoking in the office. City ordinance."

As Willows heads back to his office, I look down at his bare feet, corns, long toenails and all. Gold plops down at her desk, the one back-to-back with mine. She is perhaps in her thirties, has a plump torso and buttocks, bleach-blond hair with black roots, and a round full face. She pulls a file out of her desk and slides it over onto mine. I sit opposite her. "You're the kid from that shooting in Georgia," she says. "And Egypt."

I nod and open the file.

"Some crazy shit, huh?" she says.

"Crazy." I finger through the file. "What's the scoop?"

"The scoop?" She snorts.

"Yeah. With Garcia?"

"More crazy shit." She leans across her desk and whispers, "This is a cut-throat and dangerous operation, Powell. We write the stories others don't dare. What the hell did you take this job for?"

"Cut-throats and danger."

She snorts again, as if she's snoring. "Willows is right," she says. "You'll fit right in." She leans back in her chair, puts her feet up on her desk and says, "Garcia is a hood. Piece of crap. His tentacles are all over the city. It's your job to find the shit on him and break the story."

"Got it." I close the file and look over at her. She's watching my every move, as if she will indeed cut my throat as soon as I let my guard down. "What's your story?" I ask her.

"That's for me to know and you to find out." She talks like Detective Joe Friday from that old Dragnet show. 'Just the facts, ma'am.' What's this game she plays? "Know a place to stay?" I ask.

"You haven't checked in anywhere?"

"Just got in."

"You can crash on my couch till you find a place."

"Thanks, but just a motel is fine."

"Motel hell. I don't take no for an answer, Powell."

Damn. What's her angle? "If you insist," I say.

"I insist." She gets up and grabs her handbag. "Let's go."

I snatch the Garcia file and follow her out. "I didn't catch your first name," I say to her walking into the parking lot.

"Gold," she says.

"Okay, Gold Gold."

"Yours is Powell."

"Got it." I grin and climb into my Hummer. I follow her Mini Cooper over to South Beach, near where I had that drink. It's a good thing I pay attention and not bump into her Cooper. If I do, I'll never find her or her car.

We pull up to a modern apartment complex. She opens the security gate and I follow her into the parking garage. She pulls into a parking spot, gets out and says, "Park that monster over there."

"Right." I pull into a guest spot, barely fitting the Hummer into it. I secure my army duffle, gym bag and laptop and follow her.

We enter a small one-bedroom pad. A woman sits there in the dining room. She jumps up and Gold says to the lady, "This is Powell. Works at the paper. He's gonna crash here a couple days until he finds a place." The woman plants a kiss on Gold's lips and gives her a squeeze. "You can throw your things there," Gold says pointing at the couch. "There's your bed."

"Thanks," I say to her. "You're too kind."

She snorts. "You're funny, Powell. I think we'll get along just fine." She disappears into the bathroom.

"I'm Gina," the woman says offering her hand.

I shake it. "Pleased to meet you. Thanks for letting me crash here."

Gina is plain, skinny, and athletic. "No problem. She's a howl, isn't she?"

"That she is." I sit on the couch. "What's her first name?"

"Stacey, but never call her that or she'll kick your ass."

"Right. Got it."

Stacy, er, Gold, comes out of the bathroom. "We're going out for dinner, Powell."

"Oh. Have a nice time."

"You're coming with us."

"Thanks, but I don't want to impose."

"Impose? I swear this kid's a jokester," she says to Gina. "Swanky joint. Get dressed and we'll head out at six."

"Yes, boss." I take a shower and wait on the couch for them. I finger through the Garcia file. Classic hood, drugs, gambling and prostitution.

"Ready, Powell?" Gold says coming from the bedroom. The two girls are dressed in fancy clothes. "Going to a funeral?"

"Now who's funny?" I say, wearing the suit I bought for the funeral, minus the tie. We walk out the front of the building and right into the scene that is South Beach. I follow them to a club nearby, the Rosy Cheek, not as in face cheek.

We enter the Rosy Cheek. It's full of all types of people, young and old, straight, gay. We sit at a booth as scantily clad girls and boys dance on a stage near the bar. "Whaddaya drink, Powell?" Gold asks.

"Whiskey. Rocks."

"Kenny," she says to a passing waiter, dressed like a girl.

Kenny stops. "Hey you two." He looks at me, then away. I'm apparently not his type. I guess my long hair and bushy beard turns him off.

"Give my friend here a whiskey. Rocks. The usual for me and Gina." Kenny prances off to the bar. "So what's your pleasure, Powell?" Gold says.

"My pleasure?"

"Yeah. You like girls, boys, or something in-between?"

"Ah, Girls."

"I thought so. Me too." We watch the dancers for a minute. It seems to me the two skinny boys in their short shorts shake their asses better than the two girls do. The girls are more into provocatively sliding up and down the poles they hang on to and swing around on. Kenny serves our drinks. Gold has a bottle of beer, Gina an umbrella drink. "Thanks, Kenny," Gold says.

I nod and smile at Kenny, he forces a smirk and struts on. "So, what do you write about?" I ask Gold.

"Mostly the LGBT community. Doing a piece on heavy meth use now."

"What's Willows' story?"

"Crazy kook."

She's calling him a crazy kook?

"He's actually a great boss," she continues. "Gives us free rein. You write him a good story, with an edge, sell some papers, he'll suck your dick."

"Now who's funny?" I say.

"No, I'm serious," she says after swigging her beer.

"Oh. Then I'll pass on that."

"No, I'm joking," she says laughing.

I crack a smile, indicate a toast with my glass, and take a snort. "He's a leftover from the whacked out sixties," she says. "Never left it." With her index finger up to the side of her head, she twirls it around her ear signifying mucho loco. " A good guy though."

After dinner, the girls show me around South Beach. I compete with Gold checking out the girls. We return to the apartment where the girls turn in for the night. I stay up with a bottle of Jim and read the file on Garcia.

"What's your beat?" Stein says sitting down on the couch next to me.

"Some hood." I pass Stein my bottle of Jim.

He slugs some back. "Still drinking this cheap hooch?"

"I told you, I'm not rich." I twist Jim from his hands.

"Well, your first post. Don't fuck it up."

"Thanks for the ringing endorsement." I slam some Jim back and pass him off.

He does too. "Don't mention it."

~ * ~

I rent a one-bedroom apartment two buildings from Gold's. The usual, or some would say unusual, creatures live there. Whatever. It serves my purpose, a place to crash. I'm only there to sleep.

I settle into my desk at the paper. For the next few weeks I hang around sleazy joints this Garcia character frequents with his wise guys. I hit some up, grease them for info.

At the Grand Illusion nightclub in the seedy downtown area frequented by shyster businessmen, shady lawyers and other hoods, I hit up the bartender, Paul, a man in his seventies. He's a bald, acne-scared man. We small talk every night. He fills me in, gives me some dirt. "I used to get a cut," he says to me while wiping down the bar. "You know, on the action. But…"

"What?" I say, sipping some Glen.

He leans in closer. "Now, nothing." He looks over his shoulder. "I know this bookkeeper."

"No kidding?"

"Has some shit on Garcia."

"Think he'll talk to me?" I slide my business card from the paper across the bar over to him, wrapped in a hundred dollar bill.

He scans the bar, picks it up and pockets it in his vest. "Just keep me out of it."

I look him over. "I understand." I slide him another hundred-dollar bill. He takes that one too and pours a beer for some overweight and disheveled lawyer near me.

I sit for some time and swirl my whiskey thinking, I'm having the time of my life. I have a good first paper job, a screwy boss I never see, and no one to tell me I've had too much to drink. What more could I ask for?

A sleazy former stripper sitting nearby keeps peeking over at me and winking. She has to be in her forties and has seen better times. She has a little paunch and her breasts are already sagging. *Damn.* I ignore her, and after a while she moves on to some horny businessman. I order up another round and nurse it.

I pay Paul, hustle out and stagger to my Hummer. "Hey, Powell?"

I turn and see two goons approaching. "Yeah?" I squint, but Glen gets in my way.

The large one dressed in Armani slacks and a pink Tommy Bahama shirt with a scar similar to mine on his cheek, probably not from combat, hustles over and punches me in the face. I step back grabbing my face, my ability to react impaired. "You stick your prick in holes not meant to, it falls off." He punches me again, this time in the stomach. I crumple over, drop to my knees and spit up blood. He kicks me a couple of times and I fall over into the fetal position. "You've been warned, asshole." He kicks me again.

I lie there for a while until he helps me up. "Jesus, kid." Stein steadies me. "You let your guard down."

I wipe the blood from my mouth with my hand, getting it all over my knuckles. I think of Jimmy. "This business may be more dangerous than combat."

He laughs. I open the Hummer and find a bottle of Jim on the floor in the backseat, pop his top, swig, swish and spit the bloody mess out. Stings a bit. He takes Jim from me, wipes the neck of the bottle off on his sleeve while scowling at me and takes a swallow. "Just don't let your guard down."

"Yeah?" I twist Jim from him and swig. "I'll try and remember that." I climb into the Hummer. "Coming with me?"

"No. I'm heading into the Grand Illusion."

"Watch out for that hussy at the end of the bar."

"Got it." He goes into the bar and I drive off.

Chapter Twenty
You're A Dead Man, Powell

A week later I wait in my Hummer for the bookkeeper to show up. Setting it up, Paul warned me this character is dirty and to be careful, telling me he'll sell his soul for the right price.

Gabriel Bañuelos pulls up and parks in the lot across from me. I sip some Jim, get out of my Hummer and adjust my pants and belt, specifically the small of my back. I walk over to his car and tap on the passenger window. He unlocks the door and I climb in. "Let's have it," I say.

"I need to see the cash," he says. He's in his fifties, overweight and has a greasy face and short hair.

I toss him a cash roll. "There's a thousand. This better be worth my money."

He catches the roll and glares at me. "You use my name in any of this, you're a dead man."

"Pops, I've died a thousand deaths. Don't fuck with me."

"You got a lot of balls for a young shit."

"My balls were hatched in Iraq and Afghanistan." He narrows his eyes, pulls a file folder from beneath the seat and hands it to me. I crawl out of the car. He peels off down the street.

In my Hummer, I toss the file onto the seat next to me. I pull my Beretta out of the small of my back and toss it onto the folder and drive off.

~ * ~

The file Banuelos gave me is the mother lode. I have enough to put Garcia and his syndicate on the hook.

While working on my story, Banuelos calls me a couple days later and says he has more dirt. Late that night I rendezvous with him at our meeting place in the smelly downtown back alley. He is sweating like a pig. Granted this is Miami, it is humid, but he is sweating more than the average person would. "What's wrong?" I ask after sliding into the passenger seat.

His head jerks back and forth. He keeps peering out the windows and in the rear-view mirror. "Nothing."

"You're making me nervous. Whaddaya got?"

"Got?"

"Yeah. You called me."

"I did?"

"Okay. What the hell?" Just then, I see a man fast approaching in the passenger side mirror. I reach around, pull my Beretta out from the small of my back, and quickly pull the slide back and forth.

The driver's window implodes from a shot by another man on that side of the car. Banuelos slumps over onto the steering wheel. I jerk around, squeeze the trigger, and shoot through the window striking the man on my side of the car before he can pull the trigger on his gun. I throw open the passenger door, jump out of the car and roll onto the ground.

The man who shot Banuelos runs around to my side of the car. I shoot him in the chest as soon as he is visible and exposed. He falls down. The assassins are the same goons who beat the crap out of me the other night. I pick up the spent shell casings I fired. I only ever touched the car door handles, both inside and out, so I wipe them down with my shirttail.

I sprint back to my Hummer and peel out. *Damn.* I have killed yet again. What did Stein say about men who have hunted men? I feel ill, unlike in combat. I fumble with my flask and gulp some Jim, my hands shaking.

~ * ~

I grab my laptop and all of the files from my apartment.

I drive and end up on Highway 1 and in no time I'm driving through Key Largo. I remember the movie from a late night back home. Bogart and Bacall. What a love story, both on screen and off. It seems to me like an innocent time. I know it wasn't, however. No time is any more innocent than another.

Near nine at night I pull into Key West, another flamboyant town. I stop and park at a hotel in Old Town. I push the buzzer on the gate and it clicks open a few seconds thereafter. The concierge waits for me at the front desk. "Just a room," I say. "For the weekend." I check in and he hands me a room key.

I hit the town. I have no idea where I'm going. I just walk, as if I've been here before and know my way around. Ending up on Whitehead Street, I stand and stare at Stein's limestone house from outside the gate near the brick wall. I look around for him to greet me, but I guess he must be busy.

I mosey off, head one block over to Duval Street and end up in front of Sloppy Joes, but it doesn't look like it did, or where I remember it. It's at the corner of Duval and Greene. I look across the street. *Huh.* I shrug and go in.

The place is alive. Young tourists eat, drink and flirt. The inside doesn't look like I remember it either. It doesn't feel the same. In fact, the bar itself looks different, longer even. I see him sitting there at the bar. "Hem?" I say pulling up.

He turns around, but it's not Stein. In fact, this man is not the right age for the time Stein lived here. It's one of those men who imitate him at conventions. He has a large potbelly, a full white beard and wears a fishing vest. *A Fake.*

"Yes?" he says. "Would you like a picture with me? Just five dollars."

"No. No, thanks. Great getup though." I sit next to him.

"First time?" he asks.

"Ah, not really."

"Not really? What does that mean? Either you've been here before or you haven't."

"In a dream," I say getting the bartender's attention with a nod. "Or time-traveling. Can't quite figure it out."

"What? You're an odd one."

"Whiskey. Rocks," I say to the young female bartender with short and sassy blonde hair. She reminds me of Gelhorn and I remember Skinner. "I'm an odd one?" I say to the fake Stein. "What're ya drinking?"

"Fruit juice," he says.

"Fruit juice?" *Now I know you're not Stein.*

"Yeah. Never was much of a drinker," he says.

The bartender returns with my whiskey. "Five dollars," she says.

I drop six on the bar. "Damn. I remember when you charged fifteen cents."

She squints at me, scoops up the bills and serves someone else. "You kids today," the imitator says. "Smoking all that dope." He shakes his head, sips his fruit juice.

"Yeah, something like that." I drink. "You fish?"

"No."

"You write?"

"Course not."

"What the hell kind of a Hemingway are you?"

He frowns, picks up his fruit juice and wanders off to harass some tourists for a picture. He snags a young couple who happily pose with him and fork over five dollars.

I order up another round, wishing the real Stein would show. The young clientele flirts with one another and I glance over at the fake Stein hustling more customers. I swirl the whiskey in my tumbler around and observe everyone having a good time.

I chug back my baby, swallowing him in one gulp, and sprint for the door.

Outside, the town has rolled up the sidewalks for the night. I make it back to the hotel. There's a small side yard where three people sit by the pool drinking. *Now I'm getting somewhere.* I slink on over. "Hey."

"Hey," a middle-aged woman and a man of equal age next to her say.

"Nice night," I say.

"Yeah," says another, older man sitting there. "Need a nightcap?"

"I sure do," I say sitting down to join them.

The older man says, "Bourbon or gin?"

"Bourbon. Thanks."

He pours me a glass. "I'm Chris Hurley. This is Judy and her husband Fred."

"Nice to meet you." I tilt my glass to them and swallow.

"You a tourist?" Fred says.

"Not really. I work for a newspaper in Miami. Just had to get out of town for the weekend."

"Have you been here before?" Judy asks.

"Ah," I hesitate. "No."

"Just came down to relax then?" Hurley says.

"More or less. Guess I was looking for an old friend."

"Did you find him, or her?" Fred asks.

"No. No I didn't."

"I work for Big Apple Publishing, in New York," Hurley says.

"No kidding? I just finished at Columbia."

"Small world," he says hoisting his drink to me. "You have a card?"

I dig in my wallet and pass him my business card. He hands me his. "Have you seen the Hemingway house yet?" Fred asks.

How should I answer this? "Walked past it. Maybe go in tomorrow."

"You should," Fred says. "Say you've been there."

"Yeah. Yeah, I should." We talk for a couple hours. Judy and Fred are from a small town in Ohio and came down to scuba dive.

~ * ~

Late the next morning, I drag my drunk ass out of bed and head over to Stein's house for the tour. I wait in line at the gate. I look behind me at a car going by expecting to see that 1934 Plymouth DeLuxe four-door sedan, but it's not.

The tour begins and the docent rambles on telling stories. I pay no attention, my mind is somewhere else, in another time perhaps. We approach the front door and admire the porch that encircles the upper level of the limestone walls. A white, six-toed cat scurries past us. "Snowball," I call out to it.

The cat stops, looks back at me, comes over and twirls around my ankles. I reach down and stroke her chin. She purrs her affection. "You know your history," the female docent says to me. She then explains to the others that this cat is a descendent of Snowball, a six-toed cat given to Stein by a ship's captain. "My, she really likes you," the docent says to me. She leads the others into the house.

"I have to go," I say to Snowball. "Say hi to Papa." I think she understands because she looks up at me and scurries off into the bushes. I snap out of it, enter the foyer and see the chandelier hanging in the living room. A large, gorgeous Circassian walnut chest-on-chest sits against a far wall. I stand there dumbfounded.

The tour moves on to other rooms, yet I stand there in that living room for the longest time waiting for Stein to show up and give me a drink, but he does not. *Bastard.*

The tour comes around again and I follow it out onto the grounds where it continues, but I walk off. *I need to get a drink.*

I lounge around the pool for the next few days writing my story. Stein finally shows up at one point to proofread and edit what I've written.

~ * ~

I call and instruct Willows to meet me at a dive on South Beach. I hand him my story.

"This have anything to do with Garcia's hoods getting whacked downtown?" he says.

I squint at him, sip from my flask. He fingers through the copy, scans a passage, looks up and says, "You might want to lay low for a while. Until this blows over."

I study him and think it over. "I gotta get outta here. Hit the road. Find some stories. I'll email them in."

He nods, flicks some ash from the cigarette he holds into a tray. "You're a hell of a writer, Powell. Not afraid to get in there and mix it up."

I leave Hunter S. Thompson, er, Willows sitting there at the bar.

Chapter Twenty-One
Travels with Jim

The next day I cruise through Naples. The place is overrun with retirees and snowbirds so I keep driving. I stop at a dump, Earl's Cove, along the waterfront in Fort Myers. This is more my kind of town. I buy a copy of the *Miami Post Express* from a box outside. My article about Garcia and his arrest by the feds for racketeering adorns the front page, along with a photo of Garcia in handcuffs. I'm a dead man for sure now.

Inside, Earl's Cove hosts local anglers and drunks. Fishnets, poles and pictures of anglers with their catches hang on the walls. I look around for Stein, but he's not here. I order a burger, fries and whiskey. My phone rings. It's Kristen. "Hey."

"Are you okay, Zach?"

"I'm fine. How's Holly?"

"She's fine. I read your story online about the gangster. Are you okay? I'm worried about you."

"I'm more worried about you and Holly."

She sighs, gives up. "I'm still very sorry about, well, I guess I shouldn't say her name."

I don't respond.

"Are you still in Miami?

"No. I'm on the road. Doing some stories."

"Zach, please be careful."

"I will. Talk to you soon." I end the call.

A man, perhaps a couple years older than me, sits with his head down on a table in the corner of the room. He's on something. He looks like shit, his clothes are dirty and he has short disheveled hair, as if he just crawled out of bed, and a spotty stubbly beard. He looks up and starts screaming bloody murder, "No. I gotta go. You see that? What?"

The bartender, a kid the same age as the lunatic, yells, "Reynolds, shut the hell up. You're disturbing the customers."

The young man, Reynolds, calms down. "What's his deal?" I ask the bartender as I munch on my last French fry.

"Nuts." He looks over at Reynolds and yells, "You off your meds again, Reynolds?" Reynolds looks around the room like a startled hare. The bartender looks back at me and says, "You want a refill?"

"Sure."

He pours me another. "He was in one of those wars."

I nod. In *one of those wars? Can't he name them?* I finish my burger, lift my whiskey and go over to Reynolds. "Hey," I say to him.

He glances up, squints, then around me as if he searches for something.

"May I sit?" He doesn't respond, only stares through me. He has no food, no drink, nothing. His frame is skinny, almost to the point of emaciation. I decide to take it slow and easy. "Name's Zach." He gawks at me as if I'm an alien. "You have a name?" He nods. I wait a few moments and then say, "Can you tell me your name?"

"Ju- Ju- Ju-Justin," he squeaks.

"Nice to meet you, Justin. Would you like a coke or something?" He nods like a bobble head. "Hey," I call out to the bartender. "Can I get a coke for Justin? Thanks."

I wait for the coke to arrive. The bartender places it on the table. "Does he ever eat?"

"I give him food sometimes. He never really asks."

"Do you ever ask him if he wants some?" He frowns. "You want a burger or something, Justin?" He nods. "My treat," I say to the bartender. "With a side of fries. Thanks." The bartender goes to cook it up. I wait, and take it slow. "You live around here?"

"Live around here," he says nodding.

Damn, sounds like one of those autistics. "Really? I'm from New York. Lived in the city for a while, but I'm from upstate, near Niagara Falls."

"I'd like to see the falls," he says.

Progress. "Yeah, perhaps you could." We sit for a while, Justin peeping out the window. After a few minutes, the bartender serves Justin. He digs in and eats as if he's a ravished lion that just made a kill on a game-less drought-stricken African plain.

"I have nightmares sometimes from the wars," I say to him.

He stops eating in the middle of chewing, his mouth wide open, and looks up at me. "Me too."

"Finish chewing," I say. He does, glancing down at his food and up at me several times. I kill off Jim and signal to the bartender for another. He comes over and pours me one. "You in Afghanistan?" I ask him.

"In Iraq."

"Me too." He seems more lucid now that he has some food in him. "Where?"

"Fallujah. Op-Op-Op-Operation Vigilant Resolve." He has ketchup all over his lips. I take a napkin and offer it to him. He takes it, wipes at his lips, but doesn't get the ketchup off.

"Really? You're a Marine?"

"Marine," he says chomping on his fries.

256

While he works on his meal, I search the net on my phone and learn that Operation Vigilant Resolve was an unsuccessful attempt to capture the city beginning in April of 2004. The operation, led by the 1st Marine Expeditionary Force, began after the killing and mutilation of American contractors, some whose bodies had been dragged through the streets and strung up. The city, surrounded and cut off, was destroyed by American forces. In an attempt to route insurgents, tens of thousands of civilians evacuated the city. US forces left the city in the hands of Iraqi forces, but returned later in the year for the Second Battle of Fallujah to do it all over again. "You have someone who looks after you?" I ask.

"Looks after me."

"They have a VA around here?

"VA."

"You go there?"

"I go there."

"Do you need anything? Can I give you a ride there?"

"Ride there."

I finish my whiskey and pay for everything. "Ready?" I say.

"Ready."

I'm not sure he understands what I said, or where we're going, but I walk him out to the parking lot. He freezes in his tracks and shakes when he sees my Hummer. "It's okay," I say. He starts whimpering. *Damn. Good move, Powell.* "We're in Fort Myers," I say. "It's a civilian vehicle."

His face tightens as I lead him by his arm over to the passenger door. He gets in and hugs the inside of his door, acting as though this monster swallowed him.

I find the VA Outpatient Clinic on Winkler in Fort Myers. The GPS on my phone shows me how to get there. I pull in and park. Now he's afraid to get out of the Hummer. "It's okay," I say, coaxing him from it. As we walk away, he stares back at it as if it's the devil and he can't get away from it fast enough.

I lead him into the clinic. He stands by the door and looks the room over, his head jerking this way and that. I approach the counter where an attendant sits at the desk. "Hi," I say to her.

"How may I help you?"

"My friend over there needs some help."

"Justin Reynolds," she says shaking her head. She stands and comes out from behind the counter. I walk with her over to him. "Oh, Justin," she says taking him by the hand. "Where have you been now?"

She leads him to a chair in the waiting area. "Can you sit here for me, honey?"

He nods at her. I follow her to the counter where she fingers through some files in a cabinet. Finding one, she turns and sits. "You're a friend of his?"

"Just met him. Over at Earl's."

"I told them to call us when they see him. He goes off his meds and just wanders the city for days at a time."

"Does he have any family who can look after him?"

"His mother, but she's not in much better shape than he is. Unemployed, welfare or something. The father divorced her and is a trucker on the road all the time. Stops in town once in a while."

"So he lives with his mother?"

"Yeah, but she's no use."

"Can't you help him get a job, set up on his own?"

"We've tried, but who's gonna hire a veteran with PTSD on all sorts of psychotropic drugs? When he's on them, at best, he's able to perform simple self-regulatory functions. A job? Forget it."

"There's got to be something we can do."

She examines me. "You from around here?"

"Just passing through."

"You just find him in a bar and take an interest in his condition?"

"I'm a veteran too."

"Well, the best we can do is keep him on his meds and off the street. I'll get him in to see the doctor and get him cleaned up."

"Okay. Thanks."

I stop and say to Justin on the way out, "You take care, now, Justin. Okay?"

"Okay," he says glancing up at me, and away, his eyes darting around the room like he's watching a fly buzzing.

I return to my Hummer and sit there for the longest time staring out the window. I grab my flask, gulp and cap it off. I scribble some notes in my journal. A few minutes later I crank over the engine, pull out, and drive north out of Fort Myers.

I pick up a bottle of Jim, pull into Tampa, and find a cheap motor lodge in a seedy part of town. I grab my gym bag and my laptop and go to my room. I tap out a story on Justin describing my introduction to him at Earl's and highlight his PTSD, how it affects his ability to gain employment, and the fact that as a young man, he might need care and therapy for the rest of his life. After an edit, I hit send. It goes out into the cyber world and makes its way to Willows. I hope he can run it.

I check my bank account. There's a generous deposit on behalf of the *Miami Post Express.* Willows came though, that crazy hippie. I wire transfer half of it to Kristen's bank account.

I check emails. Nothing. I close my laptop and find a dive down the street. It's a dank little corner pool hall. A half-dozen unsavory types patronize the joint. Two bikers play pool in the back. I steer clear of them all, pull up to the bar.

I sit and have a couple rounds and grow bored. This place sucks. I head back to my cheap room and say, "Jim, my friend, it's just you and me tonight." I lie on the bed, savoring Jim, and finally read *Men Without Women* from cover to cover.

~ * ~

I drop the manuscript on the table. "I finished it," I say sitting across from him. "Damn, Harry's is dead tonight."

"Monday's are never busy," Stein says. "What did you think?"

"I liked them all, especially *The Killers, Hills Like White Elephants*, damn, that's still relevant, and I liked *In Another Country.*"

"You're too kind, Kid. You'll never make it as a critic. God knows, people who are paid to have attitudes toward things, professional critics, make me sick. Camp-following eunuchs of literature."

I signal to the bartender. He must remember me because he brings me a whiskey. Stein is drinking something else, looks like absinthe. I'll stick to whiskey, figuring that absinthe shit will kill me.

I see some flapper enter through the front door. Bushy red-gold hair, full lips and a large smile, she hurries over to us and sits down sidling up to Stein. "You must be Zach?" Hadley says after giving him a peck on the cheek.

"Yes, ma'am. Nice to finally meet you." When does he leave her? *Should I, or should I not?*

"Pleasure's all mine." She offers her hand. I kiss the back of her hand.

"Watch it, kid," he says. "There are things in life worth fighting for." He sips his potion and says, giving me a hard look, "Just remember, you can't get away from yourself by moving from one place to another."

"Thanks for the advice, but I'm not trying to get away from myself."

"Nothing can hurt you, nothing can happen, nothing means anything until the next day when you do it again."

"Enough, Tatie," she says. "He has to figure it out for himself."

"Figure what out?" I ask her.

"Fear," he says finishing his drink, slamming the glass down.

"We've been through this before," I snap.

"Look, kid. I'm afraid as the next man, maybe more so. Fear is a child's vice and while I love to feel it, as one does with vice, it is not for grown men to be afraid in the presence of true and imminent danger."

"I'm not afraid of anything. You know what I've been through." He pours himself another. I slam my whiskey back and nod for more.

He looks me over for a long moment, sips his Absinthe and finally says, "There's nothing worse than not knowing what you fear most."

I shake my head at him. "You have it all wrong."

"Tatie," she says. "Let up."

I glance at her, then over at him. *They don't know what they're talking about.*

~ * ~

I awake and adjust my eyes, the sun bleeds in through the seedy motel's curtains. *Men Without Women* lies beside me on the bed. I glance at the clock. Twelve-thirty in the afternoon. *Damn.* I look down at the near-empty bottle of Jim lying next to me like a cheap whore. I sit up, pop his top and finish him off. I toss him aside, stagger into the bathroom and stand in the shower, my long hair hanging in my eyes and down to my shoulders. I scratch at my thick beard. I haven't shaved since before last Christmas, when I last saw…I still see her riding off in that Town Car on her way to Connecticut. I have got to get her out of my mind. This happens to a lot of people. They get on with their lives, find someone else.

I think of that dream, if that's what it was. *Madness.* I have to get that nut out of my life too. I mean, I enjoy a good nip with Stein, but his crazy talk makes my head spin.

I stand there in the shower for the longest time, using up all of the hot water because it starts to cool. I check out, pay a late fee and drive north on Highway 98.

I stop at a liquor store and buy some more whiskey on my way to Mobile, a quaint little town. After filling up my flask, I take a large swallow and head into a mom and pop diner. I sit in a booth eating a delicious country-fried steak and mashed potatoes. When no one is watching, I splash some Jim in my coffee cup. I check for messages on my phone. Nothing. Where the hell is everyone?

I signal the waitress for the check, but she's waiting on someone else. I make my way to the register and wait for her to come over and ring me up, but she's busy, so I slap twenty-five on the counter, leaving a generous tip and say, "Keep it." I sprint out the door.

In my Hummer, I slam back more Jim, just to calm my nerves. I pull out and drive north on Highway 43. Transitioning onto Interstate 20, I end up in Tuscaloosa. Late, almost eleven, I stop in the enormous parking lot of Pastor Reid's mega-church. Constructed of modern glass and steel, it looks like a sports venue, or better yet, an airport terminal. It seems like a million years ago since I attended Micah's sister's wedding with Aaron and Julio on a pass before we went to Afghanistan. We had such a great time. I feel a pit in the bottom of my stomach. I slam back some more Jim and drive into town and buy some more. Good ol' boys cruise the streets in their muscle cars with their southern belles searching for action. Everyone seems happy. I find a chain motel down the road, check in and lie there in bed staring at the ceiling, cradling my best friend until I pass out.

~ * ~

The next morning I swig Jim, stagger into the shower, put my funeral suit on and drive over to the church. Just before entering Pastor Reid's house of worship, I take another drop of Jim, just to loosen me up for the Lord. I'm greeted by an usher, some young boy and sit in the back pew.

The camera operators fire up the television cameras and the Pastor comes out from behind a curtain, like the Wizard of Oz. We all stand and sing a hymn.

I am so glad that our Father in Heaven
Tells of His love in the book he has given

Wonderful things in the Bible I see
This is the dearest, that Jesus loves me

I smile at an old woman who smiles back at me. We all sit and the Pastor stands at the lectern and says, "Welcome to this glorious day. For this is the day that God our father in heaven has made for you. And his beloved son, our lord and savior Jesus, is there to shine his love down upon you. Jesus, the compassionate, the all-loving son, walks among you today. He lives in your heart. He guides you through your day. He is with you and is there for you. He only asks that you love him as he loves you. He loved the disinherited. He loves all his children."

He pauses, sips water from a glass, almost as if he's gauging his audience. He places it down on the lectern and continues, "Jesus brought us a new covenant from his father and he taught compassion. He taught forgiveness and he taught love."

We sing another hymn, the Pastor blathers on some more, this time about getting into heaven, then the whole affair is over within the hour, fits nicely into a broadcast. I notice in the program there's another performance this evening. I wait in my pew as the congregation exits the church. The Pastor shakes hands outside the door, Micah's mother at his side. When they finish, they come back in and see me in the back pew. "Son," the Pastor says, "the sermon is over."

I stand. "Yes, I know, Pastor Reid. Mrs. Reid." I shake her hand. "Nice to see you again."

"Is that you, Zachary?" he says scrutinizing my long hair and scruffy beard.

"It is, sir."

"Well, my boy, what brings you down here?"

"Passing through. Thought I'd pay my respects."

"Well, that is certainly nice of you. I must say, you have been quite the news item this past year."

"I really don't pay much attention. Well, I should be going I suppose. Good sermon, by the way. It was very relevant."

"Thank you. How so?"

"The parts about Jesus loving all his children, the disinherited. You should love him like he loves you. All of that." They walk me to the door.

"I see," the Pastor says, Mrs. Reid walking behind us.

I stop at the door, turn to her and say, "Micah loves you very much and forgives you, Mrs. Reid."

"I beg your pardon?" the Pastor says.

"Oh, I'm sorry, Pastor. I wasn't talking to you."

Mrs. Reid blurts out, "How is he?"

"Martha," the Pastor says, squinting.

"He is fine. We keep in touch."

"I think you should be going now, Zachary," the Pastor says.

"As much as I can't believe it, Pastor, in his heart, he's forgiven you too."

"I have not sinned," he says, his voice raised at me.

"You haven't? I thought we are all sinners, Pastor?"

"Yes, well, but I have not sinned in this regard."

"Oh, but you have, Pastor, sir." I open the church door. "Oh, but you have." I leave Mrs. Reid standing there engulfed in tears, the Pastor's face red. I walk to my Hummer, get in, and don't look back.

I drive north, take a turn and arrive in Memphis. I check into a sleazy downtown motel where I spot prostitutes soliciting out on the street in front of the motel. I'm tempted, but…

It burns inside me. I have to get it out, bleed it out, as Stein says, the crazy hoot. I flop down onto the bed and light up my laptop. I hammer out a story on Micah, his heroics, his Medal of Honor, and his coming out to his religious father. I re-read it, edit it one more time, then pause. I have no right to do this. Will this end our friendship? He's out, so it's not like I'm outing him.

I re-read the article again. It's such a damn good one. It will, I believe, enlighten, question, and perhaps inspire others. I throw caution to the wind, address it to Willows, copy it to Gold and hit send.

I find a rib joint and eat a great Memphis-style dish, flashing back to Uncle Clem's Barbeque in Fayetteville where the guys and I would feast. I miss those guys and those times. I remember the time she and I went to Peter's restaurant, her sitting beside me sipping wine and flirting. I splash some Jim in my coffee.

I drag my ass back to the motel and flip channels. *Band of Brothers* is playing. I can't watch it. We used to watch it at Bragg. I switch to a classic movie channel and *The Lost Weekend* with Ray Milland is on. *Damn.* I turn the television off and lie there drinking and caressing Jim until I pass out.

Chapter Twenty-Two
Move from Place to Place

I lie there gripping Alice. Micah dodges bullets at his feet and runs up the dirty Baghdad street. Someone yells from atop a building in Arabic, "Allah," then says in English, "She went that way." He points up the street.

"What's he saying?" I say.

"She went that way," Danny Cox says, pointing in the same direction with his left hand, the only one he has. He lies beside me with no legs and missing an arm.

"Who Danny?"

"I don't know, but she said she was sorry." He looks himself over. "I'd go with you, but, well, look at me."

"Okay. I'll go." I stand.

"You have to leave him." He nods at him lying there at my feet.

I look down at Jim in his paper bag. "But it hurts so much, Danny. You don't know how I need him so." I reach down and pick him up.

"I know. I know what you mean." He nods. "Go."

Jim crawls down my throat and swims around in my gut. He feels warm. I put him in my pack and, holding Alice waist-high, scurry down the street. Micah hugs the corner of a building. "I'll cover you, you know that, Zach."

I glance at him and pass by. Jimmy stands at the corner of another building. "I've got your back, Zach," he says, smiling, that big grin from ear to ear. "You've been a good friend to me."

I say nothing and see Julio at yet another corner covering me, and Aaron on the opposite corner covering me too. "We won't let you down, gringo, baby," Julio says. "She's just down that alley."

"Bro," Aaron says. "I'm not giving up on you. You saved my life."

I don't know what he means. Entering the narrow, cold and dark alley, I shiver and see her standing there staring back at me. She wears a long white dress, blowing in the gentle breeze. I know this dress. Where have I seen this dress? "Why did you leave me?" I stop in front of her at the end of alley, blood dripping from her wrist. "Why did you leave me, Mother?"

"It was so hard, Zachary," she says, tears streaming down her face. She moves close to me. I take my brain bucket off letting it drop onto the ground. I sling Alice over my shoulder and fall to my knees. She holds my head against her waist, caressing my head. "Don't make the same mistake I made."

"*It is* so hard, Mother." Tears drip from my eyes onto the dirt.

"I know, Zachary, my beautiful boy. You need to fight and you need to rise."

"I can't Mother. I just can't do it."

She turns and walks through the brick wall, as an apparition would. "Please don't leave, Mother."

Kneeling there, I look around and see I'm all alone. A cold wind blows and I shiver again, my hands shaking. My skin is clammy and my heart races as I crawl over to the wall and put my hands on it, trying to push it over, but it won't budge. Sitting up against the wall cradling Alice in my lap and gripping Jim in the other, the sun sets on me.

~ * ~

I awake in the motel in a cold sweat, Jim lying beside me. I suckle on his neck, savoring him. I stagger to the shower, sigh. I gotta get outta here. Move from place to place. Keep moving. *Stein.* You crazy SOB.

At a diner across the street, I check emails. There's one from Gold:

Powell, you nut job. That's a hell of an article on your army buddy. I'd like to do an intro, or perhaps a tag on your piece. It'll be a hit in the LGBT community. What say you? Gold I write her back:

Gold, Thanks. Sure, go for it. And who's calling who a nut job? Powell

I drive north toward Chicago.

I make my way over to Aaron's house. It's a good thing it's daytime because of the stares I receive from a couple of brothers are not welcome ones. I knock on the front door. "Yeah, coming, hold on," a woman's voice calls out.

LaShanda opens the door. "Hi, LaShanda, it's me, Zach."

"Zach? Aaron's friend from the army? I thought I was staring into the face of Jesus the way you look."

"Aaron in?"

"No. Come on in."

I follow her in and she closes the door behind me. "Is he working?"

"Not exactly."

"Why?"

"Well, he's suspended. He's in some anger management program with the police."

"Oh. What happened?"

She motions for me to sit on the sofa. "He's not right, you know." She rolls her eyes up to the corners of her sockets. "He was on the job and he almost beat some drug dealer to death. The dealer was selling drugs to kids and Aaron and his partner were making the arrest. It took his partner and

268

two guys on backup to pull him off the guy. He beat the guy unconscious. Almost died in the hospital."

The front door opens and Aaron's mother enters dressed in her nursing uniform. She sees me, but it takes her a couple of seconds to recognize me too. "Zach?"

"Yes, ma'am," I say standing.

"What're you doing here?"

"I'm driving through. Thought I'd stop and visit. I'm not staying long."

She drops her keys in a dish by the door and sets her handbag on a nearby table. "You can stay here."

"Thanks, but I don't want to impose."

"I need you to stay," she blurts out coming closer, her eyes watering.

"What is it Ma'am?" I ask her. She starts crying, moves in to hug me. Taken aback, I lift my arms around her shoulders and say, "What? What's going on?"

She sobs. "I'm losing him, Zach." We pull apart.

"Losing, how?"

She sniffles and sits on the couch. I sit beside her. "LaShanda, you don't need to hear this," she says.

"Mama, don't." She starts sniffling too. "I need to know everything so I can help too."

Damn, the water works are flowing. I hope I can hold it together.

"He doesn't sleep much. He is irritable and he won't get any help." She looks over at her daughter. "I came into his room one night and he had his service weapon up in front of his face. It was loaded, Zach. He told me he was just cleaning it."

I flash back to New Orleans.

"Why didn't you tell me, Mama?" LaShanda sobs too.

"I didn't want to worry you."

"Oh mama," she says rushing to embrace her mother.

I can't believe this whole spectacle I have stumbled into. Just as well. "You're right, Mrs. Glover," I say. "I need to stay." I mull this over while they sob together on the couch. "I have a plan."

They look over at me, listening. "It involves some deception, but it just might work."

"Anything," Aaron's mother says, "because I have tried for months now."

"Okay," I say thinking it through. "Tonight, we get him to play along. We say nothing about this and we carry on like nothing has or is going to happen." I pause, putting the pieces together in my head as I speak. "Not only are we gonna save his life, but his job." I work my phone and place a couple of calls speaking to whom I need to set things up.

~ * ~

In the kitchen with LaShanda, we are cooking juicy, thick Porterhouse steaks I bought when Aaron strolls in. "Hey, hey, hey," I say to him as he enters the kitchen.

"What the hell're you doing here?"

"What kind of a greeting is that?" I punch him on his arm.

"Damn, fool, what's with the look?"

"What? I look as handsome as ever."

"You look like one of those Taliban we used to hunt down."

"Just passing through. Writing some stories."

"What, did they run you out of Miami?"

"More or less."

He shakes his head.

We eat and tell stories. He doesn't mention anything regarding what he's going through. I wait until we're alone in the family room when he's pouring me a glass of Glen Burns. "How's work?"

"Ah, some shit happened."

"Yeah?" I sip.

270

"It's bullshit. I beat some perp and they suspended me."

"Really?"

"It'll blow over. I'll be back on the job as soon as they clear me for duty."

"Good. Good." Silence for a minute. "I have these dreams, Aaron. Nightmares, actually."

"Yeah?"

"About the wars. Some other strange shit too, but, the war stuff scares the hell outta me."

"Huh." He sips.

"You?"

He shrugs. "Sometimes. Ya know."

He tops off my drink. "Thanks."

"You might want to get some help. Maybe some counselin' or something."

I nod, wait another minute, and say, "Remember that time back in New Orleans when you guys walked in and I said I was going to clean my Beretta?"

"Yeah. Yeah, I remember that."

"Only, I wasn't cleaning my gun." He just looks at me dumfounded. "If you guys hadn't come in, well, I don't know what could've happened."

He nods. We sit in silence for some time. He doesn't say anymore. After a long pause, "Well, it's late," I say. "Hey, I have to run an errand tomorrow and I figure since you know your way around better than I do you could drive me?"

"Course." He heads up to his room while I lie awake on the sofa in the family room remembering our tours together. I think of the good times back on base and telling Jimmy I had his back. I can hear Sergeant Evans snoring, again. I see, well, her. *Dammit.* Why did she ever have to come into my life? I raid Aaron's liquor cabinet and polish off his bottle of Glen Burns. At one point Stein shows up, but never says a word. Unusual for him. He just sits next to me sharing Glen, until he pats me on my war shoulder, strolls upstairs, and meanders off down the street and into the hood. I hope those gang-bangers don't mess with him.

~ * ~

In the morning Aaron drives. "I need to pick something up there," I say. "It should only take a few minutes."

He drives me to the Edward Hines, Jr. VA Hospital on 5th Avenue and Roosevelt Road. It's a sprawling campus and medical facility covering one hundred forty seven acres. "I need you to help me carry something out," I lie to him.

He parks and we stroll in. I search the directory and lead him to a floor in one of the main buildings. At a desk, a nurse points us to where we need to go. Aaron follows me into a room where ten young men sit in a circle. A man gets up from his chair and greets us, "I'm happy you could make it, Zach." I shake his hand as Aaron hovers near the door.

Of the ten people, all multiple ethnicities, two have no legs below their knees and three are missing one or the other arm. Of these five people, all have either prosthetic arms or legs. The others appear to be physically okay. "What's goin' on?" Aaron asks.

"We just came to talk," I say turning to look at him.

"We? I'll wait for you in the car." He starts to open the door to go, but I rush him slamming the door closed, blocking his way. He steps back. "What the hell is this?" he says raising his voice.

"I just want you to stay and listen," I say.

"I don't need this shit. *You* do." He tries to push past me to open the door but I block him and hold the door shut. "Zach? Whaddaya doing? Get outta my way." He tries to reach around behind me to open the door.

I struggle to maintain my position but he's bigger and stronger than me. "I just want you to stay and hear them out. I want to help you through this, Aaron."

"Damn, fool," he says, his voice cracking. "I don't need your help. There's nothin' wrong with me."

272

"No, but I need your help."

"Then you stay here and listen to this shit." He begins to wrestle with me as if we're in a professional wrestling ring. The others in the room are on their feet, or their artificial feet, moving closer. "Dammit it, Zach. I don't wanna to hurt you." He puts me in a headlock, but I break his grip and edge away from him with my back to the door. "Let me out."

"Over my dead body."

"I warned you." He throws a punch. It lands on my eye and knocks me against the door. I rush and tackle him to the floor and he punches me again, this time hitting me in the side. I don't want to hit him, but try to immobilize him. We roll around on the floor. He kicks at me and pushes me off, the others jumping into the fray. Two guys with artificial legs and one with an artificial arm tackle him.

I get up and swing around, rush over and jump on top of everyone. We pin him to the floor. He yells, "I'm a fuckin' officer of the law and you're all under arrest."

"Yeah?" I say lying across his chest while the others hold his legs and arms to the floor. "How're you going to do that?"

"What're you gonna do, hold me here against my will?"

"If that's what it takes." I reposition myself, sitting on his waist, the others holding him firm. "Aaron, your mother and sister love you very much and are very worried about you."

"There's nothin' to worry about. I don't have a problem."

"You've thought of suicide, haven't you?"

"What?" He squirms.

"Your mother told me."

"You don't know what you're talkin' about."

"I don't know what I'm talking about? You're kidding, right?"

"You're the one who needs this." He wiggles, trying to break free. "You're the one messed up."

"I'm not letting you go. You're my friend, Aaron."

"I don't need friends like you."

"I don't want to lose you like Jimmy, Johnny and the others. You're like my brother, brother, and this is what a brother would do."

"Don't give me that brother shit white boy." He struggles to get up, but I hold him down with the help of the others. "You can't do this to me." He starts to bawl. "I'm gonna kick your punk white ass when this is over."

"It's never gonna be over. You will need me and I will need you for the rest of our pathetic lives." I signal to the others to let up. They do, slowly. After they let him go, he pushes me off and holds me to the floor by my shoulders.

Before the others can move in to intervene, he frees up one hand and raises his fist to strike, but I grab it and struggle to hold it steady. "I'm not giving up," I say. He raises his other hand to strike me, but I grip onto that one too. I can't hold this forever as my arms begin to buckle.

The others move closer, hovering. He sees them and takes his eyes off me for a split second. I twist his arms around and slam him onto his back. I gain the strength to pin him there and straddle his torso while the others hold his arms and legs again. I collapse across him, my hair dangling in his face. His strength wanes. We stay like this for more than a minute. I loosen my grip and he does not try to regain control over me. "If you don't do this," I tell him. "Then you're a dead man."

He doesn't respond, but tears roll down his cheeks.

"It's all the same, Aaron. I see Jimmy over and over and over again dying there on that street. Sometimes I see his blood all over my hands. I wake up soaked. Jimmy was a replacement and it was his first deployment. He's dead and I'm not. How can that be possible? What we went through on those tours before that one. All the shit we saw and did. How does it make any sense?" Tears stream down my face. The others in the room are kneeling next to us and some have their hands on my shoulders.

"I told Jimmy if he stuck with me he'd make it to look after his grandmother." I am blubbering now. "He was a good god-fearing boy. He loved his grandmother, the army and this country. I got his cherry popped dammit. Now he's gone and I can't forgive myself for saying that bullshit to him. That I had his back. I wasn't paying attention. I let him down. I wished that bullet would've taken me instead of him."

I lie there on top off him dripping tears onto his chest. I finally collapse and roll off. He doesn't move, but lies there with outstretched arms like Jesus on the cross.

After two, three minutes perhaps, he sniffles and then says, "I can't get it outta my head, Zach. I just keep seeing it all over and over and over in my dreams. I can't turn my head off. I see the blood. I see the arms and legs. Everywhere I look I see arms and legs and blood. I see that arm from the DFAC all the time. I get jumpy. I don't know if I can be a cop. It's all I ever wanted to do."

I say, "I can't wash Jimmy's blood off my hands, Aaron. I see the others too. All of these guys here are going through the same thing. They support one another and make it day by day. They just talk. They listen. They're here for you. When you get that way, you can call them and they'll be there. Don't ever give up, Aaron. Don't you ever give up. Your mother and sister need you. I need you. I need your damn pestering emails reminding me how crazy I am. They actually make me laugh. They make my day. I need that."

He sniffles. The other veterans have us surrounded, sitting on the floor, kneeling. A few of them are crying too, all grown men at that. Some had been the toughest fighting sons-of-bitches the military machine ever produced. "You just need the love and support of your family," I continue, "and these guys here and it will lessen and go away. When you keep busy and talk and listen and be here for one another you're gonna make it. Someone there for you, by your side, loving you and you're gonna make it, Aaron. This is what friends do. Okay?"

He wipes his tears away and nods.

"That's all you have to do is try. Never, never give up and always keep trying. Promise me that?"

He nods again, sniffling. "I'm still gonna kick your punk white ass. Look at you. You look like one of those punks, those rockers."

"Yeah? Well, I held my own just now, you big black fucker."

He chuckles through his sniffles.

We stay for three hours. Aaron and I sit on the floor with our backs to the wall listening to the others. We say nothing the entire time. The other veterans tell stories of nightmares, have trouble adjusting to civilian life, they're irritable, jumpy and some are substance abusers.

When it's over, Aaron agrees to join the group, and a sponsor, one of the veterans there, will be meeting or talking with him daily. It's like that AA program.

Chapter Twenty-Three
You're Killing Me, Jim

Two days later, I drive west. I look in my rear-view mirror at my black eye and swollen face. *Damn, my good looks aren't so good right now.*

I zip along on Interstate 80 and in Des Moines I change directions at Interstate 35 and head north through Minneapolis and on into Duluth.

It's late when I arrive so I find a chain motel and check in. In my room, I search the Net, find what I'm looking for and make a note of it. I then hammer out Aaron's story, touching on his depression and suicidal ideation. I discuss survivor's guilt and conclude the article on support groups and programs the VA has to help veterans through their pain. Two hours later, I send it to Willows. I hope he can run it with the others.

I grab a late dinner, like those people at Les Deux Magots. After I eat, I stop at a liquor store on my way back to the motel.

Inside, I find a liter of Glen sitting on the shelf smiling at me. "There you are you beautiful baby." A woman nearby looks at me and scurries on her way. I shrug. Again, I remember drinking Glen in her father's study. That day seems like a million years ago, too. I flash back to my ride with Dutch following her bouncing around atop Lilly. *What happened to the enchanted forest?* I grab Glen's ass, pay for him and slink back to my motel.

I watch *The Best Years of Our Lives* on a classic channel. *Damn, why do I do this?* During the end credits the announcer says, "Coming up, *To Have and Have Not*." I jolt up. "With Humphrey Bogart and Lauren Bacall," the squawk box continues. I've never seen it. I drop the remote beside me and settle in with Glen to watch. As the movie plays, I stare at Lauren Bacall. I can't take my eyes off her. I want the editor to cut back to her. Yes, she is beautiful, but there is more to it with the way she talks and smiles and those eyes. *Look at those eyes.*

I grab my phone and search the Net. Her first film in 1944 she is all of nineteen years old. As I read the description of her, my mouth drops open. I set the phone down. *I don't believe it.* Bacall has smoky hazel eyes. The movie is in black and white, but those eyes. The way she tilts them up at Bogart is how she...I stare at her, caressing Glen's neck after swigging. I don't even wipe the dribble off my beard. She again tilts her eyes up at Bogart and says,

You know you don't have to act with me, Steve. You don't have to say anything, and you don't have to do anything. Not a thing. Oh, maybe just whistle. You know how to whistle, don't you Steve? You just put your lips together and...blow.

I almost wet my pants.

The movie ends, but it seems different from Stein's book. In fact, Harry Morgan survives in the movie. Hollywood. Go figure.

I want to see it again, but the Warner Brothers logo, the only end credit to the movie, comes on. Peering down at Glen smirking back up at me I say, "You're not doing your job very well." I look around the room. "Where are you, Hem? No, actually, you fuckin' pest, stay away. You're contributing to my loss of sanity." Glen's a quarter full. I chug some of him and shuffle to the bathroom to take a leak. Trying to steady myself with my hand on the wall, I lean forward and close my eyes.

~ * ~

He punches me in the face. I stagger and fall backwards. "Why did you do that?" We are in his house in Ketchum.

"Call me a fucking pest, will you?" Stein comes at me again. I try to block him, but he punches me this time in the solar plexus. I double over and spit up blood.

He goes over to his desk and pours himself a drink. I stand upright and squint at him, my face sore and the wind taken out of me. "I thought you said a man shouldn't drink when he fights?" I struggle to get the words out through my sore jaw which I readjust with my hand.

"I did. I didn't say a man couldn't drink when the fight is over though." He sips rum.

"The fight is over?" I hobble over to him. He is in his fifties, full white beard and beefy. Looks like my dad.

"You're licked, kid." He hands me a glass.

I take it and sip. "I'm not licked."

"Look at yourself in the mirror. You look like shit."

I glance in a mirror against the wall and see a full head of hair hanging in my eyes, my beard scraggly and thicker than his. I peer out a large picture window and see snow-capped mountains. I sit at a square table by the window, rubbing my sore jaw. There are tall bookshelves on either side of a fireplace and wood paneling all around. "I don't get it."

"Get what?" he says sitting across from me.

"Why you visit me sometimes and why you don't at other times."

"How many times do I have to tell you? I don't come to visit with you. You come to visit with me."

"What are you talking about?" I sip.

"A little slow, kid?" He leans back in a chair. I sneer at him. "When you're busy," he says, "you don't need me. When you dated that girl, you

279

didn't need me. You only come around when you need me." I don't say anything trying to recollect whether this is the case. "When you don't need me," he says, "you'll never see me again."

"I can't imagine that I won't."

"It's not my call."

I consider this while we sit drinking and watching the sun setting behind the Rocky Mountains sprinkled with snow. He's right, this is a great place to end up.

~ * ~

I stir and discover I'm lying in the bathroom. I sit up and look around, my face hurts, there's blood on the floor and I can taste it in my mouth.

I pull myself up using the sink and look in the mirror. There's a cut on my cheek, I must have bit my tongue, and my solar plexus hurts. I stand in the shower under cold water.

After my shower, I polish Glen off, check out and drive into town. I stop and buy a bottle of Jim before finding the building in the downtown area, park in a lot and go in. "May I help you, sir?" an older woman asks from behind a desk in the lobby. She looks me up and down. I have combed my hair back and used some gel, but it still hangs in my eyes. My beard can't hide the cut on my cheek and the black eye Aaron gave me.

"Yes, please. I'm here to see David Zimmer."

"Do you have an appointment?"

"Please tell him that Zach, Zach Powell is here."

"Just a minute." She punches a number into her phone. She says, "Mr. Zimmer, a Zach Powell is here to see you. Yes, sir."

"He'll be right out."

I look around for a seat, and spot one against the wall, however, no more than ten seconds after the receptionist hung up her phone, David bursts into the lobby from an office down the hall. "Zach." It takes him a moment before he recognizes me and runs over. We embrace and he steps back. "You look like a Hasidic Jew, except for that eye."

"Makes sense. Someone thought I was Jesus the other day. How've you been?"

"Great. Come. Let's go to my office." He leads me down the hall and into his office. It's decorated with military citations, army insignia, and a picture of our platoon in Iraq. I examine it. Several of the guys are gone, all but ghosts now. I look at Jimmy standing there next to me, his arm resting on my shoulder with that large grin. I have this pit in the bottom of my stomach again. "Seems like a long time ago, huh?" he says.

"Isn't it tough to look at all the time?"

"Sometimes, I guess. Here, sit." We sit on a sofa against the wall. "What happened, there?" he says, indicting my face.

"Nothing. An old friend beat me up last night."

"Some friend."

"Yeah, he's a real pal." I look at the ring on his finger. "What is that?" I point to it.

"Yeah, I went ahead and did it."

"No kidding? Who?"

"A girl from school, Sara. She's not only the love of my life, but one hot fox."

"Listen to you. Congrats." I high-five him. "I'd love to meet her sometime."

"You're gonna meet her tonight."

"What're ya talking about? I'm just passing through."

"No you're not. You're staying with us. It's the second night of Hanukkah. The families will all be there."

"I certainly can't impose then."

"Impose. Forget it." He studies me. "You're all over the news. Looks like you're having the time of your life."

"Oh, I certainly am," I say smiling. "I certainly am."

"Still playing the field, or you have someone special?"

"No, I'm just foot-loose and fancy free. You know me, David." A long pause, then I say, "So, the insurance business?"

"Yeah. Make a great living."

"Do me a favor?"

"Sure."

"Never cancel a sick person's policy."

"Well, you know how this business works."

"Yeah I do. Just promise me that you'll go out of your way to not cut someone off when they need it most."

"I'll try," he says hesitating a little bit. "Why?"

"Just trust me."

"Okay, well, great. Let's get outta here and head to the house. We can have a cocktail and catch up some more."

"Great. I'd love a cocktail," I say following him out. *I really would love a cocktail. Damn, did I sober up from last night yet?*

I follow him to his house, in the suburbs, looks like America. He has an attached two-car garage and a split-level abode. There's a Menorah in the window. I pull up and park on the street, grab my bag and follow him in. "Sara," he calls out. "Let me take your things, Zach." He grabs my bag.

This cute little girl with bouncy black hair hurries out. "Sara, honey, this is Zach, my army buddy I told you about. The one in the news." He kisses her.

I reach out to shake her hand, but she is too kind, because she gives me a hug after registering a strange look on her face after seeing me. "It's nice to meet you, Sara."

"Yes, David has told me so much about you, Zach. It's finally nice to meet you."

"Let's get that drink and catch up, Zach," he says.

Yeah, let's. I follow him to a den. He closes the door behind me. He pours me a bourbon on the rocks and one for himself. We sit on plush leather chairs and clink. "Damn, Zach. I had a hard time with what happened to Reddens. I wanted to fly down there, but it was all over that next day and the news said you were whisked out of there by the FBI."

"Yeah, I just flew down there on a whim."

We are quiet for a moment. "You know," he says, "I drive down to Minneapolis a lot and volunteer at the VA."

"I'm ashamed to say I haven't done much volunteering."

"There's still time."

"Yeah. I guess you're right." I take a nip.

"I look at some of the guys in the hospital and I think about how lucky we are. Relatively speaking."

"Yeah, relatively." I consider him. "You have dreams?"

"You mean nightmares?"

I nod.

"Had them," he says. "Although they're becoming less frequent. I think since I got married and have Sara beside me makes it much better."

I look away.

"She understands and is right there to help me calm down and get back to sleep." He looks me over. "What about you? Nightmares?"

"No. No, not really. I think I came through it well. I keep busy and I think that's the key to things." I slam my bourbon down the hatch.

"It helps," he says. "Oh, here come the folks."

I wash up in the bathroom, comb my hair back over my head and dress in a suit, the expensive one I bought for that Thanksgiving dinner with…Note to self: Burn after use.

I meet both sets of parents, David's younger sister and Sara's older sister and brother and their young families including three children amongst them. After salutations, David's father says a blessing in Hebrew and then Sara's father says another. "I'd like you to light the second candle on the Menorah," David says to me.

"Oh, I don't want to burn your house down," I say.

"You were always the funny one, Zach. Here." He hands me the Shamash, the ninth candle used to light the others. I light the candle and they cheer and clap. "Now's who's funny," I say.

"Now we sing," David says.

"Do I know this tune?" I ask.

He chuckles. "In another life perhaps. It's Ma'oz Rzur."

They all sing a couple stanzas in Hebrew. I listen, flashing back to my time in Baghdad with David and the others.

During dinner, everyone has a story or two to tell. I tell them a funny one. "David was always the punctual one, for formations, for chow, for classes. He never missed anything, ever. Well, we had been training straight, for three weeks of twelve hours on and twelve hours off, when David went missing. It was not like him, and everyone knew it. There must be something seriously wrong, we all figured. So, the platoon looked here and there, high and low for over an hour. Nothing. Nowhere. No how. David was AWOL. Well, I had to go the bathroom and take a, well, I had some business to do. So I went in the head, and there he is, sitting on the John, leaning up against the wall, snoring away blissfully." Everyone laughs. "I wish I had a camera. He was so cute, just snoring with his mouth wide open."

I listen to David tell stories of my antics and some from the parents on David and Sara. Most of the time during dinner and thereafter, I just sit and listen to everyone talking and laughing and watch how happy everyone is.

~ * ~

The next morning, after a long breakfast with David and Sara, who are so much in love with one another, I say goodbye to them. It's around eleven A.M. and time to hit the road.

All the way back down through Minnesota I smile and laugh to myself remembering the good times we all had together. Those guys, that platoon, it was like my family, they *were* like my brothers.

At Interstate 90 I head west and at Sioux Falls turn south to Sioux City. I check into a motel in the downtown area and scan emails finding one from my bank. The paper paid me again so I wire Kristen half of the money. An email from Gold tells me to check the web version of the paper for my article on Justin. I don't.

Instead, I write an article centered on a well-adjusted veteran living in Duluth with a happy and loving family. While I slug my bottle of cheer, I detail how, with support from a loving wife, parents and a community, this boy is going to make it. I also describe how he is giving back and helping his fellow veterans by volunteering at the VA. I send it off to Willows.

The bottle I bought on the road is empty. *Damn.* I toss it in the trash. I feel sick. My hands tremble a little bit and I seem edgy. I close my laptop and walk down the street.

Sioux City is a moderately sized town with all of the usual vices. I should find something to do. What did Stein say about vices? I roll into a cowboy bar. I sit at the bar drinking and listening to a band play country music. Cowboys and cowgirls dance around on the floor in front of a band. Everyone is having a swell time.

I pay close attention to the lyrics of several songs. Great music, but as is usually the case the songs revolve around love and heartache. *I gotta get the hell outta here.*

I stroll into a pool hall not far from the cowboy bar where a few seedy characters hang. An older cowboy sits at the bar staring at his beer and a few middle-aged folks converse over drinks. Two men, one looks Native-American, the other white, play pool. They are older than I am and monstrous, probably work on a ranch or something. I order a whiskey and watch them play.

They finish a game. "You play pool?" the white one says. He's an ugly son-of-a-bitch with a fat face. He snatches two twenties from a glass on the side of the pool table.

"Not really," I lie, remembering playing pool with Jimmy and the others back at Bragg. "Well, just a little."

285

"Twenty bucks a game," he says holding a twenty up for me to inspect.

"Okay," I say. He puts one of the twenties in the glass and pockets the other. I drop twenty in and he racks 'em and breaks 'em.

We play. I don't try, so I lose the game. "Better luck next time," he says snatching the money. "Play again?"

"Sure, why not?" We play again. I order another tumbler of Jim. I try this time, and take the game.

"Back to even," he says. "Again?"

"Sure." I order another whiskey to keep me juiced. I win the game again. "Well, it's been fun, but I should be going," I say after dumping Jim down my throat.

"Gotta give me a chance to get it back," he demands. I scrutinize him, his Indian friend, and rack 'em up. I order them a round of booze. While playing, I eye the Indian, but he's eyeing me and smiling. I nod and smile back.

I beat the white boy again and he is not happy, or warming up to me. He goes over to an ATM machine against the wall and returns with a hundred dollars. He puts it all in and says, "One more time."

"I don't think it's a good idea," I say to him, but eyeing the Indian who stands up and puffs his chest out.

"Play," the white guy insists. I do. I order yet another round, try to lose, I really do, but this clown is drunker than I am. He loses.

I scoop up his hundred dollars and say, "Got an early start fellas." I get the hell out of there and hurry down the street turning up an alley to take a shortcut to my motel.

Wrong move.

"Hey, you motherfucker!" the white man shouts chasing after me followed by the Indian.

"Oh shit." I increase my speed, but they catch me. The white brute grabs and throws me against the wall of a brick building. The alley is dark, smelly and the dumpster next to me overflows with garbage. It reminds me of Baghdad. "Look, I don't want any trouble. Here, you can have your money back." I pull a wad of twenties from my pocket and hold it up to him.

He slaps at my hand, the bills scattering. "Too late for that. You're a hustler, aren't you?"

"No, I swear, just lucky."

"Well your luck has run out." He throws a punch hitting me in the face. *Damn, it was just beginning to heal.* I put my hands up and say, "Okay, okay, I get it. Listen, ranger, why don't you take Tonto here and just go?"

Oops. That wasn't smart. The Indian jumps into the fracas, rushing and throwing me to the ground. I fight back, getting in a few licks. I get up, smash the Indian in the face. *Not a good move.* Oh, what the hell? I swing around and hit the white boy too.

I try to use those close-quarter combat techniques I learned, but Jim won't let me coordinate them very well. The two goons beat the shit out of me. They hit and kick me on the ground. It's true what they say. I see stars.

Chapter Twenty-Four
The Sun Also Sets

He helps me to my feet. I shake my sore head and brush myself off. "Where the hell were you?" I ask him. "I needed you back in there." We are standing in front of a rough joint in a dusty Spanish town.

"Didn't take my advice, did you?" a younger Stein says.

"What's that?"

"Never fight when you're drunk."

"I didn't have much of a choice. They just came at me."

"Like I said, you have balls, kid. Let's go. If we hurry we can still catch the fight." He leads me down the street. We pass people dressed in simple peasant or worker clothes. A family strolls by with picnic baskets and fresh bread sticking out of the napkin it's wrapped in. The father carries a decanter of wine.

"What town is this?" I ask.

"Pamplona. The bullfight starts in ten minutes. Hadley and the others are already there."

We hand over our tickets at the gate and find our seats. Hadley, beaming radiance, smiles at me. "That's Jake Barnes," Stein says, "this lovely woman is Lady Brett Ashley, Robert Cohn and his girl Frances Clyne. Zachary Powell," he says completing the introductions.

I sit next to Lady Brett. She is lovelier than Stein described in his book. "Nice to meet you folks," I say. The fight begins and the matador starts teasing the bull, waving that red flag around and pissing him off.

"What happened to you?" Lady Brett says, sliding over a little too close to me.

"Fight," I say.

"Is Hem getting you into scuffles?"

"No. I did this one myself."

"Well, don't let him get that gorgeous face of yours hurt. You know he has the power to see to it that we live or die."

"How so?"

"With his typewriter, of course." She reaches over and strokes my leg. This makes both Barnes and Cohn agitated and they shoot daggers into me.

I smile, blush a bit. I'm clean shaven, with short brown hair, and casually dressed in a dress shirt and slacks from this time, the nineteen twenties. She leans in and whispers in my ear, "I like sex, don't you?"

I pull back, "Well, yes, but I don't think…"

She takes my arm and pulls me close, stoking my bicep. "I like it every chance I get," she whispers in my ear, her hot breath tingling me. "I can't give it up, you know." Her perfume smells sweet, reminding me of someone I knew.

"Well, I have someone…I mean, had someone…I mean, she's, well, I…I…"

"Come see me later, handsome." She sits up, looks over at Cohn and Barnes, and smiles at them. *They're gonna beat the shit out of me too.* I watch the matador slay the bull and have the greatest time drinking with them. *Damn, they can drink.*

~ * ~

Squinting from the artificial light, I sit up in a hospital bed as a nurse comes over. "Welcome back," she says. "How're you feeling?"

"I…ah…I dunno." I have an IV in my arm and chest pads with wires hooked up to beeping monitors with lines dancing up and down.

"You just need some fluids and rest for a while."

"No, I have to get going." I start pulling the pads from my chest.

"You shouldn't do that," she says. "Doctor."

This doctor, a man from Pakistan or India or somewhere, comes in. "You took quite a beating," he says.

"Yes, well, I don't remember much." I pull the IV out of my arm. They rush me, but it's too late. A bit of blood spills out on my arm. "I have to be going." I see my clothes in a bag under the bed and grab it.

"I strongly advise against this," the doctor says.

"Right. Do what you have to, but I'm checking out." The doctor frowns at the nurse.

I get dressed, struggling to put my shirt on over my back, as I am sore and bruised all over. *Bastards hit and kicked me everywhere.* I limp out to the nurses' station, the nurses pitying me as if I'm a wounded dog.

I fill out some forms and inform them I have no insurance, Willows couldn't afford it. I tell them that perhaps they can bill the VA. I call a cab and it takes me back to the motel where I check out and get the hell out of town. As I'm driving, Sioux City in my rearview mirror, I can't help but think my beating in Sioux City was worse than my beating in Egypt.

On the road, I drive and drive, heading west. I turn the radio on to a classic rock station and sip Jim from his bottle. That song by Sonny and Cher, *I got you Babe*, plays on my radio. *Damn.* It seems that is all songs are about. I search the dial and find an alternative rock station.

I stare at the road, shifting in the seat, a pain in my side harassing me.

The Gambler by the group Fun comes on the radio. It too is about shit I don't want to hear. I slap the knob turning the radio off.

I drive straight on through, except for gas and a stop at a liquor store for a bottle or two. I take a nip at times, just enough to calm me. I know just about how much to take in so I don't lose control. Although, it seems as soon as I sober up, my hands shake and my skin gets clammy. Once I get some more booze in me, I feel better.

Late one afternoon I pull off Interstate 10 and turn onto Eastern Avenue in East Los Angeles. Waiting at an intersection for the light to change, some Cholos there look at me aghast that this gringo, driving a big black Hummer, pulls into their hood. I nod and give them the Shaka sign. I guess I'm lucky the light changes before they shoot me, probably figuring the Shaka sign is a rival gang one.

Julio has moved into his own home not far from his parents. The GPS on my phone leads me to his house, a small LA style bungalow on a hill with not much street parking. A car blocks his driveway, so I pull up onto his front yard. I crawl out of the Hummer and walk up to the front door and knock. A moment later he answers the door. "What the hell?" he says.

"It's me, Zach."

"Like I said. What the hell? You look like shit."

"Yeah, I get that a lot lately. Glad to see you too."

He looks over my shoulder at the Hummer on his front yard. "That yours and you parked it on my front yard, fool?"

"Look at your grass. It's brown. Won't hurt it."

"Get your ass in here before some homie shoots you." He opens the screen door and lets me in. "What the hell're you doing here? I read your piece on that guy in Florida online. Messed up, huh?"

"Yeah, it is. Just passing through, writing some stories. Think I'll hang out around here."

"Not in this hood."

"You got that right. Thinking of waking up to the smell of the ocean. I'll look around Venice."

Jackie comes out of the kitchen carrying their child, a girl, now two and a half years old. "Hi, Jackie."

"Number two is on the way," Julio says.

"Damn, what's with you Latino's popping them out like bunnies?"

"No, two's the limit," Jackie says. "You try giving birth."

"I don't know, what will the church say?"

"Let the priests give birth before they tell me what to do," she says with a little bit of a Latina attitude.

"You tell 'im, mi amor," Julio says in a Mexican twang.

Julio grills burgers for dinner.

~ * ~

After dinner, Julio and I sit on his front porch. It's a warm December evening. He drinks a beer, and because they don't have anything harder, I drink Jim from a bottle I bought. "Sorry about your girlfriend," he says.

I shrug, think of his sisters, but decide not to bring it up. I take a large gulp. I look over at him watching me. "What?" I snap.

"Are you okay?"

"What, the bruise? I got in a fight outside a bar a few nights ago. It's nothing."

"That's not what I'm talking about."

"No, then what're you talking about?" I say, raising my voice. He doesn't respond, but looks out into the street.

Silence.

"You've got a nice little domicile going here," I say. "Everything you always wanted."

"Yeah, I do, don't I?"

"I'm happy for you." I slug Jim down my immune throat.

"You've made it too," he says.

"Made what?"

"With your writing. I mean, you found something you like to do."

"Guess so. I'm having the time of my life. No strings. Free spirit. On the road. What else could one ask for?"

He sips his beer, studying me. I don't think he bought it. "So," I say, "you've adjusted well."

He says, "It was a little rough at first, getting adjusted and all. Yeah. I mean, with Jackie, the baby, and I guess our final one on the way. I'm living the American dream, ain't I?"

"Yes you are, my friend." I clink my bottle to his beer. "Yes you are." We sit and watch the lights twinkling on the downtown skyscrapers and reminisce about our time together in Uncle Sam's Army.

~ * ~

The next day I drive down to Venice Beach and park in a lot. Walking the boardwalk, I stop at the spot where Julio, Basir and I met Chuck, the Vietnam Vet. I look around for him but see him nowhere. I stroll into the liquor store where I bought those bottles of Jim. "A vet, Chuck, used to sit out there," I say to the clerk, a young man who looks like a surfer dude. "You know where I can find him?"

He counts out some change to a patron. "He died. Three months ago."

"Really?"

"Drank himself to death, they figure. Found him face down in the sand, just over there." He points out the window.

I look to where he points. "Huh." I grab a bottle of Jim, pay the clerk and stroll north up the boardwalk. Chuck is gone. Who am I going to hang with now? I find a bench nearby and sit sipping my best buddy. Tourists with their young children sneer at me as they pass by. *Fuck them.* I get up and amble up the boardwalk.

A little farther on, I see a man sitting in a wheelchair. He glances back in my direction and watches me approach. Getting closer, I see he no legs and only one arm. *I know this guy.* Although he has long hair and a beard, similar to mine, I recognize him. "Danny? Is that you?" I pull up in front of him.

He squints at me. "Zach? Zach Powell?"

"Yes, it's me, Zach."

"No shit, man. I thought I was seeing a ghost, that Jim Morrison character, you know, the way he looked at the end of his life."

"Jesus, Moses, Jim Morrison," I say. "I've heard it all now." I high-five him on his left hand, the only one he has. A little American flag is taped to the handle of his chair and he has his Bronze Star with a V for Valor clipped to the flag. I think back to that day. He also has army stickers stuck to the chair's frame and a cardboard sign at his feet that reads: Veteran. Please help. God Bless.

"Yeah. Morrison hung around here," he says. "There's a mural of him over there on that building." He points and I look in that direction.

"You live around here?"

"Just down the boardwalk."

"I thought you were from the mid-west someplace?"

"Iowa. Nothing there for me." He looks away.

"Well, I'm gonna stay around here for a while. You want a snort?" I reveal Jim nestled in his bag.

"Hell yeah," he says.

I twist open the bottle and give it to him. He guzzles it. "Whoa," I say. He hands it back and wipes his lips. I take a good hit too. "What's with this shit?" I say sitting on the bench beside him and pointing to a jar on the ground full of bills.

"It's a living," he says, shrugging.

"A living?"

"Yeah. I get disability for, well you know, but it's never enough. This way I have money for booze, or women."

"Women?"

"Look at me. Who's gonna want me like this?"

I squint from the sun. I remember him as a skinny white boy, fast on his feet. Now, his skin is weathered and brown. "Hey," he says. "Why don't you crash at my place?"

"How can you afford a place around here on disability?"

"It's a flop-house. It's owned by this eccentric millionaire who lets us stay there for cheap. We call it Heartbreak Hotel."

"No kidding? Right up my alley." I slam back Jim and hand him off. "I'd like that."

"Never thanked you for saving my life," he says.

"Yeah?"

"At first, I was angry at you guys. I mean, what kind of a life is this? Then, what the hell? I'm having the time of my life now, right?" He raises Jim and takes a swig.

"Yeah. I guess so."

"What do you do, for money?" he asks.

I tell him all about Columbia and the paper. "Maybe I could get into Syria and get some stories."

"Why the hell would you wanna do that?"

I shrug.

~ * ~

I grab my bags from the Hummer and meet Danny at the Heartbreak Hotel. Built in the nineteen twenties, it's an actual former two story hotel and has old-style hotel rooms. Danny is on the first floor. I toss my things on the floor by the door to his room. He has a single bed, and a sofa against the wall. "You can crash there," he says pointing at the sofa.

"Great," I say. He has two titanium legs and an arm next to his bed. "What's with that?" I say.

"Yeah, awesome, huh? I don't wear them while I'm working."

"Oh." I nod and follow him into the common area where we work on killing off Jim.

As Jim kicks our asses, Danny tells me, slurring his words, "Sss oooo, sh sh eeee leffff meeee." He holds his hand out for Jim. He takes a swig and cradles the bottle in his lap. "I meee an, I doe bame 'er an awe. 'ook at me. Wooood you wa me?"

I watch him, tears dripping from his eyes. I'm frozen, speechless. After a long pause I say, "Did you love her?"

"Di I 'ove her? I sill ooooo, 'ach. I sill ooooo." He tips Jim to his lips and chugs.

"Give me that shit," I say after he finishes. I swallow hard. "Yeah, she left me too."

He doesn't hear me. He's out, cold. I wheel him to his room and tuck him into bed, not much to lift. Sitting on the sofa I finish Jim off, toss him onto the sofa, and find a liquor store and buy some more. I stumble along the boardwalk and stop at a park bench where I sit cradling Jim, gazing out at the moonlight dancing around on top of the Pacific Ocean.

~ * ~

"You're a very attractive man," Lady Brett says planting a kiss on my lips. I'm in her hotel room back in Paris.

I'm clean shaven and well groomed. I look at her bobbed hair and say, "You are more beautiful than Hem portrayed you. Don't tell him that. He'll kick my ass again."

She nibbles on my neck. "Um," she says. "You taste so divine." She pushes me down onto the bed, unbuttons my shirt, kisses my chest, and works her way down to my abdomen where she unbuttons my slacks.

"Do you think Hem will be okay with this?" I ask.

"Are you kidding? He wrote me this way." She reaches in and plays with me. I run my fingers through her hair. She smells fresh, like the ocean. She works on me.

And she works on me.

"Huh," she says peeking up. "You know, I love Jake, but I have to have sex."

"I'm sorry. I've never had this happen before."

"For him, it was the war."

296

"I'm so sorry. I'm so embarrassed." I sit up, tears falling onto my cheeks.

She puts her arm around me. "It's okay, handsome. It's okay."

~ * ~

It's cold. I'm lucky I didn't freeze to death. I sit up on the bench not realizing it got that cold here in LA overnight.

My hands tremble. I'm clammy. Irritable. I pick up Jim and discover he's a quarter full. I open, chug the rest of him and toss his empty carcass in the sand at my feet.

The shopkeepers are just arriving, opening their shops, and sweeping their stoops. On my way back to Heartbreak Hotel, I stop in a liquor store to get some more of my love. In Danny's room, I find him stirring. I fall onto the sofa. "Damn," he says. "Where you been?"

"Paris."

"What?" He swings his stumps over and climbs into his chair. "I have to piss so bad." He goes off down the hall to the shared bathroom.

When he comes back, I toss some cash at him. "Get some booze for later on."

"Sure thing." He gets ready for his boardwalk enterprise. "Hey listen. I've got some girls coming over later."

"Really?" I say, burying my head in a cushion.

"I've got just the girl for you."

"No kidding?"

"Yeah. She really does wonders with her tongue."

"I can't wait," I say, my voice muffled by the cushion.

"Okay. Seven sharp." He finishes dressing and is off. I lie there unable to move.

My War With Hemingway

~ * ~

Around noon I wake up. The first order of business, unlike my time in the military when one pees first thing, is to take a hearty swig of Jim, just to calm me. I then stumble into the common room where a radio plays tunes. I struggle to open my laptop, unable to get my hands to work the latch. I finally get it open, fire it up, but can't get my fingers to hit the right keys. I slam the cover and toss it aside. I rub my eyes with the heels of my hands.

I stagger back to Danny's room and rummage around in my duffle bag and find some cash. I see that blue box. Why have I kept it all this time? I grab and stuff it in my jacket pocket.

I purchase another bottle of my best friend from a liquor store and head to the ocean. Sitting in the sand, the waves splash up and wet my shoes. I finish one bottle of Jim and start working on the other one. At one point, while lying in the sand, some bathers come by and check to see if I'm alive. They shake me by my shoulders and I moan. They go on their way.

I sit up and reach into my jacket pocket, pulling out the blue box. I rip it open and take out the ring. I stare at it for the longest time. With the waves lapping up against my torso, I toss the ring into the surf. I smash the box and throw it aside.

My clothes are all wet and the sun sets on me. I get up, grab Jim and stagger back to Heartbreak Hotel.

Danny is in his room with two professional ladies. A blond sits on his lap kissing him. "Dude, where you been?"

"Swimming." I toss Jim on the sofa. A cute girl with short amber colored hair sits there sipping a beer. "Hey," I say to her.

"Hey to you, good-looking."

"Oh, you're too kind." I head down the hall to the shower. It's an old-fashioned bathtub with a curtain stuck in it so the water doesn't get on the floor. I throw my wet clothes on the floor and take the first shower I've had in a few days. I towel off, wrap it around my waist, and head back to Danny's room.

The blond has her hand in Danny's crotch working him over. "I'm Brett," the amber-haired girl says to me.

"Really?" I say, raising an eyebrow. "How coincidental."

"What?" she says.

"Oh, nothing." I sit next to her. She is on me lickety-split, running her hands over my bare chest, licking my nipples, stroking my penis. She kisses me all over and then goes down on me.

This seems too familiar. I try, I concentrate, I even close my eyes and try to picture her, but it's just not happening. *What the hell is wrong with me?*

She keeps working on me, but I'm dead. Nothing. I can't take it. *I gotta get out of here.* "I'm sorry," I say to her jumping up and leaving her kneeling there dumbfounded, her mouth wide open.

"Did I do something wrong?" she says. "I can try harder."

"No. No, it's not you." I dig around in my duffle bag and grab a pair of jeans, a T-shirt and pull on dry socks and sneakers. I grab a wad of cash, what's left of Jim and run for the door.

I stroll the boardwalk, finish this bottle of Jim and buy another. I find some homeless guys and share the bottle with them. We laugh, have a good time, and one of them passes out in a pool of vomit. I tilt his head so he doesn't choke on it and drown.

When we finish this one, we get another. Then another. Somehow the faucet never stops flowing. One of us finds a way to get more booze. I hang with these guys for a few days, sitting under the Santa Monica Pier. As soon as I begin to sober up, I have to get more in me, otherwise I cannot go on, I cannot stop shaking, I cannot stop dying.

My War With Hemingway

~ * ~

"I wish I had died before I ever loved anyone but her," he says.

I'm sitting with the twenty–something version of Stein again in Harry's New York Bar. It's stuffed with expatriates. "So, why did you?" I ask him.

"That is the perennial question, isn't it?" He reaches over and takes my tumbler from me.

"I'm not finished."

"You've had enough."

"What? You're one to tell me I've had enough."

"Yeah, I am. Got a lot of experience in this department, don't you know?"

I reach for the carafe of cognac sitting next to him, but he grabs my hand and holds it down and away. I struggle with him, trying to break free. "You want to step outside?" I snap.

He laughs and pushes my hand down letting it go. "You really want me to kick your ass again?"

"I should be given a rematch."

"Dammit, kid. Don't make the same mistake I made."

"What're you talking about?"

"Look at yourself in the mirror."

I stand up and look in the mirror on the wall. I am not the dapper, handsome young man of the roaring twenties I had been each time I visited Stein in Paris. Rather, it's the long haired, greasy bearded, dirty drunk from Venice Beach. I bolt from Harry's and onto the street. Well-dressed patrons heading into the bar scoff at me.

I sprint through the Paris streets until I can run no more. Couples stroll by holding hands smiling, some glaring at me with revulsion. Standing next to the Seine, gazing at the brightly lit Eiffel Tower, I collapse and pass out.

Chapter Twenty-Five
I Hope it's Not Too Late

An email pops up on the computer screen from Julio in Los Angeles:

Micah, Yes, Zach was here, went to Venice Beach and stayed with Danny Cox, but Danny said he left one night, about ten days ago, and never came back. He left his duffle, clothes, computer, everything at Danny's. He was a mess, Micah. Got into a bad fight on the road. I don't think this looks good. Julio

My name is Micah Reid. Zach, along with Julio and Aaron, is one my best friends from my army days. A lot of fun, and although he never really told you this, he did in fact look after us just as much as we looked after him, more so. I reply to Julio:

Julio, I'll catch the next flight out. Thanks, Micah

I followed Zach's articles from his road trip online with that paper in Miami. Those stories posted to the website about five days after he sent them. Then, they stopped cold. A reporter at the paper, Stacey Gold, told me she couldn't reach him either.

I noticed Zach's mood had changed those final two years together in the service. He had more of an edge, unlike the upbeat and silly Zach I first knew, always wise-cracking. The wars had changed him. Changed us all. However, I never saw him happier than with his girlfriend, Jessica. She had pulled himself out of his slump. He whispered to me when she went into the bathroom after dinner at our place in New York once that he was so much in love and that this was the girl for him. Forever.

~ * ~

While packing my bags for Los Angeles, our doorman says over the intercom, "Mr. Reid?"

"Yes, Juan?"

"There's a Jessica Patterson here to see you, sir."

I don't believe it. I hesitate. "Jessica Patterson?"

"Yes. Says she's not leaving until she sees you."

I have to see her and have her explain to me why she hurt my friend the way she did. She shows up now, when I'm packing to go find him? "Okay, send her up." I open the door a crack and wait, my blood boiling.

A few minutes later she knocks and pushes the door open. "Micah?"

"Right here."

She peeks in and closes the door. I can see she's been crying because her eyes are wet. Her clothes are crumpled, as if she has slept in them. She folds her hands, intertwining her fingers in front of her mouth, almost as if she's praying. "I'm sorry, Micah. Where's Zach?"

I can sense she wants to come closer, but holds back. "You're sorry? Really?"

Tears begin to pour from her eyes and stream down her face, dripping onto the floor. "I know you have no reason to believe me, but what I have to tell you is true. I swear to god it's all true."

I say nothing, but stare her down. If I could shoot spears from my eyes, she'd be dead from one through the heart. Standing there with my arms folded across my chest, I don't have time for this drama, I don't buy it.

"I love him, Micah. Where is he?" She sniffles.

"You have an unusual way of showin' him your love. Do you know how much you hurt him? You're lucky I'm still a good Christian, but you have a long way to go to earn my forgiveness."

"That Christmas when I got out of the car back home, my parents were waiting and my father took my phone from me right on the spot." She sniffles and wipes the tears away with her fingers. I say nothing, but continue to stare her down.

"He told me I wasn't going back to Columbia and was not to see Zach again. He checked me out of Columbia and told me I was to finish my degree at Yale. I told them fine, but I was going to see Zach and was going to marry him just as soon as he got back from Western New York." She sniffles again and tries to catch her breath.

"I stormed off into the house and tried to call Zach on the landline, but my father grabbed the phone from me and we started to struggle. Can you believe it? We were physically fighting. I'm twenty-three and he is still controlling my life? So I ran up to my room and found out that they had confiscated my computer. I ran down stairs and grabbed his car keys off the plate by the door and ran out. I beat him to the car, got in and raced off." She sways a little, but I don't move. I am so angry because Zach could be dead on the side of a road and I know that her leaving him probably contributed to all of this.

"I really don't have time for this," I say.

"Look, Micah." She sobs and pulls up her pant leg. A large scar goes the length of the tibia.

"What happened?"

"He called the police on me. I got about five miles and all of a sudden the police are chasing me. I was going to find a phone, call Zach and drive to New York and try to find him, but the roads were slippery, and the police chasing me made me speed. I lost control on a curve and crashed, hitting a rut and flipping over into a ravine." She wipes yet more tears from her eyes and has to steady herself.

I'm beginning to feel some sympathy, but she still has a lot of explaining to do. "Continue," I say.

"I woke up two days later in the hospital, badly injured, heavily sedated, but not life-threatening. I had broken ribs, this broken leg..." she sobs uncontrollably now.

I finally move over and steady her. "This is really unbelievable. Your father has a lot in common with mine." I help her to the sofa and hand her a box of tissues as she is getting her tears all over me now.

"My leg was a compound fracture, Micah," she says hysterically and burying her head in my chest. "I almost lost it."

I gently raise my arm and place it around her.

She looks up at me. "I was so mad and hurried I didn't put my seatbelt on." She catches her breath. "I was badly bruised and swollen all over and had very bad whiplash, almost broke my neck too. I couldn't move my head around for a couple weeks and they had it in a neck brace for over a month. I have bolts in my leg, Micah. For the rest of my life." She blubbers.

I shift and sigh.

"They kept me heavily sedated for days. When I finally came around, I cursed, even spit at my parents there in the hospital room. I was completely hysterical. I told them they would never keep me from Zach. You know what my father did?"

I shake my head.

"Told me that Zach is not good enough for me. He had a private detective put a whole case together on him. He pulled the file out there and told me to look at it. I threw it back at him without looking at it. He said I'd thank him someday for doing this. Can you believe that?"

"I don't know Jessica, it's been almost a year. You couldn't have called by now?"

"I just got out."

"What do you mean?"

"They put me in a hospital out in the Berkshires." She sobs again. "An institution, Micah. Can you believe that?"

304

I squeeze her shoulder.

"They made me take pills every day, to keep me calm. I was like a zombie for months. They treated me like an insane person." She once again buries her head in my chest and drips tears all over, soaking my shirt.

"I had a cast and was in a wheelchair. Then I had to have therapy to learn to walk again."

"Sweet Jesus, this sounds criminal to me. Aren't there any phones in the hospital?"

"This hospital is a tightly controlled facility. No phones, no computers, nothing." She lifts her head and wipes at her eyes with her fingers again to get the tears out. It doesn't work as more stream forth. "They lock you in your room at night." She digs in her pocket and pulls out some folded newspaper clippings. "We did get newspapers and magazines." She hands them to me.

I unfold them and see a story from *The Boston Times* about the incident in Georgia and one about Zach's escapade in Egypt.

"He could have been killed, Micah." She sobs again.

"So how did you get away?"

"They slowly decreased the dosage of the medication and I decided to play along, remain calm and escape once I got out. Four days ago they released me to my parents. I sat in the back of the car and said nothing as we rode along. When we drove through a small town, at a stop light, I bolted from the car and got about two blocks before he caught up with me. We struggled there on the street, I punched and hit him, kicked him. He backed off as a crowd gathered. My mother *finally* spoke up. It took her that long to figure it out. Finally figure out what I told them and argued with them for the two years Zach and I were together. That we love each other and there is nothing anyone can do to destroy the love between us. She pulled on my father's arm, pulling him back and said to let me go."

I rub her shoulder gently. "I'm so sorry, Jessica. I truly am so sorry."

"My father just couldn't let me go, however. He told me not to come back. That I was cut off from the money, the family, everything. Can you believe it?"

I shake my head.

"Where is he, Micah?" She looks up at me.

"I dunno. No one's heard from him for over ten days."

"Where does he live now?"

"He took a job with a paper in Miami, then hit the road to write some stories."

"Then he could be working on something," she says lifting her voice.

"I don't think so."

"What do you mean?"

"It's not good. Our friend Julio told me he got into a bad fight. He's somewhere in LA. He walked off one night in Venice leavin' all his stuff behind at a friend's place and no one's seen or heard from him since. I'm packin' to go there now."

"Then I have to go with you."

"That's not a good idea."

"Yeah," she says, trying to chuckle. "I don't know how I'd get there. I actually have no money."

"Nothin'?"

"I don't even have my ID, a wallet. I walked and hitchhiked here."

I sigh and pass her some tissues from the box and think a minute. "Okay. I'll go to LA and find him. You can stay here. I'll call Peter and tell him what's goin' on."

She sniffles again and looks up at me with those hazel eyes, tears streaming down her cheeks. I can see why Zach fell for her. "Okay, okay," I say. "You're gonna make me cry."

"Thank you, Micah." She hugs me. "Please find him."

"Okay." *I hope it's not too late.*

Chapter Twenty-Six
Zach and The General

After landing at LAX, I place a call to Julio, one to Aaron, then drive over to Venice Beach. I meet up with Julio where Venice Boulevard meets the boardwalk. We make our way over to where Danny Cox lives and find him sitting in the common room watching television. "No. He just took off and never came back," Danny says. "I heard it on the boardwalk he was spotted two days later up near the Santa Monica Pier buying booze at Pedro's Liquor Store."

"And you have all his things?" I ask him.

"In my room."

"Well, hold on to all of it for me, will ya, Danny?"

"Sure."

"Didn't he have a car?"

"A black Hummer," Julio says. "We can talk to the police. Fill out a missing person's report."

"Let's look around first and ask some questions." The three of us head up the boardwalk. With Danny motoring along in his chair, we search for Zach all the way up to the Santa Monica pier. We meet up with two homeless guys cooking over a small pocket rocket camp stove. I show them a picture of Zach standing with us on base in front of our unit HQ in Baghdad. "No," one of them says. "Doesn't look familiar."

"He would have long hair and a beard," Julio says.

"Yeah," the other one says. "I think that might be the guy who camped out a couple weeks ago. Stayed a couple of days."

"You know where he went?" I say.

"No," the second man continues. "He was really jittery. We all like a nip now and then, but this guy couldn't stop drinking. He just drank to blow his mind away."

"Shit," Julio says.

"Yeah," the first man says. "Like he was tryin' to kill himself."

Julio and I exchange glances. "Thanks," I say to the men.

We walk, and Danny rolls, back down the boardwalk to Venice where we started. Along the way we look down side streets, near the water, and ask people if they've seen him after showing them the picture. Nothing. "Follow me over to the police station," Julio says.

I give Danny my number and follow Julio over to the Pacific Division of the LAPD where we file a missing person's report. The police officer tells us that Zach's Hummer was impounded after going unclaimed in a Venice lot.

Outside, and after midnight, I stand with my back against my rental with Julio who says, "The good news is they don't have any reports of bodies matching his description in the morgue."

I frown at him. "I dunno," I say. "He has nothin'. No phone, no car. Where else could he go?"

"Don't know. I mean, he couldn't just walk all the way downtown to skid row. A lot of homeless hang out there. They give out food at the mission."

"Why not?"

"It's like, I don't know, fifteen miles."

"It's better than doing nothin'. I couldn't sleep or just sit around."

"Follow me," he says.

I follow him down the freeway and exit Interstate 110 at 6th Street. The bright lights of the downtown office buildings light the area up well.

Skid Row is squalid, people sleep on the sidewalks. I can see some people doing drugs, even shooting into their arms as we pass. We walk up one street, and down another. At each turn we're asked if we need a hit of this or would like a kilo of that. We ask almost everyone we encounter if they've seen Zach. We show them the picture, but most are so stoned they have no idea what we ask them.

We make our way over to the Midnight Mission where we find out that the Mission covers a city block and has a host of social services to help people kick addition, get off the street and back on their feet. We gain entry and search the night beds going up and down the rows. Nothing.

Back out on the sidewalk, I stand with Julio, neither of us speaks for a long moment.

Finally, "What're we gonna do?" Julio says.

"I dunno. Keep lookin'. It's all we can do."

"We could cover more ground if one stays here and one goes back to Venice," he says.

"Makes sense. I'll go back to Venice and you keep lookin' here." I drive back to Venice and walk up and down the boardwalk again searching in the alleyways, side streets, even nearby parks. Nothing. The sun begins to rise over East LA.

Julio calls and says, "I'm going home for a few hours. Sleep. Get something to eat."

"Okay. I'll go see Danny, maybe crash there for a couple hours." I end the call. On my way back to Danny's, the phone rings. It's Jessica. "I'm sorry. We haven't found him yet. I'll call you as soon as I do." I end the call. *If I do.*

I make it back to Danny's home and lie on his sofa while he goes to work, or so he tells me. I see Zach's belongings on the floor.

~ * ~

Four hours later, I wake up and check my phone. No messages from the police and nothing from Julio. If I were a cussing man, I'd scream the f-word like many guys did in the army. I call Julio. "Sorry if I woke you," I say.

"No. I'm up. I'll take a shower and trade with you, that way we might look in places where the other might not have looked."

"Good idea." It's twelve noon. I retrieve my bag from my rental and take a shower at Danny's.

I drive one way while Julio drives the other and arrive back at Skid Row at two in the afternoon. I search the internet on my phone and discover that Skid Row covers the area between 3rd Street on the north to 7th Street on the South and the LA River on the east to Wall Street on the west. I also learn that Skid Row in LA is the largest transient person's population in the United States, believed to have somewhere between three and five thousand homeless persons.

I broaden my search area and walk down San Pedro Street. I walk west on 9th Street, tracking my search using the GPS on my phone. I ask this person, I show that person the picture, I walk up to several longhaired and bearded men, often disturbing them from panhandling, usually giving them five or ten dollars.

Around ten o'clock, Julio calls. "I'm heading back for the rest of the night," he says.

"Yeah, I guess I will too." I end the call and make my way back to my rental where I parked it in a lot near 5th and San Pedro. A disheveled white woman pushing a shopping cart with her possessions passes me. She's filthy and reeks from body odor and booze. "I know you," she says flashing her black teeth.

"Excuse me?" I say trying to avoid her.

"Last night. You were asking about that man."

I stop in my tracks and turn to face her. "Have you seen him?"

"Yeah. We shared a bottle of whiskey."

"Is he okay? When? Where?"

"He's pretty messed up. Over in Pershing Square. A couple hours ago."

"Is he still there?" My heart races.

"When I left 'im."

"Pershing Square? Where's that?"

"Fifth and Hill."

"Fifth and Hill. Fifth and Hill," I say to myself searching for it on my phone. "Got it." I start to go, but turn back to face her. I hand her twenty dollars and say, "Thank you. Thank you." I run as fast as I can to the rental.

I speed over to Pershing Square. Would he still be here? She said she drank with him a couple hours ago. *Please, please God, please make him be there.*

Pulling up, I think how significant of Zach hanging out with General Pershing. He can't get the wars, or the army out of his head. I halt the car illegally in the street, run into the park at 5th and Hill and start yelling, "Zach? Zach?" I run into the center and look around. Nothing. I run to the back. Nothing. I run back up the path next to Olive and 5th and see a man lying on a bench on the northwest side of the outdoor amphitheater.

I sprint over. He lies on his stomach, his head draped over the side. There's vomit spilled all over the ground near his head. I roll him over. *Oh my God.* "Zach." I lift him by his shoulders and cradle his head in my lap. He's unconscious and unresponsive. I check for a pulse on his neck, but it's weak and slow. His breathing is shallow. I slap him on his face a couple of times. "Zach. Wake up." I grab my phone and punch in 911. "I need an ambulance now, please hurry. Pershing Square. Ah, on the left side of the amphitheater."

I sit there holding him, slapping his face again. "Zach, wake up. Zach." I check his pulse again. "Don't you die on me now." I start to cry. "We made it through the wars and you're not going to die here on a bench in Pershing Square, downtown Los Angeles. Please, Jesus. Please."

Four minutes later, I hear an ambulance. "Over here." Two paramedics rush over with a gurney. "What's wrong with him?" one asks me looking at Zach oddly as if he's a creature from outer space.

"Just get him to a hospital, any hospital, I don't care."

They check for vitals. "Weak pulse," the second paramedic says. He shines a small light into one of Zach's eyes. "No response. Jaundice. Distended belly."

They lift Zach onto the gurney and I follow them to the ambulance. "You can meet us at County General," the first paramedic says.

"I'm riding with you."

"That's not possible."

"He's an army veteran from Iraq and Afghanistan and I've come three thousand miles to find him. I'm not leaving his side. We don't have time to argue about this." I jump into the back of the ambulance before he can stop me.

"Just stay out of the way," he barks. The first paramedic drives and the second rides in the back with me. I stand aside as he hooks Zach up to wires and pads. He starts an IV as well.

We rush into the emergency room at Los Angeles County USC Medical Center. They wheel him into one of those bays where a doctor and nurse hurry over to attend to him. They make me stand back just outside the bay as they check him over. I pace back and forth, glancing in once and a while. I hear an alarm go off. Then I hear a loud beeping sound. "He's crashing." the doctor says.

I can't hear well what they say next, or understand it, but something about a central line and an IV push. I peek in and see the doctor stick this needle into his chest just below the collarbone. He then pulls a wire out of whatever he stuck in there. The monitors return to normal. After a few minutes the doctor comes out and says to me, "You next of kin?"

"Yes," I say.

"He has severe alcohol poisoning."

"Is he gonna be okay?"

"Won't know for some time. Hopefully, no permanent damage. He's young, the body can heal itself. If he's an alcoholic, he'll need care to pull through this. Support from family."

"I can give that. What will happen when he comes out of it?"

"Well, he'll have the DTs, most likely. Again, if he's an alcoholic, it's more problematic. He will crave a drink and it may be difficult to prevent him from seeking it out again."

"I understand."

"Alcoholics have to *not* want to drink again. That's where he'll need support. A lot of it. If he gets just one more drink, it could kill him."

"Okay."

"In severe cases, one experiences a host of symptoms including, anxiety, depression, irritability, nightmares, jumpiness, hallucinations, perhaps…"

"Okay. I get it," I say, stopping him.

"Once we stabilize him, and the alcohol is flushed out of him, he should be in detox. I can make the arrangements."

"Okay. Thanks, doctor." I call Julio and give him the news. I know it's early in the morning in New York, but I promised her I would call. "I found him, Jessica."

"Let me talk to him."

"It's not possible."

"I don't understand."

"He's in the hospital."

"Micah, what?"

I hesitate, then say, "Jessica, he's an alcoholic and has severe alcohol poisoning."

Silence.

"Then, I have to come out right away," she says sniffling.

"The doctor says it's not a good idea until we get him on his feet. He even said he shouldn't be in a relationship for quite some time."

"I couldn't go on, Micah. I just couldn't." She sobs.

I sigh and think. "It's really bad."

I hear her continuing to sob. "Please, Micah." She's hysterical now. "No one is going to ever keep me away from him ever again. You hear me?"

"I know, but it's just I don't want you to see him in this condition."

"I love him no matter what condition he is in." Her voice cracks. "Micah, don't do this to me. Please."

I sigh and think it over.

"Micah," she says, a stern edge in her voice.

"Okay. All right, I'll book it. Call you back." I end the call and call Aaron.

He says, "Okay. I'll fly out as soon as I can."

"You can get time off?"

"I have vacation time I've never used."

"Not really a vacation," I say.

"Yeah. But…" He ends the call.

Chapter Twenty-Seven
Detoxification

A nurse gives Zach a complete sponge bath. He has dried vomit in his crotch and on his legs. I spend the night in the chair next to his bed. They keep him medicated and sedated. The doctor told me because he is young his liver and kidneys should heal over time. However, he should never drink again.

The next day I make the flight arrangements for Jessica to fly out the following day. I check into a hotel that night to clean up and get some rest.

After two days in the hospital, they transport Zach to a detoxification center not far away. I ride with Julio.

The male orderlies wheel Zach into the facility and the staff situate him in a private room. I fill out the paperwork, give them as much history as I can, and list him as my brother. They then allow me to sit in a chair near his bed. Julio heads to the airport. Aaron is due to arrive before Jessica by one hour.

Sandy, an African-America nurse, comes in and out a couple of times checking on Zach. At one point she squeezes some medication into the plastic tube with a syringe. I sit surfing the net for alcohol poising, detoxification and recovery for alcoholics.

Zach begins to moan. He licks his dry lips. I call for Sandy. She rubs liquid-soaked swabs on his lips. His eyes flutter. He closes them again. Sandy adjusts the amount of sedation dripping into his body and he closes his eyes again and drifts off.

An hour later he moans and opens and closes his eyes many more times over the next few minutes. He starts to fidget. His eyes flutter several more times and he struggles to sit up. I help him into a half-lying and half-sitting position. He squints at me. "Zach," I say. "It's me, Micah."

He licks his lips again, moans and fidgets. He looks at the IV in his arm, reaches down to pull at it. I grab one arm while Sandy grabs the other. He struggles. "Zach, you need to lie back and keep that in."

Sandy hits a button on a monitor and says, "We'll need them after all."

He looks at me. "Micah?" he manages to squeak.

"Yes, Zach. It's me."

"Was I wounded again?"

"You're in Los Angeles, remember?"

"Los Angeles?"

"Yes. You're okay now."

"Okay?"

"Yes. Aaron and Julio are on their way." I decide not to mention her name and risk a meltdown. He tilts his head to look at Sandy.

"I'm Sandy, hon. Your nurse. If you need anything, just let me know."

"I…ah, I'm thirsty." She fetches the water canister on a tray next to his bed. A male attendant, Tom, enters the room carrying restraints. He sets them down near Zach's feet.

Sandy pours the water into a cup and raises it to his lips. He takes a sip, but then knocks the cup down splashing the water onto me. He bolts up and before we can stop him, rips the IV out of his arm. Tom and I hold him down while Sandy attaches the restraints. He fights, shaking like a leaf.

"What're you doing to me?" he says, his voice soft and raspy. He squirms in the restraints as Sandy works on hooking up the IV again.

"Zach, you almost died. I found you downtown. You have alcohol poisoning."

His pinpointed and jaundice eyes narrow at me. "Yes. I seem to remember. Los Angeles. Venice Beach. I was having the time of my life. What have you done?"

"Zach. I'm here to help you through this."

"What?"

"Zach. I've come out from New York."

"New York? I want nothing to do with New York. What are you doing here?"

"Zach. I'm here to help you."

"Huh?"

"You almost died. I'm here to help you get through this."

"Get through what? What're you talking about?"

"I'm gonna help you get sober."

"Sober?"

"Yes. I need you to be sober, for me."

He whimpers. "Just go away. Just go." Sandy finishes reattaching the IV. She pushes some medication through a syringe into the tube. "Why are you doing this to me?" He cries.

Tom leaves the room. "Because we all love you, Zach." I put my hand on his shoulder. "I don't want to lose you. We all need you."

He drifts off. I sigh and look at Sandy who straightens up. I sit back in the chair and wipe a tear from my eye.

Julio texts and says he has Aaron and they're waiting for Jessica. I really don't want her to see him like this and the intake nurse said it's not a good idea for her to be here yet. I text back telling Julio to take her to his house and wait.

An hour later Zach stirs again, struggling with the restraints. He glances at his wrists, rolls his head over and looks at me. I get up and move over to him as he squints and whimpers, "What are you doing to me?"

"I'm not giving up on you, Zach."

He starts to shiver, like from a cold breeze. "You gotta get me outta this, Micah." He squirms, again fighting the restraints. "I'm begging you." He stares at me like a trapped and wounded animal.

"I can't do that. It's for your own good."

"After all I've done for you?" He sniffles. "I was doing just fine. You've gone and messed it all up." His speech is spastic and spittle flies out. "Just fine. Just fine." He clenches his fists and struggles with the restraints again. "Just fine." He sniffles again and looks away.

I study this broken man as Sandy comes in and injects something into his IV again. He drifts off once more.

A couple hours later Aaron enters. "How is he?" he asks.

"It's not good," I say. He sits in a chair on the other side of the bed.

"How is she?" I ask him.

"A wreck. She was hysterical when we told her she couldn't see him yet. Jackie is trying her best to keep her calm, but I don't know how long we'll be able to keep her away."

"I know. The doctor said it's not a good idea for her to be here. It could push him over the edge."

Zach opens his eyes and looks at him. "Zach?" Aaron says.

"You gotta get me outta here, Aaron." He struggles with the restraints again. "I'm begging you. Please, get me outta here. I can't take it! I'll go back into combat. Anything. Just get me outta here."

"I can't do that, Zach. This is for your own good."

"My own good? What're you fools, twins?"

"Now it's my turn to help you."

"I don't want your turn. I don't want him in here either." He rolls his eyes over to the empty corner of the room behind Aaron.

Aaron looks behind him. "Who, Zach?"

"He won't leave me alone."

"Who won't leave you alone?"

"That crazy bastard. He's been following me all over the damn place."

Aaron and I look at the empty corner of the room. "Zach, there's no one there."

"He's right there."

"Who? Who is there?" Aaron says.

"Hem, dammit. You guys blind?"

Aaron looks at me. I shrug. "Well," Aaron says. "He won't hurt you."

"Won't hurt me? He kicked my ass one time. He's been driving me outta my damn my mind." He again struggles with the restraints. "I can't take this. You gotta get these off me. I gotta get outta here."

"Can't do that, Zach," Aaron says.

"What the hell are you assholes doing to me? This is against my constitutional rights. You can't hold me here." He tries to get up, but forgets he's tied down.

Sandy comes in. "Please, nurse," Zach says. "I can't take this. I promise. I'll behave. Please?"

She looks him over. "Okay, but if you don't…" She calls for an attendant. Tom arrives a minute later. They remove the restraints off his legs first, then his wrists. He rubs each wrist. They give him space. He studies us, his eyes darting back and forth. We wait, hovering. He is sweating and the jaundice is just beginning to fade.

"Zach," I say. "They need to shave you."

"No they don't. I like this look. It's very intellectual looking, ya know."

"Now that's the Zach I know," Aaron says.

"You don't know shit. You don't know me at all."

"Zach?" I say.

"What?" he whimpers. "Wait. You know what I want? I want you to get the hell outta my life. All of you. We're finished. You, me, him." He points to the empty corner of the room. "Is Julio in on this too?" he says. "Where is that fucker?" He pulls himself up in the bed, sitting against the headboard. He looks past me at that empty corner of the room and says, "What're you looking at asshole?"

Everyone looks to where he looks. We see nothing and look back at him. He puts his arms up as if he's blocking punches. "No, Hem. I'm sorry. I didn't meant it." He looks at us now. "What?" he says, his hands shaking. "Tell them who you are," he says to the ghost behind Aaron.

We wait.

"See, you hear that?" he says to us. He waits for a response from us. We don't respond. "Oh, I see what this is," he says. "It's a conspiracy. You assholes are trying to have me committed so you can feel good about yourselves. Well, I'm getting outta here." He brushes himself off as if he has crumbs on his lapel. He tries to get off the bed but Sandy and Tom push him back down. "Okay. Okay," he says lying back again. "It's cool. It's cool." He raises his shaking hands at them.

He lies there and calms down. Everyone relaxes. A few minutes pass. He just stares at us, sweating and shaking like a leaf. Aaron sits in his chair and I sit in mine. Zach sits up against the headboard, pulling his knees up to his chin and hugging his legs, his head jerking back and forth between us. Sandy and Tom edge out of the room. They leave the door wide open so they can rush back in to render assistance if needed.

We sit and watch each other for many minutes. Zach sniffles, looks down at his shaking hands. Then, like a kid jumping up from the dinner table after being excused, he bolts up and tries to get out of the bed, but Aaron and I jump up to stop him. He grabs Aaron's shirt, balling it up in his fists. "You gotta get me a drink, Aaron. I can't take it. Look at me." Aaron grabs him by one wrist while I grab his other.

"Can't do that, Zach," Aaron says. We push him back down onto the bed. He struggles with us.

"Please. I'm begging you." He whimpers and relaxes, defeated. We release him. He lies in the fetal position and cries, sweating and shaking. "Don't you get it?" he says glaring at me. "There's no point anymore." He bawls like a young child.

"The point is you have so much to live for." I blurt out, "I found her, Zach." I know I shouldn't have said that, but I want to give him a reason to live. "She came to see me."

His eyes narrow at me and he stares for the longest time. "What? Who?"

"Jessica."

He edges up in the bed like he's a jackal ready to pouch and burns his stare through me. Finally, he says, "Why would you do that to me? How can you be so cruel?"

"It's true," Aaron says. "She's at Julio's house. I just took her there."

He now bores his eyes into him. "You bastards. You fucking bastards." He wipes some tears away with his palms. "Even if she is here, I don't want to ever see that bitch again. You hear me? I don't wanna see her." He tries to get out of the bed, but Aaron pushes him down yet again. Zach throws him a look that could kill. "What, you gonna punch me again? Go ahead and punch me like you did in Chicago. You know that black eye took a couple weeks to heal."

"Yeah, it was a real good shiner, wasn't it?"

"Oh, you're trying to be funny now?" He tries to get up yet again, but Aaron restrains him.

Aaron tightens his face and holds him firmly by his wrists. Zach squirms. Tom comes in and Zach backs down so Aaron loosens his grip. Tom hovers by the door.

His whole body shakes and he catches me watching his trembling hands. He scans the room. "Well, anyway, I've got a date with my friend, Jim." He again tries to get up but Aaron blocks his way.

"You were always the wisecracker," Aaron says.

"Funny, bro. Real funny."

He sits back against the headboard again. We have a standoff. Several minutes pass and we stare one another down. Julio sends me a text saying Jessica is being difficult, and threatening to take a taxi to try and find us.

We need just a little more time I text back. "Zach," I say. "She told me the whole story. She loves you."

He shifts in the bed. "What? Who?"

"Jessica, fool," Aaron says.

"I told you assholes to stop calling me fool. I don't love her anymore. She left me. I was doing just fine on my own."

"Oh Yeah? It looks like you were doing just fine," Aaron says.

He smirks.

"I didn't believe it myself at first," I say, "but she came to see me. Told me the whole story."

"Micah, it's over. I've washed that lying bitch outta my mind. I've moved on. She left me like all the others." He is shaking like a leaf again and sweat drips from his brow. He looks at his trembling hands.

"You can't fool me, Zach."

"Look," he says, "I got a job, I support myself. I stay busy. You might have seen some of my articles?"

"And all the rest."

"Well, then, there you have it. I just had a few drinks with some friends, that's all."

"Some friends?"

"Don't judge my new friends."

Sandy looks in again. I nod that it's okay and she goes on. Tom sits in a chair next to the wall. Zach looks at his shaking hands again and says, "You're keeping me here against my will."

"I remember someone doing this to me," Aaron says.

"That's different. You had problems. Emotional ones."

"You hear how stupid that sounds?" Aaron says.

"What?" He glances at the corner of the room. "You stay outta this." He grabs and holds his left hand with his right to stop the trembling and looks back at us. "I'm fine."

"Does your friend over there believe that?" I ask him.

"So you do see him?"

"Maybe," I fib.

"He's a pompous ass." He raises his hands as if he's blocking punches again. "No…no…Hem. I didn't mean that. I'm sorry." He cowers.

"Zach, we won't be able to keep her away much longer."

"Who?" His whole body now shakes.

"Jessica."

"Are you dense? I don't want to see that bitch ever again. Tell her to go fuck that asshole father of hers." His eyes dart around the room.

"I don't want her to see you in this condition," I say.

"There's nothing wrong with my condition."

"You look like shit," Aaron says.

"Gee, thanks," he says. "You've been a real fuckin' pal." He scans our troubled faces. "Well, it's been nice chatting with you boys, but, like I said, I have a date with my old friend, Jim." He tries to get up yet again, but Aaron slams him back down.

"Dammit!" he yells. "Back off." He twists and breaks loose. "I'm through with this fuckin' mind game! You take away my freedom? Isn't this what we fought for? Don't you assholes get it?" His breathing rate increases, he's dripping in sweat, shaking all over and he cries. "I want to be left alone. Just leave me alone. Leave me alone." He looks at his arm and realizes he still has an IV. He pulls it out before we can stop him and throws it aside. Aaron grabs him and pushes him back down onto the bed, falling across him, chest against chest. He holds him down in this position. Zach, bawling, raises his arms around Aaron's back and pounds his shoulders. Aaron takes it and does not budge. Zach tires and drapes his arms around Aaron, sobbing. He's soaked in sweat. Tom rushes over to assist and Sandy hurries in and gives him a shot in the arm. He soon relaxes, staring at the ceiling and mumbling like a lunatic.

A different crew works the night shift. Zach drifts in and out of consciousness and has a conversation with someone named Him, or Hem.

My phone wakes me at one in the morning. It's Julio. "She tried to walk off down the road," he says. "She's hysterical and I can't keep her away."

"All right," I say, sighing. "I'll let the staff know. Tell her she can come over in the morning." I push end call on my phone.

Chapter Twenty-Eight
Of All the Gin Joints in All the Towns…

I open my blurry eyes and see Micah sitting in a chair on one side of the bed and Aaron in a chair on the other.

I have to get the hell out of here. I wipe my cold and clammy forehead, my hands shake and I feel anxious. I'm nauseous, tired, and weak. It feels as if an elephant is sitting on my chest, yet again. If I could just have one nip, I'd calm down, everything would be all right.

What's this game these fools play with me? I take a deep breath, exhale and sit up. Aaron sees this and acts like he's going to pounce on me again. I lie back against the headboard watching him like a child being disciplined by a parent.

Stein stands in the corner leaning against the wall picking his teeth with his pinky and annoying me. "You, you SOB," I say to him. "You've been following me all over this godforsaken world driving me outta my freakin' mind!"

"I told you, kid. I didn't come to you. You came to me."

"You know how ridiculous that sounds?"

"You know how ridiculous you look?"

"Funny." I shift in the bed. "You chose to leave this world after you said everyday above earth is a good day and the world is a fine place and worth fighting for and you'd hate very much to leave it. Why?"

"The same reason your mother did."

"Oh, don't bring my mother into this."

"Because *it is* hard, kid." He moves closer, standing next to the head of the bed. I cower, expecting him to smack me, however he says, "You have something I didn't."

"What the hell is that?" I peer over at Micah and Aaron who watch me as if I'm stark raving mad.

"You have strength, kid."

"Strength? You're stronger than me."

"Physically, yes."

"Ha, ha," I say. "I still want that rematch."

"Then I'll kick your ass again. Look, in here." He points to his heart. "I told you, I wish I had died before I loved anyone but her."

I knew I should have stopped him in Paris.

"What's that?"

"Nothing."

People are talking and approaching from outside the room. My hands shake again and I can't seem to control them. That nurse enters followed by that man dressed in a white orderly uniform like the ones they wear in asylums. Perhaps that's what this place is.

She walks in with Julio. *She comes back into my life?* Like this, here? I don't believe it, it's a ruse, she's a double. I look up at Stein nodding back at me and grinning.

Her eyes are wet with tears. She approaches, yet hesitates, as if I'm an ax-murderer. I pull myself up, shaking as if I'm standing in a winter breeze, wind-chill below zero. "No. No this is an hallucination," I say, pointing at her edging closer. I look over at Stein. "Right?"

She looks at Stein, but says to me, "No, it's me, Zach."

I close and open my eyes but she is still there, looking at me with those smoky hazel eyes. "Zach, my father did this. He took me away from you."

I snap, "Your father? That swell guy? You can't come up with anything better than that?"

"It's true, Zach," Micah says. "She told me the whole story."

"Who's talking to you?" I'm shaking so hard *I will* fall to pieces after all. *I need a drink.*

"Listen to them, kid," Stein says.

"You stay out of this." I look back at the others. "What? He's right there." I wave my arm at him.

She leans down and holds my trembling hand. I try to shake loose, but she just repositions it. "I love you, Zach." She sniffles.

"You deserve an Oscar," I say, snapping and shaking loose. "Love?" I whimper. "You said you loved me once, twice, a million times. I was such a fool to believe you. You were just like all the others." I shiver, glance at Aaron, Micah and Julio. "Please, I'm begging you, fuckers. I need a drink. Just to calm my nerves." Those fools just stare back at me and say nothing, that nurse and orderly hover next to them. *They have me surrounded.*

"I never stopped loving you and I cried myself to sleep every night."

"Yeah?" I bark. "Well, I drank myself to sleep every night."

"I know. I don't have to cry and you don't have to drink anymore." Her voice upturns.

"I want to drink. That way the pain is more bearable."

"I need *you*, Zach." She blubbers. "I need you to not drink."

"Well, I don't need you. All I need is a drink." I glare at the fools again and look back at her, saying, "Why don't you go back to your perfect little Connecticut home with those wonderful caring parents?"

"I don't need them. I need you. I want nothing to do with them." She holds my hand again, but I shake it loose. "I'm so sorry my parents did this to us."

I droop my head, stare at my sweaty, unstable hands. "You haunted me every, single, day." Tears drip from my eyes. "I saw you everywhere, even at the bottom of an empty bottle of booze. I always had to get another one just to kill the pain."

"Please, Zach. We can get through this together." She moves in and tries to embrace me, her hands trembling like mine. I pull back and everyone rises on their toes, tightening the circle around me, like a noose. I'm dripping and my body shakes again, as if I have influenza. I jolt out of the bed and fall on the floor.

Everyone rushes me. I crawl under the bed and out the other side like a chimpanzee playing a game. I jump up and run behind a chair. Aaron is the first to get to me. I grab him by his shirt, balling it up in my hands and say, "You gotta get me a drink, Aaron. To stop the shaking. I'm begging you. Please, I need a fuckin' drink." He grabs my wrists and holds them down to my side, the others hovering behind him. I break free and stand back, my heart races and the room spins.

She edges toward me, the others following. I grab Micah and twirl him around. "She's not real." I point at her standing behind him. "She's not there. Make her go away." I try to hide behind him like a child playing hide and seek. "She's the devil, that's what this is. Yeah. Can't you all see that? This is what the devil does." I look at Stein. "You told me women are devils, right? Make her go away." I push Micah aside and rush over to Stein. "You gotta get me out of this." I turn to look at the others who think I've lost my marbles. I'm over the rainbow. They creep closer and I turn back to face Stein. "Take me back to Paris. No wait, a nice warm place where we can sip whiskey. Key West. Or, back to Cuba. Well, maybe not Cuba. Can you believe it? Castro is still there after all these years. Although, your place is still there, so we could just move back in. They've kept it up real nice, you know. You could remarry Hadley. Or, bring Gellhorn, or Pauline. I don't give a shit who you bring. We could go fishing again. I really enjoyed that. But," I wave my finger at him, "I'm not chasing Nazis around the Caribbean again. That was nuts."

She closes in on me. Aaron, Micah and Julio move in too followed by the nurse and that attendant. I stand behind Stein. "Keep them away." I'm shaking so much I can't focus, can't think straight, my head hurts and my heart races so fast it's trying to crawl out of my chest. I look down, see it emerging and start to claw at it, trying to help it out of there. My gown is soaked and I'm so cold. The walls are moving in too, getting closer and closer. I fall to the floor and coil up into the fetal position. My mother kneels down putting her hand on my head, stroking my long brown hair. "We all love you, Zachary," she says to me. "We all need you."

"It's so hard." I cry. "It's so hard."

"It will get easier." She leans in, kisses me on the back of my head, and lies on the floor next to me, draping her body over mine. Now she's holding me, cradling me like she used to do when I was an infant. I look up, but it is not my mother. It is Jess.

I feel hands on my shoulders. Aaron, Micah and Julio have placed their hands on me. Oh no, that nurse, she's coming at me. She's got a needle. She's not a nurse, she's that bastard Grim Reaper. She's waving that bony finger at me and saying 'I got you now. Ha, ha, ha.' They hold me down. They're gonna give me the needle. You were right Johnny. They're giving me the needle. I'm coming, Johnny. I'm coming.

Chapter Twenty-Nine
Love Means... L.S.

I open my eyes, feeling rested, as if I've slept for a thousand years. I'm not shaking, I don't feel clammy, and I seem to be lucid, warm and I'm not sweating.

Someone is sitting in a chair next to the bed. This person's head is resting on my shoulder and their hand is holding mine. I smell something familiar and see that hair. Aaron sleeps in another chair on the other side of the bed.

She stirs. Why is she here? Why am I here? I seem to remember her coming into the room. I remember her tears. I remember Micah telling me something. I don't know why she is here. Where has she been? Why did she leave me and now come back? Is any of this real? What is this place? "Zach?" she says lifting her head to look at me.

"Jess?"

"Are you okay?"

"Don't know." I pull myself up and lean against the headboard. She sits up, still holding my hand. Those smoky hazel eyes tilt up at me and I see those lips, that face. Tears well up and I look away.

"Oh, Zach. I'm so sorry." She buries her head into my stomach. I lift my other hand, and slowly lower it, placing it on the back of her head, stoking her hair. She weeps.

I sniffle, and wipe the tears from my eyes. "I'm so sorry, Jess. I'm so sorry for putting you through this."

She looks up at me, wipes her own tears away. "We can get through this," she says. "We can do this. Together."

"I tried to find you. I went to your house and your father's office. I looked for you everywhere and no one would tell me anything."

"I didn't know that."

"I struggled to keep busy, to put you out of my mind. Everywhere I looked I saw you. In dreams. In movies." A flood of tears spill from my eyes. "I cared about nothing but booze."

"Every day, I cried myself to sleep," she says.

"Where did you go? What happened?"

She crawls into bed, puts her head on my shoulder, her arm across my torso and tells me the whole story. I listen to the nightmare, never interrupting.

When she finishes, I sit there stunned, stroking her hair. "I would have rescued you if I had only known. Some knight, and chivalry and all that." My chest is drenched with her tears.

We sit in silence for the longest time holding on to one another. I don't want to ever let go of her again, never let her out of my sight, especially with her evil father out there lurking around. I believe she doesn't want to let go of me again because she holds on tightly. She lifts her head. "Kiss me."

"Like this? You see the way I look?"

"I don't care that you look like a caveman. It's you I'm kissing, not the hair, not the beard." She leans in, and just like the first time we kissed, she grabs the back of my head and pulls me in. I taste those sweet lips, again. She holds the kiss, not letting go. Out of the corner of my eye, I see Aaron stir, nod at me, and slip out of the room.

We hold onto one another for an hour, maybe two. "How long have I been here?" I ask her.

"Four days."

"Four days? I remember almost nothing."

"It wasn't easy. You don't want to know. Let's not remember any of it. I only want to remember the rest of our lives together. I love you so much." She squeezes me again.

My eyes fill with tears and drip onto her shoulder. I don't ever want to touch another drop of booze. *Never. Ever.*

~ * ~

Tom does the honors while Jess, Micah and Aaron watch. He shaves my beard and hair off, down to the roots. I look like an inductee in the barber chair at basic training again.

Chapter Thirty
Now you Can Go, Hem

Julio retrieves my belongings from Danny Cox. Micah, Jess and I fly back to New York. Jess moves in with Micah and Peter for the time being until I complete an inpatient substance abuse rehabilitation program at the VA medical center in Brooklyn. I am diagnosed not only a substance abuser, but with separation anxiety disorder. The doctor explains how I never received appropriate treatment and counseling for the loss of my mother and witnessing her death in the bathtub that night. As a result, I descended into depression and finally alcoholism at an early age. Of course losing Jimmy and the others didn't help. Because of this, and the circumstances surrounding the disappearance of Jess, she is allowed to visit me every day and call me every few hours during the day to assure me that she is still here for me. She also texts me short notes every hour. When she visits, we sit for hours just holding one another.

Jess works for Hurley, the editor I met in Key West. He reads my war journals and convinces me to put them together into a compilation for publication.

After rehabilitation, I move in with Jess, Micah and Peter and take a job with a New York paper writing human-interest stories.

One day Micah, Jess and I take a cab to the VA Medical Center, Manhattan on East 23rd Street and check into a meeting room. A young man walks up to the podium, puts his hands on it, and, scanning the fifteen people sitting in front of him, says, "My name is Brian. I'm a veteran of Afghanistan and I'm an alcoholic and drug addict."

"Hello, Brian," everyone says. Jess squeezes my hand. We sit and listen for a while to a few heart-wrenching stories.

"Anyone else?" the sponsor says.

I raise my hand, the one that's free.

"Yes. Come on up," he says.

I make my way to the podium and say, "Hello, my name is Zach. I'm a veteran of Iraq and Afghanistan and I'm an alcoholic."

"Hello, Zach," everyone says.

I attend weekly and also enroll in an outpatient rehabilitation program for another eight months.

She wanted to do it right away before her parents found out and tried to stop it. However, we had to plan it out just a little bit so we could get everyone together and after my doctor and sponsor gave their approvals. Four months to the day after returning to New York from Los Angeles, the ceremony is all ready to begin in Great Neck on Long Island overlooking Long Island Sound.

An hour before the double ceremony, Micah, the groom, and Peter, the groom, join me, another groom, greeting people as they arrive. "Dawg," Dale says high-fiving me. "Look what the cat dragged in."

Basir follows him. "You made it," I say shaking his hand. "You revolutionary you." I pull him in for a hug.

"This is Micah and Peter," I say to them.

"Cute couple," Dale says nodding and shaking their hands. He takes a seat with the two bunnies that came with him, Basir sitting next to them.

A woman approaches along the path with two other young ladies. Micah looks at her. "Mother?"

They walk up to us. "Micah," she says, throwing her arms around him and sobbing. They hug for the longest time. He looks over at me and says, "You did this?" I nod. He then hugs his two sisters and escorts them to front row seats.

Micah and I walk to the altar. I smile at Kristen and Holly, nod at David and Sara Zimmer, and wave at Danny Cox sitting there in the front row, his titanium legs and arm shining in the sunshine. Aaron and his new girlfriend, a veteran from Afghanistan, sit with Julio and Jackie. Julio holds up a clenched fist. I shake my head. I see Bud, his wife and Duffy's wife.

Duffy escorts Jess and Peter. We two couples are married.

~ * ~

"Now you don't need me anymore," he says.

"No, I don't," I say putting my seatback into the upright position.

Stein sits in the seat across the aisle from me. "Try the fried goujon at Brasserie Lipp in St-Germain."

"Okay. I will. Anything else?"

"No. Except," he pauses, "just bleed."

"I will. I will."

I awake as the flight attendant announces, "We are beginning our decent into Paris-Charles de Gaulle Airport."

I finish my cup of coffee, squeeze Jess's hand and give her a kiss. Glancing down at the silver heart-shaped pendent resting in the crevice of her neck where the two collarbones meet, I see my refection and my eyes in their sockets. "We're going to have a beautiful honeymoon," I say. She lays her head on my shoulder and snuggles up as we land in Paris.

Statistics from official US government sources:

22 veterans commit suicide every day

One U.S. veteran of the wars in Iraq and Afghanistan attempts suicide every 65 minutes

More than 6,700 – Number of American Service Members killed in action during the wars in Iraq and Afghanistan

More than 50,000 - Number of American Service Members wounded in Iraq and Afghanistan

3,493 – Number of American Service Members awarded the Medal of Honor since President Abraham Lincoln signed the medal into law in 1863

More than 22 Million – Current number of American Veterans

147 – Number of Veterans Administration Medical Centers

90 Billion Dollars – Approximate amount of the annual Veterans Administration budget

----

Please thank a veteran for his or her service, whether or not you have agreed with the actions taken by your government, and reflect on the ultimate sacrifice made by those who died in the service of their country.

PTSD, or Post Traumatic Stress Disorder, once called "shell shock" during World War I, and later "battle fatigue" during World War II, is a scientifically proven and widely accepted clinical diagnosis that affects not only soldiers wounded in combat, but anyone who has experienced or witnessed a traumatic event.

Los Angeles hosts the largest homeless veterans population in the country, particularly along skid row. Please consider a donation to the **LA Midnight Mission**. This organization helps thousands of people to kick addition and get back on their feet.

Alcohol and drug addiction continue to afflict our veterans at a greater rate than the general population, as they have for centuries.

Quotes from Ernest Hemingway or his work:

"The world breaks everyone and afterward many are strong in the broken places." *A Farewell to Arms*

"The world is a fine place and worth fighting for and I would hate very much to leave it." *For Whom the Bell Tolls*

God knows, people who are paid to have attitudes toward things, professional critics, make me sick. Camp-following eunuchs of literature." *Letter to Sherwood Anderson, May 23, 1925.*

"No catalogue of horrors ever kept men from war…. They wrote in the old days that it is sweet and fitting to die for one's country. But in modern war, there is nothing sweet nor fitting in your dying. You will die like a dog for no good reason." *Notes on the Next War, Esquire, Sept. 1935*

"Everyday above earth is a good day…. The first and final thing you have to do in this world is to last in it, and not be smashed by it. Man is not made for defeat. A man can be destroyed but not defeated." *The Old Man and the Sea*

"Death is like an old whore in a bar. I'll buy her a drink but I won't go upstairs with her." *To Have and Have Not*

Every man's life ends the same way. It is only the details of how he lived and how he died that distinguish one man from another." As told to AE Hotchner in the 1966 biography, *Papa Hemingway: a Personal Memoir*

"People were always the limiters of happiness except for the very few that were as good as spring itself." *A Moveable Feast*

"Drinking lets you see things you normally can't when you're sober…. An intelligent man is sometimes forced to be drunk to spend time with his fools…. Drinking is the way to ending the day." *The Good Life According to Hemingway*, A.E. Hotchner

"Forget your personal tragedy. We are all … [cursed] from the start and you especially have to … hurt like hell before you can write seriously. But when you get the damned hurt, use it — don't cheat … it…." *Letter to F. Scott Fitzgerald, May 28, 1934*

"Happiness in intelligent people is the rarest thing I know." *The Garden of Eden, 1986*

"There is no hunting like the hunting of man, and those who have hunted armed men long enough and liked it, never care for anything else thereafter." *On the Blue Water' in Esquire, April 1936*

"There are no heroes in war. We all offer our bodies and only a few are chosen, but it shouldn't reflect any special credit on those that are chosen." *Letter to his parents, 1918*

The Sun Also Rises characters:

Jake Barnes, Lady Brett Ashley, Robert Cohn and Frances Clyne.

About the Author

James Charles is a U.S. Army Veteran and served in The Middle East, Central America, Europe and the United States. He is currently an administrator with the Los Angeles Unified School District.

VISIT OUR WEBSITE FOR THE FULL INVENTORY OF QUALITY BOOKS:

http://www.roguephoenixpress.com

Rogue Phoenix Press
Representing Excellence in Publishing

Quality trade paperbacks and downloads
in multiple formats,
in genres ranging from historical to
contemporary romance,
mystery and science fiction.
Visit the website then bookmark it.
We add new titles each month!

www.ingramcontent.com/pod-product-compliance
Lightning Source LLC
Chambersburg PA
CBHW070640180626
46817CB00006B/2186